BRITANNIA:

PART II: THE WATCHMEN

BRITANNIA:
PART II: THE WATCHMEN

RICHARD DENHAM & M J TROW

THISTLE
PUBLISHING

This edition first published in 2014 by:

Thistle Publishing
36 Great Smith Street
London
SW1P 3BU

www.thistlepublishing.co.uk

ISBN-13: 9781910198803

This book is dedicated with much love to
Janette, Laura and Tristan

Acknowledgements

First of all I would like to thank my agent Andrew Lownie, and David Haviland of Thistle Publishing, who allowed us to bring the Britannia series to life.

Unreserved thanks also go to Mei, whose skill, experience and talent has brought Britannia and its characters to life in the rich and colourful way that I had always dreamed of.

I would also like to thank Stephen 'Primus Lector' Shortland for all his help and for pointing out Bruno's age, and killing off a beloved hound; Lawrence Phillips, web wizard extraordinary and all those, too numerous to mention, who continue to support me in my abiding passion.

Most of all, I would like to thank Carol Trow, oracle, conduit and unsung hero of our triumvirate who has patiently put up with me all this time.

- Richard

THE WATCHMEN
LIBER I

CHAPTER ONE

Calleva Atrebatum, Decembris

'Caesar! Caesar! Caesar! Caesar!'
The roar of their thousands echoed and re-echoed through the great stone gate of the town. The wind whipped the winter cloaks and the legions' standards shifted. The VI Victrix had sent a vexillation from Eboracum in the north, the XX Valeria Victrix from Deva in the west and the II Augusta from Isca and the Saxon Shore. They had tramped the ridges, iron hard at the death of a year, the boots thudding along the roads their great-grandfathers had made. They had come to elect a Caesar, to choose from their ranks a living god. And if some of the soldiers there that day already had a god whose son was called Jesus; well, they could live with that.

A weak winter sun gilded their arms as they stood in hollow square before the granite walls of Calleva, dazzling the multitude who had come to see this day. These were the tribal lands of the Atrebates and they were there in the greatest numbers, whispering and muttering to each other in awe. It wasn't every day a new Caesar was chosen, a new emperor of the west. From the south had come the Regni and the Belgae, the people who had lived with the eagles the longest, whose old women still told tales of Vespasian and his legion from three hundred years before. The Cantiaci were there too, the men who had stood against the great Julius, slaughtering his men at the water's edge; the men who had gone down to Aulus Plautius a generation later. The Trinovantes and the Iceni, once sworn enemies in the days of the flame-haired Boudicca, stood as brothers and sisters now, watching the day. The Dobunni, the Coritani, the Silures and the rest – all of them had sent deputations, with promises and praise and presents for the new god.

Old Cerialis would not see another spring. He had been lucky to see the last two, but he was determined to be here today and make his obeisance to the Caesar. The legionary tribunes had walked forward first. They had unbuckled their damascened helmets and removed them. They had smashed their right fists against their left breasts in the time honoured way that loyal soldiers had done for centuries. Then they had laid their swords in the grass, pommel first, in front of the dais.

Now it was the civilians' turn and Cerialis was first among them. His family had ruled the Atrebates with a will of iron long before the Romans came and if he was only a member of the Ordo, the council, these days, so be it. There were still rebels, he had heard, in the north; wild men who ate each other and worshipped wood and stone. Good luck to them. If they believed they could destroy Rome after all this time, perhaps God would smile on them. Here, in the safe south, old Cerialis was a Christian. He lounged on Roman couches, ate from Roman crockery and drank Roman wine. He was at peace with the world.

'I solemnly swear,' his voice was thin and reedy over the wind, 'that I will be an enemy to those who I learn are enemies to Magnus Caesar Maximus. If I knowingly swear falsely, then may Jupiter highest and best and the Lord Jesus Christ cause me and my children to be deprived of fatherland, safety and all good fortune.'

A mighty cheer went up as he finished and he staggered to his feet to clasp the arm of the new Caesar. Magnus Maximus hugged the old man, feeling his body scrawny under the pallium he wore. He looked into the face of Cerialis, at the old eyes watering in the cold, at the pinched, blue nose. But the mouth was smiling and the heart, he knew, was good.

'Jupiter highest and best smile on you, Cerialis of the Atrebates,' Maximus said, 'and your Lord Jesus Christ.'

The old man passed along the line with the help of his people and another groveller was ready to take his place. Maximus, the purple cloak on his shoulders and a gold laurel wreath on his head, turned back to the dais for the next solemnity. At the foot of his throne, rich in velvet and studded with silver, a huge brindled mastiff lay curled, half asleep. The animal raised an eyebrow and caught his master's glance.

'I know, Bruno,' Maximus murmured. 'Boring as Hell, isn't it? But if you want to be Caesar's dog, you'll grin and bear it.' He turned to the next supplicant. 'Salve, Aulus Orderis of the Durotriges.'

Londinium

The candles guttered in the sudden draught that swept in from nowhere, rustling the parchment on the consul's desk and making the littlest child blink. She was Neria, the daughter of a river whore and a passing sailor and she was five years old. She was sitting on Honoria's lap, curled against the warmth of the woman's breasts and she felt rather smug. Because, of the eight children in the consul's secret apartments, *she* was the one on Honoria's lap and the others had to make do with the floor. They sat in a semi-circle, knees tucked under their chins, eyes wide in the candlelight.

Almost every night they came here, as dusk fell and the sounds of the day in the great city died away and became the weird whispers and rustlings of the night. And almost every night, Honoria told them stories. Stories that made their eyes widen still further and made the hairs on the backs of their necks stand on end.

When she knew they were ready, she began. 'There were once,' she murmured softly, 'four heroes of the Wall.'

'What's the Wall, Mama Honoria?' little Neria sat upright, looking at her. To Neria, Mama Honoria was the most beautiful woman in the world. And she knew all about the world, whereas little Neria knew nothing.

'It's a thing made of stone, stupid!' the curly-haired lad nearest the door said. 'They're all around the city.'

The little girl glared daggers at him, but Honoria's response was more withering. For all the boy was her own son, he could be an oaf at times and got more like his father every day. 'Not just any wall, Scipio, *the* Wall. It stretches from coast to coast of Britannia, standing against the mountains to the North. It is far, far from here and beyond it are men with one eye and their heads in their chests. They breathe fire and that single eye can turn you to stone.'

Silence filled the chamber. Sixteen eyes were glued to hers and the candles guttered again.

'Stop filling their heads with nonsense,' the consul swept in and ruffled the curls on the head of his boy.

'Your papa,' Honoria went on, smiling at them both, 'was one of those heroes.'

'That was then,' the consul said, 'when Leocadius Honorius was a flat-footed pedes, mounting his shield

5

on the Wall. All,' he looked at her indulgently, 'a long time ago.'

Honoria got up, lifting the little girl with her. 'Wouldn't you go back?' she asked him, adjusting the brooch on his shoulder. 'Even now, wouldn't you go back?'

He looked into her clear, bright eyes, the candle-flames dancing in them. 'Back to Justinus, Pat, Vit ... One of us is dead,' his gaze fell away, 'and the others? Only the gods know.' He turned to the boy at his elbow. It was like looking into a mirror. He ran his fingers along the boy's cheek. 'Don't let your mother fill your head with fairy stories, Scip,' he said.

'Aren't there monsters out there, Papa?' the boy asked, unsure, for all his eight summers, what the answer was.

'Oh, yes,' Leocadius nodded solemnly. 'Yes, there are. And I'm on my way to see one tonight.'

The consul was less than pleased. He would normally expect to hold a council with the vicarius in daylight, surrounded by his lackeys and recorded for posterity by an arse-licking scribe with a stylus. Instead, the vicarius had summoned him near midnight, and he was to come alone. He slipped out of the secret door and the city guard clicked to attention. He paused while he heard the slave bolt the door behind him and walked across the night-frosted courtyard where the fountain still played, despite the cold. The shadows fell long here, the bushes of the palace huge in the near-darkness. No moon. No stars as yet, although the night was crisp with frost.

Leocadius took the stairs two at a time and padded along the balcony. He paused at the child's door and peered in. The nursemaid was sitting asleep, snoring softly and the shutters were closed against the cold. Aelia was lying on her side, her eyes closed and little bubbles forming and breaking at her lips. Leocadius preferred her in this state and the half-light of a candle. Awake in the day she was a fractious child, with a snotty nose and her mother's whine. The consul closed the door again and was gone.

In the next chamber, Julia sat upright sewing by the light of a dozen candles. Leocadius caught her frigid stare and thought how much she looked like a Vestal Virgin in the great days of old. Such women were living goddesses in Rome, untouchable. And Leocadius had not touched Julia for a long time.

'Hope I didn't wake you,' he mumbled, striding to a press in the corner. The tone sounded as if he didn't care whether he had or not.

'I wasn't asleep,' she said, lips pursed. He glanced at her again. Sol Invictus, she was turning into her mother. 'Where are you going? To see your whore again?'

Leocadius fished a dagger out from its hiding place under some woollen cloth and held it briefly in his hand. One day … one day … He slid the blade into his sleeve. 'Affairs of state,' he told her.

'At this hour?' She arched an eyebrow.

'I can't help thinking,' Leocadius said, 'that the vicarius has the least appropriate name in the business. Civilis. *Un*civilis would be better.'

'What does he want?' Julia asked.

'Time will tell, my sweet,' the consul straightened his pallium and checked his hair in the mirror's bronze glow. 'Don't wait up.'

There was no point in doing that. Leocadius Honorius, consul of Londinium in the province of Maxima Caesariensis, ran two households. One was the household of the day where his wife Julia dutifully entertained the Ordo and the merchants of the city, travelling gentlemen and officers of the church. Here, she laid on lavish banquets for the vicarius and anybody else her husband needed to cosy up to. She did this, not because she loved Leocadius any more – in fact she seriously doubted whether she had ever loved him at all – but because she was the daughter of a consul and of a consul's wife and it was bred in her bones.

The household of the night belonged, beyond that locked and guarded door, to Honoria and her people of the streets. There were merchants here too and members of the Ordo, the city council, but they came after dark and in disguise. They came for the girls and the drink and the dice and whatever black art the consul and his whore chose to provide for them. This was home to the *real* Leocadius Honorius, who had more in common with that happy-go-lucky soldier of the Wall than he cared to admit.

'Here's to our wives and sweethearts,' as the old toast ran when the wine flowed in the secret apartments, 'may they never meet.'

He made his way east, following the river that lay silent under the night. There would be no moon but the stars were out now, winking in the inky blackness like disbelieving eyes. The consul could see the masts of the merchant ships stabbing black into the purple and he could hear their ropes creaking taut against the anchors. He turned sharp left along the Via Officionale, the broadest street in his city. To right and left the alleys lay dark and deadly, the home of the drunks, the whores and the cut-purses. Life was cheap here, death was the companion of a Roman mile. And Leocadius the consul knew every inch of them.

'Io, pedes!'

The voice came from the darkness to his right and his dagger was in his hand already. Some low-life hailing him as a common soldier; what the hell? But then, he thought it was a voice he knew. A voice from long ago, but one that would ring in his ears for ever.

'Vitalis? Vitalis Celatius?' Leocadius' own voice echoed in the alleys. 'Vit, is that you?'

A man a little younger than the consul himself strolled into the half light of the street. It had been well over two years since they had seen each other. In some ways, it was like yesterday. Leocadius sheathed the knife and slapped the man in both arms, pulling him towards him, but Vitalis held back.

'How have you been, Leo?' he asked.

'Well,' the consul laughed. He noticed Vitalis looking him up and down and he patted his own stomach. 'Too well, perhaps. I told you I could get used to the food down here. I thought you'd gone. With that Christian … what was his name?'

'Pelagius,' Vitalis said.

'That's right. You were going to Rome, weren't you? Shrine of St Petrus or some such rubbish.'

Vitalis smiled. 'It's not rubbish to Pelagius,' he said. 'Nor to me.'

Leocadius put his hands on his hips. 'So you did become a Christian after all? I haven't seen you at any of Dalmatius' services.'

Vitalis was still smiling. 'So,' he said, 'it's a mad world, isn't it, when a worshipper of Sol Invictus and Jupiter highest and best kneels down with the Bishop of Londinium?'

'Mad indeed,' Leocadius nodded, 'but while I'm wearing this pallium, it's what I have to do. I'll get over it.'

'Pelagius never went to Rome,' Vitalis told him. 'He's somewhere in the north converting pagans.'

'Good luck with that,' Leocadius grunted. 'Wild horses wouldn't get me to the north again. What are you doing now?'

'I haven't got the fire in my soul that Pelagius has. Perhaps one day, I'll go to the shrine of Petrus, but for now, I'm just staying alive,' Vitalis said. 'And that's not easy in this city of yours.'

'Mine?' Leocadius laughed. 'You'd have some argument with the vicarius over that, I think.'

'Still playing politics, eh?' Vitalis shook his head.

'Goes with the territory,' the consul shrugged. 'Look. Vit, there are places I have to be. Come to the palace tomorrow. I seem to remember you've got a good hand. I've got an opening for a scribe.' He winked at the man. 'All creeds accepted.'

Vitalis laughed. 'That's mighty Roman of you,' he said. Then, suddenly serious. 'No, thanks, Leo,' he said. 'I don't think so. Too much water. Too many bridges.'

The consul nodded. 'Suit yourself,' he said and held out a hand. Vitalis caught it.

'You still wear the ring, I see,' Leocadius smiled.

Vitalis looked down at the gold and ebony on his finger, inlaid with the four helmets. An identical one glittered on the consul's finger too.

'It's become part of my hand,' he said.

'Well, look after yourself, Christian,' Leocadius walked off into the night.

'And you, pagan.' But when the consul turned, Vitalis was already a ghost, vanished into darkness.

The vicarius' wine was good, his quarters in the huge basilica spacious and comfortable. Leocadius knew them well, because they had been his before the vicarius had arrived and Leocadius rather resented that. Civilis was the last appointment made by Count Theodosius, but that was before the Count had reached Carthago and had fallen foul of the Emperor. Now the great man was dead and all of Britannia, especially Leocadius the consul, was stuck with the great man's choice.

'You'll forgive the hour of course,' Civilis stretched back on his couch, the firelight burning in his eyes. He had dismissed his slaves and the two men sat alone as a new day dawned along the Thamesis long before the light itself crept into the east.

'I assumed you have your reasons,' Leocadius ran his index finger around the rim of the goblet. The dagger still lay up his sleeve, along with a variety of tricks, just in case.

'Magnus Maximus,' Civilis said. The elephant in the room had just trumpeted.

'Ah.'

'My scouts tell me he was at Isca Dumnoniorum a week ago, bound for Calleva.'

'He's coming east,' Leocadius nodded.

'He is,' Civilis said, 'and at every step on the way, he is being proclaimed Caesar.'

'I know.'

Civilis straightened. 'You do?'

Leocadius spread his arms, careful not to spill any of the vicarius' good wine. 'I'm the consul here,' he said. 'Not much happens without me knowing about it.'

Civilis' eyes narrowed. 'But you're a friend of his, aren't you? A hero of the Wall? The Count told me all about that in Gaul.'

'I have fought under Maximus, yes,' Leocadius said, twisting the gold and jet ring on his finger and watching it glow and sparkle in the firelight. 'But I wouldn't say we were friends.'

'Well, what would you say?' Civilis wanted to know. 'I'll be plain. My orders, from the Count himself, are to govern Britannia in his name. I expected support from the Dux Britannorum and from the consul of Londinium.'

'But …?'

'But I find that the Dux Britannorum is declaring himself Caesar at every crossroads in the country. He is stirring up the godless shits who live here to conspire against their emperor. That leaves me with a problem, Leocadius. And I want to know where my consul stands.'

Leocadius sighed and looked into the swirling darkness of his wine, then into the crumbling ruins of the burning logs. No, he would never go north again, but how much simpler life had been there, when all he had to do was march and keep watch, practise with javelin and dart and sword. When Vit had still been a human being at his elbow and Paternus was still alive and Justinus a circitor with a heart. He would swap all that for what he had now. Now he was between Scylla and Charybdis, the demons who guarded the narrow straits in men's lives.

'The problem,' he said, 'is that Maximus is doing what he's doing to avenge the murder of the very man who sent you here. He's convinced that the Count was

13

executed on the orders of the Emperor. How to get revenge? Simple. Declare yourself emperor instead and cut the vicious bastard's head off ... saving your presence, Vicarius.'

'Maximus may be right about the Emperor,' Civilis conceded, 'but I can't sit idly by while he's rousing this country into a state of open rebellion.'

'Will the Emperor send troops to rein him in?' Leocadius asked.

'I doubt it,' Civilis said. 'Too many problems nearer to home.'

'Well, there you are,' the consul smiled. 'If Maximus has a mind, he'll just take his three legions across the German Sea and tell the Emperor his fortune. We won't be involved.'

Civilis was not smiling. He was scowling, looking with contempt at the man lounging on his couch. Leocadius was over-promoted, out of his depth and quite possibly the vainest man he had ever met.

'But we will be involved, Consul, won't we?' Civilis growled, 'because if Maximus, with his delusions of grandeur, takes his three legions over the German Sea, who, in the name of any god you care to mention, is going to defend us?'

Civilis let the ominous silence answer.

'Let me tell you,' he said softly, 'how it is and how it will be. You are a popinjay. You may have been a soldier once and you may have pulled any amount of wool over Theodosius' eyes with your stories of heroics up on the Wall. But now you're an inept idiot drowning in a world you can't understand, never mind control. You are so far down the pecking order, Leocadius, that I can't tell you from the shit on my sandals. That's how it is. How it is going to be is that whatever I decide to do about Maximus, you will give me whatever limited assistance you are capable of. When I say "jump" your only question will be "How high, Vicarius?" Do I make myself clear?'

Leocadius was on his feet, the half-empty goblet on the table. He crossed to Civilis and stared into his face. 'One day,' he said softly, 'you'll push me too far, old man.'

CHAPTER TWO

Din Paladyr, Rivros in the year of the Christ 380

The hawk circled high above the fortress with its cluster of huts, scenting the smoke that rose from the fires. The great grey estuary lay far ahead, half lost in the mists of winter. She saw every movement on the ground below, the tall grasses blown by the wind. The snow was late this year though the ground was iron hard and the slower-moving streams already rimmed with ice. She saw the two fighters on the hill, circling each other in the morning air, but they were humans and she kept away from them.

The oak was in his hand as he watched his half-brother. The boy was big and strong, five years older than he was and half a man already. The arithmetic was simple and it gave the same answer every time. Eight summers is no match for thirteen summers – five more years of speed and skill and cunning. Edirne lunged, but too slow and his wooden blade rattled on Taran's before he hurtled to the wet, cold grass. His tunic was a slimy green already and his lungs hurt. His wrist ached and his tough little body was bruised and battered where Taran's blade had caught him again and again. Would the bigger boy *never* go down?

'Come on, Eddi.' Taran's taunt was more in pity than in anger. He hated mock fights with this child because it was no contest. It was like battling with a post. It never moved and it never fought back. Edirne summoned up what strength he had left and tried again. He came in low this time, too low as it turned out because he lost his balance as he reached Taran and felt his big brother's wooden blade slap him painfully around the back of the head. The impact of the blow, as well as his own momentum, sent him rolling over the rock parapet and he hit the ground with a thump that jarred his back and blew the wind from his lungs. He scrabbled to his knees but he couldn't breathe. The rocks, the windswept bushes, the sky, all reeled in his vision, his empty lungs refusing to work.

'Steady.' It was a quiet voice he hadn't heard before and the accent was strange. It was Gododdin, certainly, and yet ... He felt a gentle pressure on his chest and a firmer one on his back and he felt his lungs inflate and his heart descend from his mouth. When the blinding fog of panic had passed, he was looking up into the face of a Roman.

He was wearing a tunic, scruffy and dirty under his heavy cloak and he had a fur cap on his head. His horse, a bay gelding, cropped the grass nearby and a painted shield hung from the saddlebow.

'Io, Taran,' the Roman called to the bigger boy standing on the rock ledge, looking down at them. Taran didn't answer. He knew who this man was but had not seen him in three years and he did not know how to react.

The Roman made sure that Edirne was steady, then he retrieved his wooden sword from the grass. He weighed it in his hand, then flipped it in the air so that the pommel faced the boy. Taran watched as the Roman half-crouched and whispered something in his brother's ear. Edirne looked doubtful, but took the sword and clambered back up onto the rock. He spread his arms and circled Taran, who smiled. Was that it? Had the Roman told him to dance a jig? Somehow, Taran instinctively knew that that was going to make no difference to the outcome at all.

The younger boy lunged again, in the same old way and with the same old timing. Taran parried effortlessly, but the expected clatter of blade on blade never happened, because Edirne had suddenly thrown the sword into his left hand and he slashed it hard across Taran's ribs. The elder boy howled with shock and pain and dropped to his knees. Edirne clapped and sang, laughing at his brother's discomfort and the Roman smiled.

'You must be Edirne,' he said. 'I knew your father.'

Valentia

The lights darted like fireflies between the naked boughs of the trees. Far to the north the hill fort stood black and silent against the night and to the east sounded the restless crash of the sea. They came on rough-shod little ponies, bouncing over the heather, to the sacred grove.

A blade flashed in the darkness. 'Give the watchword,' came the guttural order.

'Light of Grannos,' the answering voice came back.

'By his rays.'

The blade slid home and the horseman dismounted, the last to arrive. His dress was strange and his hair a shining gold in the torchlights. He carried a long straight sword at his side and there was no beard on his chin.

'Welcome, Aelfrith.'

The newcomer nodded and stretched out a hand. Malwyn caught it and led him into the space. Half a dozen men stood there in a circle of stones. 'The Romans pulled this place down,' Malwyn said, seeing Aelfrith looking at it. 'It was a sacred shrine to Grannos. Not that they gave a shit about that, of course.'

'Why now?' Aelfrith eased his massive sword aside and sat down. The others also sat, crossing their legs at the ankles and sinking down effortlessly.

'Now?' Malwyn clicked his fingers. 'Wine, after your long journey?'

'Do you have no ale?'

'Ale? Of course; silly of me. Branc, ale for our guest.'

'You haven't answered my question,' Aelfrith reminded his host. 'Why have you chosen this particular time to throw your sword into the ring?'

Malwyn looked about him. They were all true men there, followers of Grannos, brothers of the sun. 'Why not?'

Aelfrith laughed. 'You'll have to do better than that, malcontent,' he said. 'You Votadini have licked Roman arse for two hundred years. Why would you stop now?'

'We aren't Votadini,' Branc said, handing the man a pitcher of ale. 'That's just what the Romans call us. We're Gododdin. Always were. Always will be.'

Aelfrith took a long, hard swig and wiped his mouth. Gododdin ale was good; but was it better than Votadini? He shook his head. 'You still haven't answered me,' he said.

'A woman rules us,' Malwyn muttered, as though the words stuck in his throat.

Aelfrith laughed again and took another draught. 'That's not new, either,' he said. 'You have goddesses and high priestesses and queens. See these?' He pointed to his leather-strapped leggings. 'You won't find a Saxon wearing a skirt, but you boys do. So do the Romans.'

Malwyn scowled at him. This man was good. Not only did he speak the Gododdin tongue like a native, he knew their customs and their history too. 'Brenna is not like other queens we've had,' he murmured. 'She was married to a Roman and has a Roman brat. You can see which way the wind is blowing, Aelfrith. A few years back there was a rebellion on the Wall. Valentinus blew it down.'

'With his fiery breath,' another man confided.

'But the bastard Romans rebuilt it,' Malwyn went on. 'Now, there's a commander of the Wall and who's to say he's not going to extend his power north? Today Aesica and Vindolanda. Tomorrow, Din Paladyr and all our sacred lands. She's too close to the sons of the She-Wolf. It's time she was stopped.'

'I'm not an assassin,' Aelfrith said, licking the ale from his lips.

'I don't need an assassin,' Malwyn said. 'I'll kill the bitch myself when the time's right. I need your men. There are idiots among us misguided enough to want to die for their queen. They'll make a fight of it. How many can you supply?'

Aelfrith waited, looking into the eyes of the queen-killers, bright in the firelight. 'What's in it for me?' he asked quietly.

'A sixth of Gododdin land, from the Wall to the sea. And a sixth of the Paladyr silver.'

Aelfrith had the ancient skill of his people not to blink or show his true feelings. The lands of the Gododdin were rich in sheep and cattle but scant of arable fields. But the Roman silver of Paladyr was legendary, like the grail the Christians talked of. 'A third of Gododdin land,' he said, stroking his chin as though he was selecting a pony in a horse-fair, 'and half the Paladyr silver.'

There were roars and hoots from everyone except Malwyn and the Saxon.

'You're a madman,' Branc shouted.

Aelfrith was on his feet. 'Thanks for the ale,' he said and turned to go. 'And good luck.'

'Wait.' Malwyn stopped him. 'We can talk about this.'

The Saxon turned back. 'We can,' he said. 'Tell me, this Brenna ... I have heard she is a passing beauty.'

'She is,' Malwyn nodded.

'Throw her in as well, then' Aelfrith said. 'Before you cut her throat, that is. And tell me, too, the opposition. This Roman, this commander of the Wall. What's his name?'

Din Paladyr

The firelight flickered on the rough beams of the domed roof, glinting sharper where it caught the eye of the rats that lived within the thatch. The smoke played tricks with the eyes, forming patterns that were now here, now there and it took a great deal of the commander's concentration to keep him in the here and now, as long dead friends and enemies whirled and eddied in the darker corners. The queen's private apartments were quiet when compared to the rough and ready company he normally kept, but even so it was full of the susurration of furs on a bed, the rustle of a dog, twitching, chasing deer in the dead rushes of the floor before the fire. And the breathing of the woman who had married his oldest friend.

'Justinus Coelius,' Brenna looked at him across the dying fire. 'It's been a long time.'

The Roman looked no older than when they had last met, but there was a weariness about him she had not noticed before, probably would never have noticed had they met more often. It was a tiredness about the eyes, a hollowness of cheek; nothing more. She had not changed either. Her eyes were still deep and dark, her laugh like the waters of the mountain streams, babbling over the shifting stones.

Justinus looked across the darkened hall to where Taran and Edirne lay asleep, wrapped in furs against the winter. 'Your boys have grown,' he said. 'Tell me about them.'

She smiled indulgently, as mothers will. She could have talked about her babies all night, but Justinus, she knew, had no children of his own. No wife. She didn't know why he was here and she didn't want to bore him. 'Taran is nearly a man,' she said. 'Rides well and loves hunting.' She twisted her mouth. 'He neglects his studies, though, Justinus,' she scolded gently. 'His written Latin ...' She raised her eyebrows.

'And Edirne?'

She smiled again. 'Just like his father, isn't he?'

Justinus looked at the sleeping boy, his freck-led face glowing in the firelight. He had not known Paternus when he was the boy's age. He had only known him as a man when the two of them had stood shoulder to shoulder on the Wall and the barbarians had killed the man's first family. Brenna and Paternus had made a political marriage, to tie the Votadini to Rome, to bring much-needed peace to Valentia. But the marriage had turned to love and Edirne was the living symbol of that love.

'You must miss him,' Justinus murmured.

She looked into those tired eyes. 'So must you,' she said. It was strange for her to imagine what Paternus must have meant to the commander of the Wall. Brenna was a woman who had found love and comfort in the man's arms but she was a queen too and a warrior. She had buckled on her helmet and swung a sword with her men and she knew comrade-ship and the need to trust the man at her elbow and the man who watched her back. Even so, she could not separate Paternus the soldier from Paternus the lover and the father of her child.

'Why are you here, Justinus?' she reached out and touched his hand. For a moment, their rings flashed together in circles of gold, the rings with the four hel-mets chased in jet. Brenna's had been Paternus' and she had taken it from his dead finger five long years ago. One day – one day soon – she would pass it on to Taran. He was not Paternus' son by blood, but by all else that was holy. And when the day came, Taran would watch over the Wall as his father had. And all would be well.

'I came to pay my respects,' he said, 'at Pat's grave. And to make sure you and the boys were all right.'

She smiled. 'We are,' she said. 'Oh, we have the odd Pictish raid for sheep and cattle – you know, the usual. But Valentinus is dead, Justinus. And I have good men around me, loyal and true.'

'Good.' He smiled back at her with words unspoken. 'Good.'

'My lady,' a voice called from the doorway. 'Is this a bad time?'

The queen and the commander of the Wall were on their feet by the dying fire, the glow throwing strange shadows on the oak uprights of the hall. 'No, no.' Brenna said. 'I was just telling Justinus how lucky I am to be surrounded by loyal men. Justinus, commander of the Wall, this is my other arm. Say salve to Malwyn.'

Pontes

General Magnus Maximus, now Caesar of the legions of Britannia, had marched north-east. His cavalry of the Heruli had splashed through the marshes at Pontes, following the old road of the II Augusta and he had set up camp in the low woods where the Thamesis forked and twisted through its long valley. This part of Britannia had been safe and peaceful for years, but it never hurt to take precautions and Maximus sat his horse by the roadside while his vexillation set to to build a camp. The centurions walked the new earth ramparts, ridged like iron in the grip of Januarius, tapping with their gnarled sticks on the backs of men they thought were slacking. The javelins, the shields and the swords stayed with the baggage as the shovels flashed silver and the axes toppled the fir trunks and lopped the branches.

By midnight, the general was lounging in his tent at the camp's centre, his principia for the night. Bruno the mastiff was lolling at his master's feet, crunching on an ox bone with marrow to die for. Maximus looked at the candle's reflections glowing in the silver wine goblet in his hand.

'Take a letter, Scribonius,' he said. 'To His Excellency Antoninus Civilis, Vicarius of Britannia, greeting.'

The clerk hurried to catch up, dipping his stylus into the ink and writing furiously. Maximus was choosing his words with care, but not great care because he had three legions under his command and a bird in the hand … '"You will have heard by now that the legions have elected me Caesar. Accordingly, I expect your allegiance when I arrive in the city and will give you three days to prepare. You will turn out the City garrison and you will bring the Ordo in person, along with the Consul. I won't trouble you with a triumph. They are *so* passé, aren't they?" That's all.

Wax it, Scribonius. I'll seal it. Oh, no, wait a minute. "Post scriptum. An ovation will do."'

Londinium

'An ovation?' Antoninus Civilis couldn't believe it. He looked up at Maximus' messenger. The man was a tribune by his scarf but he looked six. 'How old are you, Galvo?'

'Thirty one, sir.' The tribune was staring straight ahead, helmet in the crook of his arm. No one else moved. No one else spoke. All over the basilica, any number of slaves and officials could have heard a pin drop.

Civilis narrowed his eyes. 'Do you know what an ovation is?' he asked.

'Er ... not entirely, sir, no.'

Civilis nodded, his point made. 'That's because the last one held in Rome took place in the reign of Diocletian, when this place was still a cluster of miserable wooden huts. What, tell me, is the general trying to prove?'

Procopius Galvo was not a man to be intimidated. The vicarius might indeed rule all of Britannia by order of the Emperor, but Magnus Maximus was the emperor now *and* he had command of the army. It was time for lesser men to stand aside. 'The Caesar ...'

'The Caesar!' Civilis spat. 'Are we Greeks, Galvo, that we believe in democracy? Soldiers choosing their own emperor went out with the deified Julius and Marcus Aurelius.'

'Great days of our heritage,' Galvo said. He always was a traditionalist.

'Bollocks!' Civilis growled. 'This is the real world, Galvo, not some romantic, idealized past. Power is about who you know and who you can control. It's nothing to do with mindless halfwits of soldiers cheering and clapping a man on the back. Tell *General* Maximus that his request for an ovation is denied. Further, his troops are not to come within ten miles of Londinium. And, you may both rest assured, I shall be sending word of this new treachery by the fastest horse and ship to the emperor – the *real* one, that is; the one they keep in Augusta Treverorum. Now, get out.'

Procopius Galvo saluted, clapped the helmet on his head and about-faced. Maximus had warned him the interview would go something like this. And accordingly, Galvo went in search of the next man the new Caesar wanted him to find – Leocadius Honorius, the Consul.

Aquarius rose the next night with the fullness of the moon. The wind rose from the south-west, presaging storms. The sun, when it shone, was under the sign of Capricorn and the month under Juno. Along the soggy margins of the Thamesis, the stakes were sharpened and the reeds cut. Vitalis saw all this and smiled. All around him, the people of Londinium were hedging their bets. Every Sunday they trooped into the great church of Archbishop Dalmatius, summoned by bells. Yet now, in the long nights of fourteen hours with frost creeping over the planking of the bridge and crusting the walls, those same people made their sacrifices to Ossipago and Tellus Mater, to all the gods and goddesses of the hearth; just in case the Lord Jesus Christ was a figment of somebody's imagination.

Vitalis himself had no doubts. He cut the reeds with the others in the water margins because he wove baskets with them, not because it was the Roman way. He sold those baskets in the Forum and the alleys off the Via Flumenensis, but never on the Lord's day. That he kept holy.

And that Sunday he was kneeling in the inner sanctum of the little hovel he rented near the river when he heard a soft sound. Vitalis was not ashamed of his faith but he did not share it with others and he would rather die than attend Dalmatius' church, with its incense and its hypocrisy. He half rose from his makeshift altar and turned to the light streaming in through the door. For a moment he couldn't make her out. There was a halo of brightness around her hair and her hair was impossibly gold.

'Ave, Vitalis.' Her voice was soft and her Latin was from Gaul.

'Conchessa?' Was this a dream? Vitalis had not seen her for twelve years, perhaps longer. He was not a Christian then. He was not even a soldier. And the annoying little brat dogging his footsteps through the heather had been transformed into a beautiful woman. How they had fallen apart was a long story and he could not explain it now as he stood there, looking at her. They both took a step forward, half a step. He reached out and touched her outstretched hand. He saw the tears in her eyes and he held her close, so close he thought she would break.

'Little sister,' he said. 'Little sister no more.' Her body heaved with convulsive sobs and he felt her tears drip onto his tunic. His had joined them before they broke apart. She looked, smiling, into his face. It was still strong, still open, still honest, still the Vitalis who had fought her battles and squared up to the world for her. She ran her fingers over the scar on his forehead.

'What?'

'A barbarian's memento,' he said. 'Nothing more.'

She frowned suddenly and her hand fell to his chest. 'Is your heart wounded too?' she asked.

'No,' he smiled. 'No, my heart is good.'

She ran her fingers around his beard and his hair. 'It always was, big brother,' she said.

Suddenly there was silence between them. So much to say and so many years to trade in their memories. But where to begin? That was too hard for a sacred shrine in a hovel by a river, somewhere on the edge of the world.

'Er … you're married!' Vitalis saw the ring, glittering gold on her wedding finger.

'Yes,' she said. 'Yes, I am. And you?' She saw the ring on his finger too, but it was not a wedding band. It was made of gold and was chased with four helmets in blackest jet.

'No,' he said solemnly. 'This?' He held up his hand to the light. 'Another barbarian memento. I don't know why I wear it.'

They walked out into Vitalis' simple room and sat together on his narrow bed. If she was appalled by the poverty and the stark simplicity and the smell from the river, she did not show it. 'Vit,' she said, holding his hand and choking back the tears. 'I need help. I didn't know where else to go.'

'How did you find me?' he asked.

'That wasn't easy,' she smiled, sniffing. 'I went to the consul, your friend Leocadius.'

She saw his face fall. 'Friend no more,' he said.

'That's not what he says,' she told him. 'He told me all about the Wall. How you and he were heroes. We heard all about that, even in Gaul …' She was rabbiting on again, as though they were children once more and she was putting the world to rights. 'He said he'd lost touch with you for a while but when he met you again the other night, he made it his business to find out where you lived. That's how …' He stopped her with a finger on her lips.

'You said you needed help,' he reminded her.

She breathed in. For minutes, for hours, for days, for weeks, she had been putting off this moment. But now, it was here. And what she was about to ask seemed so huge, so unfair.

'My husband,' she almost whispered. 'Calpurnius. He's gone.'

Vitalis frowned. 'Left you, you mean?'

'No.' She had wrestled with this for so long now, she had not realised how it would sound to an outsider, even if the outsider was her big brother. 'No, we're happy.' She bit her lip to stop the tears falling. '*So* happy. No, he's gone, Vit, vanished into thin air. No one knows where he is.'

'Start from the beginning,' he told her, holding both of her hands.

'He was on the staff of Count Theodosius at Carthago.'

Vitalis blinked. He knew – surely the whole world knew – that Theodosius was dead, his head lopped off on the orders of the Emperor.

Conchessa sailed on. 'The last I heard, Calpurnius was transferred to the younger Theodosius, at Augusta Treverorum, in Gaul. There, one night, he just … disappeared.'

CHAPTER THREE

Londinium

A pale moon was filtering through the slats of the shutters in the private apartments of the consul. Leocadius was sitting in bed with Honoria stretched beside him. He was languidly stroking her breast while reading the latest missive from Rome.

'Nice to know I'm still in your thoughts,' she tapped the parchment in annoyance.

He laughed and threw it onto the side table. 'Sorry,' he said. 'Affairs of state.' Although he would die rather than admit it, Leocadius was out of his depth. The vicarius was right. Consuls came from old Roman families; politics and duty were born in them. Ruling was as simple to them as breathing out and breathing in. But Leo? Well, Leo was a Wall soldier when the mood took him, a lover more often. He liked his wine, his women, his dice. And now, he was a stylus-pusher, up to his neck in other peoples' problems every day. The queues of petitioners outside the basilica were testimony to that. What about the fishing rights below the bridge? When was the consul going to do something about draining the marshes? Those damned Mithraians were still worshipping in a Christian city, and what was the Consul going to do about it?

'Forget all that,' Honoria purred, sliding her hand between the consul's legs, 'at least for one night.'

'You know he wants him dead, don't you?'

Honoria sighed and pulled her hand away. It was not going to be her night. 'You'll have to be more specific, Leo, if I'm to understand what the hell you're talking about.'

'Sorry,' he said, leaning back against the wall. 'Maximus. He's coming to the old camp out to the west and he's asked Civilis for an ovation.'

Honoria frowned. She had been born with the sound of Archbishop Dalmatius' bells ringing in her ears and she knew nothing of Rome's past.

'It's a procession,' Leocadius told her, reaching across for his goblet of wine. 'When a campaigning general entered the eternal city in the good old days, he was given a triumph – chariots, music, marching, captured booty, prisoners of war – the whole Roman mile. An ovation is a smaller version of that. The general *walks* into the city, not rides, with a myrtle crown on his head. No troops, minimum of fuss.'

'So, it's to celebrate a victory?' Honoria was getting the hang of it.

Leocadius nodded.

'What victory has Maximus won?' she felt bound to ask.

'Precisely.' The consul stretched. 'Since the Valentinus rebellion was put down, he hasn't. Declaring himself Caesar seems to be victory enough.'

'And Civilis wants Maximus dead?' She folded her arms and looked at him. This was the kind of politics Honoria understood.

'Other way round.'

She sat bolt upright, 'By the gods! You mean he's going to attack the city?'

'No, no,' Leocadius calmed her. 'That's not necessary. Maximus has set his sights on the purple. Well, why not? Lesser men have done it. But to take on Rome he has to make sure all is well here first. He's had nothing but arse-kissing so far, but that's only in the south. He'll have to go north and he'll have to go west. There are tribes in both places who have no love for the eagles. No, Caesar Maximus wants me to murder Civilis.'

'He asked you?'

'Not directly. He sent a tribune to me yesterday. Galvo, I think his name was.'

'Oh, I saw him.' Honoria's eyes flashed. 'Rather gorgeous, I'd say.'

'Yes, I'm sure you would,' he laughed. 'Behave yourself. Apparently Galvo had gone to Civilis with Maximus' ovation request and had been sent away with a flea in his ear. Galvo told me all about it and said the Caesar would be ... how did he put it? "Eternally grateful if I could pray to Orcus for a solution".'

'Orcus?'

'Yes,' Leocadius sighed. 'I had to look that one up too! Dis Pater, Pluto, Thanatos – he goes by lots of names. He's the god of death.'

'But he only wants you to pray?' Honoria gave her man an old-fashioned look.

'Well, we know how useful that is. I might as well send Vitalis to do the deed. He gets on well with his god.'

Honoria patted his arm. 'Don't trouble yourself, darling,' she said, wriggling down in the bed, 'I have a few altars of my own to kneel at.' She slid back the covers and ran her hand over Leocadius' manhood. 'And speaking of kneeling …'

'Oh, all right,' he sighed. 'Do a consul's duties never end?'

And they laughed together in the moonlight.

Valentia

Justinus Coelius, commander of the Wall, rode out with Malwyn of the Votadini that dies Jovis, walking their horses over the sheep-shorn grass above the estuary. The wind was raw up here, slicing through wool and even leather as the first flurries of snow began.

'The queen tells me you've had a few Pictish raids,' Justinus said.

'You know the painted people,' Malwyn grunted. 'Never saw somebody else's sheep they didn't like.'

'I could send a vexillation,' Justinus suggested. 'A hundred men or so.'

'We can handle the Picts,' Malwyn assured him.

Justinus was already hauling in his rein, checking the bay and pointing out to sea. 'That ship,' he said. 'What's that?'

Malwyn squinted into the weather. It was difficult to make it out, but it was huge, with oars that, at this distance, silently ploughed the churning water. There was no mast or sail but the hull was decked with shields, where monsters writhed in bright colours. 'We get all sorts up here,' he said. 'It's nothing.'

'It's not Roman,' Justinus murmured. 'And it's not Votadini.'

'The Picts don't use ships,' Malwyn told him. 'Nothing to worry about.'

'Saxon?' Justinus was going through all the possibilities in his head.

'Saxon?' Malwyn frowned. 'Now what would they be doing here?'

'That's what worries me,' Justinus said. 'I'm sending you a vexillation whether you need it or not.'

All the men of Din Paladyr had gathered for the hunt the next day. The cold was as raw as ever and the animal tracks in the morning frost told their own story. It was a large pack, moving south-west.

'Not this one,' Brenna hauled her younger boy back by the scruff of his tunic. 'Not this year.'

'It's only a hunt,' Edirne whined. 'I've gone hunting before.'

'Yes,' she smiled, looking down at him, 'for rabbits. But a wolf is a different story.' She bent low to him, whispering in his ear. 'Remember old Gronw, with his one eye?'

Edirne did. The old man had terrified him ever since he could remember. A livid purple scar ran from his hair line to his lip, slicing through the dead socket where his left eye had been. He dribbled when he spoke. And when he spoke he made almost no sense to the little boy because his voice was rasping like a saw on wood.

'A wolf got him. And he was a grown man.'

'Then why can *he* go?' Edirne shrieked, waving his finger at Taran who was climbing into his saddle in the yard where the horses milled and snorted.

'Because I can,' Taran snarled at him. He pointed to the gilded torc around his neck. 'See this? It means I will be king one day. And don't you forget it, little brother.'

'Boys!' Brenna could snarl too, like any she-wolf. 'That's enough. Your time will come, Eddi. You have to be patient.'

She looked up at the Roman already in his saddle. He had left his shield in his quarters and the helmet he had brought with him just in case. Instead, he wore his fur cap. 'Look after my big boy,' she said. Taran scowled. It had taken him a long time to get used to Paternus who had become his father. But this man was different. He was cold and held himself apart. And besides, he gave Edirne fighting tips which was definitely uncalled for.

'Depend on it,' Justinus said and wheeled away.

'How are your dogs today, Piran?' Malwyn called to the hound-master.

'Fighting fit, lord.'

'Good. They'll need to be.'

Brenna held her little one close as the hunters rode out. There were waves and cheers from the women, the old men and the children and then they were gone.

They followed the old trails that snaked over the moorland, the horses' hooves crunching on the frozen heather, brown and silver now before the spring. The hounds ran on, with their easy, lazy lope, tongues lolling out of their mouths. Every now and then, one would drop its head and sniff the ground. The going was hard and the foot-runners and those on poor ponies soon fell back. They would make do with rabbits for their kill and tell tall tales of the thousand and one reasons why the wolves got away.

Had there been a sun that day it would have been high in the heavens by the time the leaders hauled rein. The pack had speeded up and they were making for the forest that lay, dark and haunted to the south. Nobody wanted to give up. Not Justinus, who had a certain reputation as commander of the Wall. Not Malwyn, who would never let himself be bested by any Roman. And not Taran, who was as much a man as any of them.

'It's noon,' Piran said, secretly glad to slide out of his saddle after the gruelling ride. 'We'd best turn back, Malwyn. The winter day is short.'

'Sod the winter day,' Malwyn growled, easing his back as best he could. 'Look.' He pointed to where Taran was urging his horse forward. 'A mere boy shows us the way. Justinus? Ready for the wolf?'

'As I'll ever be,' the Roman said.

'Watch out for Flidais, then,' Malwyn galloped on to join the future king of the Gododdin.

'Flidais?' Justinus looked vacantly at Piran who was hauling himself back into the saddle again.

'Keeper of the beasts,' the hound-master grinned, 'and spirit of the forest. She owns the wolves and she's partial to men. Let her once get her legs around you, you'll never walk again!'

Everybody laughed and they rode on.

It wasn't Justinus' imagination. The day had darkened, bringing the night earlier than usual and in the tangle of the forests it was darker still. At first the sky from the edge had lit their way, but that had gone now and they groped forward in darkness. The fast riding, thudding over the open moorland to the rhythm of hooves and the hunting songs of the Gododdin, was a thing of the past. Now they walked their horses, stroking the animals' necks to keep them calm and quiet. They could have lit flaring brands but torches would have terrified the wolves and they would never find them. As it was, Piran, the experienced hunter, knew that the pack had scented the men long ago. But the curious thing was, they were not running any more. They had slowed first to a walk, then to an amble.

The dogs knew it too, noses to the thick, brown carpet of pine needles, ears flat back, bristles upright along their spines. They didn't bark, didn't lose sight of the horsemen. No one spoke. Justinus looked at Taran. The boy looked pale and scared. He had hunted wolves before but there was something different about this hunt, something that made the hairs on his neck stand on end.

Malwyn urged his horse closer to the boy's. 'Over there,' he whispered. 'See? In the clearing.'

Taran stared. He could see nothing but the trunks of the firs, pale against the others, standing like sentinels. He could hear nothing but the moan of the trees in the top branches, Flidais singing to her children. The sky was the colour of lead with darker clouds of rusted iron rolling in from the east.

'That's a wolf, boy,' Malwyn said. 'And a big one. He's yours. Go on.'

Taran didn't move. He looked around him. Justinus had gone. So had Piran and the others. He was alone with the chief counsellor of the Gododdin, his mother's right arm.

'You're not going to let the others get there first, are you?' Malwyn's tone was mocking, scolding. He held his own rein fast as the boy took a deep breath and rammed home his heels. The pony jolted over the bracken, crashing into the open space. Taran whirled this way and that. He could see nothing in the darkness, nothing but the trees. Nothing but his own fear. He couldn't even hear the wind now, just the thud of his own heart, somewhere very near his mouth.

There was a hiss in the near darkness, something heavy and sharp hurtling through the air. Taran's horse whinnied in shock and pain as the spear bit into its shoulder and the animal staggered. The boy was thrown clear, twisting his leg as he fell. When he struggled to sit up, he was alone. The horse was dead beside him, one leg still twitching and the mouth foaming where blood had been forced up from its severed lungs. He looked back along the track for Malwyn, but the man wasn't there. There was no one there.

Taran was not given to fears. The shadows of the night held no terrors for him. He had run with his mother from the terror of the rebel Valentinus, had seen the man's silver-faced helmet through the smoke of burning villages. He had seen men die and women and children too because that was his birth-right and these were his times. A man who lived to be forty was either a miracle or a coward. No one slept without a knife by their side. All this, Taran knew.

What he did not know was who had killed his horse. What he did not know was what to do now. Because he was suddenly aware of yellow eyes looking at him from the trees. They didn't blink and they didn't look away. One by one they slunk out of the darkness – grey wolves; three of them. Their pink tongues hung out of their gaping mouths and they made no sound. In an instant, Taran realised they could smell the blood of the horse. But he was standing between them and the dead animal and his ankle throbbed in agony. He was balancing himself on one leg, slowly drawing his knife from his belt.

Each wolf weighed what he did, but they had fangs and claws. They were hungry and desperate. And there were three of them. His mouth felt bricky-dry and tears welled in his eyes. Where had they all gone, his people, who only moments ago had been riding at his elbow? And how had the wolves found him, alone like this? Piran, Malwyn, Justinus, they had vanished into the coming night, like ghosts.

The boy hobbled backwards, trying to edge past his fallen horse. He had no other weapons. His spear-bearer had long ago dropped out of the hunt. He braced himself, ready for the first wolf, but he knew he would only ever have one chance and he held his blade out, intending to slash the throat below the teeth. The animal hurled itself, ears flat, snarling. It was still in mid-air when it squealed and somersaulted before hitting the ground hard, throwing Taran off balance so that he rolled into the bracken. The second loped forward, but it was not on the attack like the first and it scented the air, confused. Its yellow, beady eyes took in the horse, the boy, its dead brother the wolf. It snarled and turned tail, loping into the forest with the third.

Somebody was running through the under-growth, crashing through the bracken and leaping the fallen trunks.

'Taran! Are you hurt?'

The boy looked up. It was the Roman, Justinus, Paternus' friend from the days of the Wall. Justinus who had come once more from nowhere to change the life of a young prince. Justinus, who always looked at the queen of the Gododdin in a way that Taran did not quite understand.

The boy nodded, letting the Roman help him up. His ankle hurt and he was shaking but he would not cry. He watched as Justinus knelt and pulled an iron dart out of the dead wolf's head. It was red with blood.

'Taran!' There was a commotion behind them and Malwyn and the others came at a run. 'Are you all right, boy?' Malwyn wanted to know. 'What happened?'

'I ... don't know,' Taran said. 'The wolves. There were three of them. Justinus saved my life.'

Piran was kneeling beside the grey killer of sheep and of men. 'Dart, Roman?' he asked.

Justinus was helping Taran onto his own saddle. He nodded. Ever since he had been a foot-slogging pedes in the army, Justinus Coelius had carried his darts. You never knew when they might come in handy.

'Good shot.' Piran hacked off the wolf's head with a single sweep of his hunting sword. 'For your saddle,' he said, holding it up.

'For Taran's saddle,' Justinus said. 'He earned it today.'

Malwyn had dismounted, looking at the headless wolf and the slaughtered horse. The others were turning back, heading for the high country and the long ride home. Justinus wrenched out the spear from Taran's horse. 'Anyone know a wolf that could throw one of these?' he asked.

'I told you,' Malwyn said, grimly. 'Flidais. She's sister to Badb Catha, the battle raven, the bringer of death.'

'Do you believe this nonsense?' Justinus asked.

'No more than you believe in Jupiter highest and best and Mithras, god of the morning,' Malwyn said, 'but ask yourself, Roman; let's just say that Flidais is real and so is Badb. Who do the evil sisters have it in for, eh? Who was the real target here today, in this darkness and this confusion? Was it a thirteen year old boy, who has never done anyone any harm? Or was it you?'

Londinium

The hum of conversation was rising to a crescendo in the largest room of the consul's suite. His slaves had been beavering away all morning to bring in more couches, more silken throws, more sconces for lighting the tapers when the light started to fail in this winter's afternoon. The effect was magical, rich and yet other worldly, so that many of the consul's guests would leave without having any firm opinion of any part of the occasion, save the food was of the very richest and the couches the softest they had ever lounged on. The food at these gatherings was often spoiled by an excess of fashion over taste. Larks' tongues stuffed into dormice, cooked in pastry and doused in honey were more a status symbol than edible and many a titbit ended up being stuffed beneath a rich silken cushion. But it was impressive; no one could say it wasn't impressive and even Julia, with a face as hard as her heart, almost smiled as she looked around her salon.

'So, you've come all the way from Gaul?' Leocadius was impressed. He lolled on his couch in the official part of his palace while Julia presided as the dutiful wife of the consul. It was one of those cenae when the great and good of the city were invited and deals were struck and gossip exchanged over the oysters and the wine. Usually, Leocadius was doing both but today he only had eyes for the beautiful girl with the golden hair, as different from Julia as chalk to cheese.

'It's not so far,' Conchessa told him.

'And with just a maid?' Leocadius had taken in the bulk of Conchessa's companion. Female she may have been, although Leocadius had no intention of proving that, but she was built like a wrestler.

'We get by,' Conchessa said. 'Adelina is a tower of strength.'

'That I can see,' Leocadius laughed. 'More wine?'

He held up the silver-chased ewer and she held the flat of her hand over her cup. 'It's good of you to invite me, Consul,' she said, 'but I have places to be.'

'No, no,' Leocadius poured for himself. 'You can't deprive me of your company yet. You're Vit's sister. I want to know all about you.' He ran a lazy finger over her forearm and looked deep into her eyes.

'I am Vit's sister,' she looked back, 'and Calpurnius' wife.'

'Ah, yes.' Leocadius knew a rebuff when he heard one, but he was not easily rebuffed, the Consul of Londinium, and Conchessa, with her full lips and taut body, was a challenge for any man. 'The Decurion.'

'Vit has agreed to go back with me,' she said, 'to find him.'

'Has he?' Leocadius raised an eyebrow. 'Well, there you are.'

'You don't sound convinced,' she said.

'What, that Vit will accompany you or that you will find your husband?'

'Either,' she said. 'Both.'

Leocadius looked into the dark depths of his wine. He seemed far away. 'There was a time,' he said, 'when Vit and I would have gone anywhere, done anything, dared the gods out of Heaven. But now ... now, he has a new God, a peacemaker. And Vit is not the same. As for your husband … who knows? He was with Count Theodosius, you say?'

'And Count Theodosius is dead; yes, I know. I have the same faith as Vit. And even more faith in my husband.'

'I'm happy for you.' Leocadius felt an invisible knife between his shoulder blades and knew that Julia was scowling at him. It was always the same. Didn't the woman know that flirting was what Leocadius did? Her father, who once wore the pallium, had done the same; it went with the job. 'Look,' he murmured, moving closer to the girl, 'I'll be honest with you; I've never left the shores of Britannia, but it doesn't take a genius to know that abroad is a bloody place. Vit can offer you one sword at best – if he's prepared to use it, that is. I can give you … what? Thirty men, forty at a pinch. It'll be your own private army. But I can't discuss it here. Come to the basilica. Tomorrow night. I'll be waiting.'

She blinked. Leocadius had been right. For two women travelling across Gaul and the German Sea it had been terrifying, with jeers and insults at every turn. The hearty Adelina had felled one man with a shovel as they halted at a wayside mansio, but even she would have been powerless had there been more of them. Conchessa had every faith in Vit, who had always been her champion in the old days. But this was a dark world and there was death on the road. Forty men. 'I …'

He could see the doubt in her eyes and leaned back, to give her space, to let her breathe. 'No strings,' he said. 'But come alone. The Vicarius has the run of the basilica these days and he and I ... well, let's just say he wouldn't approve of me helping myself to forty of the garrison for your delectation and delight. He does things by the book. Shall we say midnight?'

She leaned back too and raised an eyebrow. 'You think I'll be safe?' she asked him. 'A woman alone crossing your city at that hour?'

'Madam,' he patted her hand and smiled. 'For a woman who has crossed the German Sea, Londinium is a child's nursery.'

And they both knew that, for Conchessa, the real danger lay *inside* the basilica.

CHAPTER FOUR

Din Paladyr

'You sent for me, lady?' Justinus crossed to Brenna by her hearth-fire. The shadows of the long Gododdin night filled the chamber around them.

'Lady?' she frowned and laughed at the same time. 'That's very formal, Justinus.'

'Sorry.' He laughed too. 'Sometimes it's hard to forget I'm commander of the Wall. And that you're the queen of the Votadini.'

She closed to him, looking into his eyes and seeing, for the briefest of moments, Paternus standing there. 'I know,' she said. 'I know.' She broke away to the table, pouring wine for them both. 'You know Lug.' It was a statement, not a question, but it made Justinus start, just a little. He had not seen the old man sitting in the shadows. But then, the old man had not seen him either.

'Lug has a message,' she said, 'from beyond.'

Justinus had met Lug before. He was the high priest of the Votadini and his sightless eyes rolled in

50

his head as he walked into the circle of light from the fire. His head was shaved and he wore a torc of gold at his throat. He held out a hand and felt the Roman's chest. Then he ran his fingers upwards, over the stubbled chin and cheeks. At his eyes he stopped.

'Good,' the old man said. 'It is good, lady. This is the one.'

'You're sure?' Brenna asked, watching him carefully.

Lug nodded. 'He is the lord of battles,' he said. 'The keeper of the Wall and the master of Eagles. He is the one.'

She smiled. 'Thank you, Lug,' she said and held his hand. He half bent and kissed it, grinning up at her. Then he turned and left, as silently as he had come.

'What did he mean?' Justinus asked her. 'I am the one?'

Brenna crossed the room in powerful strides and took a spear from its rack. 'This is the weapon that killed Taran's horse?'

Justinus hefted it, looking at the silver scrolls on its barbs. 'Yes,' he said.

'You've seen these before.'

'I have,' he told her, taking it back to the weapon rack. 'It's Pictish.'

She nodded. 'But it was thrown at my boy,' she said grimly, 'and far to the south of here. A long way from the Pictish lands.'

Brenna had no maps of the Gododdin country. Maps were for Romans who needed them because they had conquered territories that were not their own and had never quite come to love the lands they had taken. But both of them knew the ground. Beyond the grassy ruins of the old wall called the Antonine, in the frozen north where the wolves ran free and the eagles soared, the red-haired, blue-skinned bastards called the Painted Ones lived and died. They built their houses of stone against the weather and knew neither mortar nor civilization. Their woollens were dark and woven with the heather and their old people wandered into the snow to die. No Roman legion had tamed them and only the Gododdin held them in check.

'You and I both know,' Brenna went on, 'that it was not a Pict who threw that.'

He nodded. 'We lost each other in the forest,' he said. 'I promised to keep your boy safe.'

'And you did,' she told him. 'I've seen the wolf's head. Taran's very proud of it.'

'As well he may be,' Justinus smiled. 'He stood his ground, even when the thing was leaping at him.'

'I don't know what's going on,' Brenna said, moving closer. 'But *something* is in the wind.' She looked at him. 'Something a vexillation can't fix.'

'You have your own troops,' he reminded her. The Votadini were not a toothless client people, unlike the old Celtic tribes to the south, men who had long ago turned their swords to corn-cutters and used their helmets to hold grain for their chickens.

They were a formidable warrior force and Brenna was their queen.

'Not the Gododdin nor all your legions can keep my boys safe,' she said. 'Not here. Not now.'

'What are you suggesting?' he asked.

She walked away from him. 'I have talked to my people,' she said.

'And?'

'The council thinks my fears are groundless. A hunting accident. They happen all the time.'

'And you?'

She turned back to him, taking a deep breath. 'I'm thinking for once like a mother. That's why I turned to Lug.'

'The blind one,' Justinus nodded.

'He sees what you and I cannot,' she told him. 'The future and the past.'

'And what does he see?' Justinus asked.

'Dragons,' she said softly. 'Dragons that come out of the east. And one dragon that stands in the west. Blood-red it is and it will never die.'

'Riddles!' Justinus laughed, sipping his wine. 'You make about as much sense as Vitalis with his crucified carpenter who came back from the dead.'

'I want you to take them south,' she said, 'to safety.'

'The boys?'

She nodded.

'You too?'

'No.' Her answer was fast and firm. 'No. Whatever is coming, I must stay. But my boys. They'll be safe on the Wall with you.'

'The Wall?' Justinus smiled grimly. 'Have you forgotten that Valentinus destroyed the Wall? If he can do it, anybody can.'

'We weren't ready then,' she reminded him. 'Any one of us. We'd grown fat and complacent. Things are different now.' She saw the doubt in his eyes. 'Please, Justinus.' She closed to him, stroking his chest. 'You were my husband's friend, the nearest thing he had to a brother. It's as though my boys are yours.'

He looked into her face, anxious and worried. For a moment, he wanted to take her in his arms and kiss away her fears, but she was queen of the Votadini and he was commander of the Wall. More, she was Pat's wife. 'All right,' he said, 'I'll take them to …'

'No.' She held her fingers to his lips. 'No, don't tell me. Now, standing here in my hall with you I can say I'd never tell a soul where the princes of the Gododdin are. But with a Pictish blade at my throat … would I be so brave?'

He laughed. 'Yes, Brenna,' he said. 'I have no doubt of that.'

It was a different Lug who stood between the fires the next night. His deerskin robes trailed the ground and the horns of the god Belatucadros stood proud from his head. The rattles echoed in the open space above the rocky scarp and the ground jumped to the thump of the drums. Justinus knew the god as Mars, the bringer of war but he was more than that. Lug and his priests whirled and chanted, swaying this way and that in the firelight as the sparks flew upward.

'I turn to the North,' Lug shouted above the wild music, 'to the shining fortress, to the winds of Heaven.'

'To the North, to the North!' the other priests chanted and the great crowd of Gododdin, as one, outside the queen's chambers, pointed to the stars of the night sky.

'To the East,' Lug had turned, 'to the keeper of the cauldron, to the fountains and the springs.'

'To the East, to the East!' the priests roared back and the people turned again, jabbing the darkness with their fingers.

'To the West,' Lug had twisted his great horns for a third time, raising his head and roaring like a stag in rut. 'To the burning fortress, to the keeper of the spear and the light.'

'To the West, to the West!'

'I turn to the South,' Lug had come full circle, his priests and his people with him, 'to the fortress of fate, to the great mother and of all deep things.'

The drumming stopped and the rattles died. Everyone there, except Justinus, had turned to face south where the moorland lay bleak and black in the darkness. The princes were led out into the centre of the circle by two priests. Each boy wore a torc around his neck and a cloak of wolfskin to the ground. They knelt solemnly before the high priest whose bony hands groped forward in his eternal darkness and he gripped a shoulder of each one.

'To the fortress of fate,' the old man whispered to them. 'May it keep you safe. To the great mother. May her love hold you. To the deep things. May you find in them wisdom.'

A single drum thudded.

Lug held up his head, the horns lifting in the firelight. 'Who will go with you?' he asked in a loud, rumbling voice.

'I will,' Justinus said. He was wearing all the regalia he had with him, his sword at his side and the spangenhelm on his head. His shield was strapped across his back. He even wore his old tribune's scarf around his neck. And of course, his ring of the four helmets, his reminder of the Wall, never left his finger.

Lug's sightless eyes stared at him. 'Belatucadros keep you,' he said, 'and bring our princes back.'

Justinus saluted in the Roman way and bowed his head as a Gododdin would in front of his god. Then he took the two boys by their shoulders and led them across the parade ground to their mother as the chanting and dancing began again.

'Bring me my boys back,' she whispered to him and she held them close.

Londinium

While the sparks flew upwards at Din Paladyr, Conchessa, many days' march to the south, was making her way across the basilica's courtyard. There was a full moon that lit her way and her own shadow loomed huge on the paving stones. She could see lights burning in the far wing, where the consul kept his offices and she reached the nearest stair. There was no one on duty here, although Leocadius had said that there would be. She hauled up her skirts and padded up the worn stone. At the top a small, black-painted door stood to the left and she took it, tapping it first. It swung open against her hand and she was inside.

Candles glowed along the walls and she followed the passageway to the brighter light at the end. The door was open here. It was the office of the consul. All day, Conchessa had been picturing this moment. Leocadius had promised her a retinue, men at her back to go with Vit and find Calpurnius. But what did he want in return? Her funds were not limitless, but she had a feeling that it was not her money Leocadius was interested in. Would she give herself to him for her husband's sake? That question, which dare not fully enter her head, had been fluttering on the fringes of her consciousness all day. That question would be answered now.

'Who are you?' A short, thick set man with a severe Roman haircut glared at her from the other side of a table, cluttered with parchment. Instinctively, Conchessa looked behind her. Had she come in through the wrong door? Perhaps he sensed her discomfort because he was chuckling. 'Are you lost, little lady?'

'No.' She stood defiant. 'I was looking for the consul.'

'At this hour?' the man smirked, laying a stylus down and leaning back in his chair. He looked the girl up and down. If this was one of Leocadius' harlots, he was impressed. He took in her fine gown and cloak with the gold ornaments at her wrist and neck. High maintenance indeed.

'I have business with him,' Conchessa said.

'He's a busy man, the consul,' the man sniggered, apparently amused by his own conversation. 'Never stops working night and day.' He stopped giggling and stared at her. 'You haven't told me who you are.'

'I am Conchessa,' she told him, 'the wife of the Decurion Calpurnius Succatus. Are you the consul's man?'

The man behind the candles laughed again, a loud, uncontrollable burst which he quickly checked, frowning. 'Never in a thousand years,' he said. 'I am Antoninus Civilis, Vicarius of Britannia. You are standing in *my* basilica, in *my* city, in *my* province. Leocadius is the shit on my sandals. Where is your husband?'

He saw her eyelids lower. 'I don't know,' she said. 'I'm trying to find him.'

Civilis burst out laughing, his face flushed. 'Well,' he spread his arms, 'he's not hiding in here. How is Leocadius involved?'

Conchessa had heard of the vicarius. He was new to the post, an appointment, men said, of the late Count Theodosius himself. 'Do you know my husband?'

'Answering a question with a question,' Civilis tutted. 'That won't do, lady.'

'Leocadius is the consul of Londinium,' Conchessa said. 'He said he could help me.'

'I'm sure he did.' He stepped out from behind his desk, 'and that would involve exploring every inch of your body.'

She blushed but stood her ground. The veins stood out on Civilis' forehead and neck, more obvious in the light of the candles. 'You didn't answer me,' she said. 'Do you know my husband?'

'I met him briefly,' Civilis told her, giggling again, 'before I left the Count. He ran the camp, didn't he? Pen-pusher?'

'He did whatever he was ordered,' Conchessa said.

Civilis laughed abruptly. 'Did he now? That's not what I heard.'

Conchessa took a step forward. 'What?' she asked him. 'What have you heard?'

'I've heard your husband was a tricky bastard,' he told her. 'Outspoken. Unruly. Takes his Christianity just that *pinch* too far.'

'He is honest, if that's what you mean.'

Civilis guffawed. 'Yes, well, honesty is the last virtue a Decurion needs. I don't know where he is but you're well rid of him. Now … what was that?' Civilis spun to the darkness behind him.

'I heard nothing,' she said.

'No, no. There. There it is again. A kind of …
waterwheel? Can't be. Did you come alone?'

'Yes,' she told him.

'Well, go the same way,' he smirked, his eyes staring wildly. 'I'm a busy man. And there's something …
you'd better go.'

And that was the best suggestion Conchessa had
heard all night.

The snow lay heavy on the ramparts of Londinium
two days later and there was an eerie stillness over the
city. Magnus Maximus had defied the vicarius and had
brought his troops to within ten miles of Londinium.
Worse, he had brought them to within a few hundred
yards. They had crossed the Fletus in the early morning, the dead reeds standing like brown sentinels to
mark his path. He had kept with him vexillations of
the II Augusta and the XX Valeria Victrix, as well as
his cavalry of the Heruli. To the inhabitants of the
city who watched from the westward walls, it looked
as if every legion of Rome was there, staring them
down, poised to attack.

To his left, Maximus saw the garrison of the
fort forming up and heard the shouted commands.
They were cranking the great ballistae into place,
ready to send rock and flame crashing into the rebel
Caesar's ranks. But Maximus knew exactly how many
men Civilis had and they would prove little trouble.
Besides, the garrison of Londinium was under the

command of Leocadius Honorius and young Leo owed all that to Magnus Maximus. In the clash of wills between the vicarius and the consul, it would be interesting to see who won. Now, it was all about holding his nerve.

'Sir! Sir! There's an army at the gate.' The slave Albinus had been here before. Leocadius was the third consul he had served, man and boy, and it seemed to be his lot in life that his consuls were consistent lie-abeds. This particular consul had fallen asleep on his couch the night before and for a moment he had no idea where he was.

'Get up, Leocadius!' Julia was more to the point. She swept through the room like a whirlwind. 'People are streaming into the city from the villages. It's chaos out there.'

'Shit!' The consul snatched up his pallium and pulled it over his head. He looked at his head slave and his wife. 'I suppose a shave is out of the question? Albinus, my sword and boots. Ought to look the part, I suppose.'

An officer, helmeted and armed, stood in the doorway. 'The garrison …' he began.

'… are almost certainly shitting themselves.' Leocadius hauled on the boots Albinus had brought and laced them furiously. 'Is it Maximus?'

The centurion nodded. 'At the west gate, sir. Lud.'

'By the river?' Leocadius frowned. 'What's he at?' The consul had never risen above the rank of

tribune and that was almost by default, a man promoted above his natural abilities. He was no general
but he knew an army pinned in along a river bank as
Maximus' was, was either asking for trouble or …

'He's not going to fight,' Leocadius murmured,
as much to convince himself as the centurion. 'He's
come to talk.'

Civilis shook and trembled on the ramparts that
looked out above Lud's gate to the west. The Fletus
was a sluggish brown ahead where he could see it
meandering through the trees and the Thamesis
roared and thundered to his left on its way to the sea.
He tried to concentrate. Maximus was all show. It all
looked very impressive, the weak winter sun glancing off helmets and shields, but he had no eagles
with him so he had no complete legion. The horses
of the Heruli would be useless against Londinium's
walls and Maximus didn't have enough men for a
siege. With the Thamesis at his elbow, Civilis had
an endless supply of fish, fresh water and above all,
a means of escape. He could hide in the marshes
north of the river for ever and beyond that lay the
German Sea.

It was this weather that was so absurd. The snow
showed no sign of melting in the sun, so why was it so
warm? He tugged at his scarf to give him air and eased
the lorica that was his battle armour. Then there was
the noise. He couldn't place it, but it sounded like
a loud and irregular thud, as though someone was

building a wall and ramming home piles of timber. But there was no work today. The wharves stood idle and the ships creaked at their moorings. Everybody who lived beyond the walls and could walk had hurtled to the Lud gate for safety and the new gate to the north of that.

'What's happening?' Leocadius had hurried west from the palace. His predecessors, snobs to a man, would have taken a litter and been surrounded by an army of slaves and retainers. He had just grabbed the nearest horse in the stables and had not even saddled it, gripping the mane and hanging on as the mare galloped over the Walbrook, her hooves drumming on the planking before slipping and sliding past the villas and the temples to where the press of people stood under the city's walls.

'Good of you to call,' Civilis growled as the consul reached the ramparts.

'Is the garrison in place?' Leocadius asked, realizing only now that he had left his helmet behind.

'They're your garrison, Consul,' Civilis reminded him. Leocadius looked at the man. The vicarius was staring and the pupils of his eyes were like pinpricks. His skin was crimson and he was sweating profusely. He clicked his fingers and a slave was at his elbow in seconds, passing him a cup of water. He drank feverishly. 'Damned warm work, Leocadius,' he said. 'Is he going to fight?'

'We'll soon know,' the consul nodded to the open fields beyond the wall.

A solitary horseman riding a chestnut gelding was making his way across the snow, trampled and muddied by peasants who had been fleeing for their lives for the last two hours. Civilis half turned on the ramparts. That bloody noise again. Whatever happened today, he was going to put a stop to that.

'The general is within bowshot, sir,' a centurion on the ramparts said to Leocadius. 'Permission to try a shot?'

'Talk to *me*, centurion!' Civilis snapped. '*I* command here.'

'No,' Leocadius ignored him. 'Look, Maximus is dismounting.'

He was. Within the garrison's bowshot, the new Caesar swung from his horse's back and unbuckled his helmet. He hooked it on the horn of his saddle and walked slowly forward, his feet silent on the snow. Slowly, deliberately, Maximus drew his spatha, the long double-edged sword of the cavalry, and he threw it downwards so that its iron tip slit the snow and bit into the ground beneath. He undid his cloak and let it fall. Then he untied the general's belt wrapped and buckled at his waist. From inside his tunic, he pulled a rough-made wreath of myrtle and placed it on his bare head.

'The ovation,' Civilis whispered. 'He's carrying it out.'

Leocadius suspected as much. So far, the south and the west had warmed to their Caesar. Londinium was his first potential check and he was not about to wrong-foot it.

'I come as your Caesar,' Maximus called to the city, 'not as your conqueror but as your loving lord and protector.'

'The barefaced cheek of the man!' Civilis snarled. He was shaking uncontrollably now.

'Will you open your gates to me?' Maximus called.

Civilis weighed his options. Maximus outnumbered him but Maximus could not maintain a siege. He had no ballistae with him so he could not smash the gates, let alone the walls. This was a bluff. But Leocadius had fought with Maximus before, in Valentia, north of the Wall and he knew the man for the brilliant soldier he was. He read the vicarius' mind. 'He'll have his ballistae beyond those woods,' he said. 'He'll have left nothing to chance.'

The vicarius was shivering so badly now that everyone along that stretch of wall was looking at him.

'You have no choice, sir,' Leocadius closed to the man, suddenly sorry for him. 'You're not well. Let me talk to him.'

'You?' Civilis' face was a livid purple. 'Let you team up with your old buddy again? Never! Clodius, my stole.'

A slave barged his way among the soldiery ranged on the ramparts and draped a gold-embroidered cloth over the vicarius' shaking shoulders. Civilis scowled briefly at Leocadius and made for the steps.

Out in the snow, Maximus waited. He heard the shouted commands and the thunder of timber as the gates swung open. He recognized the man at once. This was Antoninus Civilis, a bumptious bastard he had once met at Augusta Treverorum and now the shit was vicarius of Britannia. Annoying of Theodosius to make such a ghastly appointment, but there it was. Maximus noticed that the vicarius was wobbling, his steps erratic and more than once he turned sharply as though he had heard a sudden sound. His face, above the cloak and the stole of office was purple as an emperor's pillow and he was trembling from head to foot.

For a moment, the two men faced each other. Then Maximus held out his right hand in friendship and smiled. His smile grew wider as the vicarius went rigid. His eyes rolled in his head and he pitched forward into the snow. There was a commotion at the gate and Leocadius was running forward with three slaves and a centurion at his heels. He knelt beside the vicarius, half turning the man and feeling for a pulse. It was weak, hardly there at all. And then, the heart stopped and Antoninus Civilis was vicarius of Britannia no more.

Leocadius stood up and his eyes locked with those of Maximus. For a long moment, all that had passed between them came hurtling back, like the wild screams of a nightmare. Fire and headless men and the crash of shield on shield and a silver face that had no eyes.

'Welcome, Caesar,' Leocadius said, 'to Londinium.' And he thumped his chest in the imperial salute.

Maximus extended his arm and gripped that of the consul. 'Thank you, Leo,' he said softly and, glaring down at Civilis' body around which the slaves fussed, 'for everything.'

He whistled loudly and from nowhere a huge mastiff loped over the snow, eyes bright, studded collar flashing in the sunshine. Maximus stooped and hauled the vicarius' stole of office from the dead man's shoulders. He tied it around the dog's neck and ruffled his fur.

There was a roar of victory from the legions. And a sigh of relief from everybody else.

CHAPTER FIVE

Valentia, Februarius

They had rebuilt the forts of the Wall after Valentinus' rebellion but not those to the north. There had been legions here once along the wall named for Antoninus Pius but the painted ones had swarmed over that like ants in the reign of Commodus the mad and sad ruins told the tale. Gravestones lay at hard angles to the ground, the ground that was still like iron in Valentia, marking the burial of many a good man.

They camped at Trimontium in the high country where the old altars to Mithras and Jupiter pointed naked to the sky, overgrown with thistles and ivy. They huddled together under the crags further south and waited until the storm had passed that sent stinging hail into their faces and cold into the marrow of their bones. Taran had been this way before but the route lay deep in his nightmares and he had no clear recollection of it. He had been a small boy then, running before the barbarians who had driven the Gododdin out of Din Paladyr, hiding in villages and caves with his mother. His father was dead and there was no Paternus then to take his place and no little brother to dog his footsteps. Rome was a distant myth his mother spoke of and he had never seen the eagles in his life.

All that was different now as they trotted ever southward over the tangle of heather and the short-cropped grass. He and Edirne showed their skills with their sling-shots and every night a rabbit or two roasted on their spits or bubbled in Justinus' cooking pot. They saw no one on the road because it was deep winter and no one who was right in the head would be out in this weather.

On the fourth day, they came to Bremenium which rose like a ghost out of the mist. Edirne had never seen a Roman fort before and he stared at it in wonder. Like all the other forts of Antoninus, this one was abandoned and derelict; the weeds held sway here and the wilderness had claimed its own. While Taran tethered the horses and Justinus found a suitable place to light a fire, the younger boy ran and clambered over the crumbling stones, shouting out in the buildings that still had some kind of roof. His voice came back to him, echoing and re-echoing across the silence of the purple moors.

But Edirne couldn't see the moors. Nor could Taran. Just a swirling, grey-green that told the boys that they were at the edge of the world. 'What are these?' Edirne shouted as he looked down into two pits, dug side by side and edged to the height of a man in stone.

'Latrines,' Justinus called back.

'You shit in them,' Taran thought he ought to add by way of explanation.

There was no laugh. No response at all. Taran found that odd, but not as much as Justinus did. He was still rising from his crouching position when he saw the three figures on the wall, emerging like spirits out of the mist. They were tall and armed, with long fair hair over their shoulders and cloaks almost down to the ground. Between them, they held a little boy, whose mouth was covered with a coarse cloth and whose hands were held fast. The knife at his belt was gone and the broad blade of a sword was held horizontally under his chin.

Justinus heard Taran gasp but he raised his hand and the boy stood still.

'You're the Roman,' one of the men said, 'the one who commands the Wall.'

'You speak good Latin,' Justinus said, 'for scum from north of the Rhenus.' He knew he was taking a chance. One flick of the man's wrist and Edirne's head could join the wolf's tied to Taran's saddle. But these men were Saxons, wild, uncivilized bastards from Germania. The word was that they ate babies. They certainly smelt fear. And they would not smell it on the commander of the Wall. Not today. Not any day.

Justinus could have kicked himself. He had had a feeling for the last two days that he and Brenna's boys were not travelling quite alone, but he had seen nothing, heard nothing. He must be getting old.

The Saxon's laugh chilled the blood. 'The sword,' he pointed to the weapon at Justinus' hip. 'Lose it.'

Justinus unhooked the weapon and threw it onto the grass.

'And the darts,' the Saxon said.

'In the boss of my shield,' Justinus told him.

The Saxon gave a guttural order to the man on his right and he jumped down from the wall, striding to where Justinus' bay cropped the grass. The auxiliary's shield hung from the cantle of the saddle and the Saxon lifted it. He was still rummaging in the hollow of the boss when he heard a thud and a grunt. He spun round in time to see the man holding the boy stagger backwards, a Roman army dart embedded in his forehead and blood spurting from it.

'Run, Eddi!'

The boy needed no command from Justinus and he threw himself forward, jumping free and hurtling over the parapet to hit the wet ground of the latrine bottom. Justinus knelt and his second dart came out of nowhere, hissing through the air to thud into the second man's neck, biting through the jugular so that his blood sprayed crimson and kept on pumping as he went down, choking. The third man had already turned tail and was running for the horses that Justinus now saw tethered by a stand of trees for the first time. This time he took careful aim and as Taran stood there, open mouthed, Justinus' third dart caught the Saxon between the shoulder blades and he dropped like a stone.

The commander of the Wall reached down and fished a terrified Edirne out from his hiding place. He was a little bruised and covered in slimy moss but he would keep. Justinus ruffled his hair and the bewildered boy clung to the Roman, trying not to cry. He patted the lad and kissed the top of his head before turning to retrieve his darts. When he reached the first Saxon he had hit, the one who spoke Latin and had held his sword at Edirne's throat, he turned him over. 'One thing you don't know about us Romans,' he said to the corpse that stared at him in disbelief, 'is that we don't always carry our darts inside our shield bosses.' He slapped the man's face. 'And we don't always tell the truth.'

Londinium

'It depends which truth you want to hear,' Serapio was carefully inserting a probe up the left nostril of the late vicarius, 'Caesar Maximus' or mine.'

Leocadius looked at the man. He was Greek, of course, as all the best medici were. He had arrived with Civilis some months before and had made it clear that he had nothing but contempt for this arse-end of the Empire and the sad little people who inhabited it. 'You're telling me there's a difference?' Leocadius asked.

'Bravo, Consul,' Serapio would have applauded but he had his spare hand down the dead man's throat. 'We'll make a politician of you yet.'

'Medicus,' Leocadius came as close to the man as the proximity of a corpse would allow. 'Vicarii of provinces do not die every day. And they do not die in suspicious circumstances. The circumstances are, I take it, suspicious?'

'Crimson skin,' the medicus said, 'pin-prick pupils. I am told he complained of the heat, heard sudden sounds.'

'You're told?' Leocadius said. 'You were his medicus. Don't you know?'

'I know he had bad teeth, an ingrowing toenail on his left foot and his eyesight was deteriorating. I hadn't seen him for some time before he died. He didn't complain to me about any of the recent condition. Servants,' he explained. 'Talk to them. They see all and know all.'

'The sweating sickness, surely,' Leocadius tried the layman's approach.

'If this is the sweating sickness, I'm an Egyptian's arse. This man was poisoned.'

Leocadius frowned, looking at the dead vicarius with new eyes. 'Was he now?'

'Are you a Christian, Consul?' Serapio asked.

'Only in the sense that we all are these days,' Leocadius told him. 'Imperial edict and all that.'

'I'm for the Syrian goddess myself.'

Leocadius looked blank.

'Atargartis.'

Blanker still.

'Oh, never mind. I'm guessing belladonna, something of that sort. It's a common enough plant. It can be crushed and mixed with food.'

'A slave, then?' Leocadius said, 'from the basilica kitchens.'

'Of course,' Serapio wiped his hands on the dead man's pallium, draped over a chair, 'you're chief magistrate here, aren't you? If it comes to court, you'll be sitting in judgement.'

'Goes with the territory,' Leocadius shrugged.

Serapio looked him squarely in the face. 'If I'm right about belladonna,' he said, 'it will have been administered by someone who was with him last dies Martis or dies Mercurii.'

'Will there be any signs?' Leocadius asked, 'on the murderer, I mean?'

'None,' the medicus said. 'Welcome to my world.'

Conchessa could not sleep that night. The sleet had turned to rain, which bounced off the roof tiles and hammered on the shutters. She tried to read but the candle flame guttered and she had to give up. It must have been close to dawn in that long Londinium night when she heard it. It began as a rattle of locks and boots clattering on the stairs. Then the door of her chambers crashed back and an armed guard stood there, a circitor at their head.

'You will come with us,' he barked.

Conchessa rose slowly, hoping that her heart was not thumping as loudly to the soldiers as it was to her. 'Why?' she asked. 'Who are you?'

The circitor closed to her, his face a scowling mask. 'I'm your worst nightmare,' he said, and then, to his men, 'Bring her.'

They had allowed Conchessa to put a cloak over her nightgown, but that was all. Of the trusty Adelina there was no sign and the slaves who attended them stood meekly by while the circitor went about his business. She splashed her way, barefooted, through the puddles and they almost lifted her off the ground as they hurried up the ramp to the main gate of the basilica. She was taken into a hall with high windows and tall columns. Torches flickered in the brackets on the walls and a bronze eagle loomed over a dais at the far end of the room. On one side of the huge bird, symbol of the legions, Jupiter highest and best frowned down at the girl. There was no statue of the Lord Jesus here, no Chi-Rho nor holy lamb. This was a godless place.

'I've kept you waiting,' a voice rang from the far corner and Leocadius padded through on sandalled feet. 'My apologies.'

Conchessa stood tall and stately in front of him. 'It *is* rather early in the morning,' she said.

'It is,' he agreed and threw himself down on the throne on the dais. Uniformed officials danced attendance. One, a scribe, laid out parchment, pens and an inkwell and began to write.

'You came here,' Leocadius said, cradling his fingers together and staring hard at the girl, 'the other night, to see the vicarius.'

'I came here to see you,' she told him, her voice as strong as his.

'To see me?' His eyes narrowed.

Conchessa blinked. For the briefest of seconds, she felt her head spin and the bottom fall out of her world. What was going on? But she would not let the consul know that. 'Yes,' she said. 'As you suggested.'

'I?'

The scribe's stylus scratched on the parchment.

'Consul, I …' She took a step towards him but the guards on each side were faster and their spears clashed in front of her face.

Leocadius waved them aside. 'That's not necessary,' he said. 'What do you know of belladonna, lady?' he asked.

Before she could answer, there was a commotion at the door behind her. She turned to see her brother struggling with yet more guards at the entrance. 'Let me through!' she heard him shout.

Leocadius clicked his fingers and the guards broke away, letting Vitalis run to his sister. He held her arms, looking into her face. 'Are you all right?' he asked. 'Have they hurt you?' He looked down. 'Your feet,' he frowned.

'It's nothing, Vit,' she soothed. 'It doesn't hurt.'

Vitalis spun to the dais. For a moment, the consul expected the man to jump at him. Six years ago he would have done and six years ago he would have lost. But now? Well, Vitalis was older and wiser. Worse, the man was a Christian. Even so, Leocadius wondered, exactly how many cheeks does this man have to turn? 'What's this all about, Leo?' Vitalis asked. He was still holding his sister.

'The vicarius is dead,' the consul said.

'All Londinium knows that,' Vitalis murmured. 'What has this to do with my sister?'

'Ask her,' Leocadius said.

Conchessa took a deep breath. 'I came to see the consul,' she said, 'in the west wing of this palace. He wasn't there. The vicarius was.'

'You came to see Leocadius?' Vitalis frowned. 'Why?'

'He promised me ...'

'None of this matters now,' Leocadius interrupted, 'the best evidence I have is that the late Antoninus Civilis was poisoned by belladonna. Your sister is about to tell me what she knows about such a plant.'

'This is madness,' Vitalis shouted. 'Leo, what are you doing?'

'My job,' Leocadius told him. 'A murder in my precinct cannot go unanswered. And the vicarius of all people. Your sister can hardly have chosen a more prominent target.'

'Have you gone mad?' Vitalis asked. 'What possible motive could Conchessa have for ...?'

'She's an unknown quantity, Vit,' Leocadius said. 'From Gaul, from the court of Theodosius, where the vicarius came from. You see how it's all linked?'

'I didn't know him,' Conchessa said. 'We'd never met until the other night.'

Leocadius sat back in his chair and folded his arms. 'Tell me,' he said, 'did he try to touch you? Take you against your will?'

'Leo!' Vitalis spread his arms. 'For God's sake.'

'Mitigating circumstances,' Leocadius said. 'If that was the case, revenge would be understandable.'

'If that was the case,' Conchessa said coldly, 'I would have taken the vicarius' eyes out with my finger nails, not turned to some potion or another.'

'You got here pretty quickly, dear brother,' Leocadius said.

'Conchessa's woman sent for me,' Vitalis said. 'Told me that soldiers had taken her away. I don't know why,' he closed to the man who had been his friend, 'but I immediately thought of you.'

'Well,' Leocadius smiled, 'think of me a little longer.' His smile vanished and he barked at the guards, 'Take these two away. Separate cells.'

When they had gone, a shadowy figure emerged from the latticed screen to the side of the dais.

'Well?' Leocadius turned.

'I think he'll do,' Magnus Maximus smiled. 'Given the circumstance. Keep them for a couple of days, then bring him to the camp beyond the Lud Gate.'

'Very well,' Leocadius nodded, looking less than pleased. 'I just hope this works the way you intend it to.'

'Oh, it will,' Maximus smiled. 'You of little faith.' He turned to go, then paused and looked back over his shoulder. 'By the way,' he said. 'Who *did* kill Antoninus Civilis?'

Leocadius shook his head. 'I have no idea,' he said.

Onnum, the Wall

'Io, Circitor; three riders.'

'Can you make them out?' the circitor's voice called from below the ramparts.

'One of them's a boy.' The sentry squinted against the glare of the sky under the dark, rolling clouds. 'No, make that two.'

The circitor had joined him on the wallwalk by now and looked out at the approaching riders. 'I don't know what hopes you have, Septimus, of rising in the ranks of this army, but I may have to disappoint you, even at this early stage. That is Justinus Coelius, commander of the Wall. Your boss and mine. Look well at those features and commit them to memory, there's a good pedes.' He cuffed the man around the ear and roared the commands to the men on the ground. 'Commander of the Wall. Open the gates.'

There was a thunder of drums and the braying of a cornu as the wooden bolts slid back and the double gates were hauled open. Onnum, it had to be said, was not Justinus' favourite fort along the Wall, but it was the nearest by road from Bremenium and it had a bath house, rather a grand one with eleven rooms and to a man with cold in his bones, a bath sounded a pretty good idea by now.

Taran and Edirne looked on in amazement as soldiers formed a guard of honour, their shields bright in the afternoon and women and children cheered the three as they clattered under the gateway into a wide courtyard beyond.

'You two,' Justinus said as he slid from the saddle. 'Ever seen a Roman bath before?'

Both boys shook their heads.

Justinus smiled. 'Then you're in for a treat.'

The steam rose in the candlelight and the oil lamps glowed. Justinus hoped he could stay here for ever, soaking away the aches and pains of the long journey from Din Paladyr. He could hear Brenna's boys laughing and splashing each other in the pool next door and held out his cup for a slave to refill with wine.

'Saxons?' Decius Marcellinus was the commander at Onnum. He had known Justinus for years, when both of them served with the VI Victrix long, long ago. The world had turned since then and neither man was the young hot-head he once had been. 'That's odd.'

'You've seen none?'

Marcellinus shook his head. 'You'd have to ask at the forts further east,' he said. 'Segedunum will know, or Pons Aelius. You know the cowardly bastards only ever raid the coast and then run. The most we get here is a few tame Votadini wanting to trade south of the Wall. We check them of course. No room for complacency.'

'The three who attacked us didn't look too cowardly.' Justinus sipped his wine.

'Oh, I don't know,' the fort commander seemed to be complacency itself, no matter what he had just said. 'How much nerve does it take to hit a man and two boys? Tell me again, they're Votadini princes?'

'The heir and the spare,' Justinus nodded.

'So the queen *must* be concerned, then, up at Din Paladyr, to break her family up.'

'She is. There's something brewing, Decimus. That's why I need your men.'

'I can only spare ten, Justinus,' the commander warned. 'It's your policy not to leave any fort too light, after all.'

'Ten is fine,' Justinus said. 'Send a rider to Vindovala in the morning and to Cilurnum. I shall need eighty men ready to ride one week from today.'

'You're going back north?'

Justinus nodded. 'But first, I'm going south.'

CHAPTER SIX

Eboracum

When the other guests had gone and Rialbus the slave had cleared the meal away, Flavius Coelius and his old friend Timaeus stared into the dying embers of the fire and sampled the best wine the old man could afford. Timaeus liked this room. He himself had nowhere to call his own, but Flavius had done himself proud. He didn't have gold and silver to eat from, he had never had his hand in anyone's purse. He had a slave, a roof, a garden in which to potter and all in all, he looked as though he was a happy man. Timaeus leaned against the wool-stuffed cushion and looked at his old friend through narrowed eyes.

'Do you still keep your hand in, Flavius, with the VIth, I mean?'

Flavius Coelius had retired from the VI Victrix when his time had come. He had worked his way up from pedes to centurion and had earned his little plot of land. Then they had taken him on as hastilarius, weapons trainer, putting the foot-sloggers through their paces, march and counter-march and march a-bloody-gain. This time, though, surely, even Flavius Coelius had had enough. He chuckled. 'Can't help myself, Tim. Rialbus doesn't approve. Says I've done enough.'

Timaeus chuckled. 'You're supposed to own that man, Flavius, not be married to him.'

'Ah, he's like an old comfortable pair of sandals,' Flavius said. 'No, I get along to the parade ground every now and then. Some of those recruits don't know one end of a javelin from the other. It's all going to the dogs, you know. Not like in our day.'

'You don't know the half of it,' Timaeus Cocles had been in Eboracum for less than a day. For much of his life, since he left the Legion, he had been on the road, a tinker by trade and a picker-up of valuable information. The first place he had called was here, at his old friend Flavius'; first, because he had not seen the man for months and second, Flavius' beds were cheaper than the mansio.

'You were talking over dinner about the Empire,' Flavius said. 'Is it as bad as all that?'

'Worse. You know Valentinian died?'

'Shouting at some Germans, wasn't he?'

'Quadi envoys, yes, that's right. That man had the worst temper of anybody I've ever known. Burst a blood vessel in his brain.'

'And then?'

'Well, Gratian took over, of course.'

'Oh, yes, the son. He's a good man, though, isn't he?' Flavius said, refilling his guest's cup. 'Good soldier.'

'One of the best,' Timaeus said, 'but … well, I know we don't talk religion in the Mess, but he's a little bit too Christian, if you catch my drift.'

'What, pacifist, you mean?'

'Gods, no. Just the reverse. He's been kicking the Alemanni up and down the Rhenus like it's going out of fashion. No, he has a tendency to knock down pagan statues and insists on keeping the sun's day holy.'

'Mad, then?' Flavius wondered aloud.

'Only time will tell. Then, of course, there's Valentinian II.'

'Ah, this is Gratian's brother?'

'*Half*-brother, technically.'

'How old is he now?'

'Eight.'

'And he's co-ruler?'

Timaeus nodded. 'Declared Augustus by the army commanders when he was four.'

Flavius shook his head. Two Emperors at any one time he could understand. The Empire was huge and the job was too much for any one man, but when the army played politics, he got rattled. There was a time when the Emperor gave command of his army to his horse, but that was Caligula and nobody believed anything about Caligula. In Flavius' narrow world, a soldier fought for pay. He killed and was killed. No more. No less. It had a harsh simplicity that suited men like Flavius Coelius.

'Now,' Timaeus eased back on the hard couch, 'That's enough tittle-tattle from above. What's the news of your boy? Still holding the Wall?'

'Justinus?' Flavius sighed. 'As far as I know. I don't hear much these days.'

'You certainly don't, you old liar!' a voice boomed from the doorway. 'Which is why I just walked in to your hovel unchallenged!'

'Justinus!' Flavius was on his feet and running to his new guest.

'Hello, Pa,' Justinus laughed. 'It's been too long.'

They hugged each other and stepped back, laughing like schoolboys at some great joke.

'You bribed Rialbus again,' Flavius chuckled.

'Of course,' Justinus told him. 'I'd never have got through to you otherwise.'

'What was it this time? Wine? A woman? I've told him he's too old for all that.'

'The silver of Din Paladyr,' Justinus said. 'You know he doesn't come cheap.'

They all laughed. 'Timaeus, Timaeus Cocles, an old friend from way back. My son, Justinus, Commander of the Wall.'

The two men shook hands. 'It's been a while, Justinus,' Timaeus said.

'I remember you,' Justinus smiled. 'You taught me to throw a dart, if my memory serves.'

'That's come in handy, I trust?'

'Oh, yes,' Justinus smiled. 'More than you know. And now it's my turn for introductions. Flavius Coelius, weapons master of the VI Victrix and Timaeus Cocles, the man who taught me to throw darts ...' he stepped back and shepherded two boys into the room, 'I'd like you to meet Taran and Edirne, princes of the Votadini. And Pa ... I'd like a favour, if you don't mind ...'

The camp, west of Londinium

Through the swirling smoke of the choking incense she undulated, naked, to the rattle of the sistrum. Maximus watched her intently. Under his cloak, with his hood pulled over his head, he was as naked as she was.

'Mother Isis,' she moaned and raised the head of a god to pile on the body that already stood there. For over an hour he had watched her, as the winds of Martius moaned outside his tent and the camp settled into silence. The oil lamps glowed crimson and petals filled the floor and the low couches. She had built Osiris, the god of the underworld the Egyptians worshipped, from blocks of wood brought all the way from Leptis Magna and as each part clicked into place, she peeled a layer of clothing away and brushed herself against the general-made-Caesar.

'Behold,' she purred, rubbing her long fingers over the smooth cheeks of the god, dark green in the half light, 'Isis, your husband, your lover, murdered by the monster Set. Behold his new birth, behold his new life.' She pressed herself against the statue, closing her lips to those of the god. Then she turned and looked at Maximus under hooded lids. 'He is not complete,' she said. 'He has no phallus. Make him whole, Maximus Augustus, make him a man again.'

He stood up and let her stroke him under the cloak, rubbing his manhood to erection. Then, with only Osiris to watch them, he entered her, standing in his soldier's tent as the incense swirled and the sistrum rattled.

'Is the god whole now?' he asked her. He was sprawled on the couch, still naked, with the girl who was also a priestess naked beside him.

She laughed. 'Works every time, doesn't it?' she said.

He frowned. '*I* knew this was all a charade,' he said. 'But you're a daughter of Isis. I thought *you* might believe.'

'Oh, I do,' she assured him. 'But if you can't have a little fun with your religion, what's the point? Ever seen a happy Christian?'

He laughed. 'Point taken,' he said.

She ran her hand up his thigh again. 'How else may I please you, Caesar?'

He gently moved her hand away. 'You said you had visions,' he reminded her. 'That's why you're here. If all you wanted was a roll in the hay with your

Caesar, all you had to do was hang around the camp for a while.'

'I do have visions,' she said. 'Visions that will take you all the way to Rome.'

She stood up and pulled his cloak around her, throwing back the hood so that her long, ringletted hair shook free. She passed the statue of her god and crossed to a small camphor-lined chest she had brought with her. She pulled out a book of loose vellum, its covers dark leather, mysteriously tooled and clasped in gold.

'This,' she said, 'is the book of Aneirin, who is yet to be.'

'Yet to be?' Maximus sat up. 'What nonsense is this?'

'Aneirin has been and will be,' she said. 'Like Osiris, he will come again.'

'Lady,' the general said levelly, 'I agreed to see you because I was intrigued. You told me you had visions, that you brought the mystic powers of the East to win a crown in the West. I like riddles as much as the next man, but I have places to be and decisions to make.'

She handed him the book. 'Open it,' she said. 'Page eight.'

He took it and flicked the vellum. Each page was gilded, with strange hieroglyphics he could not read. But there, on the eighth page, was a lineage and it was written in Latin. His own name lay there, at the bottom of the page and above it Flavius Crispus and

Fausta. And above that, stretching back through time, Minerva and the emperor Constantine the Great.

'No,' Maximus said. 'No, this is wrong.'

'Will you challenge Aneirin?' Her voice rose. 'Will you question the ancients?' She closed to him and held his face in both hands. 'What is it you want, Magnus Maximus?' she asked.

He blinked, unnerved momentarily by the intensity of her gaze. 'The crown,' he almost whispered. 'Emperor in the West. Emperor of Rome.'

She nodded, her nails biting into his cheeks and temples. 'And how will you get it?'

'War,' he said. 'It's the only way.'

'And here in Britannia?'

'I must secure the peace,' he said, as though in a trance. 'Be sure that Britannia is with me.'

'And how will you do that? By asking nicely? By destroying your legions in some desolate mountain pass? You have yet to face the tribes of the West, Britannia Prima?'

'Yes,' he nodded. 'I have.'

'They won't jump to the commands of Isis,' she told him, 'Nor to the madcap lunacy of an adventurer like you from Tarraconensis. But,' she let go of his face and he felt the blood trickle down his cheeks. She tapped the open book, 'the descendant of Constantine? The man is a god throughout the Empire. Make *that* claim and they'll follow you to the ends of the earth. Especially when it is written by Aneirin, one of their own.'

She spun away and clapped her hands, twirling to the sistrum rattle that was now only in her head. 'Isis rides with you, Magnus Maximus,' she sang in a strange but melodic key. Then she was gone.

'Wait!' the general called, but she did not. 'I don't even know your name,' he shouted.

'Yes,' he heard her whisper although he could not see her at all. 'Yes, you do.'

Eboracum

The wood chips flew as the axe blades bit into the logs.

'You should have offered to marry her,' Flavius said. They were the first words he had spoken since he and Justinus tackled the log pile in the old man's back yard.

'Who?'

'Brenna.'

'She's queen of the Votadini,' Justinus said. He looked at his father and suppressed a smile. The commander of the Wall could have been Emperor of Rome and a living god but to Flavius he would still be the little whippersnapper struggling into his army boots and tripping over his shield. 'She was Pat's wife,' he reminded him.

'Ah, that was politics,' Flavius said, grateful for the chance to rest his axe now that he was feeling his years. 'From what you've told me, it sounds as if you love this woman.'

'Love her?' Justinus asked. 'Do soldiers know what that is, Pa?'

'Now, don't go all philosophical on me, boy,' the old man growled, checking the keenness of the axe-blade. 'I loved your mother well enough, Juno hold her. Time was I threw my javelin and darts and swung my sword. Now I chop wood. That's enough, really.'

'Yes,' Justinus said. 'I suppose it is. Anyway, Brenna would turn me down.'

'Would she now?'

'She'd say she'd already lost two husbands and she wouldn't want to lose a third.'

'She'd have every faith in you, then?' Flavius grinned, winking at his boy.

Both men knew what a wild world it was out there. How all things hung on a chance word, a single mistake, a wrong road taken. There seemed to be no rhyme nor reason, unless Jupiter highest and best or Sol Invictus or Mithras had plans of their own that soldiers of the VI Victrix didn't know about.

Justinus had already moved on. 'It's the Saxons I'm worried about,' he said, swinging the axe again.

'You took care of them,' Flavius reminded him.

'It's not that,' the commander of the Wall shook his head. 'It's that they knew me, knew who I was. What are the odds on that?'

'What are you saying?'

Justinus stopped swinging. 'They knew who I was because somebody sent them. They weren't a raiding party trusting to luck. They were following us – for how long, I don't know. They were assassins, sent to kill the boys.'

'And you're leaving them with me?'

Justinus laughed. 'I can't think of anywhere safer, old man,' he said. 'Rialbus will spoil them rotten and you'll make soldiers of them. If Timaeus hangs around, you'll both bore them rigid with your old boys' tales. I can't ask for more than that.'

'That I will,' Flavius promised. 'Once they learn to speak a civilised language.'

'Don't fall for that one,' Justinus chuckled. 'Their Latin is pretty good. But – and I think Brenna would want this – find a tutor for them, here in Eboracum. The days of barbarian rulers of the Votadini are over.'

'And you're going back?'

Justinus nodded. 'Just as soon as I've chopped these logs for you.'

'Chopped them for *me*?' Flavius roared. 'I thought I was doing you a favour by letting you help!'

And they laughed together as their axe blades rang on the oak.

The camp west of Londinium

The camp beyond the Lud Gate had been built eleven years ago by Count Theodosius. In the dark days of Valentinus' rebellion, no one knew who exactly the enemy was or where he would strike next. Papa Theo was a born general and he wanted a buffer in the west, something that would slow the rebels down before they reached Londinium. Now, it was a rebel who occupied this camp, a man infinitely more dangerous and unpredictable than Valentinus had ever been.

Vitalis Celatius stood in front of him now, his wrists still chafing from the chains Leocadius had ordered clapped to his arms and legs, just for the show of the thing. Magnus Maximus was lounging on a couch, throwing titbits to his dog. He looked the man up and down. 'You still wear your Wall ring,' he said, pointing to it.

'I do,' Vitalis said.

'The ring that marks you as a hero, the symbol of all that is great against the barbarians.'

'I did my job,' Vitalis said, 'as a soldier. But I am a soldier no more.'

Maximus nodded. 'Yes,' he said. 'We may have to do something about that.'

'What do you mean?'

'Tell me what you know about Theodosius.'

'Younger or elder?'

Maximus paused in his feeding of the dog. The animal looked up expectantly, saliva dripping from his massive jaws. 'I don't have time for games, Vitalis. Papa Theo is dead, just one among many victims of the emperor. We are talking about his son.'

'I barely exchanged two words with the man,' Vitalis said. 'I was a tribune then. He was a general.'

Maximus scowled at him. 'And you're a basket-maker now and I'm an emperor. Show some bloody respect.'

'Why am I here?' Vitalis asked.

Maximus leaned back. 'Because you're a hero,' he said, 'with a reputation that goes far beyond the Wall. You know Theodosius, albeit fleetingly and because you're a Christian, as is he.'

'I don't understand.'

Maximus sighed. 'I suppose expecting you to have a brain as well would be asking too much.' He got up and poured wine for them both. 'Your sister is languishing in a cell,' he said, 'on a charge of murder.'

'That's nonsense,' Vitalis told him.

'Of course it is,' Maximus smiled, 'but the graveyards are full of people wrongly accused. It was nonsense for them too.'

'So?' Vitalis frowned.

'So,' Maximus withdrew the goblet because clearly Vitalis was not going to drink, 'it can all go away.'

'It can?' Vitalis asked. 'How?'

'I'll just have a word with the consul and he'll drop the charges.'

'Why?'

'Because, Vitalis, hero of the Wall, sometime tribune now basket-maker, I have a little job for you.'

Londinium

'He wants you to go where?'

'Constantinople.'

'The Eastern Rome. Why?'

Vitalis looked into his sister's eyes. They had taken the shackles off her too and the pair were free, sitting in Vitalis' single-roomed workshop among the hoops and canes. 'Because that was the deal,' he told her, 'where I must go in exchange for your freedom.'

'But …'

He held up his hand. 'Gratian is Emperor now, at least in the West. His kid brother Valentinian – the II, I suppose we have to call him – is literally that – he's eight. You may as well give Italia and Illyricum to a flea. That's why Maximus has chosen this moment to strike. He's got three legions here in Britannia and that's a start. He intends to cross to Gaul, gaining support as he goes, forcing Gratian to recognise him.'

'All right,' she said, 'but Constantinople … it's the far side of the world.'

'It's also where Theodosius is. Or so Maximus' spies tell him. I am to take these letters,' he held up a leather satchel bound in brass, 'and to ask him personally to support Maximus.'

'Why you?' she asked him.

'Because of this.' He held up his left hand with the ring that glowed in the firelight. 'It was Theodosius' father's idea, that the four heroes of the Wall always wear this ring as a token of their comradeship, a symbol of the greatness of Rome. Theodosius, his father, Maximus and I all fought in the same war. Such things run deep.'

Conchessa shrugged. 'I get the impression,' she said, 'that Maximus would cut his mother's throat if it gave him power.'

'That's as may be,' Vitalis sighed, 'but I am not Maximus and I gave him my word.'

Conchessa held his hand, the one with the ring. 'You did this for me,' she said, her eyes bright with tears. And she held him close. 'So,' she sniffed, pulling away, 'when do we start?'

'We?' Vitalis' eyes widened. 'Oh, no.'

Conchessa stood up. 'You're not leaving me here, Vitalis,' she warned. 'I've lost a husband but I won't lose a brother.'

He looked at her. There were a thousand reasons why she should stay and none in favour of her going. Yet he knew Conchessa and knew he would argue himself hoarse before she so much as heard a word he said. 'When do we start?' she asked again, all but pressing her nose to his, 'for Constantinople?'

'Well,' he said, smiling. 'The sooner the better, really. We're going the pretty way, via Augusta Trevororum.'

CHAPTER SEVEN

Valentia, Martius

There was spring in the air as the commander of the Wall rode out from Onnum at the head of his vexillation. Before leaving Eboracum, he had prayed at the temple of Mithras and knelt in the principia before the eagle of the VI. He saw the silver helmet of the rebel Valentinus there as well, gleaming like a ghost in the candlelight. And he had talked to the praeses, Ammianus, who was delighted to see Justinus again. The old man had been a soldier-politician all his life but he was more than looking forward to retirement when he happily signed off a hundred men of his legion to march north.

At Onnum, Justinus joined up with the troops he had ordered to meet him there, from the Wall forts to the east and west. They were all soldiers of the VI, the scarlet and gold vexillum dancing at their head. At the front and at the rear, Justinus had placed his cavalry, men of the Ala Britannia, the dragon banner streaming over their heads. He had no artillery because whatever raiding party they encountered was not likely to build fortifications. And the wild asses on the road would only slow him up. He marched due north, ignoring the Roman road now and he sent his cavalry scouts ahead, just in case.

'Girl from Clusium!' he ordered and the cornice took up the braying note before the drummers steadied the tempo and the lads burst into song, their boots crunching on the heather. 'Shove! Shove! Shove!'

Justinus grinned at the tribune Arcadius. 'Nothing like a filthy song to pick up the pace, eh, Tribune?'

'No, sir,' Arcadius laughed. 'I hope there are plenty of girls at the end of all this.'

'At the end of all this,' Justinus said, watching the grey mountains to the north, 'there'll be more bad weather and blisters. What soldier of the VI would dream of asking for more?'

Din Paladyr

The council meeting had only just begun when there was a commotion outside and horsemen clattered into the great hall, servants and tables flying in all directions.

Everyone was on their feet immediately; everyone was shouting at once.

'We don't remember the lord of Din Eidyn being so unruly and so late,' Brenna said when the hubbub had died down.

Fablyr sat his snorting horse with a hawk flapping and squawking on the leather band at his wrist. The bird's bright eyes flashed in the light of the huge fire roaring in the centre of the room. 'It's a long ride along the estuary, lady,' the man growled. These two had known each other since they were children and familiarity had not led to fondness. Fablyr had grown from a gangly, sullen youth to a huge, sullen man. No one crossed him, least of all Brenna from Din Paladyr. He swung out of the saddle and passed the hawk to an attendant. Then, in accordance with tradition, he unhooked his sword and passed the blade quickly through the fire before reversing it and holding the hilt towards Brenna. She reached out and touched it and the warrior from the fort of crags sheathed it again and stood there.

'Will you take your place at the table, Fablyr of Din Eidyn?' Brenna asked. She was wearing all her finery today as it was a meeting of the council, the gold torc gleaming at her throat and a silver crown over her long, dark hair.

Fablyr did not move. He just stood there, arms folded while the council shifted uneasily in their seats and Fablyr's horsemen still kept to their saddles.

'You have a question for the council?' Malwyn asked.

Still Fablyr did not move. And he did not answer.

'You have a question for me,' Brenna said. It was a statement, not a question.

'I have, lady,' Fablyr said. 'Where are your children?'

Brenna had buried her little girls on a bare hill-side long ago, when she was not much more than a child herself. The god Arawn, the god the Romans called Dis Pater, had taken them because they were so beautiful. But everyone knew that Fablyr was not talking about them. 'My sons are safe,' she told him.

'Answer the question, lady,' Fablyr persisted.

'They are in the south.' Brenna held her ground. 'With the Romans.'

There was an uneasy shifting. Even one of Fablyr's horses whinnied and stamped as though the answer displeased it. The hawk, too, ruffled its feathers and stooped its head, watching the high table intently with one hooded eye.

'The Romans?' No one could arch an eyebrow like Fablyr, even under the rim of his helmet.

Brenna laughed at him. 'We have lived cheek by jowl with the Romans for three hundred years,' she said. 'That's a Roman saddle you were sitting on and you were taught your letters, Fablyr, by a Roman scribe – the same man who taught me mine. They are our friends, not our enemies.'

'It's because of our enemies I'm here,' Fablyr said, 'and I've brought a hundred men, waiting below the ramparts.'

'You have news?' Brenna sat forward in her carved chair. She had felt unease for quite a while and her scouts rode out every day, trotting over the heather, watching the estuary and the sea and the headlands of the Picts to the north. But there was nothing.

'The painted ones are massing north of here,' Fablyr said. 'Three days ago they were moving east.'

'Numbers?' Brenna the queen was transforming herself into Brenna the general.

'A thousand? Two? It's not clear yet.'

Brenna looked at Malwyn who shrugged.

'Do your scouts tell you this?' he asked.

'Why are they moving east?' Fablyr asked the assembled company. 'Where are they going?'

'The Saxons,' somebody around the table muttered. 'The Saesen. They'll link up with them.'

'We've seen one ship,' Malwyn reminded everybody. 'One Saxon ship in the last month. That's not much of an army.'

'Everybody knows they're cowardly bastards,' someone else chipped in, but it was the voice of hope over experience.

'Whatever the Picts are doing,' Fablyr shouted down the hubbub, 'now is not the time to have the princes elsewhere. Their place is here, at Din Paladyr. Taran should take his place in our warrior ranks.'

'He's a child,' Brenna protested.

Fablyr strode forward for the first time, kicking a sleeping hound out of the way. 'If the Picts attack in the force I'm thinking about, they're not going to care who stands against them. There'll be no children when the painted ones come looking for heads. My men would fight easier if Taran and Edirne were here, alongside their queen.'

The noise reached a crescendo and most of the council were on their feet, shouting at Brenna to do the right thing. Men who had served her all their lives suddenly felt a twinge of doubt. Yesterday she had sent her sons away. How long would it be before she ran too?

'Taran! Taran! Taran!' The boy's name was roared around the hall and the horses shifted.

Fablyr closed to the queen, resting his hands on the great table. 'Bring them back, lady,' he said. 'Time to crown a king.'

No one else heard him but Brenna, because no one else was intended to. She stood up suddenly, looking the lord of Din Eidyn in the eye. 'You are welcome, Fablyr,' she said, 'and we thank you for your kind words. You and your hundred may camp below the ramparts. Our house is your house.'

'And the princes?' Fablyr asked.

'We will let you know,' she said coldly.

He nodded and turned on his heel, striding for his horse.

Brenna turned to Malwyn. 'The inner council will attend me tomorrow night.'

'Lady,' the counsellor leaned nearer, 'you know that Fablyr is right.'

Her eyes flashed fire. 'That Taran should be king?'

'No, no,' he smiled. 'That Taran should be here. And Eddi too. If the Picts are to strike, there must be a show of solidarity. The family must be together.'

'Tomorrow night,' she said, rising. 'We'll discuss it then.'

He rose too and bowed and the rest of the council followed suit. Malwyn crossed the hall and out of the far door where Fablyr and his horsemen were milling with the squawk and flap of the hawk. Brenna's chief counsellor stroked the soft nose of Fablyr's horse and moved in as close as he could.

'Immaculate timing, as always,' he murmured.

Fablyr smiled. 'You know you can rely on me. Are our friends in the east ready?'

'Aelfrith's a tricky bastard,' Malwyn said. 'He won't do anything until our signal.'

'Will she play along, do you think, that stuck-up bitch who wears the crown? Will she send for the boys?'

'She might,' Malwyn said. 'I'll work on her. I admit I've let those little shits slip through my fingers twice now. I won't do it again.'

'Where are they?'

'That's just it,' Malwyn said. 'I haven't the faintest idea.'

Londinium

Archbishop Dalmatius was too ill to attend the solemn funeral of the late vicarius, so the long-suffering Severianus did the honours instead. The man's tomb, along the road that led out of the city from the Bishop's Gate, was the finest money could buy.

They laid the dead man reverently, east to west in the Christian way so that the vicarius could watch the sunrise and await the second coming of his lord Jesus Christ. It was perhaps unfortunate that the builders were not of that persuasion and one of them stashed an amphora of wine and a barrel of salt in the tomb before the coffin was laid in it. Another stole a couple of coins from his master and placed them with the salt, so that the otherwise penniless Civilis could afford to pay Charon, the ferryman. Without that, his soul would never cross the Styx.

They built high walls of chalk and flint with a curved roof of tiles over the top and a carved inscription extolling the virtues of Antoninus Civilis, not just for now, but for all time.

'What a load of bollocks!' Leocadius murmured to the new Caesar standing alongside him. Both men were bareheaded as the unending Londinium rain beat down on them and their cloaks were heavy with dragged mud.

For all this was a funeral, Maximus couldn't resist a chuckle. 'And here I was,' he said, 'thinking you took all this politics seriously.'

Leocadius' glance would have felled a weaker man but the general-turned-Caesar was made of sterner stuff. The great and the good of the capital of Maxima Caesariensis were there in force. As men had been saying to themselves for weeks, it was not every day that a vicarius of a province died and they all owed him that much. They filed past the tomb that would become a mausoleum and the more fervent prayed. Severianus did certainly and so did Vitalis.

The basket-maker had not been invited. He had drifted along with the mob in the downpour, steam rising from their unwashed bodies as they stared at the ostentatious wealth of their betters, the merchants of the Ordo, the men who ran Londinium. Vitalis waited until the service was over, then he crossed the road and stood in front of the priest.

'Do I know you, my son?' Severianus asked. He was not much older that Vitalis, if at all, but the basket-maker knew the conventions of the church and replied in kind.

'No, father. Not directly. I believe you knew my friend, Pelagius.'

The priest's broad face darkened. 'I knew Pelagius,' he said.

'I know his beliefs are not yours,' Vitalis said.

'You could say that.' Severianus was confused. Surely, he wasn't going to have a theological debate with a peasant by the roadside? But then, he told himself, his lord had once come in the guise of a carpenter's son when all along he had been a fisher of men.

'I need absolution,' Vitalis said.

A group of priests clustered around Severianus. Who knew these days who were God's children and who were pagans practising their black arts? The man's face was open and honest and he appeared to be unarmed. But appearances could be deceptive.

Severianus had come to his decision and he waved them on. 'I'll follow you,' he said to them. 'Dalmatius' church in one hour.' He looked at Vitalis, then up and down the road where the mourners were leaving, Leocadius and Maximus trotting away at their head. 'This is hardly the time or place,' he said.

'It will do for me,' Vitalis said. 'I have a journey to go on. At the mercy of the tide.'

'Very well,' Severianus said. He slid the embroidered stole off his shoulders and kissed it. Then he bound it loosely around Vitalis' wrists. Vitalis bowed his head. 'Forgive me, Father,' he said, 'for I have sinned.'

Severianus loosened the stole bands and took it back. 'How long has it been since your last confession?' he asked.

'I have never made confession,' Vitalis said.

Severianus looked at him. 'I'm sorry,' he said. 'When you told me you were a friend of Pelagius, I naturally assumed …'

'That I was a Christian. Yes. But I was trained as a soldier,' Vitalis told him, 'to worship Jupiter highest and best. I have received the kiss of the bull too.'

'Mithras?' Severianus crossed himself quickly.

Vitalis smiled, but there was no mirth in it. 'Signs of a misspent youth, Father,' he said.

'Te absolvo,' Severianus made the sign of the cross over the apostate.

'This man,' Vitalis said, 'the one you buried today …'

'What of him?'

'He was murdered.'

Severianus' eyes narrowed. He did not like the way this conversation was going. 'So men say,' he said.

'So the consul says,' Vitalis told him.

'The consul rules here,' Severianus nodded. 'Along with Christ, of course.'

'Then one of them is blind.'

'Careful, my son,' the priest warned. 'I will not countenance blasphemy. Not even Pelagius would go so far.'

'The consul doesn't rule here,' Vitalis ignored him. 'Maximus does. My belief? That Leocadius had the vicarius killed on Maximus' orders.'

Severianus crossed himself again. To be fair, he had heard that rumour too. Londinium was an open sewer of rumours. 'How does this concern you?' he asked.

'My sister, Conchessa, stands accused of the crime.'

'She does?' Severianus frowned. 'Why?'

'She was one of the last to be in the vicarius' presence before he was taken ill.'

'My son,' Severianus spread his arms. 'I cannot interfere in the civil or the criminal courts.'

'I'm not asking you to. Conchessa and I have been freed by Leocadius but on certain conditions. The civil authorities I can handle, but the journey we must go on will be long and difficult. I need God on our side.'

Severianus smiled. 'I don't even know your name,' he said.

'Vitalis,' the basket-maker told him. 'Vitalis Celatius.'

A light dawned in the priest's eyes. 'You were a tribune,' he said. 'The Archbishop speaks of you now and again.'

'Yes,' Vitalis said. 'I was a tribune.' He ran his fingers over the Wall ring. 'Perhaps I will be again if God wills it.'

'If He does,' Severianus said, 'He will tell you how to serve Him.'

'Can you absolve me of my sins?' Vitalis asked as the thunder rolled to the far north. 'Those I have committed and those I may commit.'

Severianus held Vitalis' shoulder with his left hand and made the sign of the cross again. 'For the sins you have committed,' he said, 'Te absolvo. For those you may commit, no, my son, I have no power to do that.' He winked at the man. 'Did you learn nothing from Pelagius?'

'So we're on our own?' Vitalis asked.

'No,' Severianus said, suddenly serious. 'Never that. Pax vobiscum, basket-maker.'

Din Paladyr

It was the first real spring sunshine Valentia had seen and it flashed on the weapons of Fablyr's little army as they fanned out across the road that led to Brenna's rocky fortress. Justinus had sent no scouts ahead of his column as close to the Votadini capital as this; he saw no need. At the villages on the way there, there were cheery waves and cups of water, loaves of bread and bowls of soup. No sign of raiding parties, no tell-tale smoke from burning villages, just the Pax Romana to welcome the sun.

The commander of the Wall halted his column and the tribune Arcadius moved his horse in close. 'Welcoming committee?' he asked.

The tribune, for all his senior rank, was as green as Valentia grass. He was promoted for his family connections not his experience or ability and sometimes it showed. Never more than now.

'Skirmish order!' Justinus bellowed and the drums thudded behind him, sending the vexillation into two dozen tight knots of men. He outnumbered the Votadini nearly two to one, and he had not deployed for battle. He was keeping his options open. If they charged him now, they would be spoiled for choice as to which five-man group to go for. And while they were wavering, Justinus would send in his cavalry to mop them up.

'I don't understand,' Arcadius said in the understatement of the entire march, 'I thought they were friendly.'

Justinus squinted to the far horizon where the huge rock of Din Paladyr lay like a mirage in the morning sun. He had been gone ... what? A little under three weeks. Could it all have changed in that time? If so, how? And if not, where was Brenna?

'When you've been on the Wall as long as I have, tribune,' he said, 'you won't call a man a friend until you've cut his throat and he's no threat to you. Always remember – we are the watchmen; the keepers of the flame.'

'Io, warriors of the Sixth!' A shout in bad Latin echoed from the Votadini ranks.

'Io, Gododdin!' Justinus replied in the local tongue.

A knot of horsemen walked their animals forward across the turf of springy heather. One of them carried the gilded horned head of Belatucadros as a banner, twisting slowly on the end of a pole. But it was the leader Justinus was watching, a big man, riding a dapple-grey that snorted and pranced, smelling battle in the wind.

'I am Fablyr,' he bellowed. 'Lord of Din Eidyn.'

'Justinus Coelius, Commander of the Wall.'

Both men saluted according to their customs and dismounted, soldiers holding their horses. They walked towards each other, then stopped within two spear lengths.

'Why are you here, Roman?' the chieftain asked.

Justinus was not much more Roman than Fablyr was. He had been born in Verulamium and had spent his entire life in Eboracum or various forts along the Wall. His Latin would barely have been understood in Rome. 'My duty,' he said. 'Keeping my promise to the queen of the Gododdin.'

'What promise was that?'

Justinus waved behind him. It was not just a casual gesture but a silent command learned over the years by men who guarded the edge of the world. The knots of soldiers changed formation like a single machine and formed two solid lines, the vexillum floating in their centre, their bright-painted shields in front of them. It was as though the ghost of the blessed Adrianus called Hadrian had risen from his grave to build a second Wall. 'To bring a little help,' Justinus smiled once the ranks stood fast and silent.

Fablyr smiled too. He knew the movement was designed to overawe him, to prove how quickly the VI could manoeuvre and how impressive even two hundred men could look drawn up in formation. 'The queen has changed her mind,' he said, looking along the line of shields, 'but thanks you for thinking of her.'

Justinus looked at the man. It was difficult to read his face, especially above the beard and below the helmet-rim. The eyes were grey and unblinking. He wasn't going to back down. 'Indeed?' he said. 'I'd like her to tell me that herself.'

Justinus stepped closer to his man. He was within a sword-thrust now. 'You're a liar, Fablyr, lord of Din Eidyn.'

The men behind the leaders saw what happened next. There was a blur of speed and a slap that echoed across the heather. Fablyr's fist had lashed out, colliding with Justinus' temple and the commander of the

Wall swayed. His head rang and his vision blurred but he was still standing.

'Stand fast!' he roared, sensing the legionary line behind him tensing to attack. The tribune's hand was already in the air but he let it fall slowly. Fablyr's Gododdin were less co-ordinated, but one or two hot heads danced out of their formation, stabbing the air with their spears and taunting the Romans. Justinus wiped the blood from his forehead where Fablyr's mailed fist had cut him. 'Swords, then,' he said. 'You and me.'

'Swords,' Fablyr nodded, a twisted smile on his face. Both men turned back to their respective seconds, unbuckling their helmets and cloaks. Justinus walked over to Arcadius, still sitting his horse.

'You're not going to fight this shit?' the tribune asked, amazed.

'That's how it works on the Wall, boy,' Justinus said. 'I call him a liar. He hits me. That's a challenge and we fight.'

'To the death?'

Justinus looked up at his second-in-command. 'Is there any other way?'

'But ...'

'There are times on the Wall,' Justinus explained, 'when you turn and run like Hell. And there are times when you stand and fight. This is one of those times.'

'But they're supposed to be our allies.'

'We've had this conversation, tribune,' Justinus said. 'If a man shakes your hand, he's an ally. If he loosens your teeth,' and Justinus eased his jaw which ached with a vengeance, 'well, you have to come to a different conclusion.'

'But what if …' the tribune barely knew how to put it. 'What if he wins?'

Justinus smiled and patted the man's knee. 'Then, Arcadius, you send in your infantry and you kick seven kinds of shit out of this riff-raff. Got it?'

'Yes, sir,' Arcadius smiled, hearing some kind of sense at last. He straightened in the saddle as Justinus turned. Then the commander turned back.

'And thanks for the thought, by the way. It's good to know you have every confidence in me.'

The two men crossed the space between them. Justinus had drawn his spatha and thrown the scabbard to the heather. Fablyr carried a heavier weapon that he twirled and tossed into the air, passing it from hand to hand to unnerve his opponent. Some men could use a sword with a left hand as well as a right and you never knew where the attack would come from. There were no shields in the way and only limited body armour. This was going to be a contest of speed and skill.

Fablyr struck first. As the aggrieved party, it was his right and the iron blades rang together in the morning. There was a roar along the Gododdin line, with guttural whoops and chants that young Arcadius had never heard before and didn't particularly want to hear again – the battle cries of the Votadini, from their wild mountains and their ancient, mystic past.

The two men circled each other, looking for an opening, a way in. Fablyr struck again, this time with a thrust aimed at Justinus' ribs. The commander parried furiously, deflecting the Celt's blade and he hacked horizontally, threatening to take Fablyr's head off. The ranks of the VI stood silent but inside each soldier there was a cheering madman, longing to leap and dance as the Votadini were doing.

Once, twice, Justinus came in to the attack and each time Fablyr beat him back. Their blades slid together until their hilts locked and they swayed back and forth. Fablyr's knee came up into Justinus' groin and he staggered back. The Celt saw his opening and hacked with his blade, scything through air until the iron ripped through cloth and flesh and Justinus' sword arm dripped red. First blood to the Gododdin and the noise was deafening.

Justinus was back on his feet now. His arm felt numb and the air in his lungs was torture. Every breath was pain. And every breath might be his last. Fablyr was half a head taller, heavier and broader than his opponent and he had that battle-madness that marked out all his race – the wild eyes and streaming hair, the flaring nostrils and the bared teeth. He had his man going backwards and it was time to end it. He tossed the sword from his right hand to his left and hacked under Justinus' raised arm. The Roman swung downwards, driving the blade tip to the heather then he smashed his left boot hard into the pit of Fablyr's stomach. The Celt floundered, fighting for air and off balance. Once, twice, Justinus' blade chopped into his body, slicing deep into the flesh of his shoulder and forearm and Fablyr went down.

There was a stunned silence. Only the rasp of the fighters' breath could be heard as Justinus prodded Fablyr's throat with his sword. He saw the blood trickling over the man's arm and knew he had no more fight in him. The Gododdin had fallen silent now, the wild dancers standing still with open mouths. Still the VI had not moved. Still the VI had not spoken. Justinus – and Arcadius – were proud of that.

But now there was unfinished business. Justinus weighed up his options. Let this man live and he would bear a grudge for the rest of his life, waiting for a chance of revenge. Kill him and the bastard would become a martyr to his people. The fair fight of today in the sunlight of Valentia would become in the retelling a knifing in a dark alley and Justinus Coelius, commander of the Wall, would be just another Roman murderer in the propaganda of history. But there was no real decision to be made. Justinus raised his sword, ready to drive the blade tip into Fablyr's throat. It was the way of the Wall.

'Stop! Justinus, stop!'

It was a woman's voice and Brenna, queen of the Votadini, the Gododdin, was galloping across the heather with Malwyn and the others of her close council. Justinus slowly let the blade droop and stood back from Fablyr's fallen body. He crouched over him. 'You're a lucky man, lord of Din Eidyn,' he growled. 'And every day, for the rest of your life, I want you to thank the queen that you're breathing at all.'

LIBER II

Chapter Eight

Londinium, Maius

Honoria had watched his arrival from the rooftops of the palace, the ones that faced east, away from Julia's compound, in the gardens of the night. Spring had come to Londinium and the sun dazzled on the whitewash and the terracotta tiles, dancing on the rippling waters of the Thamesis that were usually so sluggish and brown.

At the bridge, a huge crowd had gathered to welcome the new vicarius to the greatest city in his province and she heard the bray of the garrison's cornua and the fanfare of trumpets. Scipio was standing on tiptoe, straining to see his father against the glare of the sun.

'There he is, Mama!' he shouted, waving wildly. Honoria laughed. His father had other things to do today beside look for his little son on the rooftops. He had an arse to kiss and a new man to measure up. How, Honoria wondered, would it go this time?

She saw Leocadius in his official robes kneel before the vicarius at the bridge's head. She smiled again, because she knew what that would cost him. The gods alone knew which side of an army blanket Leocadius Honorius had been born on, but, in the words of the late Civilis, he was the shit on a vicarius' sandals. Obeisance like this was nauseating to Leocadius and merely served to confirm Civilis' observations. But Civilis was dead, his tomb beyond the Bishop's Gate already daubed with obscenities. All men, Honoria thought to herself, ended up the same, rotting in the grave or with their ashes floating on the wind. All men were the same length lying down.

Even so, the new vicarius was younger than she had expected, taller and better-looking. It was difficult to tell under his robes of office, but he looked lean and trim. His name was Chrysanthos and he had been sent by the Emperor as soon as he had heard of the death of Civilis.

'Does Papa like this man, Mama?' Scipio asked. He had never really understood why grownups knelt in front of other grownups. He and his friends wrestled and boxed, leap-frogging each other and pushing each other out of trees. Grownups didn't do that. Perhaps no grownup liked another.

'He doesn't know him, Scip,' Honoria said. 'They've only just met.'

There was a commotion below in the street, the sound of running feet and of slaves clearing the way.

It was Julia and her brat, going in their litter to join the ladies of the Ordo at the basilica, to welcome the new vicarius and make envious small talk. Honoria would not be going of course. Honoria would never be going. She knew her place, in the shadows, in the house of night. She would never share the Consul's table in the house of day, never hobnob with the great and good. But she shared Leocadius' bed, something Julia never did and she had all of Leocadius' love. That, for her, was enough.

'So,' she rolled over in the furs when they had finished. 'What's he like?'

'Who?' Leocadius poured wine for them both.

She tapped him with the leather tawse. 'Don't be coy with me, Leocadius Honorius,' she laughed. 'The new vicarius. He looked pretty dishy from a distance.'

'Yes,' Leocadius handed her the goblet, 'and that's how I'd like it to stay, please,' he said.

'Oh,' and she arched an eyebrow, sipping her wine. 'Why is that?'

He threw himself down on the bed, lying on his stomach and trailing his free hand over hers. 'He likes blondes.'

She half sat up. 'Does he now?'

'And brunettes. And redheads.'

'Is that what you talked about?' she asked him. 'A man is sent by the Emperor to come and rule a province and the first thing he tells you is his taste in women?'

'Not exactly,' Leocadius said, 'but his eyes were everywhere. Roaming over tits and arses. I thought some of the ladies of the Ordo would faint with the sheer pleasure of it all.'

'Perhaps he's been on the road too long,' she said. 'Is there a wife?'

'If there is he didn't mention her. And he hasn't brought her. Just a gruff old general with hair down to his waist.'

'A barbarian?' Honoria could be as much of a snob as Julia when she put her mind to it.

'A German. Frank, I think. Name of Andragathius – and that's not one I'll be using after a few glasses, I can tell you.'

'What is he?' Honoria asked. 'Some kind of bodyguard?'

Leocadius shrugged. 'He might need one if Civilis is anything to go by,' he said. 'What is interesting is that this Andragathius knew Papa Theo – you know, the old Count. And Stephanus, his Master of Horse.'

'It's a small world these Romans inhabit,' she said. She put down her goblet and looked hard at him. 'Tell me, Leo,' she said. 'Are you and this Chrysanthos going to get along?'

'That depends,' he said.

'On what?'

Leocadius sighed and rolled over to lie on his back. 'On how he intends to play things with Maximus.'

'What did he say about him?' she asked. Secretly, she had always liked to watch men fighting. It excited her, gave her a tension like a coiled snake in the pit of her stomach. The Emperor's man pitting his wits and his strength against a new Emperor – now that would be a contest worth seeing.

'That's just it,' Leocadius shrugged. 'It was the damnedest thing. He didn't mention Maximus. Not at all.'

Din Paladyr

'You've made an enemy of Fablyr,' Brenna said. She was sitting by the hearth, still glowing with its embers this far north, her knees under her chin. Justinus looked at her. She was a little girl again, talking about squabbling boys. About Fablyr, the boy she had known when they ran together in the heather.

'Fablyr is at war with the world,' Justinus said. He moved a stick in the fire and the embers spat and glowed. She saw the ugly wound that Fablyr's blade had made across his arm just below the elbow and she reached out instinctively and stroked it.

'He was always prickly,' she said.

'Do you want them back?' Justinus looked her full in the face. 'The boys?'

'No,' she said, then, 'yes.' Then, 'No,' again.

Justinus laughed. 'Lady,' he said, 'I believe the Gododdin expect more decision from their queen.'

'The Gododdin can go and …' her voice rose but she never finished her sentence. A wind blew from nowhere, scattering sparks in her bedchamber. She looked at him again. 'Yes, of course I want my boys back,' she said, 'because I am a mother. And I don't need those self-serving bastards on the Council telling me what to do. Nor Fablyr shooting his mouth off.' She paused. 'But you've got them safe,' she said. 'Let them stay that way, at least a while longer.'

He nodded and stood up. 'It's late,' he said. 'I must be going.'

She reached up and took his hand. 'You can stay,' she said.

For a moment, Justinus almost crumbled, almost knelt on the beaten earth and took her in his arms, planting his lips on hers, feeling their hearts beat together. Then he looked into the darkest corner where a tall soldier stood looking at him. He wore a tribune's scarf around his neck and a gold and jet ring on his finger and he was smiling. Pat. Pat the old friend. Pat the dead father and husband. And Pat would always be there. He would never scold, never complain, because Pat did not do those things. But he would be there. And for Justinus, that was enough.

'No,' the commander of the Wall said. 'No, I can't. Goodnight to you, lady.'

The Camp west of Londinium

'He's got balls,' Magnus Maximus murmured. 'I'll give him that.'

'What'll we do, Caesar?'

Maximus looked sideways at the tribune. The morning was not going well and it wasn't even the fourth hour yet.

'What we won't do is run around like headless chickens,' he said. 'Know what Crysanthos means, Galvo? In Greek, I mean?'

'No, Caesar.'

'Golden flower,' his Emperor told him, smiling. 'Well, let's see just how gilded the man's petals are, shall we? Guard of honour, Galvo and jump to it.'

'Sir!' The tribune dashed along the ramparts of the camp, bawling orders as he ran. Soldiers scurried into position, locking shields and hauling spears upright. Drums thudded beyond the Fletus and trumpets blared. Maximus stayed where he was, watching the two horsemen trotting forward from the river crossing. The man on the roan was tall and lean with a face tanned by the sun of Italia. The other one was larger, armed to the teeth and his blonde hair hung in ringlets over his wolfskin-draped shoulders.

'Armour, my lord?' A slave was suddenly at Maximus' elbow.

'No, Decimus, not today. Today, it's all about bridge-building. And testing the waters beneath. Get me that chi-rho pendant, the one you filched from that Christian in the forum. The new vicar-ius is the son of a bishop. Might as well look the part.'

With the solemnities and introductions over, Maximus and Chrysanthos sat opposite each other in the Caesar's principia, sampling an indifferent wine.

'It's local,' Maximus said, watching the vicarius' reaction to the taste. 'Yes, I know. Horse-piss, isn't it?'

Chrysanthos laughed, that tight, guarded laugh of his. 'I suppose I'd better get used to it,' he said.

'Your man,' Maximus jerked his head in the direction of the door. 'He seems sound.'

Andragathius had gone with Galvo for a tour of the camp.

'Oh, he is,' Chrysanthos nodded, easing himself back on the couch. 'If I were of the military persuasion, I can't think of anyone I'd rather have at my back.'

'Such men are useful,' Maximus nodded. He was mentally crossing swords with the man, looking for an opening, a weakness. He found none.

'And, talking of useful men,' Chrysanthos put down his wine. 'The late Civilis.'

Maximus' eyes narrowed a little. 'What of him?'

'I hear his death was a little … unusual, shall we say?'

'Say what you like, Vicarius.' Maximus refilled his cup. 'Apoplexy is always a risk when you hold high office. The blood heats and there you are … gone.'

'There are rumours in Londinium about poisoning. Belladonna.'

'There are always rumours in Londinium,' Maximus said. 'That's why I stay away. Is it any different in Rome?'

Chrysanthos laughed. 'No,' he said. 'Point taken. But there is a rumour in Rome that your legions have elected you Caesar.'

The smile still lingered on Maximus' face. 'Well,' he said, 'the rumours in Rome are wilder than the ones here, then.' There was a pause.

'I'm glad to hear it,' Chrysanthos said, 'because, had it been true, it would have placed me in a rather difficult position.'

'I can see that it would,' Maximus said.

'Where's home, Maximus?' the vicarius suddenly changed tack.

'Somewhere I haven't been in a long time,' he said. 'Hispania Terraconensis. But you knew that.'

'Did I?' Chrysanthos raised an eyebrow.

'Gratian sent you to keep an eye, didn't he? On me, I mean.'

Chrysanthos spread his arms wide. 'Just because you're Dux Britannorum, Maximus, doesn't mean that some people aren't out to get you. Gratian sent me to replace Civilis. Somebody has to run the province ... or are you doing that already?'

'In my humble capacity as a soldier,' Maximus said. 'It's my honour to serve the Emperor. He didn't need to check. No, you're the sort of man, it seems to me, who does his homework. You know where I'm from and you know my record.'

'You have a record for putting down rebellions,' Chrysanthos said. 'From the Danubius to the Wall. I can tell Gratian he can sleep easy in his bed.'

'Good,' Maximus smiled. 'Now, as new vicarius, you must have a hundred duties, but I'd take it as an honour if you would hunt with me soon. There are plenty of boar to the north-west of here and it'll be a chance for you to get to know your new province.'

'Ah, a royal progression, eh?'

'In the name of Gratian, of course.'

'Of course.' Chrysanthos finished his wine.

When he had gone and Maximus had returned to his apartments, the curtains shivered aside and the Egyptian girl stood there, eyes dark and brooding.

'Well,' he said, pouring wine for them both, 'what do your spirits tell you about him?'

'My spirits tell me nothing,' she said, staring out to the sun of the compound where the vicarius and his general were already riding away. 'But I tell you. Leave this man alone, Magnus. He has the mark of death on him.'

'Well,' Maximus said. 'That makes two of us.'

The man filled the doorway and he was not exactly Vitalis' usual kind of customer. He looked as if the only use he had for baskets was tossing enemy heads into them.

'Are you Vitalis Celatius?' he asked. The Latin was rough, Germanic, from somewhere along the Rhenus.

A shrewder man would have equivocated, dodged the question, asked who wanted to know. But Vitalis had always worn his heart on his sleeve. Double dealing he would leave to others. 'I am,' he said.

'Andragathius,' the big man said and extended an arm.

Vitalis looked blank.

'I came over with the new vicarius,' he said, 'from the Emperor.'

Vitalis took the man's hand. 'What do you need of a basket maker?' he asked warily.

Andragathius chuckled, an odd sound rumbling from the full beard. 'Of a basket maker, nothing, but the brother-in-law of Calpurnius Succatus, that's a different matter.'

'You know Calpurnius?' Vitalis frowned.

'As well as any man.'

How did you know ...?'

'About you?' Andragathius threw himself down uninvited on Vitalis' hard and solitary couch. 'The consul, Leocadius. Your friend.'

'The consul Leocadius talks too much,' Vitalis said. 'How did the subject crop up?'

Andragathius shrugged. 'It's none of my business,' he said, 'that a consul counts a basket maker as his friend. He says you are on your way to Augusta Treverorum.'

'Does he now?' Vitalis sat opposite the man on upturned barrel. 'What else does he say?'

'Oh, he was full of useless information,' Andragathius said. 'Mostly about this bloody awful city. He seems quite proud of it.'

Vitalis nodded and could not help smiling. 'He's had bureaucracy thrust upon him,' he said. 'I think he's taken quite a liking to it.'

'He's promised you soldiers, I understand, from his garrison.'

'That's right, forty men.'

'Don't take them.'

'What?'

Andragathius looked at the basket maker. 'Look, I don't know what you know or what you hope to achieve over there.'

'I want to find Calpurnius,' he said, 'for my sister's sake.'

'Is she going with you?' Andragathius asked.

Vitalis nodded.

'Tell her to take her widow's weeds.'

Vitalis stared at the man. 'Are you telling me Calpurnius is dead?' he asked.

'No,' Andragathius said, 'but I'm telling you he might as well be. He fell foul of the wrong people in Carthago.'

'Carthago?' Vitalis was confused. 'My sister thinks he was in Augusta Trevororum.'

'That's where he ran to, yes, along with the boy Theodosius. That's after they killed the Count and Stephanus.'

'You knew them?'

Andragathius' face darkened. 'Stephanus was a friend,' he said. 'He taught me to ride like a Parthian and whore like an Egyptian.' He smiled. 'Made me the barbarian I am today.'

'Who did he cross?' Vitalis asked. 'Calpurnius, I mean?'

Andragathius said nothing.

'Isn't this why you came?' Vitalis asked. 'To warn me? I can't be careful if I don't know who to be careful of.'

The German sighed. 'All right,' he said. 'The one you want is Septimus Pontus. He'll have a few toadies around him, kissing arse and making noises, but it's Pontus you're after. If anyone knows what happened to Calpurnius, he does.'

'What was Calpurnius to him?' Vitalis asked.

'One of the biggest toadies and arse lickers of them all,' Andragathius said. 'Until ...'

'Until what?'

'You won't get near to Pontus with forty men or forty thousand. Send Conchessa.'

Vitalis blinked. 'You know my sister?'

'How would I know Calpurnius and not his wife?' Andragathius asked. 'Give her my regards when you see her.' He caught sight of the ring glittering on Vitalis' finger. 'If that's all you've got,' the German said, 'beyond Conchessa's feminine wiles, may the gods smile upon you, basket maker.'

The Estuary, Valentia, Augustus

The tribune Arcadius halted his horse on the high bluff that faced the sea. A wall of cloud was rolling in from the east, like an army creeping across the crags and muffling the waters. He didn't need his outriders shouting to him, 'Io, Votadinus,' because he had seen the solitary horseman minutes before. He had been on picket duty in this godless arse-end of the world for weeks now and he had got used to the sights and sounds of the Estuary. He had watched the great gulls wheeling and dipping as they skimmed the white caps out to sea. He had seen the grey seals basking on the rocky outcrops of their island, rolling over and blinking in the sun. He knew the lonely call of the curlews at night and the distant howl of wolves in the forests to the south. He had watched the Votadini go about their business in a hundred little hamlets across the moorland, driving their sheep and goats, the children feeding the chickens and the women bringing water. He had smelt the smoke from their peat fires and watched the old men scraping their wolf and deer skins.

And now he saw a horseman, waving frantically and galloping headlong, the flanks of his sturdy little pony flecked with foam. The rider all but collided with Arcadius' outriders before they all wheeled to ride back to his picket. For all he had been here for months, the tribune had not yet mastered more than a few words of the Votadini language and he had to ask the man at his elbow for a translation.

'What's he jabbering about, Gatto?'

Gatto's face had turned as grey as the sea mist that had cut off the plateau from the rest of the world. 'Saesen, tribune,' he said in the best Latin he could muster. 'Saxons. They've landed on the shore. Five miles to the west.'

'How many?' Arcadius asked and waited for the translation.

'This man counted three ships,' he said. 'Maybe more.'

'Three ships.' Arcadius was doing a quick calculation in his head. 'Did they have horses?'

Again, the wait. Seconds only, but it could have been hours. 'No, sir. Infantry.'

'Could be …' Arcadius was weighing the options in his brain. What had begun as a pleasant little ride out in the morning was turning into a nightmare. 'Gatto, who's your best horseman?'

'Bryld.' He called the man over with a wave of a hand.

'Tell him to ride like Hell to Din Paladyr. He's to find the commander. Tell him two hundred Saxons have landed on the Estuary shore between here and Din Eidyn. I'm going to have a look.'

The translation was the work of seconds this time and Bryld hauled at his rein, lashing the sure-footed grey to a gallop as he thundered east.

Arcadius had a dozen men – eleven now that Bryld had gone – and the messenger's horse was too blown to be of much use. But if he was right that there were no horses, that gave the picket the edge. Even so, only half of the tribune's riders were Roman cavalry, trained and tested at Eboracum with the VI Victrix and with long experience of the Wall. The rest were Votadini, and they could be relied upon to charge madly at anything, achieving nothing except useless horses and, quite probably, dead riders.

'We'll advance, Gatto,' Arcadius said, signalling to his dragon-bearer, 'at the trot. No heroics. No fanfare. I want to see what these Saxons look like.'

The Saxons looked like the citizens of Hell. They had camped on a bare rocky upland within easy reach of their ships and it was the ships that Arcadius saw first. They were sleeker and faster than the biremes of the Roman fleet and had only one bank of oars, trailing in the brackish water at the Estuary's edge.

Arcadius had left his horses on the higher ground and with two of his Romans to watch his back, had crept along the misty shore. The fog was his friend today because without it the Saxons would have seen his patrol from miles away in that treeless country. There were three ships as the messenger had reported and the canvas sails were furled tight against the single spar. The prow was carved in the form of a grotesque sea monster, with snarling mouth and bared teeth. Half a dozen men were lounging on the decks of each ship, as if they were on a fishing trip and Arcadius could hear their chatter, low and incomprehensible.

He had never seen a Saxon before but he knew that they had fair hair and blue eyes. Their spears were iron-tipped and they carried the heavy, single-edged Seax at their hips, a sword the length of the Roman spatha but somehow more vicious-looking, more barbaric.

He crept away from the lapping water, careful not to slip on the shifting pebbles and made his way back through the tangled undergrowth to the high ground. Aracadius had not known what to expect but he was grateful that the Saxons had no idea of defence. They were hopelessly exposed on their bluff without a ditch or palisade in sight. They were cooking meat over their camp fires and the smell of roasting hare was tantalizing. The messenger had been right. No horses. The tribune counted heads, crouching as he was in the heather. They outnumbered his little band ten to one and as he had said to them as they rode out, there would be no heroics. Discretion was today's watchword. He left two scouts to keep watch, then he pulled back a mile. To wait.

Londinium

'Well, vicarius,' the consul handed the man a goblet of wine. 'How are you settling in?

'Fine, thanks. You have an interesting city here, Leocadius.'

'It's a small thing,' the consul said, 'but my own.' He clicked his cup with Chrysanthos.

'For the moment,' the vicarius smiled.

'I'm sorry?'

'Yes,' the new man smiled. 'I'm sure you are, but it's a little late for that now, isn't it?'

'I don't follow.'

Chrysanthos looked at the man, all carefully curled ringlets and charm. 'I've done my homework, Leocadius,' he said. 'I know all about you.'

'Good for you,' the consul beamed.

'Let me see – just stop me if I go wrong. Ten years ago, you were a pedes with the VIth Victrix stationed on the Wall. Then came Valentinus' rebellion and somehow you and three of your cronies got to be heroes. All right so far?'

'More or less,' Leocadius nodded.

'The Emperor sent Count Theodosius and Magnus Maximus to put the rebellion down and hold everything together. He was a sweet old boy was Theo and he rather took to you all, didn't he? Made you a tribune, then consul. Quite a fairy story, really.'

'Quite,' Leocadius said. 'Well, you know how it is; some have greatness thrust upon them.'

'Yes,' the vicarius nodded, 'but you also know how it is; you can take the boy out of the rank of pedes, but you can't take the pedes out of the boy.'

'Which means?'

'Which means that since you've got the palace and the basilica here, you've been running every little scam in and out of the book. Let's see; there's the rake-off from the games you illegally set up, the tribute from the wharves and tanneries. Oh, the road tax and the water cut. Not to mention the brothels and the tabernae. Have I missed anything?'

'The travellers' tolls,' Leocadius clicked his fingers. 'You forgot the travellers' tolls.'

'How remiss of me,' Chrysanthos said and he wasn't smiling.

'I think you'll find this is more or less what goes on in every major city in the Empire,' the consul refreshed his cup but did not offer one to the vicarius.

'Oh, undoubtedly,' Chrysanthos said. 'My only concern is how much of all this reaches the Emperor.'

'We're not going to fall out over figures, now, are we?' Leocadius chuckled.

'No,' Chrysanthos put his cup down. 'No, we're not. I'm putting you on notice, Consul. My people will be going over your books from dawn tomorrow. They've already, as you may have guessed, been talking to a few people. And if I find so much as a solidus by way of shortfall, you'll find yourself back on your precious Wall, wearing a louse-ridden tunic and freezing your arse off. And that's before I start enquiring as to what *really* happened to my predecessor.'

Din Paladyr

There was uproar in Brenna's hall that night. All the council had assembled and the torches guttered in the evening breeze. Lug and his priests were there, for no decision could be made without them. Malwyn sat slumped alongside the queen, a cup of wine in his hand. He was looking at Justinus, who had been reconnoitring to the east all day and had just ridden in to the fortress on the crags.

Word had spread around Din Paladyr like a forest fire of the kind men rarely saw this far north. Mothers had taken their children to them, scolding the older ones for nattering and hushing the babies at their breasts. They had watched their men leave the hurdles and the cattle, driving livestock to whatever safety they could find. They had watched them harness their lathes and seen the sparks fly from the blades of swords and axes.

As the sun had set, the scale of the panic became obvious. The trickle of refugees from the outlying villages became a torrent, a steady stream of the nervy and the dispossessed, sheep bleating and geese hissing ahead of them, columns of worried people who had heard the news and knew that their only hope of salvation was to hide behind the great stone and wooden walls of Din Paladyr. How many Saxons had been seen? More than a man could count. Their spears stretched beyond the horizon and a thousand of their devil ships had brought them here. There were so many sails that the Estuary was blocked and the sea itself was stopped. A man could walk from the south shore to the north and his feet would thud on planking all the way. And the Saxons themselves? They were tall men, half as tall again as the tallest Gododdyn and fire roared from their open mouths. They cut the throats of sleeping men and raped their wives and daughters. The fires they built were for cooking babies and the little defenceless corpses twisted on the spits above the flames.

Brenna held up her hand for silence. All day nonsense like this had flitted backwards and forwards around her council chamber. She had seen fear before. They all had. It made men irrational, short-tempered, reckless. The villagers who had run to Din Paladyr had seen it as their shield, a place of safety where their lives would go on and all would be well. But Brenna knew that Din Paladyr was a heap of wood and stone. Timber burns and the Romans, at least, had ballistae that could shatter stone. And Din Paladyr had fallen before.

Now it was time to take stock. After all the arguing, back and forth, someone had to take the bull by its horns. And that someone was the queen of the Gododdyn.

'Justinus,' she looked at him in the half light. 'We haven't heard from you.'

'This is your capital, lady,' he said quietly. 'Your fight.'

137

'You hypocritical bastard!' Needless to say, Fablyr was on his feet, pointing a finger at him. 'You came here, uninvited, with your Imperial cocksuckers and now you tell us it's our fight?'

'Fablyr!' Brenna roared, her voice of command as powerful as any man's. 'Enough.'

'I propose,' Justinus ignored the lord of Din Eidyn, 'to take my men west. If the Saxon force is as small as the messenger says, I'll match them man for man, drive them into the sea before they have a chance to get a foothold or increase their numbers.'

'The problem,' Malwyn said, running a finger around the rim of his goblet, 'is that we only have that messenger's guess on that.'

'And we don't know where they're headed,' Fablyr said. He was already on his feet and was making for the door. 'You can waste your time here if you like and you can die here. But if these bastard Saxons are moving against Din Eidyn, I know where I must be. Besides,' he paused in the doorway, his men standing with him, 'There's a smell about this place that's got right up my nose.'

Brenna called out to him but Malwyn stopped her. 'Let him go, lady,' he said softly. 'He has a right to defend his own fortress. Justinus; you won't leave tonight?'

'No,' the commander of the Wall told him. 'Wandering about in the dark in search of an enemy is a fool's game. I'll go at first light.'

'You'll take my men with you,' Brenna said. It was a statement, not a question.

'Gladly, lady,' Justinus said, 'but a hundred horsemen will do. It'll be all about speed tomorrow.'

The sun was already climbing in the heavens by the time the cavalry were drawn up. Fablyr and his Gododdyn had ridden out in the darkness, knowing the land like the backs of their hands and only their horses' shit was left to mark the way.

Justinus rode at the column's head with a vexillum of the VIth flapping behind him and the Votadini out on the fringes. He had reconsidered overnight and had taken a hundred infantry with him. There were no Roman roads this far north but the sea mist had gone now and the column could see the sun sparkling on the waves in the Estuary. The gulls wheeled and called high overhead, watching the soldiers moving west. Every now and then, Justinus' men met a straggling knot of peasants heading eastward with their lives strapped to their backs, or on the ox carts that rumbled over the heather. No, they had seen no one, except the Lord of Din Eidyn who had ridden hard past them while dawn was striking gold across the sky. They had seen no Saxons with their terrible war-cries and their flaming breath; but that did not mean they were not there, around any rocky outcrop, hiding in any long, yellow grass. It was good to know that the Wall had sent them help. The Romans were supposed to be their allies, but all they did was lounge in their forts far to the south, playing soldiers. It was time to do it for real.

CHAPTER NINE

Londinium

Chrysanthos the vicarius stood in the high window of his personal apartments in the basilica. A pale moon lent the city its full light, gilding the river and the spars of the merchant ships along the wharves like frost in the depths of winter. In fact it was unseasonably hot tonight, sticky with a humidity the vicarius did not remember from his homeland or the various parts of Empire they had sent him to.

It was the end of a long day in which he had hobnobbed with the city merchants and received deputations from the Catuvellauni who lived to the north. Didn't those people realise they were all Romans now, citizens of an Empire they didn't appreciate and didn't deserve? Why did they persist in keeping up this ancient tribal nonsense, especially when they were happy to spend Roman silver on Roman goods? Beyond the river the marshes lay like pools of silver studded with jet where the farmlands lay wet and heavy and the harvest shifted in the warm breeze.

'You sent for me?'

Her voice made him turn. She was as beautiful as he had remembered her when their litters had collided in the crowded streets beyond the Forum. Her hair was pure gold in the moonlight and her eyes bright. He lit a candle, then two and poured another cup of wine.

'I hope you like this,' he said, 'a little unpretentious Faustian but it's a favourite of mine.'

'I'm sure I'll get to like it,' she purred, taking a sip.

He smiled and clinked his cup with hers. 'To the gods,' he said. 'May they smile on us.'

She paused, her eyebrows raised. 'Somebody told me,' she said, 'that you are the son of a bishop.'

'So you find the toast odd?' He invited her to join him on a wide couch.

'A little,' she smiled. 'It's not for me to judge.'

'I am told there are more gods worshipped in this little island than in the rest of the Empire,' he said.

'I don't know,' she took another sip. 'All I know is this little island.'

'Tell me,' he said, leaning back and crossing one leg over the other. 'Why did you engineer that little accident the other day?'

She frowned at him, then laughed. 'That's funny,' she said. 'I thought you engineered it.'

He laughed too. 'If you hadn't,' he said, 'I would have had to. You see,' he leaned towards her, letting his fingers trail through the ringlet of hair that lay on her shoulder, 'I have this thing for blondes.'

'Really?' She sipped her wine again. 'That's a coincidence. I have a thing for vicarii.'

'Well, well,' he said, putting his wine down. 'A coincidence indeed. Have you eaten?'

'Not tonight.'

'Shall we?' He waved an arm in the direction of the table, large, low and circular, where platters of the most elaborate dishes were waiting. Stuffed dormice were piled high and sea-urchins, boiled in their shells and topped with sweet oil jostled with sweet-wine cakes and fried rose petal tartlets. She had never been fond of dormice, stuffed or otherwise, but she turned from the tartlets with regret. Her voice, however, betrayed nothing.

'I'm not hungry,' she purred. 'At least, not for food.'

He chuckled. Then he slipped the brooch and its gown folds off her shoulder, leaving it bare in the candlelight. The soft gleam of her oiled skin was irresistible and he leaned forward to brush it with his lips. 'They tell me,' he murmured softly, his breath warm on her neck, 'that the women of Britannia have curious ways of making love.'

'Love?' she raised an eyebrow. 'What's love got to do with it?'

He laughed aloud. 'Do you know,' he said, as she ran her fingers over his chest inside his tunic. 'I don't even know your name. My man had to track you down by the description I gave him of the accident. You *are* uninjured, aren't you?'

'Why don't you find out?' she asked him, stepping out of her gown as it pooled to the ground around her feet. 'And as for my name, it's Honoria.'

It hadn't taken Chrysanthos long to discover that the legions had indeed elected Maximus Caesar. The man had lied to his face, although, remembering his careful form of words with some bullshit about the rumours in Rome, he'd almost certainly deny it. Calling again in the camp beyond the Fletus and having it out with the new Caesar would achieve nothing. He would either lie again or slit the vicarius' throat and either way, Chrysanthos would be no further forward. He might even be dead. What he needed was a pair of eyes and ears in Maximus' camp.

'Andragathius,' the vicarius said the next morning after his slaves had washed away the delicious smell of Honoria, 'Fancy a ride to the west?'

Augusta Trevororum, Gaul

The city of Augustus in the lands of the Treveri shimmered in the summer sun, the walls of the Palastaula and the Porta Nigra a blinding white by midday. It may have been the black gate that frowned down on the trio that walked their horses through its archway, but the stone was washed with the sun today and had none of the darkness it assumed in the winter months.

Vitalis looked up at the black arrow slits overhead and noted the grooves of the portcullis mechanism as he walked between the columns. Since he, his sister and his sister's maid had left Britannia, the basket-maker had slid back into the shadows of his life and the tribune had moved forward. That way he would win acceptance. That way he would learn more. That way he might even find out what had happened to Calpurnius.

He had been on the point of taking Andragathius' advice and leaving his half century behind. But then a circitor of the garrison had come to him and told him the forty men were not available, by order of the new vicarius. Vitalis had smiled in spite of himself. So, Leo and the vicarius had clashed already. That couldn't end well.

The three had spent two months crossing the German Sea and Gaul. Conchessa and Adelina spoke Gallic like natives and even Vitalis had picked up a few basics by the time they had found their way to the east of Belgica. For much of the journey they had glided along the broad flow of the Mosa, past willows that trailed the water and watched the herons stride through the reeds. There were good army roads beyond that that brought them to the Mosella. The fields that slanted to the river were golden in their parched grass because the summer was hotter here than in Londinium and the days shorter. Nones had fallen on the fifth day and the sun, Vitalis knew and smiled at the thought, was in the sign of Leo. Ceres herself guarded the month according to the Romans and from time to time the dusty travellers had smelt the burning stubble after the harvest and seen the plumes of grey smoke drifting skywards. Along both banks of the Mosella there would be sacrifices to Diana, but these would have to be furtive and clandestine because it was well known that the Emperor wore his chi-rho like armour and he struck down pagans with the sword of God.

The guards at the gate roused themselves. Two women and a man. Nothing here to raise suspicion, but the Emperor had commanded it. No one came to his capital unchallenged. Every name must be written down.

'Vitalis Celatius, VIth Victrix.'

The circitor of the guard looked at the travel-stained rider with his women in tow, his grime and his beard. 'VIth Victrix? Where's your station?'

'Eboracum, clod,' Vitalis said, 'in the province of Britannia. And don't you riff-raff stand to attention when you salute a tribune?'

Vitalis hauled the light cloak from his shoulders to show the scarf with its distinctive colours. And it was colour that drained from the face of the circitor now and he clicked his heels. 'Yes, sir,' he babbled. 'Sorry, sir. You men,' he barked to his supporters. 'Take the tribune's horse.'

'My sister and her maid,' Vitalis said, 'need food and rest. Take them to the best mansio in the city. And point me in the direction of the garrison commander.'

Conchessa couldn't help but smile. Her big brother giving orders was something she hadn't seen before, not since they were kids, yet here he was, throwing his weight around and men were falling over themselves to do his bidding. Her heart soared, perhaps for the first time since they had left Britannia's shores. Perhaps they would find Calpurnius after all.

The Estuary, Valentia

It was past noon when the Roman column saw them and they were a mob, not an army. Justinus reined in and Arcadius' hand shot skyward. The column halted.

'Take post,' Justinus ordered. 'Battle formation.' And he muttered to his tribune, 'Let's see what these Saxons are made of.'

His soldiers ran left and right to form their line three deep, shields overlapping, javelins pointed to the sky. The two centurions prowled at their backs, tapping them into line with their gnarled sticks as their grandfathers had done before them. Justinus heard them growling, 'I'll swing for you, Ammicanius. Call yourself a soldier?' 'Buckle that strap, Celsus. Where *do* you think you are, man?' It had been the same for centuries; the old sweats keeping the kids calm. If the centurion was still grumbling, as he always did, there couldn't be much wrong, could there?

Justinus scanned their lines. It seemed a lifetime ago that he stood in the ranks like they did, throat dry as the summer dust, palm clammy on his spear-shaft. He remembered how heavy his shield had felt, how unforgiving the iron of his helmet. It was always the same; nothing changed. Once these men were in amongst the enemy they were unstoppable. The training and cohesion of the unit took over. It was just the waiting that was hard, hearts thumping in chests as each man tried to take stock of what was in front of him.

Few of them had seen Saxons before, but they knew the type. The blond bastards leaped and sang, snarling in their strange, guttural language. They had no formation worthy of the name and they had no cavalry. Justinus had both. They stood on the headland with the estuary at their backs, without ramparts or ditches. They were no more than a raiding party, unprepared for the Roman column that faced them now. And that worried Justinus.

'They're cool customers,' Arcadius said, adjusting his helmet strap, 'to take us on.'

'You read my mind,' the commander of the Wall said, easing himself in the saddle. 'What did that Votadini say, the one your patrol found – three ships?'

'"Maybe more" and I quote. But I only saw three.'

Justinus was trying to count the enemy but they kept shifting like corn in the wind, trying to puff themselves up and appear more than they were. 'Maybe less,' he muttered.

'Shall we ride them down?' Arcadius asked.

Justinus looked at him. The lad was … what? Nineteen? Twenty? Somebody's younger son, promoted before he'd finished shitting yellow. He was keen enough, perhaps too keen. And Justinus knew all too well that keenness killed men north of the Wall.

'Take the infantry,' he said. 'Steady pace. And silence. I doubt those noisy bastards will notice but silence rattles most of these foreigners. Roll them up. But if they scatter, don't give chase.'

'Where will you be, sir?' the tribune asked.

'I shall be right here, Arcadius,' Justinus said, 'watching your arse. If you hear my trumpets you break off – understand?'

'Yes, sir,' Arcadius grinned. He understood but had no intention of obeying. He could always say that, in the heat of battle, with the noise and the confusion, he hadn't heard it. That was the trouble with these commanders – they got softer as they got older; too cautious by half.

The tribune swung out of the saddle. A man on a horse at the head of an advancing line presented too much of a target. A soldier handed him a shield and he drew his sword, holding it out to his right at arm's length.

'At the march, centurion,' he roared to his senior man and the cornu blasted out its brazen order. The line lurched forward with Arcadius at its head, two ranks deep, the boots thudding over the heather as one. Justinus wheeled his horse and ordered his cavalry to close up in tight formation but he left scouts far out to his right and his left, just in case.

The Saxons were running forward, first in ones and twos, then in a mob, hurling themselves against the moving shield wall as Rome's enemies had done for centuries. The wall broke in the centre to allow Arcadius into the line and closed up again, shield against shield. There were thuds as wayward spears and arrows bounced off the iron rims or bit deep into the limewood. The line slowed a little but the ranks behind pressed forward. Justinus could see the two centurions whirling their sticks and using language that would make a fish-gutter blush.

A quarter of a mile away as they were by now, the battle sounds floated eerily on the afternoon breeze. Justinus watched as the first ranks shifted, forming three lines from the two. That was all right – the lad Arcadius was showing some initiative. The commander of the Wall could live with that. The front rank hurled their javelins, then the second. The third kept their spears in hand and he heard the swords fly free of scabbards as the first rank closed with the enemy. He knew very well what that was like, the crash as a madman threw himself against you, impaling himself on your sword bade. You saw the man's face contort in pain and rage as your blade ripped his bowels. His teeth were bared in agony and you could smell his breath. Then you smelt his blood and you batted him aside with your shield before bringing your boot down on his face and marching on, ready to take the next attack.

Arcadius had never done this before. He heard his spine click as a Saxon, in mail and braided hair, crashed into him. The terrible sword called the seax scythed to the left, knocking Arcadius' shield to one side. For a split second his body was exposed, naked to the blade but the spatha of the centurion thudded into the Saxon's body and the weight of the marching line carried him backwards. He was cursing in his strange, alien tongue, the sword gone from his grasp and his hands clawing the air. The centurion wrenched his own blade free, crimson from tip to hilt and he smashed his shield into the Saxon's face.

Arcadius felt sick. Another enemy to his right was falling forward onto him, his head smashed with a sword blade and blood and brains spattered over the tribune's helmet and face. Somehow he stayed upright and somehow he kept marching. But he'd forgotten every word of command he'd ever learned and it was the centurion who was giving the orders now, screaming at his men to close ranks if one of them fell, urging his lads forward. It was only an afternoon's work, a stroll in the park. They'd come through it.

It was the flanks that Justinus was watching. There was not an enemy alive who could smash a Roman line, but if they could hit the ends of that line, force it in on itself, then all hell would break loose and the centre would fold like the grass houses the kids built. He saw the rider first, galloping hard from the right, the pony scattering dust as it covered the ground below the scarp slope. He could see the scout was waving his arm and shouting but he couldn't make out what he was saying at that distance. He didn't need to because over the horizon came a horde far larger than the one Arcadius was introducing himself to in the broad valley ahead. He could see the standard of Belatucadros, the sun god, dancing at the head of horsemen who were rising to a trot, then a canter and heading straight for the centre of the fighting.

'They're Votadini, sir,' the dragon-bearer shouted. 'Now we'll make short work of those yellow-haired bastards.' There were whoops and cheers from the ranks of the ala at Justinus' back but he silenced them.

'Sound the recall,' he ordered.

'Sir?' The cornicen looked astonished.

'Double up, damn you,' Justinus roared and the cornu brayed out.

Arcadius in his battle line had not seen the Votadini cavalry thundering out of the north. Neither had he heard Justinus' cornu, but the centurion had.

'Sir,' he yelled above the screams and grunts. 'That's the order, sir; the order to pull back.'

'Pull back?' The tribune steadied himself. 'Don't talk bollocks, Julianus. Look, we've got them on the run.'

They had. The Saxon mob was smaller now because behind the still-advancing Roman line, bodies lay in the twisted agonies of death. The heart had gone out of the attack and the blond warriors stood dithering on the hillside, moving backwards as the blades of the VIth clanged and clashed against their wooden shields. Arcadius saw where his centurion was pointing with his sword.

'They're Votadini for God's sake,' Arcadius said. 'Come on, they're not taking this victory from me, by Christ,' and he swung forward again.

Justinus fumed in his saddle. The cornu blast was hurting his ears but it was as though Arcadius hadn't heard it. The lines were moving forward, like some giant centipede rolling leaves before it and it showed no signs of slowing. Justinus hauled his rein and galloped across the front of his horsemen to where the scout had only now reined in.

'Sir,' he gasped, as exhausted as his horse. 'They're ...'

'Fablyr's men,' Justinus said. 'Yes, I know. The only question is, whose side are they on?'

He had barely turned his horse again before he got his answer. The Gododdin from Din Eidyn crashed into Arcadius' right, the spears hurled from the saddle and the swords swinging from the sky. It was unfolding as if in some dream, some mad nightmare from which Justinus could not wake up. The Gododdin, whom the Romans called the Votadini and who had fought side by side with the legions for ever, were turning on their allies, slaughtering them on that already bloody field.

Justinus had no option now. Whatever treachery this was and whatever that mad bastard Fablyr thought he was doing, he had to stop that cavalry charge. Most of the horsemen behind him were not Roman cavalry at all, but Gododdin warriors. Never mind, they would have to do.

'The ala will advance, cornicen,' he shouted as he rode back to his place. 'Walk, march.' Again the cornu blared, a different set of notes now, wild and fierce. The horses' ears came up and their riders shortened their reins. Justinus clapped his helmet on for the first time that day and rode out two horses' lengths ahead of his line. His cavalry rode two deep, knee to knee, the horses tossing their heads as they sensed battle, snorting and champing at their bits.

Arcadius had tried to change front and face the attack from his right but he was heavily outnumbered and the line could not hold. As Justinus could have predicted, the Saxons, shaken and falling back a moment ago, were coming forward again, heartened by the roar of the Gododdin and the sight of the Romans crumbling. The Vexillum of the VIth still flew, scarlet and gold in the afternoon sun but the grinning face of Belatucadros loomed higher over the battlefield and it was rolling the Roman line up from the right.

Justinus' sword flew free of its scabbard and the line quickened its pace. The march had risen to the trot and now the canter. The commander of the Wall carried no shield and he was already within a spear shot of Fablyr's Gododdin rebels. 'Charge!' he bellowed and the cornicen blew the order loud and clear. The front line caught up with Justinus, swallowing him it seemed as they hurtled across the infantry's rear.

Iron clanged on iron as the two bodies of horsemen collided. There were far more Gododdin than Romans, but Fablyr's horsemen were at a standstill by now, skewering the infantry with their spears and hacking at their upraised shields. Justinus' cavalry sliced through them like a knife through butter and he hacked into the ribs of one man before decapitating a second. The Gododdin's head bounced off the shield of the man close to him, spattering the warrior and his horse with blood. A blade whistled over Justinus' head but he ducked, gripping the barrel of his horse for dear life and skewered another horseman.

Close behind him the cornicen went down, his larynx shattered by a sword blade. The dragon standard of the ala wobbled, fell and rose again as its bearer struggled to stay in the saddle. Justinus was looking for Fablyr. Maybe, if he could find the man and kill him, this nonsense would be over and some kind of reckoning would be had. For a moment he thought he saw him, but the press of horsemen carried him away and Justinus cursed his luck.

In the centre Arcadius the tribune had no clue what to do. The Saxons were hurling themselves against the Roman shields again, but taking their time now and parrying and hacking to good effect. Julianus the centurion could read the panic on the boy's face and hissed in his ear, 'Front rank hold fast, sir. Second and third face right.'

'Er … yes, yes, centurion. Cornicen …' he yelled to the trumpeter but the man was no longer beside him. He was kneeling in the darkness of bodies, his head dripping blood and he would never blow another note.

'Twos right,' Julianus thundered, battering his second rank's shields with his bloodied sword. 'Turn, you bastards. The enemy's over there!'

They were. The dark line of Votadini horsemen were on them now, duelling with the Roman cavalry who were trying to turn them. Julianus could see, even if Arcadius could not, that they were hopelessly outnumbered. The commander's column against the Saxon raiders made sense but no one had foreseen the twist of the turncoats now riding down their old allies.

Somehow the infantry turned, men twisting in the confined space, stumbling over the dead and dying to gain a foothold on the slippery grass. There was no time or space to form skirmish order which would have broken the cavalry up and forced them to tackle each unit almost man to man. The second and third line had stopped in their tracks, their shields locked together against the weight of the horsemen. For the briefest of moments there was a lull in the fighting, among the infantry at least. And the sounds that rose now came from hell, the moans and crying of the maimed and the rasping breath of those barely alive.

Justinus had no cornicen with him to give the signal, so like Julianus he had to yell. 'Fall back, Ala Britannica,' he roared. 'Echelon. Anybody galloping will feel my sword before nightfall.'

One by one his horsemen hauled their reins, wheeling their animals to form a diagonal line on the ground to the rear. The Gododdin were unused to this and took their cue from the Romans among them. Those still in the fight, hacking and slashing against Fablyr's men, pulled back in turn and took up the same formation behind them. Gradually, horse by horse and rider by rider, the Ala pulled out of the fight. Fablyr's horsemen jeered and spat, but nobody was giving chase. Men had the chance to look around them, to see who was living and to wonder who was dead. That they themselves were still alive was enough for most. Time to count their blessings. The butchered could be counted later.

'The cavalry's pulling back, sir,' Julianus had fought and stumbled his way back to the tribune's side. Arcadius was as white as his tunic, his eyes wide and staring. 'Permission to do the same.'

'What?' Arcadius frowned at the man. He knew he had just said something but he had no idea what it was.

'Sir!' the centurion grabbed the boy's shoulder, forcing him to focus. 'We must fall back. We'll be cut to pieces here. The commander must have lost his cornicen or he'd be sounding the recall.'

'Fall back,' Arcadius mumbled numbly. 'Yes, yes. Fall back, centurion.'

He had just turned to give his order to his front line when he pitched forward into Julianus' arms. There was a Saxon spear in his back, to the left of his spine and he was suddenly coughing blood over the centurion's mail. Crimson ran over the links and the silver Medusa heads that marked his rank. The centurion dropped his sword and held the boy, dead weight that he now was. The act of falling seemed to bring Arcadius to and he clawed at the centurion's sleeves. 'What's the matter?' he said, bewildered by the blood and the strange feeling of drowning. He was spluttering and choking, trying to understand what was happening to him.

'Nothing, lad,' Julianus said softly, though he knew the tribune could not hear him. 'Nothing's the matter now.'

Justinus sat his horse on the edge of the valley. The dragon still snarled and writhed on the rising wind at his shoulder. He had lost a quarter of his Ala but the infantry had fared worse. He had asked Julianus what had become of the tribune and the old soldier had just shaken his head.

Across the field, bright with the glow of the afternoon sun, Fablyr's Gododdin pranced and pirouetted, shouting insults at the Romans. The Saxons dropped their leggings here and there and waved their naked arses at them.

Justinus heard Fablyr's voice as he ordered his column off the field. 'That's it, Roman, run. Run to the queen. Put your sorry head on her tits and tell her what a joke you Romans are.'

Julianus was on his horse at the head of the column with Justinus beside him. 'Is that what we're going to do, sir?' he said. 'Can we at least ask the bastard if we can bury our dead?'

Justinus took up his reins. 'Burying the dead is for the winners, centurion.' He looked back at the tangle of corpses below the ridge, his own tribune among them. 'And we didn't win here today.' He rammed his heels home and trotted away.

Din Paladyr

The sky was a livid purple by the time the column saw the great black bulk of Din Paladyr and the twinkling firelights on it like stars in the heavens. No one had spoken on the way. There were no gutsy songs, no dirty jokes. This was a retreat. Only the old soldiers like Justinus and Julianus had prevented it from being a rout. The wounded had been given horses where possible or were helped along by their fitter comrades. At every step and every jolt, wounds opened again and blood seeped. Battered, tired men marched half asleep under the purple clouds that crept over the amber sun.

Where the ground had been trodden hard by the centuries and the chalk showed pale gold in the last light, fires had been lit, one on each side of the road. The wind of the night was blowing sparks from them and illuminated the paler blobs in the darkness that Justinus could not make out at first. Then he could and his blood ran cold.

'Io, Commander!' he heard through the semi-darkness. 'I am Piran. Do you know me?'

Justinus halted his battered column and urged his horse forward. He looked down. Alongside Piran stood a knot of men, some bleeding, some bruised, all shaken and afraid.

'You are the houndmaster,' Justinus said. 'Of course I know you.'

'And you know this,' Piran held out his hand in the firelight. It was a ring. Brenna's ring. The ring she had taken from the dead hand of Paternus, Justinus' friend. The Wall ring; one of four that Count Theodosius of blessed memory had given to the four heroes long, long ago. Justinus didn't feel like much of a hero tonight. The commander of the Wall looked up at the pale blobs and saw that they were heads on poles in the ground. And the heads seemed to dance in the firelight.

'Where is the queen, Piran?' he asked, and was afraid to know the answer.

'Gone, lord,' the houndmaster said. 'Fled no man knows where.'

Justinus dismounted, glad to be out of the saddle after so many hours. The horse tossed its head and shook itself, glad to be free of the weight. 'What's happened here?' he asked.

Piran took a deep breath. For hours now he had been rehearsing this moment or something like it. He knew all about messengers and what the Romans did to them. Bad news could mean a blade across the throat and he didn't relish that.

'Soon after you'd gone,' the hunter said, 'the queen was seized. And those who stood by her. There were screams in the chamber, shouting, the spilling of blood. I don't know. I wasn't there.'

'A coup?' Justinus only now remembered he was still wearing his helmet and pulled it off. 'A rebellion?'

'Yes, lord.'

'Who?'

Piran's eyelids flickered in the firelight. 'The Lord Malwyn.'

Justinus felt his shoulders droop, his head dip towards his chest. Suddenly, he saw it all. Malwyn had been planning this for weeks, maybe months. Working with Fablyr. *That* was why they had been so keen for the princes to be brought back so that the royal family would be under one roof. But Justinus had spirited the princes away *and* he had brought a vexillation from the Wall. No wonder Fablyr had called him out, challenged the commander in front of his men. *That* hadn't quite worked out as planned, but no matter. The pair must have had a fall-back position, to lure the Romans out of Din Paladyr. There *were* Saxons on the estuary it was true, but …

'A Saxon called Aelfrith came,' it was as though Piran was reading Justinus' mind. 'Malwyn threw open the gates to him. Those of us who stood firm, tried to rally behind the queen ... well, we're here.'

Piran waved to the broken little band around him and to the heads on the poles. 'The men of the council loyal to the queen,' the hunter said. 'The Lord Malwyn was keen that you should see them.'

Justinus looked at each of them in turn. There were eight of them, the loyal Gododdin who had gone to their graves for Brenna. But they had no graves as yet because their bodies were not whole and because their spirits wandered on the night air. He knew them all, at least by sight and when he came to the last one, he groaned. It was Lug, the high priest, his sightless eyes more sightless now than ever, rolled in his head and staring at the sky. There was a jagged edge below the old man's chin, dark brown with dried blood.

'It took a brave man to do that,' Justinus murmured.

'Those brave men have our families,' Piran said. 'The wives and children of every man here, alive or dead. We must go back to them, Lord. I was just told to give you a message.'

Justinus looked at the man. Beyond him and Malwyn's reminders of mortality the torches of Din Paladyr guttered along the wooden ramparts and spear points glinted there. 'What message?' he asked.

'From the Lord Malwyn,' Piran said, 'for old times' sake, he has let you live. He who could have let you ride into the fortress tonight. But you are to ride away. The Lord Malwyn is king of the Gododdin now and if he sees you again he will kill you.'

Justinus half turned. He looked up into the grim face of Julianus, at the grim faces of all his men. He knew that Malwyn had an army inside that palisade, backed by who knew how many Saxons. And he knew that Fablyr would be on his tail, perhaps not tonight but by first light. He took Brenna's ring from the hound master. Then, he took the reins and swung into the saddle, feeling every muscle in his body tensing.

'Tell Malwyn,' he leaned forward to look Piran in the face, 'he will see me again.' He looked again at Lug's dead face and led his men south.

CHAPTER TEN

Augusta Trevororum, Septembris

The city lay dumb in the sweltering heat, the Mosella lower than usual at this time of year and the mud of its banks baked hard and latticed with cracks. Moorhens dipped in the reeds which were yellow like the spurge grass all around and the tall, hunch-backed herons watched the water for fish.

The headquarters of the Schola Palatina was wedged in the narrow enclaves behind the basilica, but at least the high buildings gave shade at ground level and Vitalis was grateful for that. All the way from Londinium, he and Conchessa had been deliberating what to do when they reached the place where Calpurnius had been heard of last. He had not wanted to bring her at all but she had insisted and anyway, leaving her behind would have meant leaving her to the tender mercies of Leo, Maximus and the new vicarius, about whom Vitalis knew nothing.

So the basket-maker had become the tribune once more. He had shaved off his beard and had

gone to the west of the great city to find a post in
the field army of the Magister Militum Praesentalis.
The unit was usually based in Greece watching the
Danubius frontier but the Emperor had made a
western capital in Augusta Trevororum and three of
the army's six legions were here. The praeses known
as the magister was a reasonable man and a good
soldier, but his hands were tied. There were no
vacancies for a tribune at that precise moment, but
if Vitalis cared to return in … ooh … a year or so,
things might be different. Yes, he knew of the Wall
and the trouble there had been there a few years
back, with the rising of Valentinus. He was delighted
at last to meet one of the heroes who had put that
rebellion down, but, sorry, he still had no vacancies.
Perhaps Vitalis should try the Emperor's personal
guard.

There had been a time when these men made
and unmade emperors, when no man dared cross
them and Rome *was* the Praetorians. But that had
faded and Vitalis was not impressed by the slovenly
soldiers he had found lounging in the noonday heat.
The commander was a small, weasely man, his tunic
immaculately pressed and bright despite the sweat
that seeped everywhere on everybody else. He looked
Vitalis up and down.

'It's possible,' he said. 'The emperor has need of
good men. How many years' service?'

'Twelve,' Vitalis lied. It went against the grain of
his principles, but needs must and even as he walked

under the archway of the Porta Nigra, he realised that honesty would not get a man very far in this city.

'What house are you?' Quintilius Alfridius was a stickler for protocol.

'My own.' Vitalis stood to attention in the darkened chamber. There was a lute playing somewhere and the faint smell of incense.

'Oh dear.' Alfridius' face fell. 'No, that won't do. That won't do at all.'

'Perhaps this will.' Vitalis held out his left fist and the Wall ring gleamed in the half light. Alfridius took his hand and pulled Vitalis forward, peering at the four gold helmets on the jet base. He held the man's fingers for a shade longer than he need have, then let go.

'Count Theodosius,' Alfridius smiled, 'had those made for the men who held the Wall in Britannia.'

'You are very well informed,' Vitalis said.

'Information is power, tribune. And I work for the most powerful man in the world. You knew Theodosius?'

'I met him,' Vitalis said.

'Yes.' Alfridius leaned back and rang a little bell on the table where he sat. 'I wouldn't make too much of that around here. Theodosius is, shall we say, rather persona non grata.'

'I haven't come to name drop,' Vitalis said.

'Why have you come?'

A slave appeared at the commander's elbow and poured two cups of wine. Alfridius passed one to

Vitalis and raised his own cup. 'The Emperor!' he toasted.

'The Emperor,' and Vitalis drank.

Alfridius chuckled. 'You've no fear of poisons, I'll give you that.'

'Should I have?' Vitalis accepted the man's waved offer of a seat.

'In this city?' Alfridius raised an eyebrow. 'I won't beat about the bush. Yes. But you didn't answer my question. Why have you come?'

'After Valentinus' rebellion,' Vitalis had been preparing for this one, 'life in Britannia got a little tame. There's only so much patrolling of walls a man can take.'

'The woman with you ...' the commander began.

'My sister, Conchessa.'

'And the other one ...'

'Her maid.'

'Conchessa.' Alfridius narrowed his eyes. 'I've heard that name somewhere.'

'Do you have a vacancy in the Scola Palatina or not?' Vitalis cut to the chase. He had never enjoyed small talk and was, to be honest, a little out of his depth in the politics of the emperor's court. Leocadius would have made himself at home, tried the oysters, found a girl. But Vitalis was not, he thanked God every day, Leocadius.

'I do and I don't,' Alfridius said with an enigmatic smile on his face.

'Jesus save us,' Vitalis hissed. 'What does that mean?'

'Jesus,' Alfridius repeated. 'I've heard that name too. Do I take it you are Christian, tribune?'

'As I hope all tribunes are,' Vitalis said straight-faced.

'Of course,' Alfridius frowned right back. 'That goes without saying. All right, I'll give you a trial. See how you do after a month. It'll have to be on a circitor's pay, though, at first. You do understand?'

'Pay is not a problem,' Vitalis assured him. 'Just as long as I see some action.'

'Oh, you'll do that all right,' Alfridius grinned. And Vitalis was not at all sure he liked the way he looked at him.

The second prong of the attack took place two days later. She had had him pointed out to her before, the man called Septimus Pontus. He was the senior decurion in the emperor's city of Augusta Treverorum and although running the games was only part of his duties, he took a special interest in this and creamed off a substantial slice of the profits. The man dripped gold from every orifice and when Conchessa first saw him he was surrounded by pallium-wearing cronies and had a lovely girl on each arm. He had been wandering the forum in the early morning, sampling the fare at the street stalls, weighing the new grain and letting its dusty gold fall through his fingers. He pushed a fat finger into the cheese, chewed off a hunk of bread and tasted the wine. The look on his face said it all and, as his entourage swept on, two burly soldiers in the uniform of the Scola Palatina dismantled the stall in his wake and roughed up the stall-holder who had failed to please.

Then he made for the slave market and Conchessa followed. The crowd had been there for some time and the auctioneer was already in full swing.

'My lady ...' Adelina was tugging at the girl's cloak. It was unseemly for a woman to be seen in places like this. Like much else that was Roman, the buying and selling of slaves was a man's work. Conchessa tapped her hand away and pulled herself together. She had grown up with slaves, with that double standard that said a slave was a man like any other and the equal of his master. Yet at the same time, he was nothing, a gap in the line, a space in the darkness of the universe. But Conchessa had never seen a man bought and sold before. Nor would she today, because it quickly became obvious that this was a specialist sale. There were no men on the circular wheel of the dais at all, just girls. They ranged in age perhaps from ten to thirty, all shapes and sizes, bound loosely around the neck with silken bonds.

The clientele was male, however. In fact, Conchessa was the only free woman there. She stood out like a sore thumb, ignoring the mutterings and whisperings of the men around her. One by one the girl under the hammer was led forward and put through her paces; made to turn to her left and to her right, to kneel, first on one knee, then the other. Occasionally a punter strolled up to the dais and prodded the girl's ankles or looked up her dress.

Conchessa wandered as casually as she knew how across the back of the auction crowd. The sun was gilding the roof tops now and it would not be long until it shone full on the market, throwing the shadows of the slaves for sale across the striped awnings of the basilica. Now she was close enough to Pontus to hear his conversation.

'Shame on you, Septimus,' one of his friends was swigging from a goatskin sack. 'It hasn't been legal to buy a girl to do *that* since the days of Diocletian.'

'Bugger Diocletian,' another of them laughed. 'Septimus has got that look in his eye again. Who's your money on, Septimus? The black one?'

A beautiful African girl, perhaps eighteen, was at the front of the dais now and there was a forest of hands in the air. Fat old lechers jostled with each other and Adelina kept as close to her mistress as she could, the hand under Conchessa's stole clenched into a fist.

'Let's see what we're getting,' Pontus shouted and the auctioneer dashed across the dais and ripped the girl's dress from her shoulders. She gasped and shuddered, much to the delight of the watching men and stood there, trembling. She knew better than to try to cover her nakedness. This was what the punters had come for and she had been sold before.

'The teeth,' Septimus shouted and the auctioneer forced his short-gripped whip against the girl's full lips to make her open them.

'I think the horse fair is next week, Septimus,' a third crony sniggered. 'But I grant you you'd probably have more fun riding her.'

There were guffaws all round. But Septimus Pontus did not bid. The black girl was gorgeous with rounded breasts and a trim waist. But the senior decurion was already looking elsewhere and the girl from Africa was sold to someone else.

Next on the dais was a smaller offering, fine-boned and beautiful. Her dark eyes were huge and her hair hung black and shiny over her shoulders. Conchessa could not be sure of her age, perhaps fifteen. She looked out at the crowd with pure hatred written on her face. If the girl had ever cried, she would not cry now. Not in front of these animals.

'Again, auctioneer,' Pontus called. 'Let's have a look.'

There were roars and sniggers. When a man like Septimus Pontus was buying, he could make up his own rules and many a man in that crowd had no money at all. They had just come for the show.

'Let's not.' A voice stopped the auctioneer in his tracks. Stopped him because the voice was female. All eyes turned to Conchessa who stood like an angel at the mouth of Hell, all gold and glowing in the morning.

Pontus smiled that lop-sided smile of his. 'A solidus, auctioneer,' he shouted, 'says the dress comes off.'

'Two says it doesn't,' Conchessa countered.

There were titters and whispers from the crowd, a collective sucking-in of breath.

'Do you wish to buy this girl, madam?' Pontus asked Conchessa while barely looking at her.

'Do you?' Conchessa asked. Now she turned to him for the first time. 'Or have you just come to drool and play with yourself?'

There were no more titters and the banter had stopped. The only sound in the market place was the creak of the dais as it rocked on its housings, ready to be cranked round for the next slave. A crony at Pontus' elbow broke the silence with a snigger and he nudged his overlord. 'Come on, Septimus. Put her in her place. Five solidi for the slave girl.'

There were gasps anew and everybody looked at everybody else. This was ludicrous money.

'Are you bidding for her yourself, Milo?' Pontus asked, still smiling.

'Er ... no ... five solidi ... God, no. I thought you ...'

'...wouldn't want to be outdone by a slip of a thing, eh?' He looked Conchessa up and down and immediately like what he saw. 'Quite right,' he said, 'but let's be realistic, shall we? Four, auctioneer.'

'Four solidi.' The auctioneer brought the crowd to order.

'Five,' Conchessa said.

'Six,' the decurion said.

There were murmurs all round as male dominance asserted itself. The girl on the dais hadn't moved but she was praying with all her might that the beautiful blonde lady would win in this duel for her life.

'Seven,' Conchessa said.

There was silence again. Adelina gnawed her lip. She knew exactly what Conchessa was doing and why, but the whole process frightened her. Adelina had been born a slave. She had never been bought or sold but she felt for every girl on that dais as if she'd been her own daughter.

'Eight solidi,' Pontus stood like a rock in the midst of his people. The bejewelled girls on his arm had both clung closer to him, as though to retain their own positions in his life. This black-haired slip of a thing wasn't going to muscle in on *their* territory. And they had nails and teeth to make sure of it.

Conchessa looked across at him. Already she had offered to spend half the silver she had in the world. This man might go on for ever because he had the riches of the emperor behind him. She gathered up her skirts and pushed her way through the throng of men, Adelina at her elbow, nudging them aside. Close to, the girl on the dais looked very afraid. Her defiance had gone now and a little girl looked down at her would-be saviour.

'Kneel down, child,' Conchessa said softly.

There were guffaws and ribald laughter from the crowd. 'Aye, aye.'

'I say,' somebody called. 'Steady on, now. I mean, we're all men of the world.'

The girl knelt on the hard oak of the turntable, looking pleadingly into Conchessa's eyes.

'How old are you? Conchessa asked.

'Fourteen,' the girl said. 'I think.'

'Where are you from?'

The girl blinked back her tears. 'I should tell you, lady. I am a Jew.'

Conchessa's eyes widened a little. She had never met a Jew before. She had heard, of course, that they ate babies but looking at the girl now, she found that hard to believe. Conchessa took the girl's hands and helped her up. Then she turned to the auctioneer. 'Nine solidi,' she said in a calm, clear voice.

There was another gasp from the crowd. She looked at Pontus, his face a mask of annoyance. Then he smiled his crooked smile and turned away, his people with him jabbering in his wake.

Londinium

Another city. Another time. The rain drifted across Londinium, peppering the river with yet more water. The rats scurried along the waterfront, up the wooden posts that held the cargo ships at anchor. They paused on their nightly travels, sniffing the air in search of food. There. There was the place. A bireme with oars levelled and stowed, torch lights flickering under canvas. There would be men there. And where there were men, there was food.

Leocadius placed the dice to his lips and kissed them. He looked at the others around the table. Varro of the Black Knives who slit men's throats for a living. Bromilius, procurer of girls. Lucius Quadratus the money- lender. But most of all, he watched the Arab, Sabatha. The man's Latin was excellent, but he wore the strange robes of the East and his gods were unknown this far to the West. All night the Arab had been winning as if his dice were made of pure gold. As if his dice were …

Leocadius threw the bone cubes that bounced and clattered on the board. There was a roar from the others at the table and from their hangers on peering in intently to watch the roll of the dice.

'They're not falling for you tonight, consul,' Sabatha said, scooping Leocadius' coins into his hands. He clicked his fingers and a slave rushed forward to pick them up. Suddenly the man jerked back, a knife point quivering in the woodwork where his fingers had been. All the Arabs were on their feet, daggers drawn, jabbering and shouting all at once. Sabatha quietened them with his hand in the air. He leaned back in his seat and folded his arms.

'Is there a problem, consul?' he asked.

Leocadius reached forward to retrieve his knife. 'I believe there is,' he said. 'Your dice.'

'What of them?'

'They're loaded.'

More cries of outrage from Sabatha's people.

'Strong words,' said Sabatha when the noise had subsided.

It was Leocadius' turn to lean back and fold his arms although the dagger was still in his right hand, concealed under his tunic sleeve. 'Ask anyone,' he said. 'I don't tend to lose at dice. Hand – well, that can go either way. But dice proper? No.'

'We can all have bad luck,' the Arab said.

'We can,' Leocadius conceded, 'but not as consistently as this.'

'So what do you propose?' Sabatha asked.

'My money back,' the consul told him, 'plus the money of all these gentlemen you've been fleecing all night … and half your pot too.'

There was silence in the room until the wind caught the moored ship and it swung slightly, wobbling the candles and creaking on the housings up on deck.

'Where I come from,' Sabatha said slowly, 'if a man accuses another man of cheating, he must expect to defend the charge with his life.'

'Ah' a cheeky grin spread over Leocadius' face, 'but this is Londinium, sheikh. We do things differently here.'

'It's a ticklish thing, protocol,' Sabatha said. 'Technically, on my ship you are in my country and you play by my rules. On the other hand, I am moored in your waters so I play by yours. How shall we resolve it?'

Leocadius' left hand was in the air, flicking a coin that flashed as it turned and clattered on the table. His right hand lay in his lap, still holding the knife. 'A denarius of the Emperor Gratian,' he said, 'newly minted, I believe, in Augusta Treverorum. You may check to see how many heads the coin has.'

The Arab picked it up and looked at it. Gratian stared to his left with a studded crown on his head above the laurel wreath. Sabatha flicked it and saw a gateway on the reverse, the Porta Nigra of the Treveri. 'Very pretty,' he said.

'Let the coin decide,' Leocadius said. 'If I win, all this,' he pointed to the pot, 'comes with me.'

'And if you lose?'

Leocadius smiled again. 'If I lose, the pot is yours. And with it, my life.'

It was time for noise from the consul's people. Lucius, Varro, Bromilius, they were all on their feet, shouting and waving their arms in the air. And it was Leocadius' turn to quieten them. 'It's all right, boys,' he said. 'I'm in no danger. Sheikh.'

Sabatha took the coin and threw it to Lucius. 'You toss it,' he said.

The money-lender looked doubtfully at Leocadius who nodded and the coin spun in the air, glittering in the candle flames as it fell. It landed with a clatter and Lucius' hand was over it before anyone could see.

'Call,' Sabatha said.

'Heads,' Leocadius said. 'I've always had a soft spot for the Emperor.'

Lucius took his hand away and the grim walls of the Porta Nigra glinted in the candlelight.

For a moment, no one moved. Then Varro opened his mouth. 'Leo ...'

But the consul held up his hand. 'Gentlemen,' he said, 'I'll bid you good night.'

Bromilius was on his feet first. This was madness, but it was madness of the consul's own making. If he wanted to throw his life away on the spin of a coin, well, so be it. The others stumbled after him, making for the steps that led to the rain-washed deck. Varro paused and patted Leocadius' shoulder. It was useful, in his line of work, to have a consul who looked the other way when it came to highway robbery, but he could survive without him. As for Bromilius, he couldn't imagine any consul of Londinium closing down the city's brothels, cut or no cut. That just wasn't done. Bromilius kept his council to himself. Whatever happened in the next few minutes, he wasn't going to be the one to break the news to Honoria; that much was certain.

Sabatha waited until he heard their feet thud away overhead and felt his ship sway as his guests trod the gangplank to the relative safety of the Londinium waterfront. He dismissed his people with a flap of his hand and sat looking at the consul. 'Well,' he said. 'That was all very dramatic.'

'Wasn't it, though?' Leocadius smiled. He always enjoyed putting on a good show. 'Let's get one thing straight first. The dice *are* loaded, aren't they?'

Sabatha laughed. 'Of course,' he said. 'I wouldn't use them if they weren't.'

Leocadius laughed too. 'Right,' he said. 'Well, let's get on with it, shall we?'

The camp, west of Londinium

'You don't think my chin looks too big in this?' Magnus Maximus was studying the drawings on the table in front of him. The autumn storms were lashing outside, the wind whipping the leather of his tents and tugging at the guy ropes. Here in the principia he was warm and dry but the weather had turned; there was no doubt of that.

The Egyptian leaned forward, naked except for the wolfskin cloak she had wrapped loosely around her waist. She looked at the drawings too. Within a circle, the head of Magnus Maximus Imp. looked stern and unyielding, as befitted a man who had recently proclaimed himself emperor. There was a cloak around his neck and a simple wreath on his head. She looked at the design for the obverse where a kneeling goddess gave the laurels to the general, in full armour, fresh from the fight.

'Where will you have the coins struck?' she asked him. 'In Londinium?'

He chuckled. 'I thought, sorceress,' he said, 'that you would know that already. Why settle for Londinium when you can have Augusta Treverorum? I have a hankering to say hello to my old friend Gratian.'

There was a sound from the doorway and Andragathius stood there, dripping wet with his hair plastered to his forehead. 'Have I chosen a bad moment?' he asked, in his gruff Latin.

The girl rolled away and backed into the shadows. It was her way and few men dared comment on it. She seemed to be taking up more and more of the Caesar's time and cynics began to wonder whether he would so much as fart without her permission.

'Andragathius.' Magnus threw the designs to one side. 'I'm thinking of taking the II Augusta north.'

'A winter campaign?' The German frowned.

'Not a campaign exactly,' the Caesar said. 'Hopefully, there's no one to fight. No, I'm thinking more of war games. Putting the lads through their paces.'

'Where?'

'Britannia Prima. I've never been there myself but the II have. We'll pick up their cohorts from Isca.'

Andragathius looked blank.

'Sorry,' Maximus said. 'I keep forgetting you don't know the country. Over here,' and he crossed to the far wall where a map of Britannia had been pinned. 'We are here. Londinium. Here,' he pointed to a land mass beyond a river mouth, 'is Isca. I thought we'd move north, along this ridge to ... here.' The Caesar's finger halted at another estuary. 'Horrea Classis.'

'What's that?' Andragathius asked. 'A two week march?'

'About that,' Magnus nodded. 'Care to come along? Or does the vicarius have a job for you here? It must be gripping stuff, counting sheep-pens.'

The German smiled. 'It would be pleasant to see those mountains,' he said.

'Ah, they're nothing like the ones you're used to,' Magnus warned. 'But I've been told they have a charm of their own. And in answer to your earlier question, no. This won't be a winter campaign. You can carry on counting your sheep pens until spring.'

Londinium

Dorio was getting too old for this game. Ever since he was a boy he had been working this stretch of the river, wading waist deep in freezing, brackish water, mending his lines and spreading his nets. Was it him or were the salmon smaller than they used to be, the trout in fewer numbers? He'd done everything he could think of. He'd sent incense to Sol Invictus, cut a lamb's throat for Mithras. Gods, he'd even gone to stand through one of Archbishop Dalmatius' endless Christian sermons – and that *was* taking religion too far. But nothing had worked. He was still barely making a living, still had the same nagging wife who'd been bending his ear for the last twenty years, still had the same layabout kids who thought the river-fishing business was beneath them. Could it get any worse?

Yes it could and it did that morning as he hobbled over the marshes, the mud sucking at his boots. He could see something floating with the tide, a bundle of rags that had obviously got tangled up together somewhere up stream. Well, he'd have a look. Maybe if he hauled the cloth ashore he could dry it out and make a little profit on it. He gasped as the cold water reached his knees. He never got used to it, although he had done this every day for years. Damn. The bundle was floating away from him, on one of those infuriating eddies that developed a yard or so out as the wind took it. He grabbed a stick from the reed beds and, checking his footing, poked it into the fabric. It held fast, but the bundle was heavier than he expected and it carried him along for a few yards until he could steady himself.

Dorio would need two hands for this and he launched himself, throwing the stick away and pulling at the water-logged load. It rolled towards him in the darkling waters, dripping with weed and tangled with ropes. Dorio stood up sharply and almost let go. The cloth was wrapped around a body and the body was dead. It was a man; the fisherman was sure of that. The hair was black and the clothes good, expensive and new. The face was a pulp of smashed flesh, bloody and bruised where the keel of some ship had collided with it. But Dorio wasn't looking at the face. He was looking at the gilt chain still partly hooked to the cloth at the shoulder.

And Dorio sent up a prayer to every god he could think of, just in case. Because that was a chain of office that he had seen many times when he had taken his fish to market. It was the chain of the consul of Londinium.

CHAPTER ELEVEN

Valentia

Justinus' battered soldiers reached Onnum two days later. His Gododdin cavalry had gone with him, hoping to find their queen somewhere in the wilderness of Valentia. But of Brenna there was no sign. No one in the villages they rode through had seen her but they were alarmed to see the condition of the little army that trotted through their settlements. Din Paladyr was far to the north and the villagers had little to do with that. They tended their flocks as they had always done and prepared for the autumn slaughter, sharpening their knives for the ritual throat-cutting and bringing salt from the sea to the east. Every year, it was the same; the endless struggle for survival. A man could feed his family but he could not feed his sheep as well when the grass lay buried under feet of snow and the animals could not feed themselves. In-fighting and treachery in Din Paladyr? Those who heard of it just shrugged. What had any of that to do with them?

'Should we be on our guard, then?' Decius Marcellinus the fort commander asked Justinus as they soaked in Onnum's baths once more.

'Step up the cavalry patrols,' the commander of the Wall advised, 'but I don't think they'll take us on. Winter's coming and Malwyn has to win over a few hearts at home first. He's threatened me with the fires of Hell if I ever go north again, but I don't think he'll come south. He's won himself a kingdom with little blood shed. He'll be happy with that for now.'

Decius looked at his master. A man like Justinus Coelius was difficult to read. Victory? Defeat? He took both those things on the chin and above that chin was an unchanging face. 'What will you do?' he asked.

'Reinforce the Wall,' Justinus said. 'It'll mean going cap in hand to Ammianus again, to raid his headquarters for men, but it has to be. He's a reasonable man. He knows I can't leave the Wall undefended.'

'And Brenna?'

Justinus looked across at Decius. For all these two went way back, he had never really liked the man. 'She's a survivor,' he said. 'She's done it before. She'll do it again.' A sudden thought occurred to him. 'And she's proud. Don't expect her to come here – or to any fort – and beg for help. It's not in her nature.'

'What about Din Paladyr?' Decius asked.

Justinus scowled at him, then stared into the steam swirling around his sweating body. 'There will be a time,' he said softly.

Londinium

Old Dorio knelt on the cold floor of the basilica. The light of a new day was streaming in through the high windows, dappling the mosaics in front of the dais.

'Get up, man' Chrysanthos said impatiently. 'You've done no wrong. Have you?'

'No, sir.' The fisherman struggled to his feet. Years in the water and the cold had taken their toll. Grovelling was in his nature, but it took him notice-ably longer to do it these days. 'No, sir. I just found him floating.'

'And the chain,' Chrysanthos held it in his hands now, before passing it to an underling. 'That's what caught your eye?'

'Yes sir. As soon as I saw it I knew. I knew I should come to the basilica, sir, to tell you what I'd found.'

Chrysanthos leaned back on his carved oak chair. 'You hoped for a reward,' he said.

'Reward, sir?' Dorio blustered. 'Why, no, it never crossed my mind. I was just doing my duty, sir, as any citizen should.'

'Yes.' Chrysanthos' smile was mirthless. 'Very commendable. You know the river, fisherman?'

'Man and boy, sir, these forty years.'

'So the body,' Chrysanthos wanted answers. 'How did it get to where you found it?'

'She's a tricky one, the Thamesis, sir,' Dorio said, warming to his theme now and realizing that, for all the bureaucratic lackeys lounging around the room, *he* was the expert here. 'She has her ways.'

Chrysanthos waited. He was not a man known for his patience and this old idiot was trying it sorely this morning.

'It's my guess,' the fisherman went on, 'he went in somewhere around the Walbrook.'

'Went in?' Chrysanthos checked him. 'You mean slipped? Fell? Was pushed?'

'I'm sure I don't know, sir,' Dorio said. This was not his field of expertise and he felt the conversation slipping away from him.

'All right,' the vicarius said. 'What then?'

'The tide would have carried him downstream, then back up again, depending on when he went in.'

'And that we don't know.' Chrysanthos was thinking aloud. 'All right, fisherman. And our thanks.'

'Er …' Dorio dithered. He was being dismissed and with not so much as a denarius for his trouble. He had hauled the body ashore, laid it out on his own fish-gutting table, walked all the way to the basilica carrying a chain that represented five years' profits. All right, he would never have been able to sell it, the device was too well known. Neither did Dorio know anyone who could melt the gold down. No, his plan had been to walk away with a packet from a grateful authority who would pat him on the head for being an upright citizen and put silver in his purse. This way, not even a pat on the head.

'That will be all,' the vicarius said and Dorio became all too aware of two very large guards standing at his elbow. He barely had time to tug his forelock before they were helping him rapidly to the door.

Chrysanthos left his chair of office and strode to a side door, half-hidden behind a column. The statue of the deified Constantine watched him go and he padded on sandalled feet down the twisting spiral of the stone stairs until he reached the next level. It was cold and damp down here in the bowels of the building, where the stone foundation rose from the Londinium clay. He took a torch from its bracket in the wall and made his way to an ante-room beyond a studded door.

'Serapio,' he nodded to the medicus of the late consul Civilis who was peering into the left ear of the corpse on his slab.

'Vicarius,' the man bowed.

'What can you tell me?' Chrysanthos was looking at the body that Dorio the fisherman had recovered from the river. It was naked now, washed of the Thamesis weed and filth and it was slowly turning dark green.

'He was in his late twenties, I'd say,' the medicus murmured. 'No sign of manual work. Well muscled, though. And … see these?' He half turned the body, pointing to pale tracks across the skin high in the ribs. 'Old scars. Our man could have been a gladiator. Or a soldier.'

Chrysanthos tapped the arm muscles, then the thighs. Lastly he prodded a finger against the abdomen, 'Too scrawny for a barleyman,' he said. 'Anyway, we all know the Emperor's edict against gladiators. They're a thing of the past, surely.'

The medicus shrugged. Both men knew there was a world of difference between the edicts that came out of Rome or Augusta Treverorum and what actually happened at the arse-end of the Empire.

'Is that what killed him?' Chrysanthos was pointing to the smashed head, the unrecognizable face.

'Possibly,' Serapio said, 'but I think that's got more to do with the buffetings in the river. The place is choked with ships this time of year. He could have hit any one of them. No,' he grabbed the hair and pulled the body upright so that it half sat on the marble, 'I think what killed him is this,' and he pointed to an ugly knife wound just below the hairline. 'A single downward thrust with what I'd say was a curved blade. It would have ripped his lung. He'd have bled to death.'

He let the body drop back.

'Do you know this man, Serapio?'

The medicus sighed. 'I've been hearing rumours for the last two days that this is Leocadius Honorius, the consul. Has anyone heard from him?'

Chrysanthos looked at the man. 'No,' he said. 'Not for the last two days.'

'It's been two days now,' Honoria's eyes flashed fire as she prowled the room. This was *her* domain, *her* lair, the palace of the night and these scum were dithering in front of her, shifting like naughty schoolboys from foot to foot, avoiding her gaze. 'One of you must know *something*.'

'Honoria ...'

She spun to face him. She had whored for this man, more than once, and she knew him for the shit he was. 'Don't "Honoria" me, Bromilius. When did you see him last?'

'Er ... dies Mercurii, wasn't it, Lucius? The old memory, you know,' he tapped his temple lightly with his knuckles and tried to grin, 'plays tricks these days.'

Lucius Quadratus knew a buck when it was passed his way. 'He was well ...'

He froze in mid-sentence, feeling the woman's eyes burn into him. They all knew Honoria's reputation. There was a rumour that she had knifed Longinus the old consul, so that Leocadius could have his job. There was a rumour that she had poisoned Civilis the vicarius so that he could keep it. The gods alone knew what she'd do to Chrysanthos. And indeed to anyone who crossed her.

'When?' She looked into Lucius' eyes. 'When was he well?'

The money-lender's lips were dry. He knew Leocadius' whore too, the speed at which her fury rose and the suddenness with which she struck. But he'd dug himself in too far now. 'On the ship, at the tables.'

'The tables?' Honoria's voice was gravel. 'You were playing dice. Whose ship?'

'The Arab's,' Bromilius said. 'The Arab Sabatha.'

Honoria nodded. She remembered Leo talking about this man, how rich he was, how ripe for the plucking. He had a whole fleet of grain ships and dealt in the spices and perfumes of Arabia. He had more money than Leocadius had ever seen. She felt suddenly cold and straightened to her full height. 'What was the wager?' she asked them all, 'the size of the bet?'

Silence. Then her eyes fell on Varro. The big man shifted uneasily. 'His life,' he grunted.

The speed of what followed surprised them all and she slapped him hard across the face. He reeled backwards, his knife in his hand, his face a mask of anger. 'You bastards,' she growled at them all. 'You left him there to die. You, Bromilius, you snivelling little shit,' and with each word she smashed the rings on her fingers into his face. The man stumbled away, bleeding and in pain, his lip swelling already. Lucius took one look at the mistress of the consul and ran, ducking out of the room and scurrying down the steps.

Varro stood there, his knife still in hand, his cheek stinging.

'Are you going to use that, you piece of shit?' she asked him levelly, 'or am I going to cut your balls off?'

He slid the knife away. 'He's no bloody loss,' he said, 'neither use nor ornament, if you ask me.'

'He made you, you moron,' she snarled. 'Without him the Black Knives will have to go back to robbing old ladies. Well, it's what you do best, I suppose.'

Varro was furious. In his weaker moments he had to admit he felt a little guilty at leaving Leo to his own devices, but to be told his fortune by this tart was intolerable. Threatening women was beneath him, however and he spun on his heel and left.

'Where's Papa, Mama?' little Aelia asked. Julia looked at her. The girl was becoming more irritating by the day, if only because, every day, she looked more like her father.

'He's gone away, darling,' she said as the maid combed her hair and looped it up with the ivory combs high on her head. It looked a little old-fashioned but it befitted a widow of a consul and at least her mother, Matidia, would approve.

'Where's he gone, Mama?'

She looked at the girl. She was nearly nine. What do you tell a child of that age, that the rumour was that her father had been murdered over a sordid game of dice among thieves and cut-throats; the father who was supposed to be the Emperor's man in Londinium, keeping the flame and making the streets safe for women and children?

'He's away on the Emperor's business,' Julia lied.

'When will he be back?' Little Aelia was combing her hair up like her mother's, turning her head from side to side to see it in the glow of the copper mirror.

'We don't know, darling,' Julia said, glancing at the maid. 'One day. One day we'll see him again.'

She didn't cry. Julia had done her crying a long time ago, when she first realized that Leo didn't love her; had probably never loved her. When she'd first heard the rumour that there were others, many others, especially that bitch called Honoria. When he was away at night, he was not burning the midnight oil on the affairs of the city. He had turned out to be just like Julia's own father, chasing anything in a dress. And then, there was that strange area beyond the palace wall, that gate eternally locked and guarded, the house she could not see into. As for the guards who patrolled there, they were the consul's men. And he had long ago bought their absolute obedience. And their silence.

Honoria didn't cry either. She'd forgotten how. She paced her apartments in the house of the night, only yards away from where Julia primped and preened. She bore the woman no ill-will. Julia had never deserved Leo and if she shed any tears for him they would be in public and timed to perfection, as the city went through some ghastly form of burial for him. Honoria half smiled to herself. Archbishop Dalmatius, they said, was close to death so it would be that simpering nobody Severianus who conducted the service. They would lay the consul's body east to west as the Christians did; the consul who didn't have a Christian bone in his body and, if he prayed at all, prayed to Sol Invictus and to Mithras, god of the morning.

No, Honoria did not cry. Instead, she had gone to the waterfront. No, said the harbour master, the Arab's ship was not here. It had sailed with the tide two days ago. Where was it going? Gaul, he'd heard, but once at sea, of course, ship owners and their captains could always change their minds. As she lit candles to Sol Invictus that night, Honoria vowed to get even. Varro, Bromilius, Lucius, the unholy trio who had let her man die, they would all feel her wrath in the coming weeks. And she sharpened her knife and prepared her potions.

Only little Scipio cried. Not in front of his mother because he knew somehow that her heart had turned to stone. He cried alone in his bed for the papa he had lost; the papa he would never see again.

Augusta Treverorum

Quintilius Alfridius secretly enjoyed the Emperor's bashes. They were very informal little cenae where anybody who was anybody at Gratian's court mingled and the gossip flowed with the wine. No uniforms today, no ceremony. Everybody wore civvies and ate and drank their fill. Sessions like this gave Alfridius a chance to look over any new men who had arrived, although at the moment he was still rather smitten with his new tribune, Vitalis Celatius.

'Septimus,' the commander of the Scola Palatina tapped on the sleeve of the latest arrival. 'I'd like you to meet my new tribune, from Britannia.'

'Britannia, eh?' Septimus Pontus shook the man's hand. 'We've been hearing rather curious tales from that quarter, haven't we, Quintilius?'

'We have indeed.' Alfridius clicked his fingers in the general direction of the slaves, milling around with ewers in their hands. 'Well, I'm sure Vitalis can fill you in. He's here with his sister.'

'Oh?'

Vitalis took stock of this man. Septimus Pontus looked as oily and snake-like as Andragathius had described, even if he was younger and better-looking than he had expected. Here was the man that forty thousand troops could not get near. Yet Vitalis' sister might.

'My sister, Conchessa,' the tribune said.

Pontus' face fell for a second before the lop-sided grin took over. 'Oh, yes,' he said. 'We've met, your sister and I.'

Vitalis knew that perfectly well. And the evidence for it was a Jewish slave girl installed in his household. 'Have you really?' he beamed, hating himself all over again for yet more subterfuge.

'She could haggle for Rome, that one,' Pontus said, without elaborating. 'Tell me, is she ... attached?'

'A widow,' Vitalis said, 'in all probability.'

'That's rather cryptic, tribune,' another man next to Pontus cut in. He extended a hand. 'Milo

Belarius.' He jerked his head to Pontus and the others alongside him. 'We're all on the Emperor's staff.'

'In all probability,' Pontus repeated. 'You'll have to explain that one, Vitalis.'

'I mean, we must assume her husband is dead in that no one has seen him for over a year. Perhaps you know him? Calpurnius Succatus?'

Milo's face flickered for a moment and another man gulped down a swig of wine.

'No,' Pontus said, looking haughtily around them all. 'It rings no bells for me.'

'That's odd,' Vitalis sipped his wine slowly. 'Because Calpurnius was on the Emperor's staff too. A Decurion, like yourselves.'

'Where was this?' Pontus asked.

'Carthago. Under the late Count Theodosius.'

It was one of those moments when time stops. Nothing moved in the atrium. There was no sound. Then Pontus broke the moment like the snapping of twig. 'Carthago,' he said. 'All that was a long time ago.'

'Gentlemen,' an official had stepped into the room and he slammed a staff of office to the ground. 'The Emperor.'

Every man there was suddenly on his feet, smashing his right fist to his left breast and then holding the hand out in front of him in the old Roman salute. Vitalis had never seen the Emperor before; had never seen *any* Emperor before. Yet, here he was, Flavius Gratianus Augustus. And he was just a man.

Londinium

They buried Leocadius Honorius that wet Friday as the month turned. Chrysanthos spared nothing. There were full honours, as befitted the status of a consul and a hero of the Wall. The garrison turned out with cornua and standards and the even carried a vexillum of the VI Victrix in honour of Leocadius' old legion. The great and good were there , the Ordo and their wives and children, going through the motions in Dalmatius' church near the bishop's gate as Severianus kissed Chrysanthos' ring and led the service for the dead.

There was a low chanting. And the solemn tolling of a bell. This was the public show, the passing of a consul. The new Caesar was there, riding a black horse for the occasion and Chrysanthos' man Andragathius who was slowly becoming Magnus's, sat his roan beside him in the church square. The vexillation from Magnus' camp west of the Fletus lowered their spears as the coffin passed them, carried on the broad shoulders of the city's watermen. Old Dorio came to pay his last respects, hoping that somebody would listen to his story and buy him a drink on the strength of it. Nobody did.

But the night was different. This was the private show, not for a dead consul but for a dead friend. For good old Leo. If Julia, stoic and graven as an image had led the mourners in the day, Honoria led them now, in the taberna by the Walbrook that had been

Leo's second home. Anyone who had diced with the dead man was there, wrestled with him in the street, stood him a drink or shared a woman with him; they all toasted the friend they had lost. Honoria knew the women there and their specialities. She had grown up with half of them and she could understand why Leo had gone with them. Men like Leocadius could never be faithful, even to two women. That would be asking too much.

There was a dice game going on by the time the newcomer arrived. It was still raining out there and his cloak dripped water. He watched the dice roll and bounce, heard the roar as one man won and another lost, heard the shrieks of the girls and the slaps as their backsides were hit just for luck, just for the habit of the thing. He had not taken his hood off and only his beard and lips showed in the candlelight. He accepted a goblet of wine and the hunk of cheese and the crust of bread. And he waited.

Honoria was not at the table. That was because Varro was winning and she found it difficult to stay in the same room with the man. Suddenly, she noticed a stillness. The shouting and the music had stopped and she could hear the rain on the roof. She found herself drawn to the table and could not look away. Varro was leaning back with the dice in his hand, throwing them casually in the air and he was looking at the far end of the table where the man in the cloak still sat.

'Double or nothing,' he said, a greedy glint in his eye.

'I don't know,' the cloaked man said. 'I hear you're pretty good with those.'

'Well,' Varro grinned, 'if it's too rich for you ...'

'Oh, no,' his new opponent smiled. 'In fact, it's not rich enough. Let's spice it up a little, shall we? Let's throw in your life.'

Varro's grin vanished. 'Who am I playing against?' he asked. 'Take that hood off and show your face.'

The stranger raised both hands and let the velvet fall. There were gasps all round, not least from Honoria. Sitting across the table from Varro, his face grim, sat General Magnus Maximus, the Caesar.

Nobody knew quite how to react. Half the people in the room were on their feet, some bowing, some saluting. The sensible ones had slipped out of the door. Others hadn't moved at all.

'Caesar!' somebody said before throwing his arm out ahead of him.

'Not tonight,' Maximus said quietly. 'Tonight, I've just come to play dice. And to pay respects to an old friend.' He raised his goblet. 'Jupiter highest and best smile on you, Leocadius Honorius,' he said in a loud, clear voice. 'I solemnly swear that I will be an enemy to those I learn are the enemies of Leocadius Honorius. If I knowingly swear falsely, then may Jupiter highest and best cause me to be deprived of fatherland, safety and all good fortune.' And he emptied his cup. 'Well, Varro,' he said, 'are you ready to place your last bet?'

The leader of the Black Knives looked around him. His men, who had been carousing at his elbow moments before, were suddenly absent and sullen faces stared at him. He knew them all, the men he had drunk with and the women he had taken up against every wall in the city. People he thought were *his* people. And now, in the eerie stillness of the taberna, they were not.

His knife lay in its sheath at his left hip. All he had to do was to transfer the dice or lose them and he could claw the weapon free. He knew this place like the back of his hand and the alleyways outside. He'd be able to lose this bastard in the darkness and anyway, knife fighting was what Varro did. Magnus Maximus may be a general; he might even be bloody Caesar, but men like him never got their hands dirty. They had people for the rough stuff.

Varro threw the dice in the air, high so that they rolled and spun in the candlelight. His right hand was on his knife hilt when his life left him. It did it in a split-second. There was a sudden jolting thud and a burning pain in his throat. He felt his head crash back against the tall chair he was sitting in. his fingers fluttered uselessly at his hip and he couldn't see anything. He couldn't move either. Something was pinning him fast to the back of the chair. What was going on? The room was dimming and he was having difficulty breathing. And all this seemed to go on for hours. The dice clattered onto the boards but

Varro did not hear them. He did not see them either because Varro of the Black Knives was dead.

Maximus got out of his seat and crossed the room in three strides. He glanced down at the dice. 'Well, well,' he said. 'Two sixes. My lucky number.' Then he wrenched his knife out of Varro's throat and the dead man pitched forward, blood pooling under his head. Maximus wiped the blade on his cloak and made for the door. On the way he passed Honoria and smiled at her. 'For Leo,' he said

Augusta Treverorum

He watched her astride the dappled grey as it trotted down the hillside. At the bottom, a tributary of the Mosella twisted and babbled over stones, its sound musical in the morning. He checked the horizon. No brother. No maid. No retinue of slaves. Just her. Just Conchessa, the widow who was not a widow.

He tapped his bay with his heels and rose to a canter following the old goat path that led to the ford. Augusta Treverorum with its gates and turrets, its arena and its circus, lay over the hill out of sight. This spot, sheltered by the horse chestnuts, could have been anywhere in the world, an oasis of calm and peace.

He waved to her as he drew rein and waited for the grey to reach him.

'Have you come to buy the slave girl from me, decurion?' she asked him.

He laughed, and looked younger than his years. 'I have enough slave girls to last me a lifetime,' Pontus said, 'but I'll wager you don't.'

'I am not a betting woman,' she said.

'Good.' He sprang down from his saddle and tethered the bay to a bush. 'I'm glad to hear it. Won't you join me?'

She looked at him with her head on one side. 'What's this?' she said. 'A picnic?'

'I forgot the wine,' he said, 'not to mention the bread and cheese. Can we at least enjoy the view? I love this spot.'

She swung down and looped the rein over the same bush. 'It's prettier than Carthago, I'll wager.'

His smile vanished and he sat down, cross-legged. 'And I thought you weren't a betting woman,' he said.

'You know who I am.' She sat too, her feet tucked under her, her cloak trailing on the grass. 'And who my husband is.'

'I know who your husband was, lady,' he said, looking at her closely.

Her mouth opened with a slight gasp but she could not show her shock now. 'That's funny,' she said, looking back at him. 'When my brother mentioned Calpurnius you had never heard the name.'

'When your brother asked, I was in a forgetful mood.'

'And now you've remembered.'

He chuckled. 'Conchessa … may I call you that?'

She nodded.

'Conchessa, I can duel with you all day. You bought that wretched girl in the slave market just so that I would notice you, didn't you? You didn't have to do that, you know. I would have noticed you anyway.'

'Because I was a woman at a slave auction?'

He was suddenly, almost grimly, serious. 'Because you are the most beautiful woman I've ever seen.'

She felt herself blushing and felt annoyed with herself that she was. 'Of course,' she said, 'and I'm not a betting woman, but I'll wager you say that to all the girls.'

Pontus laughed. 'Most of them,' he said. 'But in your case I'm afraid it's true.'

Conchessa looked at the man. Had she misjudged him? Had Andragathius been right? That Septimus Pontus was a man with something to hide; that forty thousand troops could not touch him? She had seen his annoyance at the slave market. But she had not seen this side of him, yet. Here was a soft-spoken gentle man, like her own dear Vitalis when he wasn't dressed up playing soldiers. Was that it? Was it the uniform that turned men in the service of Rome? Were they all biddable little boys who became monsters in their pallia and armour and decurion's robes? Even Calpurnius … and that was why she was here; that was why she had ridden out this morning, knowing that Pontus came this way.

'So you've remembered my husband?' she asked, her heart thudding against her ribs.

'Of course,' he said. 'He was on my staff at Carthago. And you're right. That place is nowhere as pretty as this. It's all sand and burning heat and flies. What was it the great Cato used to say after every speech of his in the Senate? "Carthago must be destroyed". He got that right.'

Conchessa leaned forward. Before she knew it, her hand was on the sleeve of the senior decurion. 'What happened to Calpurnius?' she asked in a voice not much above a whisper.

He looked at her for a long time, then he took her hand and held it in his. 'I don't know,' he said. 'He was sent on here after Theodosius died. We had orders to move. I sent him ahead to prepare …'

'And?' She was leaning forward, squeezing his hand, willing him to answer.

'And that was the last any of us saw of him,' Pontus shrugged. 'He wasn't here. Not in the basilica, any of the mansios, the palaces, the army camps. No one remembered seeing him. I had my men out for days, combing the city, the back alleys. We … we even dragged a section of the river.'

'Nothing?'

He shook his head. 'Nothing,' he told her.

He felt her sag against him, smelt her hair as he pressed his face against it. 'There are thieves out there, Conchessa,' he whispered. 'On any road in the Empire. The Pax Romana isn't what it was.'

She nodded, but her cheeks were wet with tears and she didn't want him to see them. But he did. He lifted her head and looked into her eyes, big with tears.

'But you're going to go on looking, aren't you?' he said.

'Yes,' she told him. 'I am.'

Chapter Twelve

Eboracum, Rivros

There were rumours along the Wall for weeks and the weeks turned into months. The Saturnalia came and went and the snow lay heavy on the black moorlands and dropped softly through the pines of the woodlands. Justinus Coelius, commander of the Wall, inspected his forts and his milecastles as always, the snow stinging his eyes and the frost coating his beard. His staff rode with him these days, just in case. A man could get lost in the sudden blizzards that the winter threw up, the wind ripping through crevices in the broken stones that marked the Wall's outposts.

Now and again they trotted past wayside crosses or smaller shrines to Mithras, the soldiers' god. Now and then they broke bread with the locals and held their hands gratefully over their roaring fires. But of Malwyn and his renegade Gododdin there was no sign.

No one had heard of Brenna the queen for so long. There was no news at Segedunum on its high bluff over the Tynus; nothing at Vindovala and less than nothing at Vercovicium, teetering on the edge of its rock crest. Justinus left word with his fort commanders to be ever vigilant; then he left his staff to return to Onnum and he rode south.

The weather turned vicious again on his way and he took shelter in what was left of a crofter's cottage. Most of the roof had gone, but the walls still held and he was able to huddle in the dankness of the collapsed wattle, his horse alongside him for warmth. It took him six days to reach Eboracum and he was never so glad to see civilization in his life. The river was partly frozen as he walked the horse over the bridge, its planks slick with ice. It wasn't dawn yet and the fires of the night in the canabae had not long gone out. The homeless ones stirred under their rags, snoring and farting as they prepared to face another day with frostbitten fingers outstretched, begging for their bread.

Justinus looped the animal's reins over the rail of his father's house. It had become a joke between them for years now – that the boy would try to creep up on the man, get the better of him, prove his military worth. That Justinus had done that a hundred times, in Valentia and along the Wall, could not be doubted. But all that was in the outside world. This was personal, between father and son and old Flavius had set the bar high.

So, cold as he was, tired as he was, hungry as he was, Justinus went through the motions. He eased his sword from its scabbard and inched open the gate. There were no lights in the house and no sign of Rialbus the slave. The man was slipping. He was nearly as old as old Flavius, but that was no excuse. Justinus closed the gate behind him, careful not to rattle the bolt or jar the hinge. He breathed shallow so that the vapour snaking ahead of him didn't betray his presence.

Ahead of him, beyond the well, the stairs rose to the left. Along the landing slept the old man, with his bed to the right and his head towards the door. So far, it looked good and tired and cold as he was, Justinus warmed to the challenge. One day, he had promised himself, he would get the better of the old bugger and the father would be proud of the son.

In fact, he hadn't even reached the bottom stair when he felt something push him hard from his left, lurking in the shadows. He would usually have just stepped sideways, regained his balance and faced whoever was there. Instead, he found himself stumbling against something curled up so close to his right leg that he fell over it, sprawling and cursing under his breath. The sword had gone from his grasp and when he looked up, there were two spear points inches from his throat. At the other end of the shafts, two boys with curly hair and elfin grins stood looking at him.

'You'll have to do better than that!' Flavius Coelius was suddenly at the top of the stairs, arms folded and beaming with pride. 'You've met my new guard dogs, Taran and Edirne? Rialbus, you lazy shit, get out of that bed and get some stew for my son.'

Throughout breakfast, which Justinus wolfed down with the hunger of the road, he couldn't help admiring the boys who sat in front of him. He had not seen them for the best part of a year and they had grown. Taran was a man in all but name, his shoulders brawny and the softness of his skin was becoming darker and tanned against the summer sun and the winter wind. Little Eddi was little no more. The boy was eleven now, not that much shorter than his half-brother and every time he smiled, Justinus could see the boy's father, his old friend Paternus there. It was in his grey eyes, his thatch of hair, the way he carried his head.

With the meal done and the clash and hurry of the great city of Eboracum echoing all around the walled house, Flavius put the boys through their paces. They were good with sword and shield, outstanding with daggers and darts. Only the lack of space prevented Justinus from telling how good their archery was. He laughed and clapped them from bout to bout and was delighted to see that Eddi wasn't always on the losing end. And they made a formidable team – they'd proved that already by their ambush on him in the half light.

'Right!' Flavius clapped his hands to bring the war games to an end. 'Latin lessons!'

There was an explosion as both boys complained, one voice deep and reasonable, the other still treble and more so as it became more pleading.

'Let them off today.' Justinus let his voice join the boys'.

'No exceptions.' The old hastilarius leaned back against the wall, arms folded again; a sure sign he could not be moved. 'Get a move on. Last one to the magister's house does four laps of the parade ground. Full pack.'

And the boys tumbled over each other in their eagerness to get to their lessons.

'You're a hard man, Flavius Coelius,' Justinus smiled, helping himself to more bread. 'And you've made a good job of those two. I'm impressed. Now, what do I tell them about their mother?'

'No news?' Flavius asked.

'Nothing. It's as though the ground has opened up and swallowed her.'

'Would she have left Valentia?'

'Not willingly.'

'You don't think ...?' There was a sudden look of concern on Flavius' face.

'Suicide?' Justinus read his father's mind. 'That's not the Votadini way, Pa. It's what we Romans do, given the right circumstances, but not Brenna's people. And certainly not Brenna.'

'The right circumstances?' Flavius repeated.

'Yes, you know. Shame. Defeat. Disgrace.' He leaned forward so that his nose was close to his father's. 'Extreme old age.'

And he only winced a little as the old man hit him around the head with a skillet.

Augusta Treverorum

The snows lay thick on the ramparts of the Emperor's capital too, the stones of the Porta Nigra powdered white. Soldiers with frozen feet trudged along the parapet, trying to stay warm, moving their fingers constantly on the shafts of their spears, in an effort to keep frost-bite at bay.

The Emperor Gratian was warming his arse in front of a roaring log fire in the basilica that morning. He had worn the purple for six years and looked older than the twenty two summers he had reached. He had the large eyes that women loved and the tight sneer that men loathed. And there were few who loved this man for himself. Many loved him for what he was; because a friend of the Emperor was bound to be going places, spiralling upwards on a heady mix of power, moving in the right circles and making for the light.

For all his youth, Gratian was a good judge of men. And most of the men below him – because they all *were* below him – he could read like a book. They were crawlers, arse-lickers, sycophants who would happily butcher their own mothers for a post in his entourage. But the man standing before him this morning was not like them. He stood to attention in the full dress uniform of the Schola Palatina, now that the legion's commander had given him full rank and status.

'Vitalis, isn't it?'

'Sire,' Vitalis saluted.

'At ease, man, at ease. Some spiced wine on this cold morning?'

'Thank you, sire.'

From nowhere a slave carried a silver tray and goblets full of steaming ruby, shining in the firelight. These were the Emperor's private chambers and in the corner, a hawk flapped and screeched on its perch. Gratian crossed to the bird, dipped a dead chick into the warm wine and let the hawk's razor beak rip the little yellow body to pieces.

Gratian chuckled. 'Pontus tells me I'll lose a finger one day, doing that. But there it is. Now, Vitalis; they tell me you have recently arrived from Britannia.'

'Some months ago now, sire.'

'Yes, yes, quite.' Gratian wiped his bloody fingers on the hair of a slave girl and slapped her backside. 'Oh, forgive me,' he said. 'Where are my manners? Does she please you, this one? I can have her sent to your quarters.'

'No, thank you, sire; honoured though I am.'

It was not everyone who turned down such an offer and from the Emperor himself. Gratian looked at him. 'Not Greek, are you?' he frowned. 'I mean, I know Alfridius has his moments, a boy in every port, that sort of thing.'

'Er ... no, sire, not Greek.'

'Good.' Gratian sipped his wine. 'Good. Glad to hear it. Now,' he offered Vitalis a seat. 'To cases. When you left Britannia, what news was there of Magnus Maximus?'

Vitalis sat on the gilded couch. Maximus had sent him with urgent letters for young Theodosius. But young Theodosius was, when last heard of, in Constantinople. And Vitalis had dallied here for too long, on behalf of Conchessa, asking questions covering the whereabouts of a man he had never met.

'When I left Britannia, sire,' Vitalis said, 'the general had declared himself Caesar.'

Gratian was sitting on his own couch alongside the fire and he waved his goblet at a slave to refill it. 'Yes,' he said. 'That's what I heard. How many legions does he have?'

'Sire,' Vitalis shifted uneasily, 'I was not a tribune in Britannia. At least, I was, but I resigned my commission.'

'Does that answer my question?' the Emperor snapped. He was used to more toadying than this, even if less truth went with it.

'Your Imperial Majesty knows the strength of your forces in Britannia,' Vitalis hedged.

'Yes, I do,' Gratian shouted suddenly. 'To give them their old names – the II Augusta, the VI Victrix and the XX Valeria Victrix.'

'Three legions,' Vitalis shrugged.

'And how many more?' Gratian hissed. 'Auxiliaries? Client kings? Mercenaries?'

'Sire,' Vitalis spread his arms. 'I don't know.'

Gratian stood up and started pacing the room. Then he stopped. 'More to the point,' he said, 'what does he intend to do with them?'

'Again, sire,' Vitalis stood up too, 'I don't know.'

Gratian looked hard into the tribune's face. 'All right,' he said. 'Let me put it another way; what would *you* do?'

'Me?' Vitalis laughed. 'I'd no more declare myself Caesar than fly.'

'But if you were Maximus?' Gratian persisted.

Vitalis thought for a moment and put down his cup. 'If I were Maximus,' he said, 'I would cross the German Sea and I would take all this,' he gestured around the lamp-lit room, 'from you.'

Londinium, Martius

'He's going, then?' Chrysanthos sat alone at the head of a long table eating his cena, every now and then passing small pieces of chicken to the cat that sat on the table, purring and flicking its tail.

'By the end of the month.' Andragathius stood dripping in front of him. It had been raining hard for days in Britannia and spring seemed very far away. All the way from Maximus' camp the water had been driving into his face so that his clothes and armour were wet through and his eyes were red-rimmed and bleary.

'War games?' Chrysanthos said. 'You're sure that's what he said?'

'He's been talking about it for weeks,' the German helped himself to wine. 'I told you.'

'Yes, I know. I know. But all the same …'

'I thought I'd go with him,' Andragathius said.

Chrysanthos looked up at the man. He and the German had worked together all over the Empire for more years than he cared to remember. He had become part of the furniture. 'I see,' he said. 'I was rather hoping you'd take up the post of the late Honorius.'

'Consul?' Andragathius guffawed, sounding gruffer and more foreign than ever when he was laughing. 'Me, a pen pusher? Come on, Chrysanthos. Can you see it?'

The vicarius smiled and wiped his greasy fingers on the cat who purred indulgently, as though honoured by the gesture. 'No, I suppose not. Well, then,' he sighed and stood up. 'Make use of yourself. Wherever Maximus is going, send me word. There'll be local scouts that can be bought even if his soldiers are loyal. Send me frequent reports. I need to keep the Emperor informed.'

Andragathius nodded, saluted and turned.

'Oh, and Andragathius,' Chrysanthos stopped him as he reached the door. 'You won't forget who the Emperor is, will you?'

Andragathius smiled.

'End of the month, you say?' Chrysanthos called.

'Something like that.'

It was nothing like that. In reality Maximus had struck his tents that night and marched out. He did it in darkness. No drums, no cornua. A thousand men marching northwest in the driving rain, their boots squelching in the mud of the Thamesis' floodplain. Frogs croaking in the marshes watched them go, grim-faced men in fur caps plastered to their heads, their long cloaks dragging in the ooze. They carried their shields on their backs and their helmets and camping gear dangled from poles that wore grooves in their shoulders. There were no lights, no music. Men marched all the better to the rhythm of *The Girl From Clusium* but that was not how the Caesar had ordered it. They called this war games in the officers' quarters and the principia, manoeuvres in the field. But it was marching, bloody marching whatever you called it. And at the end of each day's march, picks and shovels would smash into the clay to raise earthworks and stakes. All right, there were no enemies among the Atrebates, who had grovelled to Rome now for three hundred years. But that wasn't the point. This was the II Augusta, the great, great grandsons of the men who had marched with the deified Vespasian and this, as far as any man knew, was war.

At the edge of the water-logged meadows, Magnus Maximus sat his grey. He had chosen this animal carefully – a mare calm for battle but with a near-white hide that shone in the dark and dazzled in the sun. Wherever he was and whatever time of night or day, every man would know where the Caesar was and rally to him.

The dragon standards of the cavalry dripped in the rain and the hunched horsemen moved their

215

animals at a walk. The gods alone knew how far they
were going or where, but they had to be steady and
ready for anything. The scouts had ridden out before
it was truly dark, marking the way and checking the
ground. Behind the horsemen was the place the
Caesar would ride. A silver eagle bobbed above the
marching heads, wings spread wide and cruel beak
jutting forward. Below it and behind the covered
canvas litter of the Caesar's sorceress was carried
by six solid slaves chosen for their brawn and staying power. Behind that her carriage, laden with her
charts and amulets, the carved body parts of Osiris
and her book of Aneirin. Then came the footsloggers
of the II Augusta, only a vexillation as yet but that
would swell to a full legion when they reached Isca
Augusta. And behind them, the heavy artillery, the
wild asses and the ballistae, squealing and groaning
as the axles turned under the weight and artillery-
men scurried alongside, hauling timbers here, pressing shoulders to the wheel there. The oxen with their
massive horns dragged the ammunition carts, piled
high with stones under canvas, each one painted with
the obscenity of death – 'Taste this, cocksucker'. No
nice girl would want to take a soldier of the II Augusta
home to meet mother. Last came the cavalry of the
reserve, Andragathius at their head, as bedraggled
and wet through as their colleagues at the column's
head.

Maximus wheeled his grey and splashed over to
the road where a slave held his mastiff on a short

leash. The Caesar bent low in the saddle and patted the dog's wet head. 'Not this time, Bruno,' he murmured. 'We'll be gone for too long and the years aren't with you anymore.'

The mastiff looked up at him through loving and uncomprehending eyes. The Caesar patted him for one last time, running the velvet ears through his fingers. Then, he swung his horse away. 'Look after him, Ramilius,' he called back to the slave. 'See that he wants for nothing. And see that when his natural time in this world is done, he dies in his sleep.'

Augusta Treverorum

There was a smell of spring along the Mosella that evening. The day had been warm and the sun bright. He had invited her to join him in his private apartments behind the basilica and she had accepted.

There were moments – and this was one of them – when Conchessa hated herself. She had looked in the copper mirror as Adelina had braided her hair, curling each golden strand with the white ribbons she loved. She was dressing in her best for Septimus Pontus, a man who may have had a hand in the death, or at least the disappearance, of her husband; yet here she was, going to dine with him. The invitation had come for her alone. Usually it was for Vitalis too, but Vitalis had always made his excuses. He didn't like Pontus and he didn't trust him and he was less happy each day with the fact that Conchessa, apparently, did.

For her part – and she hated herself even more for this – she found it difficult to remember Calpurnius' face. That was silly; they were man and wife, for God's sake, half each other's souls, yet every time she tried to focus her mind, his features were a blur, as if he was not there. As if he had never been.

'I asked you here for a reason,' Pontus said, pouring more wine once the meal was over.

She waited.

'I have some news.'

'About Calpurnius?' She sat upright on her couch.

He nodded. 'He was seen, here in Augusta, not long ago.'

'When?' she wanted to know. 'By whom?'

'One question at a time,' he said softly. She started as he took her hand. 'What if I told you I didn't want him to be here? Not now.'

She took her hand away. 'When was he seen?' she asked levelly. 'And by whom?'

He sighed and leaned back on his couch. 'When was just before Saturnalia.'

'But I was here,' she frowned. 'I was here in Augusta then. Why didn't you tell me?'

'Because I didn't know myself until yesterday. That's why I invited you tonight.'

'Who saw him?'

'Well, that's the problem. His name is Marcus Cotta; he's a cavalry officer of the Schola Palatina.'

'The Emperor's Guard?' she blinked. 'That's my brother's unit.'

Pontus nodded. 'Augusta Treverorum may be the capital of the Western Empire,' he said, 'but it's still a small world.'

'Why is it a problem?' Conchessa was on her feet, ready to leave, anxious to find this man.

'Because Cotta isn't here. He rode out on a mission for the Emperor yesterday morning. All I can tell you is what he told me.'

'Which is?' Conchessa was not giving up this easily. For months now, she and Vitalis had been making enquiries, he through the army and the court, she in the streets and market places and at the wives' gatherings. They had met nothing but dead ends, puzzled frowns, faces that looked away. Here, at last, she had something. And from Septimus Pontus, the man she had been told to be wary of, the man she had been told not to trust.

'He saw him fleetingly and it was dark. He could have been mistaken.'

'Where was this?'

'In the Via Damnati.'

She frowned, struggling to understand. 'The brothels? No, that can't be.'

'I'm sorry, Conchessa.' He looked into her eyes. 'I hope Cotta was wrong.'

She gnawed her lip, trying not to cry because she had promised herself she would never cry again in front of Septimus Pontus. 'What if he wasn't?' she asked. 'Why would Calpurnius ...?'

Pontus spread his arms and shook his head. 'Visit houses of ill-repute when he had you? I don't know, but …'

'Yes?' She was leaning towards him, looking up into his face, silently pleading for an answer.

'There's something you don't know. Something I should have told you.'

'What?' She felt her heart pounding against her ribs. Her eyes were wide. 'What should you have told me?'

He put down his goblet and stared at her. Then he took her in his arms, holding her firmly and staring into her face. 'Calpurnius was corrupt, Conchessa,' he said. 'He was milking the system, robbing the Emperor blind in Carthago.'

'No,' she was shaking her head and frowning. This was not the Calpurnius she knew. Not the Calpurnius she loved.

'Count Theodosius found out about it. He offered your husband a choice; he was to fall on his sword or the Emperor would be told.'

'But …'

'But he turned the tables on Theodosius. Don't ask me how, but he did. It was Theodosius who stood accused of corruption and Gratian had him executed. There was nothing any of us could do. The Emperor is as stubborn as a mule and Calpurnius poisoned his mind against the Count. He is hiding from the Emperor, who now knows the truth.'

Conchessa could barely find her voice. 'Why didn't you tell me all this?' she managed.

He looked at her. 'How are you feeling?' he asked.

'Empty,' she said. 'Dead.'

He nodded. 'That's why I didn't tell you.'

For a moment, she swayed, the room spinning in her vision, the candlelight blurring into a sudden whirlpool of light.

'But he's alive,' she said, although it didn't sound like her own voice.

She wanted to say more, wanted to thank Pontus for his information, but no words came out. She would go to the Via Damnati, to look for Calpurnius. But when she found him, *if* she found him, would it ever be the same? What he had done, what he had become – could she live with that? In her marriage vows, before the priest and before God, she had promised to love her husband, for better, for worse. But how much worse could it be?

She was leaning against Pontus, feeling strangely relieved now that she knew; now that she had, at least, a partial answer. She felt strangely warm and the candles weren't spinning any more. She looked up into his face and saw the lop-sided smile. Then her mouth opened and he kissed her, lifting her up in his strong arms and carrying her through a curtain to the dark, perfumed room beyond.

He sat her down on the wolfskins spread over the bed and sat beside her, stroking her cheek and the sheen of her golden hair.

'I should go,' she whispered.

'Yes,' he said softly. 'Yes, you should.'

CHAPTER THIRTEEN

Britannia Prima, Aprilis

Maximus' scouts had ridden due west to Isca and they had been ferried across the river by surly oarsmen of the Silures. The great fortress of the II Augusta was not what it had been. There was a time when its granite walls stood as a bastion against the wild chieftains who followed Caratacus. Its barracks were huge and the II Augusta was the most impressive legion in the whole of Britannia; some said in the whole of the Empire.

But that was then. Peace had come to Britannia Prima and the legion, like all the others, was scaled down, cohorts being sent north to Horrea Classis to join the VIth. Many of its barracks stood empty and they would be emptier still when the commander received the scout's orders. He was to send a thousand of his best men, cavalry and infantry. A small artillery unit would be useful, but nothing elaborate. Three wild asses should do it.

'Three wild asses?' the commander had spluttered at the centurion in front of him. 'Who the hell does this Maximus think he is?'

'He thinks he's Caesar of the Western Empire, sir,' the scout said calmly. Would you like to tell him otherwise?'

Maximus himself had swung north, along the old Antonine Road that led along the tribal boundaries of the Dobunni. The way took him along rolling hills and sheep-filled valleys where they hadn't seen soldiers for years. It was Aprilis and the Nones fell on the fifth day. The sun was in the sign of Aries, the ram and the month was under the protection of Venus. Through every village and hamlet they passed, the locals were washing their sheep in their streams and only broke off the ritual to stand and gawp at the army tramping through. Now that the rain had stopped and spring was here, Maximus' troops picked up their paces and were managing fifteen miles a day. It wasn't enough and every night he berated the cohort commanders in his makeshift principia. The slowest man must become the fastest man. Get the artillery moving. Was that a baggage train or a snail crawling at the rear? There'd be short rations to any man who wasn't pulling his weight.

And Maximus was not the kind of soldier who led from the rear. On most days he dismounted and marched with the foot sloggers, grabbing the shield of one and the baggage of another. When he wasn't doing that, he had his shoulder to the wheel of a wild ass, grunting and swearing with the others, lashing the oxen and sliding in the mud. He drank the men's cheap, sour wine or the ale the locals gave them as they passed and sat at the roadside with them, gnawing on his crust of bread and cracking dirty jokes. The II Augusta came to love Magnus Maximus, there was no doubt of that. But not for one minute did they forget that he was the Caesar.

He was riding ahead with the advance cavalry on the day they reached Viroconium, the old capital of the Cornovii. All day the horses had plodded uphill, leaving the road so that they could find the high ground. There were the remains of a camp here, desolate, remote, wild, the tall grasses bent flat with the winds of winter that snarled this way. An old shrine to Mithras had long ago collapsed into its crevice in the stones and what had once been the principia was an empty shell, full of the whispering wind and little more.

Magnus reined in his horse, the grey, and let the animal chomp the grass at its feet. In the broad plain below the high hill, he could see a river meandering and beyond it the red-tiled walls of Viroconium, spreading to east and west, a reminder that, edge of the world though it might be, Rome still ruled here. This was the fourth largest city in Britannia and it offered sleep and baths and food and women for the Caesar's tired men. He would take all that gladly.

'Take yourself on a ride, circitor,' he said to the dragon-bearer on his right. 'My compliments to the garrison commander and can he put us all up for a day or two?'

The garrison commander had gone to endless trouble. His city was no longer a legionary base but he had three hundred men at his beck and call and they had to shift for themselves while Maximus' II Augusta took their contuberniae with barely a word. Contuberniae weren't the most luxurious accommodation in the Empire, but a bed is a bed and when you've slept with other men all your adult life, the snoring and the farting didn't matter anymore.

Maximus himself, with his Egyptian whore as the garrison commander quietly called her, far behind Maximus' back, had the run of his quarters and he kicked out the leader of the Ordo who in turn ... it was the way of it when the Caesar came calling.

That night, as the watch patrolled the star-kissed ramparts of Viroconium, the Caesar lay half-submerged in his bath, topped up every now and then by his slaves.

'We'll spend a few days here,' he was talking to Andragathius soaking in his own bath a few feet away, but his eyes were shut and it looked, for all the world, as if the Caesar was fast asleep. 'Then, depending on the Egyptian, we'll move on to Deva and pick a fight with the XX. Set up some sort of battle situation.'

'What if the Egyptian says No?' Andragathius asked, feeling his long moustache ends curling in the steam.

Maximus narrowed his eyes at the man, then he chuckled. 'I don't know what gods you barbarians north of the Rhenus worship, but I expect more support from my Master of Horse.'

It was Andragathius' turn to chuckle. 'Sorry, sire,' he said. 'It's really none of my business.'

'No, it isn't,' Maximus told him flatly. 'Mithras, Sol Invictus, the carpenter from Nazareth, who knows which of them is real? And that's before we get on to the nonsense the locals round here worship.'

'Who is it this month?' Andragathius asked him, reaching out for his goblet of wine. 'The Egyptian, I mean?'

'Isis,' his commander told him. 'She's making sacrifices to the Pharos.'

'The what?'

'It's some sort of lighthouse, apparently, in Alexandria. It's a wonder of the world. The Egyptians worship it. Even though it keeps falling down.'

Andragathius laughed. 'Do I detect a note of disenchantment with your enchantress?'

'You detect what you like, barbarian,' Maximus scowled at him. 'She hasn't been wrong yet. I need to secure Britannia before I pay young Gratian a visit and I need these western tribes behind me. I've already sent emissaries ahead. They'll follow me if they believe I am descended from the deified Constantine.'

'Are you?' Andragathius raised an eyebrow.

'Do bears shit in the woods?' Maximus asked.

'In Germania they certainly do,' Andragathius told him.

'Well, there you are, then. You stick to soldiering, Master of the Horse and leave the politics to us grown-ups.'

And the men laughed together in the steam and the half-light.

Londinium

Chrysanthos the vicarius moved into the consul's palace that spring. He had sent word to Julia, expressing his regret at the death of her husband, the late consul Leocadius Honorius and saying how sorry he was for her loss. Oh, and could she vacate the premises by the Ides? There was a small villa available for her and her daughter and staff to the north of the new gate, beyond the wall. They would not lack for anything.

One of the first decisions that Honoria made was to demolish the gate that lay between the house of the day and the house of the night. It was all one now and if the vicarius chose to hold wild parties with his concubine's street people, then so be it. But it was the other side of the solidus that pleased Honoria most. The vicarius had no wife; or if he had, he had left her behind somewhere in the Empire. So Honoria took pride of place. Chrysanthos didn't ask her to marry him, of course; that would raise too many eyebrows and the church wouldn't approve and altogether, it was too much trouble. So Honoria had all the trappings of marriage without its drawbacks.

As the lady of the vicarius, she mixed with all the best people. The women of the Ordo, the rich merchants' wives, who had crossed the road to avoid her only months ago, now invited her to their cenae and she presided with effortless ease over their boring little committees, hanging on her every word. Their husbands, of course, had always found Honoria interesting, but now they could do so openly, flirting at functions, kissing her hand, fondling her arm. On more than one occasion she had to remind them that the vicarius would not approve of their hands being *there*; and if that didn't work, she hadn't forgotten how to use her knee and her fingernails.

And all this, she reminded herself sometimes, she had achieved by lying on her back. And occasionally kneeling up.

Chrysanthos heard little from the messengers sent by Andragathius. In Aprilis they had rested at Viroconium but from then on, the intention was that Maximus would take his troops into the mountain country in the far north of Britannia Prima. He had a legion's strength now and it was Andragathius' belief that he planned to add the XX Valeria Victrix to it any day. Then the messages stopped and the messengers came no more. Chrysanthos asked his council, the men who knew Britannia best. What kind of place was that, beyond Viroconium? The tribe there, the Deceangli, what manner of people were they?

In the long watches of the night, with Honoria in his bed sleeping the sleep of the unjust, the vicarius wrote his own letters to be sent by ship and the fastest horses. He wrote to the Emperor, to Gratian at Augusta Treverorum. He wrote that Maximus was on the march. And he felt pretty sure he was marching east.

Augusta Treverorum

The slave girl had been in the lady Conchessa's household now for five months. Adelina had taken the child under her wing because Adelina was like that; everybody's mother. The girl was a good cook and she could press and fold clothes like no other. No task was too big or too small for her and she was eager to please. And never more eager than when the tribune Vitalis came calling. He had his own quarters at the Emperor's back-gate with the Schola Palatina, but he visited Conchessa when he could and the girl noticed they talked in riddles, about a man called Calpurnius. A man who had vanished into thin air. It was a name she had heard before.

The early summer sun was streaming in through the open door and Vitalis sat in his chair, letting the girl unlace his boots and sink his tired feet into the hot water. All morning he had been drilling the Schola. March and counter-march. Left wheel. Right wheel. Battle order. He hadn't done this for so long, he was surprised how quickly it all came back to him.

He was also surprised at how out of condition he was and this girl's hands caressing his soles were pure Heaven.

He hadn't really noticed her before, although she'd usually been there when he called. Conchessa liked her and was impressed by her work, though whether she would ever merit the solidi she had paid for her was open to question.

'You're called Rebekah, aren't you?' he asked her, watching the sun glinting off her black hair.

'Yes, sir,' she said, not looking him in the face.

'Do you like it here, Rebekah?'

'Oh, yes, sir,' the girl smiled, her dark eyes bright, her smile broad. Now she did look him in the face, this handsome soldier, with his armour and his tribune's scarf. She felt her heart thump and she looked away. 'Everybody's very kind,' she murmured.

'Tell me about yourself,' Vitalis said, leaning back as she dried his feet with clean linen.

'There's nothing to tell, sir,' she assured him. 'I am a slave. And a Jew.'

'And I am a soldier and a Christian,' he said. 'But my Lord Jesus Christ was a Jew. You and he are of the same people.'

'I know nothing about that, sir,' she said.

'Where are you from?' he asked.

'My people are from the holy land, sir. From Judea. But ...'

'Yes?'

Rebekah looked suddenly afraid. She gnawed her lip and picked up the bowl, as though to go. Vitalis stopped her. 'But?' He held her arm fast.

'There are Jews here, in the city. I see them sometimes. We pray together.'

'You do?' Vitalis smiled. 'When you speak to God, what do you call him?'

'Yahweh, sir. The all-seeing. But if I understand it right, your God and mine are the same. It is just in the matter of the messiah we are at odds. And when *you* speak to Yahweh, what do you call him?'

Vitalis smiled to see the little slave so animated when it came to her religion. He had believed in many gods in his life and had seldom met someone so young and so certain of her faith. 'We think of God as all-loving. He has many names, but to us he is usually simply the one God. Your Yahweh is the Roman Jove, Jupiter Highest and Best. You have swapped gods with your conquerors.'

'No,' she said firmly. 'Yahweh has no conqueror. He is above earthly things.'

'Well,' Vitalis said, letting go of her arm. 'We can agree, at least, on that. Where are these Jews?' he asked. 'The people who are not your people?'

Her face darkened again. 'They are lost, sir. The damned.' She suddenly closed to him so that her face was closer to his than any slave should ever be to a free man. 'Promise me,' she said. 'Promise me you won't try to find them.'

Vitalis blinked. This little girl with the dazzling eyes and the raven hair had, a moment ago, been washing his feet, all subservience and silence. Now she was in his face, demanding that he make a solemn vow.

'No.' He shook his head. 'I won't. I promise that.'

She bobbed quickly then spun away, nearly colliding with Conchessa in the atrium. She bobbed to her too and was gone.

'What was all that about?' she asked Vitalis.

The tribune sat down again and started lacing his boots back on. 'I'm not sure,' he said, looking out of the door into the courtyard where Rebekah had run, her bare feet padding softly on the stones. He looked up at his sister. She looked radiant this morning. In fact, she had looked radiant for days now. And she had a spring in her step that Vitalis had not seen for a long time.

'Conchessa,' he said, retying his scarf ready to get back to the barracks. 'I gave Maximus my word before we left Britannia. I have to go east, to find Theodosius.'

She looked at him. 'I know,' she said, 'but I have to go to the Via Damnati.'

'No!' He stood up sharply. 'We've had this conversation, sister. You're not going there.'

'Why not?'

'I told you,' he almost shouted, then he relented. 'Without wishing to sound too much like Mama, it's no place for you.'

233

'But …'

'But Septimus Pontus says that Marcus Cotta says he saw a man, in fading light who might or might not be Calpurnius; yes, I know.'

'It's all we've got, Vit,' she said. 'After all these months of searching, following every lead, starting at every shadow.'

'Precisely,' he nodded. 'And here's another one.' He read the disappointment in her face and he took her hand. 'Has it never occurred to you,' he said, 'that perhaps Calpurnius doesn't want to be found?'

She blinked back the tears and he looked down. On her wrist was a gold bracelet, beautifully wrought with vine leaves and clusters of grapes. He knew it was a gift from Pontus. 'And perhaps,' he said, 'deep down, you don't want to find him.'

Her eyes flashed fire and she lashed out, slapping him hard across the face. She wasn't, in her mind, hitting the brother she loved more than anyone in the world. She was hitting out at Calpurnius, the man who had deserted her. At Pontus, the man who was starting to fill her life as she, when the devil took her, wanted to fill his bed. She regretted it instantly, but what was done was done and she spun on her heel.

Vitalis' head sang from the power of the slap. He shook his vision clear and finished tying his scarf. What was going on today? What was the matter, suddenly, with the women in his life?

Valentia, Iunius

'Saesen,' Justinus nodded. 'There's no doubt about it. They're Saxons.'

The commander of the Wall had ridden out with a patrol from Segedunum that morning, skirting the sea that shone like chiselled glass to the east.

'How many do you see, circitor?'

The man at his elbow squinted against the sun. 'I count twenty, sir,' he said. 'Give or take.'

Justinus nodded. He was outnumbered two to one and this time the enemy had horses, the sturdy mountain ponies they had borrowed from the Votadini. Over the months since Din Paladyr had fallen, the Gododdin people of the south had stayed loyal to Rome. Those in the north, near the estuary and the great fortress itself, had gone over to Malwyn and his Saxon allies.

The raiding party had already struck; the smoke of the village they had targeted was proof of that. Justinus' patrol had ridden through it an hour ago, patching up the wounded as best they could and leaving the survivors to bury their dead. The Saxons had some stolen women with them – the sharp-eyed circitor counted six, tied behind their captors' horses, stumbling over the heather, too tired and too terrified to cry.

'Anybody speak their language?' Justinus asked. Nobody in his patrol did. It would have been unlikely if they had. The Saxons were renegades from far beyond the German Sea, beyond the Rhenus in dark, forested regions none of the Wall men had ever heard of. The commander sighed. 'Then we'll have to do it the old-fashioned way. Skirmish order.'

He hadn't shouted. He just gave the command in a steady, gravel voice that each man there knew meant business. They wheeled their horses into line with a horse's width between each one and they braced their lances against their shoulders. Justinus took his place at their head and drew his sword, watching the long blade gleam silver in his hand. He walked his chestnut out alone and went through the motions even though he knew his words were like chaff in the wind.

'You have committed a grave offence,' he said, 'against the Pax Romana. Let those women go now and you will live.'

There were jeers from the Saxons. One of them dismounted, rolled down his leggings and waggled his arse at the Romans. His comrades laughed, pounding their saddles and slapping each other at the man's bravado.

'Who's your best archer, circitor?' Justinus half turned in the saddle.

'Mallobaudes.' The circitor motioned the man forward.

'Cut that man a new arsehole,' Justinus commanded. Mallobaudes was quick, but he wasn't that quick. By the time he'd passed his spear to a mate and strung his bow, the Saxon had rolled up his leggings and was mounting his horse again.

'On second thoughts,' Justinus said, 'split his bollocks.'

Mallobaudes sucked in his breath. The wind was to his right, drifting in from the sea and the sun was in his eyes. Even so, a command was a command. There was a hiss as the arrow left the bow and the archer's horse recoiled, pawing the ground. There was a scream from the Saxon as he felt an indescribable pain in his crotch. The Roman shaft had thudded into his groin and blood spurted over the sheepskin slung over his saddle. He doubled up, desperately trying to staunch the bleeding. The jeering had stopped now and the taunts turned to angry shouts and threats.

'Bit high, sir, I'm afraid,' Mallobaudes said. 'Sorry.'

'Sorry be buggered, semisallis,' Justinus grinned. 'That's good enough for me. You got two pricks for the price of one.'

'Er … that's pedes, sir,' the ever-humble Mallobaudes reminded him.

'Don't you recognize promotion when you see it, soldier?' the commander smiled. 'I'm feeling generous today. Battle order!'

This time the command *was* shouted.

'You're going to die for that, Roman!' Justinus heard a language he recognized drifting across the open ground.

'Well, well,' the commander said, resting his sword blade on his shoulder. 'That was an attempt at Latin, I think. We *are* honoured. They're annoyed now, boys,' he said. 'They'll make mistakes.'

As they closed in to form a tight line with Justinus in their centre, they watched the Saxons ramming their heels into their horses' flanks and thunder forward, hooves flying over the short-cropped grass and thudding on the iron ground of summer. Their line was ragged and broken.

'As I thought,' Justinus said. 'They're keeping men back to protect the women. And they'll kill them when we gain the upper hand. Circitor, you and the new semisallis there, hang back. Form a second line. Deal with them, will you?'

'Sir.' The man hauled on his rein and Mallobaudes, still glowing with pride, swung his horse alongside him.

Justinus' sword was in the air. 'The patrol will advance,' he called. 'Walk. March.'

The horses whinnied, sensing battle. They shook their heads and the bits jangled. A steady line was creeping out over the headland, like a wave rippling on a beach, driving the driftwood before it, ready to crash against the rocks of the Saxon attack. No one in Justinus' patrol made any sound, but they were met with a wall of noise. The Saxons fought like any barbarians, wild and disordered, relying on the speed of their charge and the roar of their numbers. But that was all smoke and mirrors, and it had no substance. By the time the waves collided, the Romans had risen to a canter whereas several of the Saxon horses were blown already, having galloped up the slope, to get at the enemy.

Justinus ducked a sword slash and drove his blade tip into the body of the man who would not make another mistake. He wrenched the sword out and drove his horse into a second man, crushing his thigh before smashing his face with his blade. Around him the spears of his men were finding their mark, thudding into leather-strapped chests and skewering faces. There were screams and blood and the whole murderous mess that went hand in hand with defending the Wall. Justinus had been here before.

The circitor and the semisallis had broken off before their front line reached the Saxons. They galloped, one to the left, one to the right and converged on the men sitting their horses, milling around the women tethered to the animals.

'Which two would you like, circitor?' Mallobaudes shouted over the thudding hooves and the sudden screams of the women.

'I hope you're referring to the enemy, soldier, and not these nice ladies.'

'Naturally,' Mallobaudes said and hacked the first man from the saddle so that he bounced on the ground, a crimson gash spreading across his chest and shoulder.

'Well, that's good,' the circitor shouted, lunging with his sword into the ribs of the second man, 'because I don't think the commander's going to promote you any further today.'

Mallobaudes now found himself facing a problem. One of the Saxons guarding the women had pulled his horse across so that the semisallis was riding at two of them. He parried the first sword blow but the second slid over the top of his shield and caught his neck just below the helmet cheek plate. He felt his teeth lock and he swung his horse away. The circitor was racing across to his defence, but he was too late. One of the women, dragged behind a riderless horse, had caught hold of its dead owner's sword and had cut herself free. She threw the sword to another woman who hacked her bonds too. Then both of them jumped up on the back of a Saxon's horse and dragged the rider down. He shouted and cursed as he went down but there were fingernails deep in his eye sockets and he was writhing on the ground with the other woman's teeth in his wrist.

Before the circitor could reach the one remaining Saxon, the blond bastard had hauled his rein and was galloping to the north as fast as the animal could go, foam flying from its bit and lashing tongue.

Mallobaudes steadied his horse and dropped his shield. He felt the jagged wound along his jawline. It was open and slippery but he was too numb with shock yet to feel any pain. The circitor rode in alongside him and checked the wound.

'You'll live,' he said. 'By the way,' he jerked his head down to the women. All of them were free now and the two who had brought down the Saxon were busy cutting his throat before they hauled down his leggings and hacked off his manhood. 'Glad they're on our side, aren't you?'

Mallobaudes nodded. He didn't realise how difficult talking was until he was halfway through his sentence. 'A few more of those,' he mumbled, 'and we'd be out of a job.'

Now the Romans roared. The barritus rose from the half dozen men still able to sit their horses in Justinus' line. Two were dead and a third was trying to claw his way out from under his dead horse. For the Saxons, it had been butchery. Three of the twenty were lashing their animals away to the north, leaving the others dead or wounded on the ground. Justinus had wiped his crimson blade on a Saxon's tunic and he dismounted.

'Which of you,' he shouted to the Saxons still able to hear him, 'is the one who speaks Latin?'

He half expected the man to be dead. Or if he was living, refusing, in his sullen defeat, to respond. 'I do,' a voice near him growled. Justinus looked at him. The man had pale auburn hair and an old scar across his forehead. His new scar was self-evident. A sword blade had ripped his arm from shoulder to wrist. A Roman surgeon would amputate, but the chances were this man would bleed to death.

'Are you from the fortress?' Justinus asked him, 'from Din Paladyr?'

The Saxon nodded, holding his arm close to his body with his other hand, pressing hard to try to stop the bleeding.

'Does Malwyn still rule there?' the commander wanted to know.

'He does. With Aelfrith.'

'Aelfrith?' This wasn't a name that Justinus knew.

'My lord,' the Saxon grunted.

'What of Brenna?' Justinus asked. 'What of the queen?'

The Saxon looked up at him, crouching as he was on the grass, his arm useless, dripping blood on the heather. 'She's there,' he croaked. 'At Din Paladyr. Men have her every day. Aelfrith was first, as was his right.'

'His right?' Justinus repeated, anger rising deep inside him.

'That was the deal he struck with Malwyn. Well, part of it anyway. He was to have half the queen's silver and all of the queen. But he tired of her soon enough. So she was passed to us all, anyone in the end. I had her once,' he grinned, watching Justinus' face and smiling, as though at the memory of it. 'She was good. Tight. Like a young girl. She ...'

But the Saxon never finished his sentence, because Justinus' sword blade thudded through his throat. His eyes crossed, he spat blood and gurgled, pitching forward as the Wall commander ripped the weapon free. He looked at the men standing around and those still in the saddle.

'Circitor,' he said. 'We've got dead to bury. And men to patch up. Then we'll get these women home.'

'And the Saxons, sir?' the circitor asked.

'We're not burying them,' Justinus said. 'It's a waste of sweat.'

'I meant the living ones, sir,' the circitor said.

'Living ones?' Justinus looked the man in the face. 'I don't see any living ones.'

CHAPTER FOURTEEN

Deceangli Territory, Britannia Prima

The lamps flickered blue that night in the principia of Magnus Maximus. For nights now he had listened to the sistrum rattle of the sorceress, heard her soft prayers to Isis of Pharos, that strange goddess and that wonder of the world so far away that few men here had heard of either, still less understood them.

The Caesar stretched and yawned. He hauled the tunic over his head and unlaced his boots before slipping off his subligaculum. Naked, he stretched on the bed. There was nothing to compare with the comfort of a campaign bed. It was hard and it wobbled on uneven ground, but lying on one made him feel he was home. Home itself was far away in Tarraconensis, but here, beyond the ramparts of the makeshift camp, there were mountains like those of his homeland. He could smell the pine and the firs and listen to the sighing of the wind over the headland. And he drifted to sleep …

Suddenly, he woke, half sitting up. He wanted to look around him, to find out where that noise had come from, the one that had woken him. But he couldn't move his head because there was a dagger-tip just under his chin, tickling his beard. He started to swing one leg to the floor, but the knife prodded upwards and he thought better of it.

'Too late for that, Macsen Wledig,' a voice whispered. It was a woman's voice.

Instinctively, he groped for some bedclothes, to cover himself.

'Too late for that too,' he heard her chuckle.

Then the blade disappeared and she let him sit up properly, throwing him a wolfskin to lay across his lap. He could make out the vaguest of shapes in the darkness. Long hair, a cloak. Nothing more.

'Who are you?' he asked, wondering where the hell his guards were.

'Your worst nightmare,' she said, standing away from him now. 'Someone who can get past your legion and murder you while you sleep.'

He was still sitting on the bed, letting his eyes get used to the darkness. 'Why didn't you?' he asked.

'Why would I?' and he heard the sound of a knife being sheathed. 'We're allies, you and I.'

He hurled himself across the room, grabbing his sword as he went. In an instant, the blade was glinting at the girl's throat; the tables turned. 'Let me ask you again,' he growled. 'Who are you?'

'My name is Elen,' she said.

He closed to her, now that he could see more clearly. She was beautiful, with a mass of tawny hair under her hood. She pulled that back so that he could see her properly. Her face was proud, arrogant, even, and her eyes showed no fear.

'You might consider,' she said, glancing down, 'getting dressed.'

He glanced down too. The wolfskin had fallen to the floor and he was naked again. 'Not until you tell me what you're doing here,' he said.

'I am Elen,' she repeated, 'the daughter of Eudaf, chieftain of the Deceangli, prince of what you call Britannia Prima.'

'Does the prince send his children to treat with Rome?'

She moved across the room, ignoring his still extended sword arm. 'Are you Rome?' she asked him.

'I will be,' he said. 'Just give me time.'

'If you weren't here with an army, Macsen Wledig,' she said, 'I doubt I'd give you the time of day.'

He chuckled and sheathed his sword before reaching for his cloak and covering his nakedness. 'Not a social call then?'

'I came,' she said, 'because my father is old and ill. He wanted to come himself but he can't manage the journey.'

'Would he have come as you have?' Maximus asked. 'Like a thief in the night?'

'Assassin would be more apt,' she said. 'Your security is sloppy.'

'Clearly,' he lit a candle, then another. She started as soon as she saw his face, then composed herself again. Elen, the daughter of Eudaf, was the most beautiful woman Maximus had ever seen. And Magnus Maximus had seen a lot of beautiful women. He poured them both a cup of wine and handed one to her. 'How did you ...?'

'Get through two ditches, past a gate and four guards?'

Put like that, Maximus appeared an idiot.

'Let's just say I have my ways, Macsen, and leave it at that.'

'What's that you're calling me?' he asked. 'Macsen ...?'

'Macsen Wledig.' She sipped her wine. 'Maximus the ruler. It's what my people call you.'

'And what should I call you, princess? Elen?'

'That will do,' she smiled. 'When you know me better, you might call me Elen Lwyddog – Elen of the armies.'

'That sounds fierce,' he chuckled.

Suddenly, Magnus Maximus, Macsen Wledig, the Caesar, was flat on his back on the ground, his own sword blade pointing to his manhood where the cloak had flapped open.

'Doesn't it, though?' she asked, eyes glinting in the candlelight. She threw the sword down and hauled him upright. The pain in Maximus' pride was intense.

'I could ride before I could walk,' she told him, 'and can shoot the eye of a raven at three hundred paces. I killed my first man when I was twelve. He was a Roman.' She sipped her wine.

He looked at her. 'How's your flower arranging?' he asked and held his breath. He already felt he knew this woman – discovering whether or not she had a sense of humour might turn out to be the death of him. She stared back at him for a long moment, and then threw her head back and laughed. And, after a sigh of relief, Maximus joined in.

Elen of the armies slipped out as noiselessly as she had come, promising to be back in a more conventional way in two days. The Caesar cursed himself. He should have felt a fool, bested by a slip of a girl. *And* he'd been bollock naked at the time. Usually, when he was in that position, the girl wasn't wearing much either. But he consoled himself with the fact that this was no ordinary girl. She had indeed penetrated the security of his camp, held him at knife point and could have killed him. And to up-end a hardened soldier like … what had she called him? Macsen Wledig? That took some doing.

So the next morning he snarled at everybody. The guard was to be doubled. Anyone found dozing would be flogged and put on half rations. The earthworks were made three feet higher, the palisades extended with murderously sharp iron along the outer walls, sunk into the timbers. By the day's end, Maximus was satisfied, smiling at the improvements. Let Elen Lwyddog get through that lot!

They came from the north-west, as she had promised, two days later, out of the dawn with the golden-pink light gilding their weapons and banners. They were the Deceangli, the wild tribe from the north of Britannia Prima who had once fought the Romans to a standstill and whose priests, the Druids, had burned the eagles on their altars. There were no Druids today, for they had been destroyed long ago, but their priests leapt and pranced in front of the rolling army that crept over the hills like ants foraging through the tall grass. Their carnyces brayed, brass tongues clattering on copper mouths and their drums thudded, keeping time for the marching troops and shaking the ground.

'Impressive,' Andragathius murmured to Maximus. They sat their horses on the parade ground in front of the camp, the legion drawn up in all the pride of war. The eagle of the II Augusta flashed silver in the early morning sun and the dragon standards of the cavalry flapped in the breeze.

From the wings of the Deceangli, horsemen lashed their ponies hard, charging each other and striking their shields with their lances. At each crash, there was a banshee shriek and scream from the on-coming army.

'Not bad riders, either,' Andragathius muttered. He was wearing his bearskin cloak today, that stretched to his heels and spread out over his horse's crupper.

'Good thing they're on our side, eh?' Maximus winked at him.

'Jupiter highest and best!' Andragathius didn't often invoke a Roman god, but when he did, men knew there was a reason for it. He nodded to the centre of the Deceangli line where a tall beautiful woman was riding a black horse. She wore armour like her men, but chased and studded with silver, a velvet cloak pinned to her shoulders, Roman-style. Only her head was bare, the blond locks flying out behind her in the stiffening breeze.

'What's the matter, Master of Horse?' Maximus smiled. 'Never seen a girl before?'

'Not in full armour, no,' the German frowned. 'I thought their king was called Eudaf.'

'Their king is,' Maximus said. 'This is his little girl.'

'Little girl?' It would be a while before Andragathius could come to terms with this. 'What an insult!'

Maximus chuckled. 'You old German,' he said. 'I thought it was us Romans who were the sexist ones.' He raised his hand and the legions' trumpeters blasted their welcome. Elen raised hers and the Deceangli line halted, the horses snorting, the spears of the infantry held aloft, pointing forward as though challenging the Roman line.

Maximus unbuckled his helmet and swung out of the saddle as a groom took the reins.

'You're not going to …?' Andragathius started to say, but Maximus wasn't listening. He was striding out over the heathland, drawing his sword. The spears lowered in ceremonial gesture, with a single guttural roar from the spearmen. Before he reached them, Maximus raised his naked blade high then brought it crashing down across his thigh so that the iron snapped and he threw the pieces aside.

Another roar and the spears shot skyward again, their butts thudding to the ground. Elen of the armies dropped from the saddle and walked out from her people. As they met, Maximus dropped to one knee and bowed his head.

'Jupiter highest and best,' Andragathius muttered, shaking his head. First the Egyptian whore and now this woman who rode like a man. What was the world coming to?

'Welcome, Caesar Maximus,' Elen said in perfect Latin. 'Welcome to Britannia Prima.' She held out her hand and he took it, to stand facing her. For a brief moment she looked solemnly at him, then, in her own tongue, she said, 'Welcome, Macsen Wledig, to my homeland.'

Augusta Treverorum, Iulius

It was the time of the Games. In Rome's great past, great men had ordered the munera, the funeral rites, in which gladiators had fought to the death in honour of the departed. That had grown over the years and over the centuries so that the Games became a part of every festival and holy days were not holy without the spilling of blood in the great sacrifice. The crowd roared their blood lust as blades flashed in some sun-baked arena and Emperors from the deified Augustus onwards had given the mob what they wanted – bread and circuses.

But that was then. And old men muttered about the good old days when a man was a man. The young men scoffed at them, but what did they know? Today, it was all the Christ and soft manners and *love*. Jupiter highest and best, it defied belief! But Gratian was a man apart, a throwback some said to Commodus the mad. He had brought the Games back, at least in Augusta Treverorum. But he was not content to watch the show from the awning that shielded emperors from the sun. He had to be there himself, down there in the sand, to feel the pulse of blood and smell the fear.

The crowds had long ago settled in to their seats in the great arena at Augusta. The flags of the empire flew from its walls and the stall-holders and trinket-sellers were having a field day at the gate. The acrobats had been and gone, hitting each other with pigs' bladders and slipping in the entrails of goats. The children squealed and shrieked their delight and did it again when the noxii were brought out, the convicted criminals marked for death. They were dishevelled, bleeding from the scrape of their irons, their backs ripped by the cat with the nine tails, each one thonged with sharp bone.

Conchessa didn't want to be here, but Septimus Pontus had invited her and told her it was by special invitation of the Emperor, so how could she refuse? She sat with the ladies of the court, but Pontus was next to her, surreptitiously stroking her hand that rested by her side on the cushioned bench. She felt like a girl again, in the throes of her first love. The others had noticed – how could they not – and whispered together. It's just another in Pontus' endless list, some said; some who had once sat where Conchessa sat today. It wouldn't last. With Pontus it never did. Oh, they were all his undying loves at the time – until the next time. And anyway, wasn't this woman married? To a man who had disappeared? No, she was a widow, surely? Perhaps, but she was the sister of the new man in the Schola, the tribune who never laughed. He wouldn't take this lightly.

The tribune who never laughed was officer of the day and he was with the Emperor now, in the dark of the animal pens under the arena. Above, they could hear the roar and stamp of the mob as the noxii died, one by one; ritual murder by order of the Christian Emperor of the West. It was difficult to believe that feet above them, the day was hot and the sky cloudless. Here, it was cool and water trickled down the walls. The gladiators were being laced into their armour ready for the events of the afternoon. The

Myrmidon with his huge fish-eyed helmet, the Thrax with his murderous curved blade, the Retiarius making sweeps with his lead-weighted net. The doctores scuttled among them, strapping webbing and giving last minute advice – 'Keep your guard up,' 'Watch the left-hander,' 'Are you going to do it like that?' The doctores were the trainers, gladiators themselves who had won the rudus, the wooden sword of honour and their freedom, but they could no more keep away from the ring than fly.

As the Emperor passed among them in his flowing robes, they broke off their moves and their hum of conversation and saluted him. He nodded to them.

'Keeper,' he called to a surly-looking man half-hidden in the shadows. 'What have you got for me?'

'A worthy selection, Sire,' the man bowed and stood aside. Vitalis followed Gratian along a narrow passageway lit by flickering torches until the noise of the gladiators died away and a strange, almost suffocating smell hit his nostrils. There were rows of cages here, each one containing a beast. There was a bear, two or three wolves, two lions and a leopard. They were growling as they prowled, their paws silent and their eyes watchful. Gratian took a torch from the wall bracket and held it towards one cage. All the cats roared and hissed, their whiskers flexing as they bared their teeth.

'They don't like the fire,' Gratian said, chuckling.

He passed the guttering brand to Vitalis. 'Which one would you face, tribune?' he asked him.

Vitalis' eyes widened. Was this man mad? 'None of them, Sire,' he said.

'But if you had to,' Gratian persisted.

'The one with no teeth,' Vitalis told him, straight-faced.

For a moment, Gratian looked at the man, then burst out laughing. 'Very good.' The Emperor walked to the far end of the cages and walked along them, running his hand over the iron bars. Half way along the leopard went for him, throwing itself against the iron and slashing with its claws, hissing and spitting. Gratian dodged back. 'That one,' he said to the keeper. 'Make him ready.'

He turned to Vitalis who was looking in disbelief at the animal, slinking backwards, its tail long and lashing. It was still snarling, its little eyes yellow and unblinking. 'Imagine that skin spread over your saddle, Vitalis, eh? Yes, keeper, we'll take him.'

Conchessa closed her eyes as another of the noxii went down, target practice for the gladiators. Now there was a mere handful left, a huddle of desperate souls and, at a command from one of them, they all knelt down and raised their faces to the sky.

'What are they doing?' Conchessa asked aloud, although she knew the answer already.

Pontus was talking animatedly to a decurion on his right, but he broke off to answer her. 'They're Jews,' he said. 'They're praying. Much good may it do them.'

'Pontus.' The senior decurion leapt up at the sound of his name. The Emperor was back on the dais from the bowels of the arena and the entire court was on its collective feet.

'Sire?'

Gratian pointed with his studded staff with its eagle-head. 'These people are dying too easily. Where are they from?'

'I believe they're locals, Sire. From the ghetto.'

'The ghetto,' Gratian nodded, looking thoughtful. 'I've been too generous in that direction, Pontus. Come and see me tomorrow. Augusta Treverorum is a Christian city or it's nothing.'

Everyone had their sweetmeats and wine on the Emperor's terrace and then the fun really began. The gladiators went through their paces, the barleymen twirling and pirouetting in the sand. Swords clashed together and blades clattered on shields. Only one bout was advertised to the death and Conchessa was dreading it.

'Sister.' Vitalis had summoned her from his place alongside the throne. He was thinking desperately for an excuse to get her out of there, knowing how she was feeling. She turned and half rose but Pontus touched her arm and she stayed. In that one moment, Vitalis' worst fears were realized. All the time he had been at Augusta, he had heard nothing but evil of Septimus Pontus. 'No,' Conchessa had said to him when he had voiced his fears. 'He's not like that. He's just misunderstood. Men like him make enemies.'

They did. And from today, Vitalis Celatius was one of them. His little sister, so wise, so much older than her years, had gone over to the enemy. He had lost her.

There was a sudden roar from the crowd and Conchessa buried her face in her hands rather than watch the arena. To one side of the ring, a Myrmidon, his huge helmet flashing with silver facets like diamonds in the sun, stood over a Retiarius. The man's net lay spread in the sand and he himself was half-crouching, his trident gone and his hand raised in supplication.

Conchessa's heart thudded, it seemed to her, even above the noise of the crowd. She looked from left to right, saw the scowling faces, the glittering, hate-filled eyes. There was to be another death in the arena and the crowd was screaming for it. All around her and across the far side of the tiered seats, men, women and children were drawing their thumbs across their throats. She glanced down to the Retiarius, whose chest was heaving with the exertion of the fight and the terror of what was to come. Conchessa could not imagine what was going on in the man's mind, he who had been trained like an animal to kill or be killed.

It was the Emperor's decision and his alone. All eyes were on him now, even Conchessa's. Some were shrieking at His Greatness to give the order; others were willing it in their minds. But, to her amazement, Gratian was looking at her. He saw the tears trickling down her beautiful face and the pleading in her eyes. He raised his hand, the thumb held horizontally at his ear, ready to pull it back through the air. The Myrmidon had dropped his shield and stood over his beaten enemy, legs planted astride him with sword held high, the point downwards towards the net-man's bare neck. He too was watching the Emperor. At least the death would be quick. Conchessa's mouth opened and she felt herself slowly shake her head. The Emperor smiled and his thumb came to the upright. There was another roar from the crowd, a wail of disappointment that turned to rapturous applause, because it was treason to disapprove of Gratian. And the thumb that pointed skywards today could easily slice throats tomorrow – their throats.

The Myrmidon symbolically thrust his blade into the sand and marched in triumph to the Gate of Life, followed, at a respectful and grateful distance, by the Retiarius. Conchessa let out a sigh and mouthed a silent 'Thank you' to Gratian, who nodded and half-bowed.

'With me, tribune,' he said to Vitalis and he leapt up onto the parapet. He raised both hands until the crowd's roar had dwindled to a rumbling murmur and finally silence.

'I have failed you,' Gratian yelled so that his voice echoed around the archways and bounced off the columns. 'I have let you down.'

There were cries of protest from every angle, shouts of 'No! No!'

The Emperor held up his hands again. 'Let me make it up to you,' he shouted and unbuckling his cloak, passed it to Vitalis. He turned to him. 'If things go wrong in the next few minutes,' he said, 'sell that for what it's worth. But dip it in my blood first.'

Then he turned and leapt down to the sand, landing squarely where the Retiarius had gone down. There was a stunned silence. What was happening? Men and women turned to each other, asking the same question. Had the Emperor gone mad? From the Gate of Life, four torch bearers came at the run, brands flickering in their hands. Gratian unbuckled his sandals and kicked them off, pawing the ground and making sure his soles didn't slip. 'Tribune!' he yelled up to Vitalis, looking down, as were all the court except Conchessa, from the royal parapet. 'Your sword, if you please.'

Vitalis looked at the eager faces around him. Yes, the Emperor had gone mad. He drew his sword, reversed it and threw it down. Gratian caught the hilt cleanly and felt its weight in his hand, slashing the air left and right to the roar of the crowd. The man was the Emperor, the lord of the greatest Empire on earth, the superior of any gladiator who ever lived. And even those Christians who worshipped their own God, were looking at another god today.

The torch bearers stood, two by two, on each side of a grilled gate on the far side of the arena from the Emperor's dais. Gratian held his sword in the air and the grille flew upwards with a rattle of iron. For a moment nothing happened. Everyone there craned to get a view, staring at the black void in that wall. Gratian was watching it too, beads of perspiration on his lip, his eyes fixed, his focus total.

Suddenly, a spotted shape hurtled into the sunshine. The crowd roared and the women screamed. Conchessa stared. She couldn't look away. Moments ago she could not look as one man was about to kill another. But *this*, this was so different. She couldn't find words for it, but try as she might, she could not tear her eyes away.

If the crowd had been roaring for a kill moments ago, they were ecstatic now. The leopard swung left, snarling and clawing at a torch bearer who whirled his flaming brand to keep the beast back. Half those who watched had never seen a leopard before but they could see at a glance what it could do. One hundred and fifty librae of bone and muscle, with razor claws and teeth that clamped to bone and flesh. It spun away from the fire, but the second torch bearer was not fast enough and the animal leapt at him, batting aside the brand so that it dropped in the sand and went out. Instantly, the cat's jaws were around the screaming man's head and it was ripping his bowels open with its hind claws.

The other torch bearers beat the beast back with their brands and the leopard slunk off out of their reach. The three still on their feet circled the cat warily, listening to the sobs of their dying comrade. The leopard licked its whiskers, tasting the blood drops that glittered there. It went first for one man, then another, but each time they were faster, keeping the flames between it and them. They were driving the animal out across the centre of the arena, towards the one man who had no torch at all. The leopard saw him and the torch-bearers fell back.

The crowd were silent now, watching in horror as a man with just a sword stood facing one of the most deadly killing machines on earth. For a second, two, three, Gratian stared into the smouldering yellow eyes. The leopard was crouching, lashing its tail in the sand and its ears were flat to its head. Its spotted fur stood on end over the rippling muscles and Gratian knew he had one chance. If he missed that, it would all be over and he would be dead before he hit the ground.

The beast leapt, sinews taut and claws outstretched. Gratian felt the rip across his cheek and smelt the rancid, blood-filled breath from the leopard's mouth. He closed his eyes and lunged for all he was worth. His blade slid between the animal's teeth, slicing its tongue and embedding itself with a sickening squelch and crack of bone into its brain. The impact of the attack carried Gratian backwards and he fell under the leopard's dead weight as the blood ran down his arm, still holding the sword.

The torch-bearers leapt forward and dragged the spotted carcase off their Emperor. They helped the shaking Gratian to his feet. His look of terror had changed to a broad – and very lucky – grin. 'Don't damage that pelt,' he wheezed. 'I want it over my saddle by nightfall.' Then he staggered out alone, sword in hand, crimson to the hilt and called through the agony of his desperate lungs, his head throbbing with the wound to his temple. 'Are you content?'

The roar in response was deafening. Everyone in the arena was on their feet, cheering, jumping up and down, hugging friends, family and total strangers. Conchessa, in spite of herself, hugged Pontus and he hugged her back, laughing. The Emperor's bloodless cloak still dangled in the hands of the tribune Vitalis. He wouldn't have to sell it after all. And, in spite of himself, he looked down at Gratian and laughed with the rest.

CHAPTER FIFTEEN

Segontium, Britannia Prima, Augustus

Maximus' army had marched due west through Deceangli country with the wild Hibernian Sea on their right flank. The purple mountains from which the snows had gone rose dumb and silent in the summer heat and sheep wandering the upland pastures bleated at them as they passed.

On the open ground the Romans and the Deceangli fought each other with wooden swords, with trophies for the victors and a lot of Roman wine and Deceangli ale. Laughter flowed with the drink and all was well. On the third day of the leisurely jaunt west to the Deceangli capital of Caer Llyn, there was a wedding; one of Elen's women was marrying one of her warriors. There was music and dancing and more laughter among the tall grasses and the flowers.

'This is Elysium,' Maximus said, sitting on the ground with his arms resting on his knees, 'this kingdom of yours.'

Elen laughed. 'You should see it in winter,' she said, clinking her cup with his, 'if you can see it at all. The fog covers everything, from the mountain tops to the valley passes. Green, it is and swirling, with the faces of the mountain spirits in it, beckoning and calling. Many's the shepherd who has been lured to his death.'

Maximus shook his head. 'My homeland is like this,' he said. 'Too hot to hold a sword in the summer and in Januarius your bollocks would freeze solid on the hillside.'

She closed to him. 'I have heard a rumour, Macsen Wledig,' she said.

'Oh?' He raised an eyebrow. He would love to forget politics for a while, just for a day; this special day for the two young lovers dancing to the drums and harps, but that was not to be.

'They say you are descended from the great Constantine.'

'Do they?' he said, smiling at her.

'They say more,' Elen went on, running her finger around the cup's rim. 'They say your grandfather was Crispus and your great grandmother the daughter of Maximillian. You are the great grandson of the Empress Elen, my namesake.'

'And all this is important?' Maximus asked ruefully, refilling their goblets.

'It is to my father,' she said. 'He is an old man. He believes in dreams and prophecies and swords that live in water. Oh, second childhood perhaps, but if he believes it, the Deceangli believe it. And they will follow you.'

'Follow me?' he paused in mid-swig. 'Where am I going, Elen of the armies?'

'Like the deified Constantine,' she said, 'you are going to Rome, to claim your rightful inheritance. And you need troops. You have your own legions of course, but a few thousand auxiliaries wouldn't hurt, would they?'

'And what about you?' he said. 'Will you follow me?'

She laughed, that sound like the babble of the mountain streams. 'Oh, no,' she said, suddenly arch and proud. 'You'll have to do better than a family tree to impress me.'

That night they came to Caer Llyn, the stronghold of the Deceangli and the Lord Eudaf was there to greet them. The old man would never see seventy summers again and his old eyes could not stand the sun any more. Even torchlight hurt them and walking was agony for him. But the Romans had come to Caer Llyn; Macsen Wledig himself had come. He who was spoken of in the book of Aneurin; Aneurin who was and will be again.

Eudaf sat on his gilded throne in the great entranceway to his palace. The night was warm and the stars bright as the fires blazed to light the path of Macsen Wledig. The Caesar walked bareheaded, as he had when he had met Elen, as far as the world knew, for the first time. He drew his sword and weighed it in his hand before tossing it into the fire.

'To the fire,' he called to the king in the words of the Deceangli that Elen had taught him. 'Iron to the fire. Iron to the water.'

The old man nodded, his eyes bright with tears. 'Iron to the fire.' Slowly and with difficulty he clawed his own sword from his studded belt and threw it into the flames to join Maximus' blade. 'Iron to the fire. Iron to the water.'

Maximus bowed before him and knelt, the legion at his back and all of Caer Llyn in front and on both sides.

'Welcome,' the old man said in his reedy voice, 'Welcome, Macsen Wledig.'

'Thank you, gransha Eudaf,' Maximus said. He stood up and helped the king to his feet, clasping his forearm in the Roman way. He towered over Eudaf whose snow white hair lay tangled under his golden crown. More gold shone at his neck, a torc twisted into tight spirals, peppered with stones that flashed and caught the firelight. The old man looked up into the dark, bearded face. He frowned and ran his fingers over Maximus' cheeks, nose and forehead. 'You remind me …' he said and his voice trailed away.

There was the thump of a drum from the legions and the soldiers parted to allow the Egyptian sorceress through. She was draped in a richly embroidered black cloak, the hem heavy with gold thread and pearls. And in her arms she carried the book bound in leather, curiously studded with silver and gilt. She knelt before Maximus and the king.

'The book of Aneurin,' Maximus said, still speaking the words that Elen had taught him. 'Who was and who will be.'

The king's daughter was suddenly at his elbow. The old man barely looked at the book, still less at the smouldering siren who had brought it. She took Maximus' arm and that of her father. 'That doesn't matter,' she said in Latin. 'I knew it the first time I saw you, Macsen Wledig and I brought word to my father. You are the living image of his eldest son, the brother I barely remember. He died when I was a child, but the old man loves him still.'

'So all this ...' Maximus frowned, stopping short of saying 'nonsense'.

Elen shook her head and leaned in to the Caesar. 'You need all the help you can get, adventurer,' she said, stopping short of calling him 'usurper'. 'Ritual. Riddles. Books written by men who have not yet been born. Faces that are familiar as the wind that rocked our cradles. It all works, Macsen; you can depend on it.'

The old man had grown increasingly impatient in recent months, staring his gods in the face as he was. And he was impatient now. All this Latin prattle. Enough of that. 'Elen,' he said to the girl. 'Tell our guests they are welcome ...'

But the king never finished his sentence because there were suddenly shouts and running feet, torches darting with men scurrying down the slope from the great fortress. A horseman leapt from the saddle, his horse blowing and its hide flecked white. He dropped to one knee in front of Eudaf and Elen and gabbled something Maximus and the Egyptian couldn't understand.

'What's the trouble?' the Caesar asked.

Elen's face was a pale mask in the torchlight. 'The Roman Fort on Mona,' she said. 'It's been attacked.'

'Attacked?' Maximus repeated. 'By whom?'

Elen looked at him with her steady grey eyes. The old man's little girl, the princess of the Deceangli, was a general again.

'The Painted Ones, the Scotti,' she said, 'and the Attacotti, eaters of men.'

Augusta Treverorum

The blade glowed in the fire, smoking red hot along its length. The Emperor sat naked from the waist up, sweat running from his hairline. His medici had cleaned the leopard's wound but its claws were infected, they said. Stitches would not do it. The gash across his cheek must be seared along its length with hot iron and the beast's poisons burned out.

It was the early hours now and Gratian had become more delirious as time had passed. They had bled him and tried various potions, but nothing was working. They were anxious to get on, to cauterize the wound before the infection took hold and killed him. But the Emperor had other ideas and he started at the click of a scabbard hilt in the doorway.

'Ah, tribune. Come here.'

Vitalis handed his helmet to an orderly and stood by the Emperor's side. Gratian's body was sheened with sweat and he was trembling. His face was hideously swollen with the black gashes of the leopard's claws under his eye socket and the eye itself purple and almost closed.

'Now,' Gratian hissed and rammed a leather pad into his own mouth. A surgeon seized the moment, grabbed the red-hot iron and pressed it against the man's cheek. Gratian bucked and jerked, sweat flying from his hair and tears filling his eyes. Then he sat still and spat out the pad. 'You saw?' he grabbed Vitalis' tunic front. 'No one held me. I did not cry out.'

'I saw, Sire,' Vitalis said softly.

'And you saw today, in the arena?'

Vitalis nodded.

Gratian used both hands to claw his way upright, hauling on the tribune's tunic and scarf to do it. When he was level with the man's face, impassive in the firelight, he hissed, 'Get back to Britannia,' he said. 'Find your friend Maximus. Tell him what you saw today. Tell him he does not want to tangle with an Emperor like his. Tell him … tell him he can keep Britannia if he wants it, but no more.'

'He is not my friend, Sire,' Vitalis insisted.

'Heroes of the Wall,' Gratian muttered, the room starting to spin with the pain. 'I know all about you.'

He grabbed Vitalis' hand and held the jet ring up to his face. 'From Count Theodosius at Carthago. Oh, I was not much more than a boy then, but I remember it. He glowed when he told us. And I can remember your names still. Justinus, the circitor; Paternus the semisallis and Leocadius and Vitalis, the pedites. You rose from nothing and look at you now, standing toe to toe with your Emperor. And I know Maximus – he's always been easily impressed. He was impressed by you, you watchmen on the Wall. And he'll be impressed by me. Tell him. And tell him not to come to Augusta Treverorum or it will be to his grave.'

'Sire,' and Vitalis saluted and turned on his heel. He didn't see the man sink to the floor.

'I'm not going, Vitalis.' Conchessa stood like an ox in the furrow.

He crossed the atrium to her and looked into her eyes. Then he took both her hands. 'You can't stay here,' he said.

'Yes, I can,' and she held her head high. 'I will have the protection of the Emperor.'

Vitalis snorted and let her hands fall. 'That man is mad,' he said. 'I'm convinced of that now.'

She shook her head. 'No,' she said. 'He's afraid of Maximus, that's all.'

'What? He faces leopards and he can't face the Caesar.'

'The Caesar?' she repeated. 'That's treason around here, isn't it, calling Maximus that?'

Vitalis smiled. He thought the politics of Londinium were vicious enough, but against Augusta Treverorum, it was like a child's playground. Then his smile vanished and he looked at his sister again. 'You mean you have the protection of Septimus Pontus,' he said.

She ignored him. 'I cannot leave until I have found Calpurnius,' she said. 'And you have to go. The Emperor has commanded it.'

For a moment he hesitated. Maximus had sent him with orders to find the younger Theodosius and he had not accomplished that. There was so much he wanted to say to her, so many words he couldn't find. There was a gulf between them already and now there would be so many miles. 'Yes,' he said sadly. 'The Emperor has commanded it.' He took her in his arms, holding her so tight he thought she might break and she rocked gently, tears welling in her eyes. When at last they parted, he held her at arm's length. 'Take care of yourself, Con,' he whispered. 'Please.'

And he turned on his heel. In the passageway, the girl Rebekah stood, holding his helmet. He took it from her and saw tears glistening in her eyes too. 'Are you coming back, sir?' she asked him, afraid to hear the answer.

'Of course I am,' he said, surprised by her question and her tears. 'Look after your mistress for me, Rebekah.'

And he was gone.

Londinium

Fast horses took the tribune by the army roads across
Gallia Belgica to the coast in fifteen days and he
thumbed a lift on a navy transport carrying horses to
the Thamesis. The weather was turning as he splashed
through the marshes south of the river, the harvest
due and anxious farmers scanning the skies for more
of the rain that promised destruction from the west.
After Augusta, Londinium looked pitifully small and
parochial, but Vitalis had forgotten how much he
missed his little workshop in the huddle of buildings
along the wharves, where the rats ran and the river
stank. He saw it briefly as he urged his horse over
the bridge and through the great gate reinforced by
Count Theodosius when Vitalis had been a tribune
for the first time. Then he was at the basilica and soldiers were saluting him and taking his horse.

Chrysanthos the vicarius was a busy man and he
had a province to run, but a messenger from the
Emperor could not be ignored. He looked up at the
tribune standing in front of his table and recognised
the uniform of the Schola Palatina, the Emperor's
personal guard.

'How goes it with His Greatness?' he asked Vitalis,
clicking his fingers to a slave, who brought the messenger wine.

'I have the Emperor's message for Caesar
Maximus,' the tribune said.

Chrysanthos leaned back, pushing the ledger and the stylus away from him. 'I am vicarius here,' he said. 'Whatever message you have you will give to me.'

Vitalis shook his head at the slave and refused the wine. 'With respect, sir,' he said, 'I will not.'

Chrysanthos narrowed his eyes. 'Not?'

'No, sir,' Vitalis said. 'The Emperor was most insistent. His words are for Maximus alone.'

'Well, well,' Chrysanthos smiled. 'We mustn't upset the Emperor, must we? The truth of the matter is, tribune, I don't know where Maximus is. He's on manoeuvres somewhere up country. Do you know Britannia?'

'Very well,' Vitalis nodded.

Chrysanthos took him across to a map of the country, marked with roads and cities and forts. 'The last I heard,' he said, looking up at it, 'he was somewhere here, south of Deva.'

'The headquarters of the XX Valeria Victrix,' Vitalis nodded.

'That's right,' Chrysanthos said. This man knew more about Britannia than its vicarius. 'How do you know this place again?'

'I was born here,' Vitalis said. 'It's my home.'

Chrysanthos frowned. 'What did you say your name was?'

'Vitalis Celatius,' he told him.

'My God,' the vicarius was amazed. 'You're a Hero of the Wall.'

Vitalis smiled and waved his ring in the air. 'Funny how shit sticks, isn't it?'

'My dear fellow,' Chrysanthos gushed, shaking the tribune's hands warmly. 'I had no idea. I've been rude. Forgive me. You'll take cena?'

'No, thank you, sir,' Vitalis said. 'I was hoping to pay my respects to the consul.'

Chrysanthos' face darkened. 'The consul?' he repeated. 'Ah. Of course, you were friends, weren't you?'

'We were,' Vitalis said. 'Old comrades in the VIth. All that seems a long time ago now.'

'I have sad news, Vitalis Celatius,' Chrysanthos said. 'Leocadius Honorius is dead.'

Vitalis blinked. 'How?' he asked. Leo was only a year older than he was, but then, he didn't live Vitalis' lifestyle.

'Murdered, I fear. And his murderer sailed for the east months ago. I made all the usual enquiries, of course, but it was useless. I'm sorry.'

'Yes,' said Vitalis. 'So am I.'

Chrysanthos was a kind man at heart and he wouldn't add to Vitalis' sorrow by telling him how depleted the city treasury had been at Leocadius' departure from this vale of tears.

There was a sudden movement in the gallery overhead and both men looked up. Vitalis recognized the face at once. It was Honoria, more gorgeous than ever, wearing the robes of a wealthy matron. He half turned to talk to her, but she glanced down as if he wasn't there. She looked right at him and right through him and she walked on.

'You're determined to find Maximus?' Chrysanthos asked.

'I have my orders,' Vitalis told him.

'Well, at least stay the night. Join me in the palace.'

Vitalis watched where slaves bobbed and opened doors for Honoria. 'No,' he said. 'Thank you, but no. There's nothing to keep me here now.'

Segontium, Britannia Prima

Maximus and Andragathius had ridden out with Elen across the heather that morning. The sea mist rolled in from the straits and they could barely make out the island of Mona, a black rock above the grey. The German was still unhappy to have a woman alongside him. Women had their place, as he had often told the Caesar; underneath him in bed, cooking over a camp fire, rocking the cradle. But riding to war? No, that made no sense at all.

The three of them tethered their horses to the low bushes and crept forward until they were lying flat on their stomachs on the headland, looking down at the sea crashing, white-capped feet below.

'They've come before?' Maximus asked Elen.

'Most summers,' she said. 'Across the Hibernian Sea. They're raiding parties, hoping to strike lucky.'

Maximus nodded. Both men had met this all their lives – the discontented and the disconnected who hung like camp dogs around the edges of the Empire. From Palmyra in the east to Pannonia in the centre and Germania to the north, robbers nibbled at the fabric of Rome's greatness, never daring to take her on directly, but hitting fast and running away, like naughty children knocking doors in Augusta Treverorum.

'From what your messenger said,' Andragathius grunted, 'this is no raiding party.'

'They'll have heard that my father is ill,' Elen said, watching the mist wreathe and curl below them. 'They'll think the time is right.'

'They didn't reckon on us,' Maximus said.

'This isn't your fight,' she said, looking at him.

'I don't know,' Andragathius sighed. 'We came on manoeuvres and end up in the middle of a bloody war. How big is the fort on that island?'

'Two hundred men, if memory serves,' Maximus said. 'It's just an outpost.'

'And at Segontium?' the German wanted to know.

'Another five hundred,' Elen chipped in before Maximus could answer. She caught the look on his face. 'Know your enemy,' and she winked at him.

'Now I am confused!' Andragathius shrugged. 'Jupiter highest and best.'

He was pointing out beyond the mist, suddenly rolling away from the west. Along the shore, set carefully on the high points of land across the straits, a row of stakes stood tall in the morning and on top of each one, a battered, bloody head had been transfixed.

'That's your garrison at Caer Sacrum,' she murmured. 'And if the Attacotti are there, they'll have no eyes. The Attacotti will have had those for breakfast.'

Augusta Treverorum

Conchessa had waited until the household slept, then she crept from her bed and dressed simply, in her oldest clothes. She stuffed a dagger into the folds of her belt, but she had no real idea what she would do if she was called upon to use it. She strapped her sandals high and dispensed with the cloak. The night was still warm and she wanted to be able to lift her skirts and run if necessary. She checked Adelina's door. The woman was snoring her head off as usual and would not wake for another three hours yet. She padded down the steps to where Rebekah, the slave girl, lay curled on the couch. She was dead to the world.

Conchessa slipped through the door into the broad street, then struck right, out across the city. She had rarely been on these narrow pavements or cobbled streets after dark and she had always been in company, either of Vitalis or Pontus, or, at the very least, Adelina. Now she was alone and it felt strange. In fact, Conchessa had rarely been alone in her life. There had always been a father, a mother, a big brother, a husband there, to guide and comfort, to hold her hand, to light her way. Now there was nothing and as she left the main thoroughfares where the torch brackets guttered and the guards patrolled, their spear-butts trailing the ground, she felt suddenly, utterly alone.

A cat mewed at her from a high wall and for the briefest of moments, she was back in that arena, staring at what Gratian had faced. But that was silly, she told herself. This was somebody's pet. She reached up and stroked it and it purred, rubbing itself against her hand. She walked on. The streets were narrower here, darker, but they had noises of their own.

There was drunken laughter coming from a tavern on the corner where the lights burned low and from somewhere came the soft lament of a lute, each note struck as though played by a blind hand that could not find the chord. There was a couple up against a wall, the girl with her head hitting the brickwork each time the man rammed into her. He turned his head and saw Conchessa. 'Your turn next, darling,' he grunted.

'Piss off!' the girl hissed at her clearly unwilling to share her lover with anyone else.

Conchessa stepped lightly over a puddle. She had quizzed Pontus on exactly where Marcus Cotta had seen the man who so resembled Calpurnius. The husband who had become a ghost had been walking along the Via Damnati, the street of the damned, moving east. To the north, she knew, stood the great circus where the chariot teams vied with each other with their screaming whips and their colours of white and blue. The grid of streets, with their order and symmetry and right angles, lost their way here and the alleyways were a dark, impenetrable tangle where the houses closed in and sudden dead ends stopped the unwary in their tracks.

'Hello, gorgeous,' a voice in the darkness sounded slimy, unreal. 'We haven't seen you here before.'

'What brings a nice girl like you to a place like this?' another voice slithered.

She would have ignored them, but first one face, then another emerged from the shadows and she realised she couldn't walk on. She turned sharply to go back, but a third man had stopped her with his bulk. 'I'm looking for someone,' she said, in as strong a voice as she could.

'Oh, yeah?' the third man said. 'Who might that be?'

'My husband,' she said.

There were guffaws all round. 'Come to fetch him home, have you, darling?' the first man asked. 'Past his bedtime?'

'Talking of bedtime,' the second man was hauling up his tunic, pulling his manhood into the open.

'Now, now, Lucio,' the third man said. 'What we have here is a lady. She doesn't want low life like you.'

'Ah, they're all the same length lying down,' Lucio reminded him, 'lady or not.'

'Gagging for it,' said the first man, following Lucio's example and rubbing himself. 'That's why you're really here, isn't it, sweetheart?'

Conchessa tried to dodge past the third man, desperate to get away, but he was too big and too fast and he blocked her retreat. Her knife flashed in the darkness and there were whoops and jeers from the men.

'Watch yourself now, Metellus,' the second man said. 'She's armed and dangerous.' He was trying to peer over her shoulder. 'Nice tits, though.'

While he distracted her, Metellus lashed out with his fist and knocked the knife from Conchessa's hand. She heard it clatter on the cobbles somewhere behind her. All three men moved in, giggling and cursing as their intent became more urgent.

'One at a time, boys,' the first man said. 'And I saw her first.'

'Actually, you didn't.' A fourth voice rang out clear in the darkness and the first man spun like a top, blood spraying out in an arc from his neck. He gurgled and staggered against the wall, his erection, like his life, suddenly gone.

She felt a hand grab her arm and pull her out of the alleyway. Then she was running with her saviour, her skirt lifted, her sandals skidding on the cobbles. They turned a corner and, fighting for breath and still on the edge of panic, she looked up into his face.

'Hello, Conchessa,' he said.

LIBER III

CHAPTER SIXTEEN

Augusta Treverorum

'Leo!' Conchessa gasped. 'Leocadius Honorius. What are you doing here?'

'You're an intelligent woman, Conchessa,' he smiled. 'Can't you do better than clichés like that?' He was looking around the corner to where the girl's attackers were muttering together in the darkness of the alleyway. 'Let's just say I got tired of Londinium.'

'Talking of clichés,' she said, heart still pounding and eyes still wide, 'they say when a man's tired of Londinium, he's tired of life.'

'Yes.' Leocadius was leading her away from the corner. 'I wouldn't go so far as all that. What's that shambles of a brother doing, leaving you alone in a place like this?'

She stood on her dignity. '*You're* alone in a place like this,' she said.

He laughed. 'Never quite alone,' he said and flashed his knife blade. 'Come on. We'll lose them in the forum.'

Segontium, Deceangli Territory

Clodius Vettens was the commander of the Roman fort at Segontium and these days he was a martyr to gout. The endless, driving rain that marked every winter and most springs and autumns in Britannia Prima had taken its toll and had rusted his joints. To alleviate the pain he imbibed more than was good for a fort commander and that inflamed his joints even more. Some days – and this was one of them – he couldn't get out of bed.

Elen of the armies was used to seeing men in bed, her own father and Macsen Wledig among them, so she was unfazed by the wreck that lay in the Principia that morning. Vettens, as much a politician as a soldier, as a commander had to be these days, was embarrassed and he tried to rise. She held his shoulder. 'Don't stir yourself, Clodius,' she said, 'but we have what you might call a situation and I want you to be ready.'

'The Painted Ones,' the commander nodded, gratified to be allowed to rest his head back on the pillow. 'Yes, I heard. Any idea of numbers?'

'If they took the fort on Mona,' Elen was pacing the room, thinking like a general, 'which we know they did, they must have at least a thousand. They wouldn't risk an all-out attack like that with less.'

'Some raiding party,' Vettens grunted. The sun wasn't over the mountains yet and he longed for a drink. He grabbed the pitcher by his bed. 'Hair of the dog?' he offered her a swig.

She shook her head, then, on a sudden impulse snatched the jug from him. 'We have a plan, Clodius,' she said. 'But I need you to concentrate on this problem and this alone. And for that I need you to stay sober. Can you do that for me?'

Luguvallum, the Wall

A chill autumn was coming to the northernmost reaches of Gratian's empire, a cold rain that turned to sleet across the grey-purple of the moorlands. Justinus Coelius felt a *little* ashamed of himself for staying so long in the comforts of Luguvallum, but it was not the raiding season and the clash with the Saxons in the east had been repeated nowhere north of the Wall. Luguvallum had been the capital of the Carvetii, part of the great Brigantes confederacy, and had been an unprepossessing cluster of mud huts until the Romans got there. Now, along with the cohort of the XX Valeria Victrix with its knees firmly under the table, there was a forum, baths, even a basilica of sorts. It was here that Maximus' messenger found him one morning before the sun was high.

Justinus took the despatch and read it. Maximus' seal, Maximus' own hand if he remembered right. He looked at the messenger. The man was clearly exhausted, his cloak and boots soaking wet and heavy with Brigantian mud. But he was also a centurion, so he would be more in the know than the average rider who carried the post all over the Empire.

'The Painted Ones,' Justinus was re-reading the letter, 'and the Scotti. You've seen them?'

'Yes, sir,' the rider told him. 'They've taken all of Mona.'

'So they'll move on Segontium next,' Justinus was thinking ahead. 'Tell me, centurion, has the Caesar asked for help from the XX at Deva?'

'He has, sir, but he's not sure they'll be enough.'

Justinus frowned. If an entire legion as well as the II Augusta could not hold those barbarians, what hope was there? Maximus had asked for as many men as Justinus felt he could spare, but that meant stripping the forts along the Wall and that was a risk that no Wall commander could take. The centurion read the commander's mind. 'He doesn't ask lightly, sir,' he said. 'This is no raiding party. They aren't going to sail home again at the sight of an eagle. They've taken those before.'

Justinus knew that. The Painted Ones were natural born killers, with their limed hair and the swirling patterns on their skin. They fought nearly naked and took men's heads as souvenirs of a good night out. As for the Hiberni, the commander of the Wall had seen them only once and had never faced them in battle. The taller the men, the taller the stories but, like every Roman, Justinus was happy with the fact that, dead, they took up no more than six pedes of earth.

'It's not the raiding season,' he was thinking aloud. The Painted Ones, the Hiberni, the Saxons, all of them waited until spring to go marauding, attacked in the summer when the days were long in the land. Then they sailed home in the twilight of the year, to roar and drink and boast around their camp fires. It had been the way of it for three hundred years. He looked up at the centurion. 'They've come to stay,' he said.

'What answer shall I take back to the Caesar?' the messenger asked, standing as straight as his exhaustion would let him.

'Get yourself some food, man,' Justinus said, 'and a night's sleep. You'll have fresh horses for the morning. That'll give me time to compose a reply.' And time, he added silently to himself, to pray for Mithras for a miracle.

Deceangli Territory

The place to stop an army was at the coast, on the wet sands of the beach or the jagged rocks at the cliff face. Hands would slip here, feet fail to make firm ground and all the time the crashing tide and tugging current would be in the faces of the attackers.

All the more surprising, then, that Elen of the armies had not done that. Her warriors, the tall men of the Deceangli, had hung back as the autumn days shortened and the spiders spun their webs. Magnus Maximus, watching them go from the palisades of

Segontium, had seen them do it. The II Augusta had upped stakes and marched to the east, beyond the reach of the Scotti scouts who might be foraging inland. Andragathius led them. And Andragathius had been told to wait.

The Caesar had said his goodbyes in the Principia, beyond the room where Clodius Vettens, increasingly these days, saw curious little Celtic creatures crawling in and out of his walls. Over the days and weeks he had known her, Elen of the armies, Elen of the gold-tawny hair and the dark eyes, had become oddly important to Magnus Maximus. That she could handle herself with a knife or sword he didn't doubt, but out there, against what he had heard were the most fearsome warriors in the world, how would that go?

'You *will* follow the plan?' he had asked her.

She had laughed. 'Would I do anything else?' she said.

And the Caesar wasn't sure.

The Painted Ones and the Scotti had drawn up their skirmish line between two rocky outcrops where stands of pines clustered. At their head, in the centre, with his own horse to the rear, stood Colla Mor, the under-king from Laigan. There was a simple circle of spiralled gold around his head and he wore a coat of mail, the links glistening like dew in the morning. Elen had seen him before. When she was a small girl, his men had raided the estuaries of her homeland and stolen cattle and sheep. They had burned villages and the stench of scorching timbers and the heat of blazing thatch lingered in her nostrils still, after all the years. Beside him and to his left, stood his banner, the red upraised hand of Ulaid, the one he had taken in battle from the king of the northern province. To his right stood a giant of a man, the aire-echta, the king's champion. A livid scar, white across the darkness of his face, gave him a terrifying look but the man who Elen was afraid of was the man who gave him that scar.

'We are the Eriu,' Colla Mor shouted. 'We have many names. You know us as the Scotti. The Romans call us Hiberni. And we're going to kill you anyway.' He looked at the Deceangli drawn up in battle array before him. 'Will anyone face my champion?'

The giant took three paces forward and dropped a leather sack on the ground between his feet. One by one he pulled out three heads. Roman heads. They had no eyes, just black holes dried with blood and their mouths gaped open.

'This one,' Colla Mor yelled as the first head appeared, 'was Aulus, commander of the Roman fort on Mona. The last time that mouth moved he was crying for his mother. This one,' he waited until the second head was held aloft, 'is his second in command, Gracchus. We had to clean him up a bit because he'd shat himself. And this ...' a broad grin crossed the Scotti's face, 'this is my favourite.' A penis had been rammed into the open mouth. 'I don't know his name but you can guess what his pastime was.'

Elen of the armies spoke enough of this man's language to get the gist of what he was saying. 'What is your point, cattle thief?' she called across the open space between them. There was a rattle of iron on wicker as Colla Mor's warriors bashed their shields with their sword blades so that the sound echoed and re-echoed around the headland, bouncing off the rocks and down the inland valleys. Colla Mor quietened them with a wave of his hand.

'My point is,' the king said, 'that all of Mona is ours. I'm man enough to acknowledge that the Romans are the foremost fighters in the world. Until today. Today,' he pointed to the grass in front of him, 'they lie at our feet. What have you got to stop me, cumhal?'

Again the rattle of the swords on the shields. Fighting talk to drive his men to fever pitch. Cumhal. Elen knew what that meant. Slave. 'Why don't you come and find out?' she asked, her voice as strong and steady as any man's.

The rattle of shields was increased by wails and cat calls. Again, Colla Mor silenced them.

'Are you the one they call Elen Llwyddog?' he asked her.

'I am, sheep-shagger,' she smiled. The Deceangli clapped and whistled now.

Colla Mor folded his arms and muttered to his standard bearer, 'She's mine when this is over. The rest of you will have to take turns.' He raised his voice again. 'All right,' he said. 'Little girl who fights for her father. Are you man enough to take on the aire-echta?'

The champion drew his sword with a slow, deliberate movement, scanning the line of the Deceangli ahead of him. There didn't seem to be very many of them. For an instant Elen considered it, her knuckles white on her sword pommel, her jaw flexing. Then she remembered what had she promised Maximus and steadied herself.

'Caradog,' she murmured to a warrior on her left. 'Is that oaf within spearshot?'

Caradog smiled. He looked up to the pale sun peeping now and again above the clouds. He licked his finger and raised it in the air. 'Very likely, lady,' he said.

'Do the honours, then,' she smiled.

Caradog hefted the ash shaft in his hand. Then he took two paces backwards and launched himself, hurling the javelin for all he was worth. It hissed through the air, twisting and spinning as it went, to crash against the champion's shield and bounce uselessly onto the grass.

'Is that it?' Colla Mor shouted. 'Is he the best you've got?'

'No,' Elen yelled back. 'We had to leave his granny back at Caer Llyn. She's busy this morning.'

Colla Mor had had enough. He hadn't come to trade insults with this whore of the Deceangli and he drew his sword, slashing the air with it in what was clearly a signal. Elen had seen the king before. She had seen his raiding parties. But she had never seen his army and she had to admit, she was impressed. All along the battle-front, the huge warriors called the fianna were Colla Mor's bodyguard. They engulfed him now as they crept forward, the giant champion at their head. Their green banners, stiff in the morning breeze, streamed high overhead – the man hanging from a tree, the triple spears called the Terrible Sheaf. There flashed the Torch of Battle and the Three Legs; there the Bright Light and the Golden One. And there wasn't a single Painted One in sight.

A rain of arrows hissed through the air from behind the Scotti's charging front. The Deceangli shields came up and the field was alive with the thud of barbed iron biting deep into limewood.

'Pull back!' Elen roared to her warriors who were steadying themselves for the impact of the Scotti. 'Pull back!'

For the first time in their lives, the Decenagli turned tail and ran, dodging between the double row of bowmen Elen had drawn up to their rear. That went hard with these men, who had never run from anything in their lives. They just hoped their general knew what she was doing. The archers let fly and the shafts hit the Scotti line running. Men somersaulted in mid-air with the impact, iron slicing through foreheads, faces, shoulders, chests. Wherever the line wavered and crumpled, others from behind closed in and the wave came on. The archers fell back to reload but a second volley from the Scotti found their marks and brought them down, men twisting in the air to fall, bleeding, onto the men already dead.

Elen pulled her line back, steadying them every hundred pedes or so, screaming at her archers to reload and fire each time they stopped. The noise was deafening, the attackers, roaring defiance and tearing up the ground, their boots slipping on the now-bloody grass of the valley. Then, at her signal, the entire Deceangli line broke and it was every man for himself, crashing through the bracken and hurtling down the rivulets and gullies at their back, scattering through the heather like rabbits in a hunt.

With difficulty, Colla Mor halted his men. One or two of the more foolhardy, their blood up and sensing victory, got caught in the ravines they did not know and were hacked down by Elen's timid warriors. Most of the Scotti had come to a halt now, wheezing and out of breath, but elated. The Deceangli had barely dented their line and just look at them; they were running through the heather as if the hounds of Hell were after them. They laughed and pounded each other, pointing at the vanquished and calling them every kind of coward under the sun.

'I'll never live this down,' Caradog muttered to Elen, who had not even drawn her sword today. He was shaking his head. What would his old granny say?

Elen smiled at him. 'Take it up with Macsen Wledig,' she said, but somewhere inside her, she felt the same.

Across the field, some of Colla Mor's men were rolling over corpses and flicking their eyes out of their sockets with greedy knife-points. To the victors, the spoils. And the wailing victory songs began.

Augusta Treverorum, Septembris

'What do you have for me, Pontus?' The Emperor was staring out of the window of the basilica as the leaves on the silver birch were turning to gold.

The decurion obeyed his lord in all things but he was not as rabid as Gratian and he could see that the little plan the man had in mind was fraught with difficulties. 'We estimate that there are still well over a hundred Jews in the city, Sire,' he said.

'Tell me something I don't know,' Gratian snapped, watching the Schola Palatina drilling in the courtyard below. 'Where are they?'

'Well, that's just it, Sire,' Pontus said. 'We believe they're hiding in the old watercourses, the cisterns beyond the circus. It's a rabbit warren down there. There aren't any plans.'

Gratian looked at the man. Neither of them was an architect and the men who had built the under-ground passages were dead or had moved on. Until the Emperor arrived, Augusta's Jews had lived in the poorest vicus, a shanty town beyond the walls, near the cemetery where they buried gladiators, whores and thieves. The noxii lay there, without coffin or shroud, four to a grave. No one left markers or came to pay their respects. But the ruler of the Christian world in the West was not happy with freedom for the men who called themselves the Chosen People. They were idolators, deniers of Christ and did not deserve to breathe the same air as a free man.

So he denied them air. On a cold morning in the darkness of the year, the Schola Palatinae and the garrison of Augusta had descended on the ghetto, burning and looting, hauling people out of their beds, kicking them downstairs. Those who protested were hacked down, their womenfolk raped in front of their eyes. The rest, mumbling their strange foreign prayers, were marched to the circus, to be spat at by the locals before being consigned to the dark tunnels that ran under the city. Any of them found above ground would automatically become a slave. Or, if it pleased the Emperor, they would have been nailed to a cross, once the deserved punishment for traitors and idolators.

'Seeing them in the arena,' Gratian was remembering the day he had faced the leopard, 'made me realise that the situation cannot go on. I want them removed. All of them.'

'What is your will, Sire?' Pontus asked, although he knew what the answer would be.

'Kill them, Pontus.' Gratian waved a slave over to pour his wine. 'Kill them all.'

'I don't think I've seen one before.' Leocadius was staring at the slave girl, Rebekah.

293

'They're not far removed from us,' Conchessa laughed. 'Almost human, really.'

He caught her gaze and laughed with her. 'All right,' he said. 'But I've still never seen one. Not in Londinium. And certainly not on the Wall.'

'Don't you miss them. Leo?' she asked. 'Your family, I mean.'

The soldier who had once been the consul of Londinium looked out over Conchessa's shoulder to the autumn sun kissing the vines on her portico. 'My official family, no. Julia is as cold as Januarius in Valentia and the girl's just like her. As for Honoria and Scip … well,' he shook himself free of the memory, 'that was then.'

Leocadius had moved in with Conchessa. Eyebrows were raised among the ladies of Gratian's court, but she explained, rightly, that he was an old friend of her brother and was looking out for her in his absence. And that was all there was to it.

'That's all there is to it, Pontus,' she had told the senior decurion when the news reached him. She couldn't tell whether he was jealous. Her fondness for Pontus had grown over the weeks and months she had been at Augusta. They had been seen in public many times, at the Games, at the chariot races, at the dozens of bashes the Emperor threw, dining off silver plates and drinking from gilt goblets. As for Pontus' bed, Conchessa had not been there. She had not been there because of the flame she still carried for Calpurnius. But that flame, she hardly dared admit, even to herself, was guttering in the winds of Pontus and the court and each time it sparked into life again it was smaller and smokier than before. 'Will you go back for me?' she asked Leocadius that morning. 'Back to the Via Damnati?'

'My second home,' he smiled.

'But those men,' she frowned. 'The ones who attacked me. Won't they be looking for you?'

'I won't be hard to find,' he told her.

'Here.' She rummaged in the folds of her gown and passed him a locket, chased in gold. He took it and clicked the catch at the side. There was a face, painted in lacquer, staring back at him. The hair was dark and curly, the eyes a shade too close together for honesty.

'This is Calpurnius?' he asked her.

Conchessa nodded. 'As I remember him,' she said. 'But I haven't seen him for nearly two years, Leo. He could have changed.'

He tucked the locket away and patted her hand. 'If he's there,' he said, 'I'll find him.'

'But why?' Conchessa asked, her eyes brimming with tears. 'Why *would* he be there?'

Leocadius shrugged. 'From what you've told me, there's a price on his head.' He knew what it was to be outcast, cut adrift from the world of light. 'The street of the damned is where he belongs.' He chuckled. 'Where *I* belong.'

She nodded. On the face of it, this was the same Leocadius she had met in Londinium those months before, strong, devil-may-care, but there was a sadness to him now, a depth she hadn't seen before. It made her sad too.

'What if,' he said as he turned to go, choosing his words carefully, 'what if Calpurnius doesn't want to be found?'

She let out a breath she seemed to have been holding for nearly two years. 'Then I will have to accept that,' she said, 'and let him go.'

Segontium

The tribune Vitalis Celatius had seen army camps before and permanent forts like Segontium. It was rare for him to be fired on by his own side however and he hauled in his rein sharply as the flaming arrow bit into the ground by his horse's forehooves and fizzled out.

'Who goes?' There was a commotion in the stunted bushes that lay black in the greyness just before dawn and a picket leapt into the open, spears pointing at him.

'Vitalis Celatius, Tribune of the Schola Palatinae.'

The spears stayed erect. 'Schola Palatinae?' a semisallis repeated.

'The Emperor's bodyguard, pillow-chewer.'

'You're a long way from home, sir.' The semisallis saluted and the spears came down.

'Aren't we all?' Vitalis said. 'I'm looking for the Caesar Magnus Maximus.'

'Gone east, sir,' the semisallis told him. 'No man knows where.'

'East?' Vitalis frowned. He had been on the road for days, trailing Maximus' army as the autumn gilded the land of Britannia Prima. It was like chasing a will 'o' the wisp, the corpse lights that floated over marsh and mountain, the wandering spirits of the dead. Everywhere he had ridden, soaked through with the mountain rains and bitten by the northern winds, he had heard the same story. Yes, an army had passed this way. They had helped themselves to anything that was not nailed down, but that was to be expected. At one point, Vitalis had come across two soldiers, naked but for their boots, dangling from a tree. Around the neck of both men hung a placard that read, 'I used to be a rapist.' Vitalis didn't need to read a signature carved into the flimsy wood. These two had ignored the friendly advice of their general. They would not do that again.

'You're at great readiness, semisallis,' the tribune said, impressed by the alertness of the picket.

'We've got trouble here, sir. Barbarians. Thousands of them.'

CHAPTER SEVENTEEN

Segontium

It wasn't every day that a tribune of the Schola Palatinae arrived at an outpost on the arse-end of the empire. Ordinarily, Clodius Vettens would have been impressed. He would have ordered a full turn-out of the guard, had an ox roasted and had pheasants stuffed with dormice. But this was not ordinarily. This was now and Segontium was under siege from the north.

'So where are they?' Vitalis asked the camp commander. The man had at least struggled out of his bed today and was sitting in his principia wrapped in furs. It wasn't as cold as that, but Vettens couldn't stop his teeth from chattering. So many little faces grinned at him from the curtains on the walls that he had long ago stopped noticing them. No doubt everybody else had too.

'To the north,' the commander told him, sipping his wine as though his life depended on it. 'We see them sometimes. They come out of the forest, laughing at us.'

'Who are they?'

'Scotti, Picti, Attacotti. Every painted bastard from the edges of the world. They're coming for me, Vitalis. They're coming for me.'

'How many, would you say?'

Shit. This man was irritating. First Vettens had had that egomaniac Maximus. Then the deranged Elen of the armies, more of a man than anybody under Vettens' command. Now he had this kid, still wet behind the ears and, no doubt, about to offer his wisdom and experience.

'Last week, my scouts reported they'd camped as far south as the estuary and as far east as the gold mines.'

'Gold?' Vitalis looked at the shivering man. 'Is that why they're here?'

'How the Hell should I know why they're here? All part of Caesar's plan, I shouldn't wonder.'

'His plan?' Vitalis was confused. Ever since he had left the vicarius in Londinium he had heard stories about Magnus Maximus. The man had sold his soul to whatever monstrous gods his Egyptian whore worshipped. He had drunk the blood of newborn babies – no less than four villages had told Vitalis that. He had proclaimed himself a god as the old Emperors had done and went to bed with sheep and little boys. But nowhere in this nonsense was there talk of any *plan*.

Vettens sighed. He should have been back home in Tuscania now, selecting the finest grapes from his vineyards, dandling his grandchildren on his knee. Instead, he was staring destruction in the face. And he was staring at it through the long, dark glass stem of a bottle.

'I am to fall back,' he said. 'At the first sight of an attack from the enemy, I am to abandon Segontium.'

'Abandon Segontium? You heard this from Maximus himself?'

'His whore.'

'The Egyptian?'

'The Deceangle. Elen of the armies as men call her.'

Vitalis shook his head. He had never heard of this woman until three days ago, when hopeful villagers he passed spoke of her. She could kill a man with one stare of her glittering dark eyes, they had said. No one could predict what would happen when she and the Caesar met. But all would be well. She was Eudaf's daughter. And that was enough.

'Abandoning a fortified camp is contrary to every Imperial order ...' Vitalis began.

'Don't lecture me on Imperial orders, Tribune!' Vettens snapped. 'How long has it taken you to reach me from Gratian?'

'About a month,' he said.

'Well, a month from now, there won't be any of us left, especially if I try to hold this god-forsaken place. If the Emperor values Segontium, let him come and defend it himself.'

'But it's madness,' Vitalis persisted. 'If there are as many of the enemy as you claim, what hope will your men have out in the open?'

'Maximus knows what he's doing,' Vettens persisted, as only a drowning man can. He took another hefty swig of his wine. There was a silence between them. 'He's marched east,' the commander said, 'to join up with the XX. Will you follow him?'

'No,' Vitalis said. 'My message from the Emperor can wait in view of this little local difficulty. With your permission, sir, I'd like to stay.'

'Suit yourself,' Vettens shrugged. 'But when those bastards attack, don't get in my way.'

Olenacum, the Wall

It went against every notion of military practice and common sense, but an order was an order and men like Justinus Coelius obeyed instinctively, especially when the order came from Magnus Maximus. He had sent word by gallopers all along the Wall from Segedunum to Maia, high on its sea crags. He ordered a mixed vexillation, horse and foot, under the command of two tribunes and the best part of twelve hundred men met him at Olenacum. He rested them, especially those who had marched from the east; then they hoisted the standards and marched southwest, towards Britannia Prima with its dark mountains wreathed in cloud. Justinus Coelius had stripped the Wall of its finest and best, the cavalry, infantry and artillery of the VI Victrix and he prayed with all his heart that Jupiter Highest and Best – and Mithras too – would watch over these ramparts in his absence.

Augusta Treverorum

No one had seen the man in the portrait Leocadius carried. He looked a *little* familiar to one of the tavern keepers and a whore along the Via Damnati swore that he had robbed her at knife point only the other night. One night was very much like all the others in this Hell hole in Gratian's new capital. Drunks lurched in the dark, dead alleyways, tarts hitched up their skirts for business; Greeks did the same with their tunics. Everything was for sale here. Everything had its price. Leocadius had spent hours combing the back alleys under the jutting walls of the great circus where the chariots raced in the sunshine. This was Londinium writ large. More taverns, more brothels, more gambling dens than the little city on the Thamesis could possibly hold. But to Leocadius Honorius, the former consul, the hero of the Wall, it was a giant haystack. But he wasn't looking for a needle; he was looking for a wisp of straw.

'Well, well, well,' a cold voice made him turn. In front of him, his wine lay beside a set of dice on a gnarled wooden table. He had made a few solidi tonight in the course of asking his questions but had got nowhere. And now it looked as though his luck had run out. The man behind him he recognized at once. The last time Leocadius had seen him he had knifed his companion. The former consul, the hero of the Wall, wondered again what he was doing here. Drifting like the renegade he was, taking his chances at the blade's edge, flying, like Icarus, to the sun. But the sun burned, like the flames that guttered in the tavern.

'Care to chance your arm, friend?' he asked the man, gesturing to the dice.

'Tell me your name,' the man grunted. 'I always like to make killing a personal thing.' He passed Leocadius out of arm's length and sat down opposite him at the table. Two of his friends joined him, so that three of them faced the chancer with the dice.

'My name is Leocadius Honorius,' he said, smiling.

'Never heard of you,' the second man grunted.

'Your loss,' Leocadius shrugged. 'Are you rolling?' He picked up the bones and rattled them in his hand.

'He's a cocky shit, isn't he?' the third man chipped in.

Leocadius stopped the rattle and frowned at the man. 'You I don't remember,' he said. 'If you weren't there the other night, upsetting my lady friend, I suggest you run along. I've no quarrel with you.'

'Ah,' the first man said. 'But we've a quarrel with you. All of us.'

'You have?' Leocadius took a sip of wine.

'Trebonius,' the man said. 'He was the friend of mine you cut the throat of the other night. I don't know whether there's a God or not. But if there is, he's great indeed, dropping you into our laps like this.'

'Trebonius,' the second man said. 'He had a wife and kids.'

'Really?' Leocadius raised an eyebrow. 'See me giving a shit about that?'

He kicked the table legs hard and the whole thing fell forwards into the laps of the three on the other side. One of them dodged aside and Leocadius' knife was already in his stomach. He jerked as the blade struck home and reached out with clawing fingers, his eyes glazing and blood gurgling from his lips. The second man came for Leocadius, knife flashing in the half light. There were screams and the crash of furniture as people dashed to get out of the way. Iron rang on iron and Leocadius darted backwards, parrying for his life. The first man attacked too, lunging and scything, until the hero of the Wall had his back to one and there was nowhere else to go.

'Mother of God!' A female voice shrieked as the door crashed back. The fight in the narrow room was instantly forgotten because a bigger problem had just arrived.

'Jupiter highest and best!' Every god in the heavens was being called upon at that moment because the army had arrived. The curling two-headed dragons on their shields flickered in the candlelight.

Then, those lights went out and everybody dived for cover.

'This isn't over, pretty boy,' Conchessa's attacker snarled at Leocadius as he dashed for the back door.

'Missing you already!' Leocadius called after him. He turned to face the troops who were filling the room. Time was he would have stood shoulder to shoulder with these men, the calcei chafing his feet and the iron heavy on his head. In yet another time he would have barked orders at them, expecting them to jump and skip to his command. Now he was a nobody, a ruffian in a tavern with a knife in his hand.

'Any Jews here?' a semisallis barked as his men overturned tables and chairs, driving people into the street.

'Why do you want them?' Leocadius was almost surprised to hear his own voice asking the question. Was he turning into a *real* hero, for the first time in his life?

The semisallis, a big man with attitude, looked him up and down. 'Our first mistake,' he grunted to the soldiery around him, 'was not forcing these animals to wear yellow.'

'Yes,' a comrade muttered. 'They all look like us, don't they?'

The semisallis chuckled. 'One way to find out,' he said, staring into Leocadius' face. 'Those Chosen People cut their boys with flint knives. Well, let's see how much foreskin you've got left, big mouth.'

Leocadius straightened and opened his eyes wide. 'Semisallis,' he giggled, swaying his hips. 'Not here.' He winked. 'Not in front of the men.'

A ripple of laughter ran round the suddenly silent room but the semisallis was not amused. His sword came up to the level but it wasn't fast enough. Leocadius' knife tip thudded into his forehead just under the helmet rim and the man tumbled backwards. Blades flashed in the half-dark but the chancer had gone, leaping over tables before he reached the street. There were more soldiers to his right, a wall of oval shields blocking the cobbled road and making straight for him. Over their heads, torches guttered in the wind. They had dogs with them, shaggy in the darkness, snarling and snapping on their short leashes.

Leocadius ran left, ducking under the shadow of the circus. He caught his breath. He didn't know all of the twists and turns of Augusta yet; he hadn't been here long enough. And he wasn't sure where he was. Shouts from his right told him that the soldiers were coming that way too. They were combing the back alleys, methodically driving the locals out into the open. He heard the roar, spit and crackle as they torched one house after another. They were burning out vermin. They had come for the Jews. But Leocadius was not a Jew. And yet …

Someone grabbed his sleeve and he spun sideways, forcing his attacker against the wall. He'd lost his knife and now he'd have to use his bare hands.

'It's me, sir,' a strangled voice said. 'Don't ...'

Leocadius checked himself, relaxed his grip. The throat he held belonged to a slave girl; Conchessa's slave girl, Rebekah.

'This way,' she mumbled. 'This way.'

For a moment, he hesitated. The girl was leading him into the pitch darkness and the unknown. On the other hand, there were a few hundred armed men behind him and most of them had murder in mind. He followed her.

Caer Llyn

He sat alone on a gilded throne, his legs crossed at the ankles, his head buried in his hands. Around him his attendants stood, silent. He had heard their words, listened to the arguments. He had read their entreaties, the petitions from all the corners of his empire, the letters of outrage and the songs of protest. They ate and drank, his court, but he did not join them. They hunted, but he did not ride with them. They brought him wine and trinkets, fine horses and beautiful women, but he turned them all down.

He turned them all down because of her. He could not eat nor sleep nor think of anything else but the lovely girl he had once seen. Her beauty had blinded him like the sun at the highest in the heavens. He had gazed on her long golden hair, the shift of white silk slashed with scarlet and the rubies that

307

glittered on her brow. And he whispered her name. 'Elen.'

She smiled in her sleep. Then she laughed. Then she frowned, because the name was still there. Even as she woke and the familiar darkness of her room filled her vision, she heard her own name. His face was in front of hers, smiling. And he leaned forward and kissed her. She sat upright, suddenly, with an inrush of breath, scrabbling to her knees on the bed and looking around frantically for her weapons.

He moved back, knowing how dangerous this woman could be. 'You were dreaming,' he said.

She nodded. 'The dream of Macsen Wledig,' she said. 'And here you are.'

'I seem to remember,' Maximus said, 'the last time we did this, the tables were reversed and you held a blade at my throat. Would you like to do that again?'

She stood up, clutching her gown around her. 'No need,' she said.

'We're allies now.'

'We were allies then,' she reminded him. 'And you got past *my* guards this time.'

'They were gentle with me,' he laughed. 'Tell me, do you ever offer your ally any wine?'

It was her turn to laugh. 'It has been known,' she said, and she poured them both a cup from the ewer on the table.

'Were you really dreaming about me?' he asked her.

'If I say "no", you'll be disappointed. If I say "yes" your head won't fit through your tent flap. What would you like me to say?'

'I'd like you to say, "Come into my bed, Macsen Wledig. Lie beside me until the morning." I'd like you to say, "Love me, if you can." And if you can't,' he looked at her levelly, 'at least let me love you.'

Despite herself, Elen of the armies' mouth fell open and for a moment she was lost for words. 'And I thought you'd brought a progress report,' she regained herself. 'Brought news.'

'I have,' he said, as business-like and matter-of-fact as she was. 'Our friends have spread out across the coast as far as the estuary. It's nearly October so the raiding season is over. They intend to stay. I expect an attack on Segontium in the next few days.'

'So we're next.'

'You are,' Maximus nodded. 'The XX Valeria will be with me by dies Saturni and I've sent to the commander of the Wall for reinforcements.'

She nodded. 'You're not taking any chances,' she said.

'I told you,' he smiled. 'If I'm going to take on Gratian and his legions I need to be sure that Britannia's safe.'

'And that's why you need me,' she nodded.

He laughed. Why hadn't he met this woman years ago? She thought like a man. Rode like one. Fought like one. Then, another thought occurred to the Caesar. She was his other half, what the Romans call

309

divida anima mea, half my soul. He stood up and put down his wine. Then he took her hand and kissed it, before looking deeply into her eyes. 'That's not the only reason,' he said and lowered his lips to hers.

She held her fingers against them. 'You have the Egyptian,' she said. 'The nameless one. You have women without number. That's the way of it with generals.'

'Yes,' he said, smiling. 'The harlots of the Empire waiting with their legs open. Any one of them has had access here,' and he took her hand and pressed it against his groin. 'But in here,' he took her other hand and placed it against his temple, 'that's different. Not one of them has been here.'

She closed her eyes and he kissed her, long and deep, their tongues curling in the darkness. She pulled back a little, taking his hand and leading him towards the bed. 'The dream,' she whispered, 'of Macsen Wledig.'

Augusta Treverorum

Leocadius was secretly glad he had the girl's hand to hold because he had no idea where he was going. Rebekah led him along the wall by the chariot stables, dark now and silent except for the occasional stamp and soft whinny of a horse. Then she pulled him to the left and they slid through a wicket gate into a long passageway. They both felt their way here, hands scrabbling on rough stones, coarse-faced and cold.

In fact it was the cold Leocadius was most aware of. That and the smell. It didn't take an engineer to know that they were going down into the cisterns of the city where the water dripped and dappled, a greenish light shimmering on the surface that lay so far below the streets.

'They'll find us here,' she said, even her whisper echoing like a shout. 'We must move on.' They skirted the huge liquid pools and ducked under a low archway. A glimmer of light here told them that the street was above. They pressed themselves into the shadows as shafts of torchlight flared above their heads and boots rattled and thudded on iron grilles.

'What's happening, Rebekah?' For all his new-found worldliness, Leocadius was at heart a Wall soldier. He was out of his depth in Gratian's orbit.

'Those men,' she whispered, looking into his face. 'They're the Schola Palatinae, the Emperor's own guard. The Emperor wants us dead. Us Jews.'

'Why?'

She was smiling at him, despite herself. 'If you ever find an answer to that,' she said, 'let me know.'

She pulled him along an old watercourse, where the rats ran huge and black and she hurried up some steps to a door at the top. She tapped on it. Once. Twice. Then three times in quick succession. It swung open and she gabbled something to someone inside. Leocadius felt himself thrown backwards against a wall and a sword tip was pressed against his throat.

'He wants to know who you are,' Rebekah said.

311

Leocadius held up both hands and tried to smile. 'Some of my best friends are Jews,' he said.

He felt the point press harder and shut his eyes. Was this it? He who had cheated death so often? Was he going to die here in the alien dark?

Rebekah spoke urgently to the swordsman and the blade fell away. Leocadius swallowed again and felt blood trickle down his chest.

'Rebekah says you are a friend,' the man said. He was older than Leocadius, dark with worried eyes.

'I'd like to think so,' Leocadius said.

'We've been expecting this.'

'We?' Leocadius frowned. 'Who are you?'

'The Children of Israel,' the man said. 'Men call me Ezekiel.'

'Leocadius.'

'You're Roman.'

'No,' Leocadius laughed. 'I'm from Britannia, but don't hold that against me.'

'Well, I'm from Gaul,' Ezekiel smiled. 'Mad world, isn't it? Come and meet the others. We'll have to make a run for it. We've women and children down here and the Schola Palatinae mean business.'

He led the way. Torches guttered in the foetid air and the three of them were descending still further along a narrow path over a sheer drop. Leocadius allowed himself one brief look down then swept on. There was no doubt about it. He was standing on the mouth of Hell. It wasn't some ghastly punishment the Christians fretted about, which would face the

evil-doers when they died. It was right here. On earth.
In Augusta Treverorum.

Ezekiel shoulder-barged a large door, studded
with iron. 'The Romans built these tunnels,' he said,
'long before our time. Part of a water-course they
never finished. We've been here for months. It's
been our home. Here we are.'

Beyond the studded door lay a sort of courtyard
with a low domed ceiling. Torches flickered here and
the air was a little fresher. There were homes crowded
into recesses. Old men and women were cowering in
the niches, younger women were strapping what they
could carry onto their backs and the men were standing in sullen knots, shaking their bearded heads and
readying what makeshift weapons they had.

'We'll have to make our way out under the circus,' Ezekiel said. 'Leocadius, Rebekah, how much
time do we have?'

The girl looked helpless, lost. 'Half an hour,'
Leocadius said. 'Maybe less.'

'Right,' Ezekiel nodded, and he was gone, making his way through the gathering throng, slapping
backs and helping with loads. Children were crying.
Old men were praying, facing the broken bricks of
their sewer homes and nodding fervently. Rebekah
slipped away too. 'I must help them,' she said.

Leocadius wandered the courtyard, trying to take
all this in. A tribe lived here, as lost as any the Ancients
wrote about. Their skin was pallid, their eyes frightened. Then he came face to face with a little mob of

men, sickles and pitchforks in their hands. And in the centre of them, a face he knew. The eyes were darker and haunted, and a straggly beard had grown over the once clean-shaven chin.

'I know you,' he said in Latin.

No one moved. No one looked at him.

'You.' He prodded the man in the chest. 'Look at me. I am Leocadius Honorius.'

'What of it?' the man asked him.

Leocadius smiled. 'I've brought you a message,' he said. 'From Conchessa. From your wife. Hello, Calpurnius.'

Chapter Eighteen

Segontium

The cornices brayed out in the morning and Vitalis woke to the sound of running feet. He knew that sound all too well. The fort was coming under attack. He hauled on his tunic and grabbed his helmet and sword, clattering up the steps from his quarters in the Principia. On the ramparts, the II Augusta stood to their arms, a line of shields and spears inside the sharpened stakes of the palisades; grim-faced men who had been waiting for this moment for weeks.

Vitalis squinted against the early rays of the September sun and watched the line of the enemy stretching as far as he could see. For days in the Principia there had been endless speculation about these men. How many were there? Were they the Painted Ones? The Hiberni? The Attacotti? All three? Vitalis did not know their banners lifting in the morning breeze, but the red hand in the centre caught his eye. He knew legionary standards with the same device fashioned in bronze; the raised hand that said 'Stop! You will go no further.'

A rattling sound rose from the enemy lines, swords and axes battering on wicker shields. It got louder, like thunder from the north. And the lightning would follow. One by one the large warriors along the front began to place stones in a pile, so that slowly a cairn rose up.

'It's how they count their dead.' Clodius Vettens was at Vitalis' side. He looked pale and nervous but he was wearing his armour and the insignia of a fort commander.

'I don't understand,' Vitalis said.

'Each warrior leaves a stone. When the fight is over, he returns for it. If he doesn't return, he is dead. It's simple arithmetic, really.'

'Those banners.' Vitalis pointed to them. 'What are they? Tribal units?'

'God knows,' the commander said. 'Some magic nonsense, I suppose.'

A solitary swordsman walked out from the lines and rammed a spear into the ground. 'I am Colla Mor of the Eriu,' he shouted. 'My children and I have sharpened their weapons on the Column of Combat. We outnumber you five to one.' He waited as silence drifted across the vallum.

'What's he talking about?' Vitalis asked the older man.

Vettens shrugged. 'Damned if I know,' he said. 'They're the Hiberni, from the land of eternal winter.

They worship stones and sleep with sheep, that's all I know about them.'

'Five to one,' Colla Mor went on in his own language. 'And that's before we call upon our friends.'

He raised his right arm and there was a roar to his left. Out of the trees, still dark in the morning light, mounted warriors whooped and yelled, their spear points like flames in the forest. Their hair was stiff with lime and their bodies slashed and spiralled with blue.

'The Painted Ones,' Vitalis nodded grimly. There must have been as many of them as Colla Mor's Hiberni and they were whipping themselves into a frenzy for the fight.

'You've faced them before?' Vettens asked.

Vitalis nodded.

'Well,' the commander sighed. 'You won't have to face them today. White flag, signifer.' He waved to the standard bearer on the ramparts below him.

'White flag?' Vitalis spun to him. 'Why? What are you doing?'

Vettens blinked at the man, his bluff called. 'I told you,' he said. 'Following orders. In the event of an attack, the Caesar told me to fall back, abandon the fort. What part of fall back didn't you understand?'

The white flag was lifted high by the standard bearer, his helmet wrapped in the wolfskin of his rank.

'No,' Vitalis screamed at him. 'Raise the vexillum of the II.'

The man dithered, confused now and unsure of what to do.

'Damn you, sir,' Vettens snapped at Vitalis. 'Keep your nose out of this. Primus pilus,' and he turned to the senior centurion at his elbow. 'You will take the white flag out to these people. Somebody in the camp must be able to make himself understood. Arrange safe conduct for us. All baggage, cattle, sheep, arms to be left behind.'

'Sir,' Vitalis grated. 'Even if you can negotiate with this man, do you think he will honour his word? And what will we do without our weapons, like whipped children?'

'Primus pilus …' Vettens began, but Vitalis cut him short.

'Primus pilus,' he said softly. 'The commander is the commander no longer. Clodius Vettens, by order of His Serene Highness the Emperor Gratian, I am removing you from command of Segontium. You will give me your sword.'

For a moment, Clodius Vettens gnawed his lip. That a mere tribune and a boy at that, should humiliate him in this way! But then, Clodius Vettens was beyond humiliation. His shoulders slumped and he slid his spatha from its scabbard. For the briefest of seconds he held the point towards the tribune's chest, then he relented, reversed it and Vitalis took the hilt. He saluted the ex-commander with the sword and tossed it to the centurion. 'Primus pilus,' he said, 'you will place the commander in the Principia. Under close arrest.'

'Sir.' The man clicked to attention.

'You!' Vitalis yelled down to the signifer who was still holding the white flag of truce aloft. 'The next time I see that rag I expect to see you wiping your arse with it. Now, raise the vexillum of the II Augusta!'

As the scarlet and gold flag came up a roar burst from the ramparts around Vitalis. But the tribune was already watching a tired, defeated old man crossing the courtyard below him on his way to house arrest. Clodius Vettens needed a drink. And Vitalis Celatius, the Christian who had not killed a man for years, looked out over the windswept vallum to face demons of his own.

Augusta Treverorum

The passageway was full of the sound of running feet and the torches of the Schola Palatina threw their fierce shafts over wet brickwork. They weren't far behind now but Marcus Cotta's men had no room in those endless tunnels to use their shields. Leocadius at least was grateful for that. He hung back with Ezekiel, forming a rearguard to give the women and children time to get to the hatches that led to the upper world.

Shrieks and screams echoing and re-echoing in the darkness told the Jews that some of them had been found. They had taken a wrong turning, one that led to a brick wall, or worse, right into the path of the pursuing soldiery. And these men were not soldiers tonight. They were murderers, slaughtering the innocent wherever they found them. Men, women, children, it didn't matter.

'Where are the others?' a circitor demanded to know of a little boy. Your father? Your mother? Where are they?'

Nothing. Silence and sullenness. The circitor had no time to waste. He brought his blade down once and kicked the child's body aside. As he turned a corner, he felt his feet whipped from under him and a strong grip held him fast. He felt his head rammed again and again into crumbling brickwork until he passed out and knew no more. He didn't feel Leocadius snatch the sword from his hand; nor did he feel Leocadius draw the blade across his throat so that his blood ran mingling with the little Jewish boy's.

Leocadius leapt over the man's body and clawed his way up the steps where he had seen Ezekiel moments before. With them was Calpurnius and Leocadius had no intention of losing him again. Conchessa would never forgive him. He glanced down to see the torchlight flashing on the Roman helmets and he dodged into darkness. The killing went on.

A cold rain was driving across Augusta, the capital of the Treveri, as dawn broke. There would be no sun today, just a leaden sky shedding its tears for the dead.

Septimus Pontus had spent the last hour in that freezing rain, the water soaking into his cloak and hood. Marcus Cotta had been very thorough. His men had personally despatched seventy eight of the vermin that infested the city's sewers. He had lost sixteen of his company, including a promising circitor whose loss would be felt. His clerk had written all the details down and Pontus would pass it to the Emperor. All in all a good night's work.

'You've closed down their tunnels?' Gratian was up early, his breakfast spread before him.

'All but the cistern channels,' Pontus told him. Cold and wet as he was, he had not been asked to join the Emperor at his table and he stood there, dripping.

'So,' Gratian savoured his wine with greater relish than usual. 'We've cleansed Augusta of this filth.'

'I cannot be entirely sure of that, Sire,' Pontus told him.

The Emperor leaned back, looking the man in the face. 'Pontus,' he said. 'You are my chief decurion; some would say my right hand man. But make no mistake. If I find any Jew in this city who is not already a slave, you will be removed. Do I make myself clear?'

'You do, Sire.'

'I couldn't tell you.' Calpurnius sat on Conchessa's bed. 'I didn't even know you were here until …'

'…Until Rebekah told you about me,' Conchessa nodded. When, an hour or two ago on a night that shed rain and blood, she had seen her husband's face for the first time after so long, she had thrown her arms around his neck and cried. He had cried too. For all that had been and might have been.

Conchessa's heart was in a turmoil. Leocadius, brave, impetuous Leocadius, had done what he said he would do. He had found Calpurnius Succatus, the decurion who had vanished like a ghost from the streets of Augusta, the man who, Conchessa had feared from the outset, was dead. And Rebekah, the slave girl who had said she did not know where she had come from or where she belonged … Rebekah had come from that strange city beneath the city where the rats and the killers of Christ lived out their pitiful existence. Had the girl known about Calpurnius from the beginning? She had clearly told him about Conchessa. Why hadn't she returned the favour and told her about Calpurnius?

'What happened?' Conchessa's voice was harder than he remembered. He looked at her. It had been two years since they had last met. Were her eyes always that cold? The months of his hiding had taken its toll and he was no longer the confident courtier he had once been. 'What happened at Carthago?'

He sighed. He had to face the truth now. He owed his Conchessa that much. 'Carthago was a long time ago,' he said. Her eyes flashed fire. Was he still, even now, lying to her? 'We had our hands in the coffer chests,' he said, unable to look her in the face. 'Pontus and I.'

'Pontus?'

He looked up. 'Yes. Do you know him?'

She nodded. 'I know him,' she said.

'Oh, it's expected, of course, to an extent,' Calpurnius went on, too far gone in his confession to change course now. 'Everybody from chief decurion to litter-bearer helps himself here and there. But Pontus and I were falsifying accounts, claiming for troops where there were no troops. Theodosius found out.'

'Count Theodosius?'

Calpurnius nodded. 'You met him,' he reminded her.

'I did. Before we were married. I liked him.'

Calpurnius closed his eyes. 'Everybody did,' he said. 'And rightly. *There* was a man to occupy Gratian's throne. Had an honest streak a mile wide did old Theodosius. So, Pontus went to Gratian. Told him that the Count was fleecing him. Gratian doesn't care about the solidi, but he does care about loyalty. To him, a traitor is the worst form of life on God's earth.'

'What did Theodosius say?'

'Nothing.' Calpurnius poured himself another wine. It had been a long time since he had savoured the good stuff. 'What's fine, what's Roman,' he said. 'Theodosius would no sooner betray a colleague than he'd cut off his own right arm. That's what Pontus was counting on. Gratian dispensed with the niceties of a trial, playing right into Pontus' hands of course. Theodosius was executed; his Master of Horse with him. I've never seen men die more bravely.'

'What did you do?' she was almost afraid to ask.

'You mean what *should* I have done?' Calpurnius got up and wandered the room, drinking in the daylight through the window. 'I *should* have gone to the Emperor and confessed my sins. I should have turned in Pontus and I should have saved Theodosius' life.' He paused. 'What *did* I do? I ran. Pontus saw me as a weak link, a conspirator he couldn't trust. If he could bring down a man like Theodosius, he'd squash me like a fly. The young Theodosius ran too, before the Emperor banished him. Went east, we heard, to Constantinople.'

'And you came here?'

Calpurnius managed a bitter laugh. 'Out of the frying pan into the fire, eh? I didn't know the court was to move to this very city. I was going to contact you, sort it all out ... sort *us* out, if that was possible. Then Gratian's outriders arrived at the Porta Nigra and I ... I hid.'

'In the sewers.'

'In the sewers,' he said softly, 'with the outlawed and the dispossessed, like the rat I am.' He looked at her, into the eyes that were still cold but now glistened with tears. 'What now?' Calpurnius asked. 'What happens now?'

She had not been drinking but she took the ewer and refilled his cup. 'There is still, I take it, a price on your head?'

'Of sorts,' he said.

'Then we'll have to get you out of the city. No one knows you were in those tunnels, not for certain. We'll go west – to Britannia.'

'We?' His sad face lifted.

She held up a hand. 'You are my husband,' she said. 'I took vows before you and before God. But there is something I must do first.'

For a moment he reached out to her. He wanted to hold her close, to kiss away her tears and his. He wanted to make it all right. But he couldn't, because she had gone.

In the passageway at the top of the house, Leocadius was still nursing the bruised cheek he'd got from his run-in in the taverna.

'Pontus?' He raised an eyebrow.

'You were listening!' she snapped.

'Forgive me, lady,' he smiled. 'I don't usually eavesdrop, but these are extraordinary times.' He hauled up the heavy spatha he had taken from the dead circitor in the sewers. 'If you want the man dead,' he said levelly, 'you only have to say the word.'

Her look of horror said it all.

'It's what I do, Conchessa,' he said. 'I am a Wall soldier.' And he held up the glittering ring of gold and ebony, the one that old Theodosius had given him so long ago. 'Besides, the Count and I went way back. I owe him this.'

She reached out and patted the ring and the hand that wore it. 'So do I,' she said.

Segontium

The sun was high by the time the chanting stopped. It was designed, of course, like all war chants, to demoralize the enemy, to rattle the Romans already overawed by the sheer numbers. The II Augusta had cut its teeth under the blessed Vespasian to the south of Britannia when they had come ashore under the general who would become an emperor, trailed by the fleet off the coast. Whole forts had fallen to him but the II could hold fortresses as well as take them. Vitalis walked the ramparts. He could see at a glance that he had six ballistae in place, the hand-shooters that sent heavy, iron-tipped bolts that could skewer three men standing one behind the other in tight battle formation. And he had four wild asses, the onagers that tossed rocks high into the air to smash attacking lines and shatter skulls as they came down, obeying the power that brought them to earth.

The chanting had stopped but now an unearthly scream rose from the throats of the enemy and the whole line moved forward. At first they came on like Romans, in formation and at a steady pace. Then the usual battle-frenzy took over and the units became a wild, screaming rabble, each man, Hibernus, Pictus, Attacottus, racing to be the first one to reach the ramparts; to be the first one to die.

'At one hundred and eighty paces, primus pilus,' Vitalis' right hand was in the air. The arrows began to hiss from the charging lines, in ones and twos at first, then by the hundred, so thick it snowed wood and iron. Most of them fell short, thudding into the broad grass of the vallum or bouncing off the upright palisades, too spent to bite home.

Vitalis looked along his line. Grim faces in profile watched the assault rolling forward, like a mist from the sea, with wave after wave behind that. Hadn't it always been this way? A thin line of the She-Wolf's sons standing against the world, facing death; facing glory.

'Now!' Vitalis' hand came down and the ballistae bucked and kicked, the bolts hissing deadly across the vallum to thud into the Hiberni. The impact blew them backwards, punching irregular holes in their lines. Then the rocks hurtled high against the autumn clouds, to smash down through heads and shoulders and backs. The lines wavered. Colla Mor's men had fought Romans before and they had taken stone raths without number at home in the lands of winter. But a *Roman* fort, manned with Roman missiles? That was different.

'Reload!' Vitalis yelled and the gunners hauled on the creaking ropes and groaning frames, lifting rocks into the cradles and steadying their machinery.

The Hiberni line had all but stopped now but the Painted Ones were coming from their left. They had abandoned their tough, short-legged horses, those wild men from the far north, because, like the Romans, they fought best on foot. Their lithe bodies flashed blue as they dashed across the vallum, leaping over the Hiberni dead and screaming their battle cries.

'Archers of the II!' Vitalis swung his arm in the time-honoured order to his bowmen. A line of heads appeared over the stockade spikes and a hundred arrows hissed deadly, thudding into the naked blue bodies and bringing them down. The artillery opened up again, the rocks crashing into the wavering, surging mob. And the archers fired again, angling their shots downward now and pinning the floundering Picti to the earth that was not theirs, but would become their burial ground for all that.

Then they broke, the green banners of the Hiberni pulling back to the safety of the forest and the Painted Ones dancing away, hurling insults and waggling their arses at the men in the camp. Cheers rose from the palisades and helmets were thrown in the air here and there.

'Stand fast!' Vitalis bellowed to his men. 'That was just the gustatio, gentlemen. The cena has yet to begin.'

Cornovii Territory

The rains had washed away the roads on the bleak moors south of the Wall and no one in the vexillation of Justinus Coelius felt like singing. To a man they were wet through, exhausted by the punishing pace the commander of the Wall kept up and they were close to mutiny. These men were auxiliaries and cohorts of the VI Victrix, but they were Wall soldiers and most of them had served there all their lives. Now they were going south-west into alien country without so much as a star to guide them.

Justinus rode back along the cursing, trudging line, the mud slimy up to his horse's flanks and his own boots heavy with the brown, cloying stuff. He splashed past his sullen infantry, past his wild asses to reach the cavalry of his rearguard.

'Still there, I see,' he nodded to the centurion in command.

'They are, sir,' he grunted, 'and I'm getting a crick in my neck watching them.'

'Only two?' Justinus asked.

'We've seen no more. And they always keep back, just out of bowshot. I can't make out their faces in this bloody rain.'

Justinus looked back along his marching column. What was left of the road curved west through a stand of trees, dark conifers hugging the hillside. 'Give me two of your best men, Sextilius. I want them with me now.'

The centurion barked his order and the two cavalrymen rode ahead in the wake of the commander. For a while they took their places among the horsemen that led the column, then all three men fell by the wayside, one by one, to hide in the darkness of the trees.

For three days now the two horsemen had been following Justinus' column, like ghost soldiers wandering the moors. They weren't Saxons, Justinus was sure of that. If they were volunteers, looking for action, why didn't they come forward? Within reason, such men would be welcome. As the pair reached the woods they were wary. The last of the column was almost out of sight now in the driving rain. They peered into the darkness of the trees. If there was ever a perfect place for an ambush, this was it.

Suddenly, Sextilius' best horsemen crashed out onto the road, shields raised, spears at the ready. The pair hauled their reins and tried to turn but when they did, all they faced was another rider; Justinus Coelius, commander of the Wall.

'Taran. Edirne,' Justinus smiled. 'The least you can do when you meet an old friend on the road, is to say hello.'

Augusta Treverorum

Septimus Pontus stretched and yawned. It was the end of another long day in the service of his Emperor and he was tired. Only Gratian seemed pleased that the Jews had gone. No one else seemed to notice. The Chosen People had lived like moles for so long that no one missed them above ground.

He closed his eyes and let his head fall back on the pillows. There was a sound to his left, soft, subtle, like the whisper of linen. Septimus Pontus never slept far from his dagger. After all, this was Gratian's Augusta and no one felt truly safe. 'Most people come announced,' he murmured. 'By the front door.'

'I didn't think you'd want this visit made public,' a soft voice answered him.

He sat bolt upright. 'Conchessa?' he said. 'It's very late.'

'Am I not welcome?' she swept noiselessly into his chamber, her silken cloak trailing the ground.

'Always,' he smiled. He got up and took her hand, kissing it before he removed her cloak.

'I have found Calpurnius,' she said.

Few men could second guess Septimus Pontus. His face, they said, was as immoveable as the Tarpeian Rock in Rome. But tonight his jaw dropped just a little as he took in the news. 'Is he ... well?' he asked, pouring wine for them both.

'In his body, yes,' she told him. 'But his heart ... well, we shall see.'

'Where did you find him?' Pontus asked as if Conchessa had left him somewhere, like a discarded piece of jewellery.

'Hiding in the sewers,' she said.

'With the Jews?' he frowned.

'He seemed to have an affinity with them. Outcasts all.'

'Right here in Augusta,' Pontus mused, smiling. 'Ironic, that.'

She sipped her wine. 'Isn't it?'

For a long moment they looked at each other. Then she put her cup down.

'Did you come here to say goodbye?' he asked her.

'Yes,' she told him. Then she drew a knife from the folds of her dress and threw it down on the bed.

'You came here to kill me,' he almost whispered.

Her face was a mask of pain. 'Pontus, I'm not very good at this. Calpurnius says it was you. You who stole from Gratian and poisoned his mind against Theodosius. You who wanted Calpurnius dead because he knew the truth.'

Pontus' face broke into a smile. 'I can debate truth all night with you, lady,' he said. 'It wouldn't get us anywhere.'

'Is it true?' she persisted, 'what Calpurnius says. Is it true?' Her eyes burned fiercely through a mist of tears.

'If you have to ask that …' he said. He snatched up the knife, sliding it free from its sheath. Then he reversed the blade, holding the hilt towards her. 'Yes,' he said sharply. 'It's true. All of it. I betrayed the emperor, Theodosius, everything I am supposed to hold most dear. So did Calpurnius. We both have to live with that; with men's blood on our consciences. Calpurnius must find that harder to do than I. So why don't you finish the job, Conchessa? It only takes one thrust. Here,' he pointed to his throat. 'Or here.' He pointed to his heart. 'I won't try to stop you.'

The hilt jutted inches from her hand and she trembled, the tears trickling down her cheeks. She shook her head slowly. 'I can't,' she mumbled. 'I can't.'

'Why not?' he asked her, bending his head to hers.

'Because ...' she blinked back the tears, 'because I have fallen in love with you.'

The granite face of Septimus Pontus cracked again. How many women had he had, from consul's wives to street whores and slaves? And how many of them had ever said that? 'And I with you,' he said and brushed the long hair from her face. Gently, as if she might break, he kissed the wet cheek. Then he threw the knife away and folded her in his arms, feeling her body jerk convulsively as she cried, all the fears and sorrows of the years flowing from her like the waters of the Mosella that ran below the shuttered windows.

He let his fingers wander over her shoulders, releasing the gold clasps that held her gown in place. It fell noiselessly to the floor and he moved his lips into the curve of her neck. She was warm and responsive as her tears dried and his hands roved over her breasts in the candlelight.

'Pontus,' she said. 'I must be with my husband.'

'Of course,' he said. 'Of course you must. But not tonight. Tonight,' he trailed his right hand down the contours of her body, 'belongs to us.'

Chapter Nineteen

Segontium

Colla Mor had tested Segontium's defences and had counted the number of Clodius Vettens' ballistae with the bodies of his men. Time was not on his side. He could march on beyond the fort and raid the villages to the south before attacking Eudaf's stronghold at Caer Llyn. But if he did that, he would always have Segontium at his back, a spear-point held permanently between his shoulder blades. The weather, too, was closing in and some of his Eriu were getting restless. The harvest was done but winter was coming on and the great fogs would roll into the estuaries and the land the Romans call Hibernia would be lost to view, perhaps for ever. There was grain here, sheep and cattle to eat and horses to race. Ale was plentiful and women too. But for some of Colla Mor's men, *any* women would not do. They had wives at home and children. And the nights were long.

The Eriu streamed past the fort, east and west and encircled it. Vitalis ordered his camp marshal make an inventory – ballistae, shot, wine, salt, grain. The fort had been built on a water-course, dammed and channelled by Roman ingenuity so the well was bottomless and Vitalis had no worries on that score. His casualties were light but he had no idea where Magnus Maximus was and Clodius Vettens was no help. Most days the old man drank to forget and by nightfall had forgotten almost everything.

Elen's scouts watched all this with misgivings. Their princess-general had told them that the Romans were supposed to fall back, surrender the fort if necessary and open their gates to the barbarians. But that hadn't happened and they rode back to report.

She sent other riders out, on fresh mountain ponies from Caer Llyn. They galloped north east towards Deva and found the Caesar in his marching camp to the south of it, waiting for their news.

'He did *what?*' Maximus was on his feet in his Principia, staring down Elen's scout who had the misfortune to be able to speak Latin.

'He's sitting there, Caesar,' the man muttered, 'holding on.'

'And the Hibernii? The Picti?'

'Sitting with him,' the scout said. 'Perhaps for the winter.'

Maximus sent his wine goblet and its ewer hurtling across the room. He was a good judge of men. And he hadn't had Clodius Vettens down for a stubborn idiot. The man was a drunk, at the end of his career. What was he hoping to achieve by this show of guts? There was a time to stand like an ox in the furrow and die with the eagles. And a place. This was neither the time nor the place.

'Shit!' He whirled around the room. 'I'll nail the old bastard's skin to his own palisade. Right.' He flashed a glowering glance at the scout. 'Tell your princess,' he said, 'I am not waiting for reinforcements. I'm marching on Segontium. If I can't choose my own battlefield to face these bastards down, so be it. I'll do it on theirs.'

Cornovii Territory, Flavia Caesariensis

'So you came looking for me?' Justinus sat before the fire's glow. His message to Maximus had told him that speed was essential, so he broke with convention and did not build a makeshift camp every night. Instead, his men camped in the open with mounted pickets keeping watch under the stars.

Edirne nodded, chewing the lamb-bone on the commander's left.

'No,' said Taran. 'We came looking for our mother.'

Justinus was afraid of that. He looked at the boy who was a boy no more. Taran had just passed his seventeenth summer. His back was broad, his face already etched with the chiselled features of a man. And he was Lord of the Votadini, prince of the Gododdin. It was the way of it, the young bucks rutting and locking horns with the old stags.

'You've travelled the Wall,' Taran said to Justinus. 'Has there been no word?'

'Whispers,' the Wall commander told him. 'Nothing more. I've sent scouts, made enquiries. There was a woman north of Vindolanda. Her mind had gone.'

'And?'

Justinus shook his head. 'I went to see her myself. It was not Brenna. Not your mother.'

Edirne blinked. He had lived as an orphan now for two years and he wasn't expecting much by way of news. It was Taran, in his own way, who had never given up; who would never give up.

'So old Flavius let you go, then?' Justinus nudged the younger boy, trying to lighten the moment.

'He said I should keep my Latin up,' Edirne grunted.

Justinus laughed. 'Yes, he would.'

'What would it take?' Taran wasn't laughing. He was looking the Wall commander in the face. 'What would it take to hire your army?'

'My army?' Justinus stirred the fire's embers with a stick and it crackled and spat, sparks hurtling up into the gathered night. 'Look around you, boy,' he waved to the bivouac, black against the purple. 'What you see is what you get.'

'You've got half a legion.' Taran could count too.

Justinus smiled. Old Flavius had taught these boys to be soldiers, to ride and fight with sword, spear and shield. Tactics were another matter; strategy a world beyond that. 'And what do you want me to do?' he asked the boy, 'with my half a legion?'

Taran's face had not changed in the last half an hour. 'I want you to take Din Paladyr,' he said. 'Help me get my throne back.'

'*Your* throne?' Justinus queried.

'She's dead, Justinus,' Taran said. This was the first time he had said it. Even when little Eddi snuggled in to him in his narrow bed at Eboracum, crying for his mother in the early days, he hadn't said it. Taran would never give up; but that meant never giving up his quest for justice. For his mother, it was too late. The Lord of the Votadini leaned forward. 'I want to feel my blade slicing through Malwyn's throat,' he said, sending a chill up Justinus' spine. 'And that Saesen shit he teamed up with.'

Justinus nodded. 'Half a legion against Din Paladyr,' he said. 'You might as well piss into the wind.'

'You won't help?' A muscle twitched in Taran's jaw. The boy who had become a man had an unreasonable streak. And he was as stubborn as his mother.

'No.' Justinus raised his head. 'Not until this current little business is over. The Caesar has asked for my help, for my half a legion. When that's over, we'll see.'

Taran was on his feet, staring down at the Wall commander. 'And I thought my mother meant something to you,' he growled.

Justinus stood up with him. He was still an inch or two taller than the boy. 'She does,' he said, 'but the Caesar means more.'

'Duty!' Taran barked. 'Is it *so* important?'

'Yes,' Justinus told him. 'It is.'

Eddi scrambled to his feet and the boys marched away from the fire.

'Where are you going?' Justinus called after them.

'Anywhere!' Taran shouted. 'Away from the smell of Rome.'

Justinus sat back down. 'I should stick around if I were you,' he said. 'In a few days, unless I miss my guess, you'll see a full-blown Roman army in action. You might pick up a few tips for when we take Din Paladyr.'

Augusta Treverorum

They thought it best to wait until night fell. The Emperor seemed pleased with the clearing of the city's tunnels, but Calpurnius knew – they all knew – that there was still a price on his head. And Pontus had been right; disloyalty was not something that Gratian could forgive.

The slave girl Rebekah had not come back. Where the Jews had gone, and nowhere was truly safe for them, the girl with the raven hair and the smoulder-ing eyes had gone and Conchessa had lost her invest-ment. Adelina and Leocadius had loaded the pack animals with whatever they could carry and they led them out under the frosted stars, clattering along the cobbles until they reached the massive black bulk of the Porta Nigra where the flames of the night watch guttered and the studs of the calligae rattled on the stones.

Calpurnius had never been to Britannia before and the stories the others told him didn't exactly fill him with enchantment. But whatever it held, Britannia was a new chance, a new life; and realistically speaking, how many more new chances could the man expect? He was lucky to escape with his life from Carthago. And now, again, from Augusta. Surely, now, his God would have mercy on him?

There was a sudden commotion beyond the bridge. Dogs were barking and a knot of horsemen were galloping for the wooden planks, cloaks flying in the night. The watch jumped to attention, trumpets braying and men clicking into position. Calpurnius' little party had just reached the bastion when the lathered horses were reined in below the parapet.

'On the Emperor's business,' the first rider called. He threw something gold and glittering to the circitor of the watch and the man thumped his chest and threw his arm forward in salute. The horsemen rode on, their hooves thundering on the bridge. Then they were gone, clattering up the cobbled streets that led to the basilica.

'Papers!' the circitor turned to Calpurnius.

'Lady,' he bowed to Conchessa. Tonight Calpurnius Succatus, decurion, once a right hand man of the Emperor, was a humble slave. Conchessa handed the necessary documents to the sentry who looked at her. A lady, certainly, with two slaves and what appeared to be a servant, perhaps a freedman, an insolent shit who didn't avert his gaze.

'On your way,' he barked and the party moved off over the bridge.

'Mother of God!' Calpurnius hissed when they had crossed the Mosella, winding dark and deep below them.

'Jupiter Highest and Best!' Leocadius echoed, sharing his companion's thoughts.

Adelina had no idea what was going on, but Conchessa did. She half-turned to Calpurnius. 'Wasn't that …?'

'The younger Theodosius,' he nodded.

'I knew him in Britannia,' Leocadius muttered. 'Pompous little shit, I thought.'

'You thought right,' Calpurnius agreed, 'but if he's here, that means that Gratian wants to kiss and make up. He needs him. He banished him from his court and now he's back.'

'By invitation?' Leocadius asked.

'Has to be.' Calpurnius slapped the ass's rump ahead of him. 'Do you see an army?'

They didn't. Just the darkness of the night stretching cold ahead.

'There's something in the wind,' the former decurion said. He knew Gratian and how his mind worked.

Leocadius smiled. 'Magnus Maximus,' he said. 'The Caesar.'

Caer Llyn

'What does the Egyptian say?' Elen asked him as they lay together in her private chambers that night.

He rolled over and teased the hair from her face. 'Since when do the Deceangli care about predictions from the East?'

'You care about them,' she said. 'And therefore, so do I. I'm not talking about my people.'

He smiled. 'She says the time is right.' He saw her eyes bright in the candlelight. 'She has seen a dragon in the West.'

'And Colla Mor?'

Magnus Maximus shook his head. 'I'm not talking about that,' he said. 'That's just a little local difficulty.' He stared into the darkness beyond the circles of light. 'I'm talking about Gratian.'

'I know you are,' she said, tracing the skin of his arm with her fingers. 'What kind of man is he?'

He looked at her, then he laughed. 'He's yesterday's man,' he said. 'Now,' he rolled over her and pinned her arms to the bed, 'the little local difficulty. If I told you I wanted you to stay here, to hold Caer Llyn, what would you say?'

She pulled his head down by the hair and whispered in his ear. He pushed himself up on his arms.

'Lady,' he said, 'I haven't heard words like that since I left Rome.'

'Well, then' she laughed her musical laugh, 'you have your answer.'

Deceangli Territory

The cornicines saluted each other across the purple of the heather. Ravens wheeled in the skies over the crags and the morning promised rain. Clouds were building into thunder heads as the two armies marched. From the north-east came the little column of the VI Victrix, defenders of the Wall, their commander riding at their head. Beside him, on sturdy little ponies, two boys wearing the golden torcs of princes of the Votadini kept to the high ground beneath the vexillum in its red and gold.

Across the valley from them, the cohorts of the XX Valeria Victrix, half a day's march from their legionary base at Deva, stood in full battle order, helmets buckled to their chins, shields at the rest, spears piercing the sky. At the head of the cavalry screen across their front, a large German with waist-length hair sat in his black bearskin watching the reinforcements come on.

As the trumpets sounded, the column from the north halted and three horsemen trotted out towards the lines of the XX. They all dismounted and crossed the heather to the waiting cavalry.

'All hail to the Caesar, Magnus Maximus,' their leader shouted.

'All power to him.' The German's Latin wasn't bad.

'Justinus Coelius, commander of the Wall,' he announced himself.

'Andragathius, Master of the Caesar's Horse,' and he swung out of the saddle before grasping Justinus with both hands. It was like being hugged by a bear. 'Your sons?' Andragathius nodded to the boys.

'My sons,' Justinus repeated.

Eddi's heart leapt. Ever since Justinus had picked him up, wounded and winded in that mock fight with Taran all that time ago, the boy had hero-worshipped him. He could barely remember Paternus, his real father, but he knew that he and Justinus had been friends, comrades-in-arms along the Wall and that was enough for him. Taran was less impressed.

'We are princes of the Votadini,' he told the German.

'Good for you,' Andragathius smiled. 'Welcome to … wherever the Hell we are, gentlemen.'

It was raining in the high country. The Deceangli did not march like Romans. They were a mob, a swarming army with their bows and spears slung on their shoulders and their shields dangling down their backs. Rain droplets stung like hail as they bounced off heads and hair was matted onto faces, grim in the dull, glinting light. There was one road here, the Roman one that ran from Deva to Segontium. Elsewhere the older sheep trails criss-crossed over the heather and the great grey-green crags stood as sentinels to Elen's army.

She had said her goodbyes to Eudaf who had watched her go with tears in his eyes. That she would survive he had no doubt; but him ...? Crossing his own chamber was agony these days and he couldn't stand for long without sticks. Again and again as winter threatened from the north he cursed his years. *He* should have been riding out against those bastard raiders. His people never crossed the Winter Sea to raid among the wild bastards who called themselves the Eriu; why should they come to him?

'They're jealous, Gransha Eudaf,' Elen had told him on the night before she had ridden out from Caer Llyn. 'They haven't got sheep like ours or horses like ours, or ...' she fluttered her eyelashes at him, 'girls like ours!'

'That's enough of that, my girl,' he scolded her, but his eyes were creased in smiles. He would always miss the son who lay under the heather on the hills west of Caer Llyn, but he couldn't wish for a finer general to lead his armies now.

The Deceangli had their dogs with them, loping over the slick, wet ground and snuffling in the sheep-cropped grass. Boys hoping to be men ran with the baggage wagons, loaded with grain, salt, flour and apples. Each one carried a knife at his belt. Each one was prepared to take a life or lose one. That was how it was and how it had always been. Cornovii, Ordovices, Eriu, Scotti, Picti, Romani – they had all been the enemies of the Deceangli since time began. It was how it was and how it had always been.

Elen rode with her cavalry, her hood thrown back so that all men could see her, her long hair plastered to her shoulders and her eyes clear and bright. She was riding west, to her destiny.

Magnus Maximus, the Caesar, was marching too, in parallel with the Deceangli but to their north. His was the typical formation that Rome had used for centuries. His scouts rode ahead, watching the crags and the places that had 'ambush' written all over them. The eagle of the II Augusta shone dully in the grey weather and the rain bounced off its silver wings. Maximus rode bareheaded today, his hands cold on the pommel of his saddle, his cavalry of the Heruli around him, bristling with weapons. Only their eyes showed above the cheekplates of their helmets and the rain dripped from their cloaks and boots.

Behind them, the infantry slogged, their feet slipping and sliding despite the studs of their calcei. Their baggage was behind them with the train because Maximus had no idea *exactly* where the enemy were. Spears wore grooves into shoulders but they could come to the upright in an instant and their deadly tips could be buried in a Scotti throat seconds after that. The Caesar allowed no singing this morning. Other than the steady thud of boots and hooves, the whinny of horses and the creak of artillery wheels, a strange silence hung over the army of Magnus Maximus. He had not wanted it like this. He had wanted Clodius Vettens to surrender Segontium so that the raiders would take it and stream ever further south, away from their ships, so that he, Maximus, could deal with them. Now that the insubordinate idiot had held on there, he had to strike fast, moving with the sea to his right, cutting the bastards off from their escape. Well, that was how war went; you couldn't plan it and you couldn't reason with it. A war just had to be fought.

The Caesar turned in his saddle to see his legion behind him. Somewhere beyond that fog, through the mountain passes, rode Andragathius and the XX Valeria. And, he hoped, Justinus Coelius and his reinforcements from the Wall.

Segontium

The insubordinate idiot stood on the ramparts of Segontium that morning as the rain lashed down. It was late in the year for barbarian raids; no man enjoyed pillage in weather like this. So today would probably be another day of watching and waiting.

Vitalis looked down into the yard where his men were going through their paces with clashes of sword on shield. Every now and then a circitor would snarl, a centurion would bring his gnarled stick down. 'Not like that, Aulus, you Greek's subligaculum' 'How long have you been in this bloody army?' 'I'll have you, Titus, you just wait.' 'Mithras save us!'

Vitalis smiled in spite of himself. His camp was surrounded by the Hibernii, a wild, inhospitable people not used to siege warfare and the strain was beginning to tell on his little command. So he kept them busy, march and counter march, wheel into line, battle order, skirmish order. Then he inspected their weapons. 'Your sword, please, pedes,' he would bark at a hapless soldier. 'I can't see my face in it,' as he checked the blade. 'Double pace around the walls; full pack.' He barely remembered old Flavius, Justinus' father, the hastiliarus of the VI, but he was starting to sound just like him.

Vitalis had sent messages out before the Hibernii tightened their circle. To the commander of the II Augusta at Deva. To Magnus Maximus, somewhere on the road in this bleak country that God had forgotten. To *anybody* who might take pity on a Roman command lost in a green sea of Hibernii. He needed reinforcements. And he needed them now.

There was a scream from the fringe of forest to his left and he walked the ramparts in that direction. Nervous guards gripped their spear shafts, sodden in the wet and squinted through the rain to see what was happening. A single horseman was cantering forward, a stolen bearskin cloak over his shoulders and his auburn hair shaking droplets as he rode. He swung his pony this way and that, yelling a challenge to the camp. His cries were blood curdling, all the more terrifying because no one understood him.

Vitalis looked at the faces of his men. Four or five times a day something like this happened. Some hot-head would ride or run out, shake his arse at the fort and curse them all. It was harmless in itself, but Vitalis knew it was taking its toll. For nearly a month now his command had endured these taunts, sometimes accompanied by the hissing sting of arrows, falling short into the grass of the vallum or biting into the uprights of the palisades.

'Permission to try a shot, sir?' an archer asked him. Vitalis looked at the boy. What was he? Seventeen? Eighteen? It had not been that long since the tribune had stood where he did, a boy standing guard on another wall, one at the edge of the world.

'And waste an arrow?' Vitalis raised an eyebrow at him. 'He's out of range, sagittarius.'

The lad knew that, but he had to do something. His face said it all, a turmoil of suppressed emotions that showed too in the white knuckles around his bow.

'How's your voice?' the tribune asked him.

'Sir?'

Vitalis turned to the courtyard below. 'Centurion!' he bellowed.

'Sir?' The man saluted.

'Break off. I want every man on this wall. Now.'

'Sir!' He spun to the soldiers in mid-practice. 'You heard that officer of the Schola Palatina. Double up, damn it!'

There was a thud and a clatter as men sheathed their swords and scrambled up the ladders. When they were all on the ramparts, looking ahead at the single Hiberni, still prancing on his horse, Vitalis shouted along the line, 'We have had a request from that gentleman,' he said. 'He loves our legionary songs. What's your favourite?'

Every man looked at the one next to him. One or two ragged voices broke out with tentative suggestions. The unfortunate pedes who called out 'Goodbye Mother' got a clip around his ear and the general roar went up, 'The Girl From Clusium'.

Vitalis smiled. 'Now, *there's* a surprise,' he said. 'Right, lads. Let's drown out that Hibernii shit, shall we? And, when it comes to the chorus, give it all you've got!'

The whole rampart burst into song, the ribald dog Latin hurtling over the vallum to the dark trees beyond. 'She's up. She's down. She's the best girl in town. She's the one who taught me to love. Is it kisses and flowers and romantic hours? No! It's Shove! Shove! Shove!' and the men nearest the palisade suited the action to the words.

Vitalis watched as the lone Hibernii reined in his horse. He heard the baritone rumble from the camp and his own shrieking trailed away. When he saw a hundred men thrusting their genitals at him, he turned tail and disappeared into the woods.

'Oh, dear,' Vitalis frowned. 'He didn't like it. Got anything else in your repertoire, lads?'

'Goodbye Mother,' a timid voice called out.

The lad was buried with cuffs and buffets and the laughter rang to the sea.

Chapter Twenty

Augusta Treverorum

The Emperor had dismissed his people and sat alone on the throne in the palace. Torches flickered on the walls, throwing lurid shadows on the stones – a face leered here, a gorgon grinned there, dragons coiled everywhere. He was wearing a simple tunic and no crown because he wanted to face Theodosius as a man, not as a living god.

Theodosius had not seen Gratian for four years. And the last time they had met, the Emperor had exiled the man from Carthago and told him he was lucky he still had his life. He had been on the road from the south for nearly three weeks, pushing his horsemen hard and catching sleep where he could. From Caesaraugustus they had taken the high country north of the meandering Iberus and made for the Montes Pyrenaei. Snow was already filling the mountain passes and the horses trudged up to their knees, Theodosius' fur-wrapped feet gliding over the silver-studded whiteness. Gallia Lugdunensis had been warmer, with its flat, treeless plains and its stunted olive groves and they had taken the Rhodanus on the cattle boats before mounting again in Gallia Belgica and galloping for Augusta.

'I wasn't sure you'd come,' Gratian left his throne, the loneliest seat in the world, and handed Theodosius a cup of wine. The man hesitated. Theodosius was half a head taller than his Emperor and his face wore a permanent mark of superiority, as though there were a perpetual smell under his nose.

'I wasn't sure I would either,' he said and took the cup.

So far, so good. Theodosius had travelled half way across Gratian's Western Empire to get here. And now he was accepting Gratian's hospitality.

'About your father ...' Gratian wasn't going to let the ghost of Count Theodosius haunt his every move from now on. His son held up his hand.

'Let it lie, Sire,' he said. 'You believed my father was a thief and a traitor.'

'I did,' Gratian nodded. 'I believe it still.'

'And you are wrong.' Theodosius looked the man squarely in the face.

A silence. Then, 'Can you live with that?' the Emperor asked.

Theodosius put his cup down on a table and sat, unbidden, on a couch. 'That all depends,' he said.

Gratian sat opposite him. 'On what?' he asked.

'On what you want,' came the reply. 'On what you're offering.'

'Who says I want anything?' Gratian was good at games like this. Men who stole other men's thrones had to be.

Theodosius was on his feet. He was no longer the underling, the snot-nosed kid hanging on his father's cloak. He looked down at Gratian. 'Thanks,' he said. 'I really enjoyed the exercise of freezing my arse off crossing those lands of yours. I'll send you my expenses.'

'Magnus Maximus,' Gratian said, scowling at the man's face.

'Ah.' Theodosius sat down again. The battle-elephant in the room had trumpeted at last.

'My best intelligence tells me his Britannic legions have elected him Caesar. He's gathering his troops and he's coming here.'

'For you?'

Gratian chuckled. 'We've already got two Emperors,' he said, 'at least in name. And two Caesars. There's no room for another.'

'It would be a little cluttered,' Theodosius sampled the wine for the first time. He'd tasted nothing so fine for months. 'Where do I come in?'

Gratian got up and paced the room. 'I've only met Maximus once, and I wasn't impressed, not on a personal level. But you know him – you fought alongside him in Britannia.'

'In Valentinus' rebellion, yes,' Theodosius nodded, 'although I didn't actually see much fighting personally.'

'What kind of man is he?'

'Ruthless,' Theodosius said. 'He'd slit his own grandmother's throat in exchange for power. It's like an elixir to some people,' he shot a sideways glance to Gratian, 'and of course, he's a natural-born killer. If it were Maximus standing before you rather than Theodosius, you'd be dead by now.'

Gratian took a swig of his wine. He was no coward; he'd proved that a hundred times, in battle with men and beasts. He tolerated no opposition and he took no prisoners; there were plenty of Jewish dead to testify to that. But there was something about Magnus Maximus, about the *legend* of Magnus Maximus, that chilled his blood. And he was starting to care less and less who knew that. 'They say,' he murmured, 'he has an Egyptian sorceress with him, a seer who can read men's minds.'

Theodosius chuckled. 'In Tarraconensis,' he said, 'I knew a man who talked to his goats.'

'So?'

'So, the goats talked back.'

Gratian found himself laughing in spite of himself. He knew that if Maximus crossed the German Sea and stood toe to toe with him, all would be well. But all he faced now was rumour and a growing monster writhing in the darkness of his nights.

'Prophecies and dreams,' Theodosius said. 'Rome has fretted about them for centuries. Time to give them up. I'm a Christian.'

'So am I!' Gratian was suddenly stung to think that this upstart courtier was likening him to some superstitious ancestor, rattling bones and not leaving his house on the Ides of March.

'Then your God will sustain you.' Theodosius spread his arms as if by way of explanation. 'As He will me. Magnus Maximus worships Mithras, the bull-killer. He prays to Jupiter they used to call highest and best before we knew better. Now, you tell me he's listening to sistrum rattles and breathing in the smoke of incense. Let him come, Gratian. The man's been in Britannia too long; it's addled his brain.'

Gratian sighed. It was strangely good to hear straight talking for a change. Pontus, Alfridius, all his cronies in Augusta sensed the Emperor's mood and followed accordingly. Arse-lickers all, they gave him no comfort.

'Is that it?' Theodosius asked. 'Is that what you wanted to hear?'

'I want to hear the *truth*!' Gratian snapped, suddenly afraid that Theodosius was here to trick him after all.

'The truth is,' Theodosius stood up, facing his Emperor, 'that Magnus Maximus, confused in his faith as he may be, is the best soldier in your Empire, West or East. He'll take some stopping.'

'Precisely,' Gratian looked into the man's eyes. '*That's* why you're here.'

'I?'

'Don't play the arena clown with me, Theodosius. You're no slouch in the field yourself and with your father's reputation ...'

'… which you destroyed.'

Gratian ignored him. 'With all that, I need you as a second sword. Perhaps Maximus will think twice if he knows you're with me.'

Theodosius put his cup down and crossed to Gratian's throne where the great gilded eagle spread its wings on the wall behind it. 'And what,' he asked, his back to Gratian, 'do I get in return?'

Another silence.

Theodosius half-turned.

'The Eastern Empire,' Gratian almost whispered.

Now Theodosius turned fully to the man. '*All* of it?'

'All of it,' Gratian nodded. 'From Mesopotamia to Dalmatia. You'll have it all.'

'And what about Valentinian?

'Who?' Gratian sipped his wine.

'Your half-brother.' Theodosius half-smiled.

'I repeat,' Gratian said, 'who? His bollocks haven't dropped yet and the army will follow whoever I give them.'

'What else?' Theodosius asked.

Gratian rounded on him. 'Good God, man. I've just given you half the Roman Empire on a plate. What more do you want?'

Theodosius moved closer, so that his face was almost touching Gratian's hairline. 'I want my father's reputation back,' he said. 'Intact. In a public ceremony. Right here in Augusta.' He moved away, sipping the wine again. 'And until that happens, I don't so much as draw my sword.'

Gratian's jaw flexed and he felt the nagging ache he got occasionally from the wound of the leopard. His first instinct was to fell this man on the spot, drive a dagger into his demanding guts and twist it before kicking him to the ground. But the rising spirit of Magnus Maximus would not let that happen.

'Do we have a deal?' Theodosius extended a hand.

Gratian caught it. 'We have a deal,' he said.

Londinium

It had taken Calpurnius, Conchessa, Leocadius and Adelina over four months to reach Londinium. The city along the Thamesis was, to be fair, wasn't home to any of them, but Leocadius enjoyed breathing in the smell of fish along the wharves again. Conchessa was glad to be safe at last and away from the pressures of Gratian's court. But Gratian's court meant Pontus and she found it hard to shake the memory of him. Especially now that she was carrying what she thought might be his child. Adelina, the all-noticing, had spotted it first. No other woman could miss the signs; the nausea, coming in waves not once, but many times a day; the tender breasts, that Conchessa cradled to give herself ease whenever she thought no one was looking; the swell of the belly and the glow in the eye and skin. And

Adelina could count backwards as well as anyone. Calpurnius, on the other hand, had not noticed as yet and would almost certainly, with manly hubris, assume that he was the father. But if he was the father of the baby in Conchessa's belly, it would be a miracle. But Christians believed in miracles and the bump that was as yet hardly a bump might be God's way of bringing Calpurnius and Conchessa together again, not just as husband and wife but as mother and father. Leocadius had kept away as much as possible when his children were still inconvenient swellings at the waist of his women; he wouldn't give Conchessa's game away, because he didn't understand the game, nor want to.

As Conchessa pondered what had been and what might still be, she thought of the brother she had not seen now for nearly six months. He had ridden north-west to find Magnus Maximus and no-one talked of Magnus Maximus in Londinium, unless it was worn-out mothers, whispering his name to terrify their fractious children into silence.

Calpurnius had his own peace to make, not to mention a living to earn. He bathed, shaved off his straggly beard and dressed appropriately to see the vicarius. His robes of office and the Imperial orders he had worn at Carthago had long gone, exchanged for food and shelter along the lost, lonely roads of an outlaw. So a new tunic and cloak was the best he could run to and even that was bought with almost the last of Conchessa's savings.

'Calpurnius Succatus,' Chrysanthos the vicarius was tucking into a chicken when the man arrived, tearing off a leg and throwing titbits to the cat.

'If this is a bad time, vicarius …'

'No, no. Wine?' Chrysanthos held out a cup.

'Thank you, no. I was hoping for a job.'

Chrysanthos gulped his own wine. 'I am used to decurions being a little more circumspect, a little more round-the-houses as they say here in Britannia.'

'Sorry, I … decurion?' Calpurnius frowned. 'You know who I am?'

'Of course.' Chrysanthos was wrestling with a particularly recalcitrant piece of chicken. 'I know everybody who crosses that portico. If I don't, they don't cross it.'

Calpurnius understood that. Gratian's court was just the same. Trust was just a word that nobody believed in. 'Well, then,' he said. 'You know …'

'That you were on Gratian's staff at Carthago, yes. With the late Count Theodosius and Septimus Pontus. Er … I assume he isn't late? Is he?'

'Not that I know of, vicarius, no.'

'No,' Chrysanthos murmured. 'Well, there it is. People like Pontus live forever. So, you want a job?'

'Forgive me, sir,' Calpurnius straightened. 'I was forgetting my manners. What I meant was, I wondered whether you had a position, a vacancy.'

'Hmm,' Chrysanthos wiped his mouth and fingers and a slave took the chicken carcase away. 'Forgetting your manners, yes. It's like that when you're on the run, I expect.'

'Sir, I …' Calpurnius frowned.

'You disappeared from Carthago after that wretched business involving the elder Theodosius,' the vicarius interrupted. 'Since then, only you know where you've been and what you've been doing. Can you give me a single reason why I should employ you?'

'Holy charity,' Calpurnius answered him.

Chrysanthos opened his eyes wide. 'Holy charity?' he repeated. Then he laughed. 'Well, you don't see too much of that these days.' He slid back his chair and walked to the basilica's windows, one of the large ones that looked out over the smoke of the city, the river grey in the morning and the mud flats of the south bank glistening wet after the ebb of the tide. He suddenly turned back to the supplicant in his hall. 'Half pay,' he said, 'on a month's trial.'

'Fair enough,' Calpurnius nodded.

Chrysanthos crossed to him. 'I'm going to give you every shitty job in the book, Calpurnius Succatus. *And* I'll be watching you. If I get so much as a whiff of the Carthago nonsense, you will, I fear, be history.'

All in all, it was more than Calpurnius could have hoped for.

Deceangli Territory

'Scotti,' Elen's second-in-command murmured. 'No doubt about it. Look there.' Morganwg pointed with his sword to where the enemy chieftains cantered their ponies along their line. 'The saffron tunics. They think the stuff kills lice.'

Elen shook her head. 'Morganwg,' she smiled. 'The breadth of your knowledge never ceases to amaze me. And does it?'

'Does it what?'

She looked across at him, easing herself in the saddle, suddenly doubting what she had just said. It was never wise to pay a man a compliment. 'Does saffron kill lice?'

'No,' he laughed, 'the Deceangli do. And we kill the Scotti they hide on, too!'

'That we do. Send a rider to Macsen Wledig. Tell him we've sighted Scotti a day's march west of Caer Llyn and we engaged them.'

'Shall we tell him we beat them, Elen Llwyddog?' he asked, winking.

'We're very chirpy this morning, Morganwg,' she said. 'Get lucky with a sheep last night?' It was her turn to wink. 'Get on with it!'

While Morganwg's messenger rode north east in search of the Caesar, Elen of the armies weighed up her options. The Scotti were drawn up on sloping ground ahead, a solid mass perhaps twenty deep, their spears piercing the leaden sky. It had rained in the night but the ground up here was relatively dry. At least there was no mud to slow her cavalry. And that was the best news. The Scotti, true to form, had some archers, a solid phalanx of spearmen and slingers whose shooting was legendary. But the only horses were those ridden by their chieftains. They were not natural horsemen like the Goidel from further south in their winter vastnesses and they fought better on foot.

Elen yelled at her leaders, the men whose great-great grandfathers had fought for Caratacus against Rome and they scattered into their formations, taking their people with them. Three hundred years of watching the Romans had taught the Deceangli well. They would never fight in tight, legionary formations, advancing in silence until the barritus roared out, deep and defiant. They would never sing the Girl from Clusium or any other ribald marching song the legions knew. But they knew how to fight barbarians who had never seen a real Roman army before.

The girl-general nudged her horse with her heels and trotted along her lines. The priests were standing in front of each unit, beating their drums and calling out their prayers. No Christian God and his carpenter son had come this far north, not into these mountains, and any missionary who had tried had been sent packing. So it was the old gods and the old prayers that floated over the field this morning.

There was a sudden barked shout from the valley floor and the whole Scotti line began to move. The men at the front, the chieftains from Ulaid with their bright plaids and their red hair, had dismounted and were jogging forward, shields across their chests, spears upright. The line was gaining speed, each man elbow to elbow with his comrade; each man watching the Deceangli formations immobile ahead of him.

The priests had finished their prayers now and a beautiful, haunting music rose from the whole of Elen's army. It was a slow dirge, mournful and sad, a requiem for all who were about to die. The Scotti could barely hear this for the noise they were making, their feet thudding over the hard ground, their wild banshee wails echoing and re-echoing off the mountains high to their left.

'Now!' Elen's voice shrilled over the singing and as one, each spearman dropped to one knee. From behind each phalanx, archers the Scotti hadn't seen until now, let fly with their arrows. The hiss of their flight was like a man's last breath and so it was for the front and second ranks of the Scotti who went down with iron barbs in the heads, necks or shoulders. Men behind leapt over the fallen or stumbled headlong before scrambling upright and running on. Then they stopped, as abruptly as they started and stood, shields square to the Deceangli, panting in their exertion. From nowhere, the slingers burrowed their way through the tight press of men and whirled their leather slings as one. The missiles hurtled through the air to splat onto shields and heads as Elen's spearmen rose to protect their archers.

'What in the name of ...?' Morganwg's face was awash with blood and a grey slime, dripping from his helmet rim and trickling into his mouth.

'Brains,' Elen said. 'It's what they do, those unnatural bastards. What's coming out of the sky now used to be our people. Archers!' She raised her voice and her hand. The shrillness of a moment ago had gone and the voice of Elen of the armies was as deep as any man's. 'I want those slinging bastards gone.'

Again, the infantry dropped. Again the archers let fly, their arrows thudding into the defenceless slingers who barely had time to reload. This time, those still standing were firing stones, sharp-edged pebbles that clattered into the Deceangli like hail. Men fell back, their shields peppered, their eyes gone, their faces a mask of blood, this time their own.

'I wondered when they'd stop being nice,' Morganwg grunted to Elen, but she had already wheeled her horse and was riding along her front line, waving her men to their feet. She whirled to the attack as the Scotti came on again, treading the dead and wounded slingers into the ground and breaking into a run. The earth, it seemed, shook with their charge. Their blood was up and there was no stopping them now. This was the army, their chieftains had told them, that broke before the Roman camp at Segontium. They had no stomach for a real fight and their leader was a girl. Well, they could fight over her later, draw lots to see who would have her legs around them up against which tree. But for now, they'd give her rabble a lesson they'd never forget.

Elen's raised arm came down again and the whole Deceangli line ran forward, chanting and screaming like the Scotti they faced. Except that the Scotti had just run half a mile and their lungs were tortured and their legs were like lead. As for the Deceangli, they had not yet begun to fight. And most of them had grannies they had to impress.

The smoke of their fires drifted up from the headland beyond the dunes, mingling with the mist that rolled in from the sea. The Scotti had come to stay. They had pillaged the villages along the water's edge, hacking and slaughtering, cutting off heads and chopping brains to fit their slings. The nets they had left because, like the Deceangli they had murdered, they fished for a living too.

Maximus' scouts reported back. They'd seen four villages with perhaps fifty men in each and twenty three ships drawn up on the white sand beaches. The Caesar had smiled at the news. 'Time for a picnic, gentlemen,' he said to his cohort commanders.

This time the artillery were left behind with the baggage. Maximus led his cavalry against the villages, trotting forward under their dragon banners, the Heruli who had never seen this wild country before but who would leave their mark on it nonetheless. Dawn was still creeping over the dunes when the infantry hit the beaches. They came on at a jogging pace, boots thudding on the dry sand and harness rattling. No one spoke. No one shouted. And the enemy were particularly dozy that morning.

'Romans!' A guard who had been fast asleep yelled in his native tongue, pointing horrified to where half a legion was running towards him. There were flaming brands in the hands of the front rank and they hurled these into the ships. The ropes caught fire first as the pitch brands hit home, the tongues of flame spreading over the decks and up the mast. Men leapt out of their beds on the planking and into the sea, gasping as the cold hit them. They grabbed spears, swords, axes, whatever came to hand but the first ship was already ablaze, sparks flying upwards and timbers cracking as it wallowed in the shallows.

The Scotti tried to form a defensive wall with their shields on the sand, but it was hopeless. Now the barritus went up, the bass roar of the II Augusta that those raiders had never heard before. That most of them would never hear again. The front line sent their spears as javelins hurtling through the air to thud into limewood shields and slice through flesh and bone. They drew their swords with one fluid, practiced movement and came on, not at the run now but at a steady pace, hacking against the flimsy Scotti line and driving them back. The broad Roman blades struck home, ripping through sinews and muscle. The heavy shields batted the dying men aside and the studded calicei came down to grind faces into the sand, wet here with the tide and the blood.

One by one the ships went up, sparks flying in the sea breeze from one deck to another. The timbers cracked and split as decks collapsed and the hulls buckled, the furled sails disintegrating and blowing in burning fragments out to sea.

It was all over in half an hour. Every single ship had gone and with it any realistic hope of the Scotti getting home. Bewildered, terrified men threw away their weapons and ran. Some ran along the shore where the razorbills and guillemots wheeled, looking down at them with contempt. Others ran inland, into the welcoming arms of Magnus Maximus' cavalry. A few, bleeding and in pain, made for the sea, thrashing uselessly in the grey, surging tide.

'It's a long swim back home, boys!' one of the infantry called after them and the archers of the II used them for target practice.

The scout lashed his horse over the heather, riding for the smoke. Villages were burning inland and the rout here, too, was complete. The Heruli were trotting backwards and forwards, swinging out of their saddles to make sure of their kills. These men were not the savages they had just beaten, but if they found a man with a human head tied to his belt or rammed onto a pole outside the hovel he had stolen, they hacked off his head too and kicked it into the nearest ditch.

'The praeses' compliments, Caesar,' the scout of the II saluted when he reined in in front of Maximus, still sitting his grey at the edge of a village. 'He reports all Scotti ships destroyed.'

'Excellent!' Maximus smiled. 'Casualties?'

'Well,' the scout looked grim-faced. 'Circitor Ostius burned his thumb rather badly, but he'll be all right.'

Londinium

He hadn't seen Lepidina for a long time, but in some ways it was as though they had never parted. She lay under him that autumn night as the wind howled along the Thamesis, rattling shutters in its fury. Neither of them heard that. All Leocadius heard was her ragged breathing in his ear, rising to a scream. All she heard was the grinding of his teeth. All she felt was his manhood thrusting into her and then it was all a blur. He grunted and then lay still as the ceiling and his curly hair swirled in her vision. He lifted himself up on his arms and smiled down at her.

She shook her head to clear her vision and smiled back. 'I've missed you,' she said, laughing.

'So I see,' and he laughed with her. 'How have you been, Lep?'

'Usually,' she raised her eyebrows, 'people ask that of old friends *before* they leap on them.'

Leo laughed again and pulled out of her, gently, rolling to one side. 'Think yourself flattered,' he said. 'I haven't met old Quintus yet. Sol Invictus knows what I'll do to him!'

Their laughter rose above the wind. Then, suddenly, she was serious. 'Leo,' she said. This was more like it. Lepidina had a body to die for and the stamina of an army mule, but when she wasn't in action in somebody's bed, she could whine with the best of them. Leo had missed her too, but he hadn't missed that whine. It usually came before a request for money. Rather a lot of money. 'What happened?' she asked, turning on her side and looking at him. 'To you, I mean.'

He didn't look at her but kept his eyes trained on the ceiling. 'Let's just say I needed a change,' he said.

'A different bed?' she asked him.

'Different bed. Different road. Different life,' he shrugged.

'And now you've come back.'

'The other man's grass isn't always greenest,' he said. It was his turn to face her. He ran an appreciative finger over her breasts, teasing her nipples to erection again. She giggled.

'What's the news of Honoria?' he asked.

Lepidina wasn't giggling now. She pulled away from him, sitting up, the bedclothes wrapped around her as though she was building a wall between her and her lover. This wasn't like her. Even when Leocadius was consul, living with Julia and sleeping with Honoria, he always had time for Lepidina. And Octavia, Melissa, Flavia, one or two others. 'I haven't seen her,' she said.

Leocadius sat up with her and pulled her face towards him. 'Lep,' he growled, cocking his head to one side. 'What is it you're not telling me?'

She gnawed her lip. For a moment he thought she might cry. Instead, she whined. 'Oh, Leo …'

'Tell me,' he insisted.

'We haven't seen her because she's a fine lady now. She's living with the vicarius.'

'Chrysanthos?'

Lepidina nodded. 'I see her sometimes, with the ladies of the Ordo. She travels everywhere in a litter, with slaves and servants.'

Leocadius nodded. Honoria had become Julia. The house of day and the house of night had blended to become one. 'What about Scip?' he asked.

'Your boy? I've only seen him once. He was riding with the vicarius, going on a hunt, I think.' She looked into his eyes and saw the hurt there. 'Forget all that, Leo,' she said, fondling his arm, stroking his hair. 'Different bed. Different road. Different life.'

'No,' he said softly. 'I was wrong. There's only one life and I've got to live it again.'

CHAPTER TWENTY-ONE

Deceangli Territory

The Scotti dead lay in heaps where they had battered themselves against the Deceangli. The Deceangli dead were buried in the large pits dug by their comrades and blessed by their priests. And the fires burned long into the night.

'You didn't get past my guards tonight,' Elen smiled. The Caesar had ridden openly into the camp and had been escorted all the way. She handed Maximus a cup of wine. He took it but saw she was wounded and put it down.

'You're hurt,' he said.

'It's nothing.' She turned away from him.

'It's everything,' he said and led her into the guttering candlelight under the tent's awning. The wind shook the leather walls and made the guy-ropes dance, but the light rain that had laced the evening had stopped and the priests could carry on their laments dry-shod. The gash on the girl's arm had been stitched and wrapped with butter under clean linen. Even so the blood had seeped through, staining the whiteness.

'I was wrong to leave you,' he said.

She pulled her arm away and passed him the wine again. 'I told you …' she began.

'Yes, I know.' He stopped her. 'You killed your first man when you were twelve.'

'And he was a Roman,' she reminded him. 'How did your men do today?'

'Like taking honeycomb from a baby,' Maximus said, sitting next to Elen on her couch. 'They sleep late, these Scotti; weren't expecting us. It'll be different tomorrow, I fancy.'

'You'll go on?'

'I will.' He sipped the wine, enjoying the warmth of her next to him. 'I won't bore you with the figures, but there are an awful lot of murderous bastards who won't be going home any time soon. Those who got away will have run west, to tell the others. They'll be waiting for us.'

'And you'll oblige them?'

'Yes, but not for a day, perhaps two. I need Andragathius to catch up with me. It'll be good to see Justinus again, assuming he's with him.'

'Ah, yes,' she smiled. 'Your hero of the Wall.'

'He's a good man,' Maximus laughed, unsure whether Elen was being serious or not with the admiration in her voice. 'Loyal. In fact, I'd go further. Justinus Coelius is the best soldier west of the Rhodanus. Except me, of course.'

She waited and when he said no more, jabbed a finger into his ribs. 'And me!' she shouted, laughing.

'Oh, of course,' he nodded wisely. 'Present company always excepted, of course!'

She pulled him nearer, by grabbing a handful of hair, something no man under the Caesar's command dare do. 'You're saying "of course" too often for my liking, Macsen Wledig,' she growled and they kissed in the candlelight, the wind in the night outside bidding its own plaintive farewell to the Deceangli dead.

Segontium

'There's something going on.' Vitalis was talking to his second-in-command. 'Look, there, beyond the trees.'

The view was only possible on a clear day and now that the sea mist had rolled back, the estuary sparkled clear, white caps, wind-driven, rolling east. The Hibernii, who had been camped in villages and bivouacs at the forest's edge, were formed up in a massive column, ready to march out.

'They're pulling up stakes,' the junior officer said. 'My god, they're going!' He whipped off his helmet and began to wave it, shouting and whooping.

'Stand fast, Severus!' Vitalis said, putting a warning hand out. 'How do we know it isn't a ploy? To draw us out into the open?'

'Oh.' The lad looked crestfallen. 'I hadn't thought of that,' he admitted.

'Don't worry,' Vitalis smiled at him. 'That's what they pay me for. Keep watch. And let me know if anything changes.'

Londinium

It seemed so long since he had seen it, his consular palace by the Thamesis. There stood Chrysanthos' guards at the gate, stamping on the ground and breathing on their hands to keep warm as their breath snaked out onto the night air. He had no intention of trading insults with them, still less offering awkward explanations. He swept past them, his cloak over his face just in case and he ducked into the dark alley alongside the wall. The ivy branches curled strong here, tracing the old pattern up the brickwork and plaster. They took his weight as they always did and he was at the top.

Behind him the river slid like a silver torrent under the full moon. He could have done without this light, but beggars cannot be choosers and tonight, he was very much the beggar. To be fair, he didn't look it. Leocadius had won a great deal of money with his dice over the last few days and if he was no longer consul of Londinium, he could certainly pass for one. Ahead, the garden lay bright in the moonlight. This was the house of the night, but the little door in the wall that separated it from the house of the day had gone and only a moonlit arch shed its light onto the lawn.

Leocadius hauled himself over the parapet and dropped silently to the stones below. He pressed his back against the wall, hugging the darkness for as long as he could. The night air was crisp indeed and he breathed softly so that no one should see the vapour in the half light.

Honoria's window was in darkness. In fact, the whole of this wing of the palace seemed dead and empty. Lights burned in the house of the day, beyond the wall and Leocadus ducked through the archway, brushing aside the dying grape vines that clustered there, the leaves yellow and brittle. He crept closer, like a thief in the night. He could see Chrysanthos, the vicarius, sitting at table with oil lamps, papers and quills around him. 'Poor bastard,' Leocadius murmured to himself. So it wasn't only he who had to burn the midnight oil; it obviously went with the job for any man who helped run the Empire.

Chrysanthos was alone, except for a tabby cat that stretched out on a couch next to him, yawning and flexing its claws. Leocadius made for the steps that led to the upper storey. The kitchens were deserted at this time of night and it would be several hours before the slaves were up, waking the palace with their clash and carry. His sandals padded up the stones, worn smooth over the years by other feet and he reached the landing. Would Honoria have moved into Julia's old room, he wondered. Casual flirting with a lady of the Ordo had earned him the valuable information that the new vicarius had kicked Leocadius' 'widow' out into the sticks. The room was beautiful, large and airy. It would appeal to Honoria, ever ambitious, always out for the main chance.

She didn't hear him come in. She didn't hear anything until his hand was clamped firmly over her mouth and there was a dagger-tip just under her chin. 'Hello, Honoria,' he breathed in her ear. 'How have you been?'

When he thought she wouldn't scream, he relaxed his hand and let the dagger drop, sliding it back into its sheath. She spun to face him, eyes darting fire and mouth open in disbelief. Then her eyes narrowed and she flung back her right hand, bringing it round before he could stop her to slap him hard across the face.

'Leocadius Honorius,' she said through gritted teeth. 'You utter shit!'

He clicked his jaw, frowning with the shock and pain. 'Yes,' he said. 'I suppose I had that coming.'

It took Honoria a while to marshal her thoughts. Part of her wanted to scream, to summon the guard and call for Chrysanthos. Part of her wanted to bury Leocadius' own knife in his ribs. Parts of her … but those parts, she could control. What she wanted now was answers. 'Whose body was it?' she asked.

'Sorry?'

'The one the fisherman pulled out of the river. The one we buried with the full honours of Rome. The one we all thought was you.'

'Ah, yes.' He looked a little crestfallen. 'Some layabout. He'd had a skinful and fetched up in the Thamesis on the wrong end of somebody's knife, apparently. Oh, nothing to do with me, I assure you. Fortuitous though, wasn't it?'

'But why did you do it?' she asked, moving closer.

Leocadius shrugged. 'Chrysanthos was breathing down my neck,' he said, whining like Lepidina now. 'Maximus was going to cause trouble any day. He'd already killed one vicarius.'

'What?' She blinked.

'Civilis. Had him poisoned.'

'Oh, Leo.' There was sadness in Honoria's face that he had not seen in a long time; perhaps had never seen – he couldn't be sure. 'That wasn't Maximus. That was … you still don't understand, do you? That was me.'

'You?' His mouth hung open.

'I killed Civilis just like I killed Longinus. Remember? Julia's father? Your predecessor?'

Leocadius was nodding. He remembered. He understood.

'And why do you think I did that?' she asked him.

'For me?' he whispered.

She nodded. There were tears glistening in her eyes in the candlelight. He buried his face in his hands and then ran his fingers through his hair. 'What kind of idiot have I been?' he asked her. And he was asking himself the same question.

She shook her head. 'So you ran away for nothing?'

He nodded. 'I came to a paying arrangement with the Arab, Sabatha. For a considerable number of solidi from the city's treasury, he would provide a handy corpse – they're not hard to come by, as you know, along the wharves – and take me east. I ended up in Augusta Treverorum.'

'And you came back.' She was looking at him now, her eyes dry, her mind made up.

'I can hardly say "to take up where I left off",' he smiled, looking around at Honoria's room, which had been Julia's.

'No, you can't,' she said and crossed to the table where wine and goblets stood.

'You and Chrysanthos …?'

'We're not married, if that's what you're asking. He's the vicarius of Britannia and all Londinium knows that I have a certain reputation. He can't make it official. But I have all the perks. I go to all the best parties. And women who would've crossed the street to avoid me in the old days hang on my every word now. I like it, Leo.'

She passed him a cup and he took it.

'You still wear the ring,' she noticed. 'The one Count Theodosius gave you.'

Leocadius chuckled. 'I do,' he said. 'All that seems rather a long time ago now. A different world. How's Scip?'

Honoria's face darkened. She loved her boy but every day he got to look more like his father and was taking after him too. He hadn't discovered girls yet – although that was only a matter of time – but his speed and luck with dice were already legendary where the children of the great and the good gathered. Suddenly and because of Scip, her mind was made up. 'Here's to you, Leocadius Honorius,' she said, holding up her cup. 'Welcome back.'

He raised his cup too. 'It's good to be back,' he said and he drained it. Then he crossed to her and kissed her hard on the lips but she pulled away, turning her back to him. 'We have to be careful,' she said. 'Chrysanthos is not a fool.'

'And there is no house of the night anymore,' he said.

'No.' She held her head up. 'No, there isn't.' There was a soft thud from somewhere beyond the curtain and they both turned. 'You must go,' she whispered.

'Before I do; Maximus – where is he?'

'The Caesar? I don't know. Why?'

'I have a little message for him. I think young Theodosius has joined Gratian. But all that will have to wait. I must see you again.'

'The weavers' quarter. Tomorrow night. The eleventh hour.'

'The eleventh hour it is,' and he kissed her cheek before slipping into the darkness.

She waited, running a finger around the rim of her cup. A face appeared around the curtain that led to her bed. 'Lemnius,' she said as the slave bowed. 'The ring.' She tapped her left hand to indicate where Leocadius wore it. 'It shouldn't take long. See that he ends up in the river.' Lemnius hadn't seen the fine powder that Honoria had slipped into Leocadius' goblet, the powder that she had carefully ground from the hemlock root that grows along the Fletus.

It didn't take long. Lemnius kept to the shadows, unlike the dying man he was following, who was weaving erratically into the moonlight, lurching against walls and vomiting into the street. Three, four, five times, Leocadius' body tried to clear the poison that was tearing at his insides, roaring through his bloodstream like acid fire. Them his jaw locked and he couldn't see. He felt his head hit a wall and he was suddenly writhing in a gutter, his teeth clenched, his back arched. He jack-knifed with the agony of it, then shuddered and lay still.

Lemnius sauntered from the darkness. A man had died of a seizure in the night. It happened all the time. He lifted Leocadius' left hand and tore off the gilt and ebony ring that shone under the moon. He slipped it into his purse then hauled the dead man upright before tossing him over his shoulder. It was only a short walk to the river and the water was high tonight, the tide not yet turned. He shouldered the weight and let it fall forward with a splash.

There would be no Dorio tonight, no watchful fisherman to pull the consul of Londinium from the weeds. The body of Leocadius Honorius floated out to the black deeps and the wide sea.

Deceangli Territory

The Caesar had been right. The next time he clashed with the enemy, it would not be so easy. Between them, Maximus and Elen had knocked the fight out of most of the Scotti. Their ships had gone, so the dazed and bleeding remnants hobbled westward to find their wild allies, the Painted Ones, who lay between Segontium and the estuary.

Two days had passed and there was still no sign of Andragathius and the XX Valeria Victrix; no sign of Justinus Coelius. Maximus didn't know the numbers ranged against him despite the best efforts of his scouts to keep him informed and to cap it all, it was raining again.

He had been here before. Not on this particular headland with the slate slabs high to his right and the valley broad below him. But he had faced the Picti before and they never changed. He ordered Elen's Deceangli to rest and give them time to lick their wounds. They had borne the brunt of the fighting three days ago. All Maximus' II Augusta had done was mopping up operations, skirmishing against an enemy all too ready to run. It would be different with the Painted Ones. They ran from nobody.

They pranced in the field below him now, their checkered trousers covering brawny legs that stamped the grass flat or hugged the barrels of their short-legged ponies. Even through the driving rain, the general could count two thousand of them, outnumbering his own command to nearly two to one. Maximus looked along his line. His Heruli horsemen sat on the wings, to left and right, the animals pawing the ground in their keenness for battle. Above their heads, the long-tailed dracos, the dragon standards, howled their challenge as the wind rushed through them. On either side of Maximus, sitting his horse under the red flag of a general and the silver eagle of the II Augusta, the infantry stood silent and grim, their shields facing forward to present an impenetrable wall to the enemy, their spears upright. Julianus of blessed memory would have known this formation; so would Vespasian, Pompeius Magnus and the deified Julius. Some things never changed, not in nearly four hundred years. Some things never would.

They came on in the same old way, whooping and leaping, the rain bouncing off their naked shoulders and washing away the blue talismans painted there. Some of the Picti designs were tattoos, not paint and only blood could wash them away. The Caesar was happy to oblige in that service. Maximus was impressed at the extent that the Painted Ones had tried to match even his formation, with their cavalry on the wings, like his. They had more horses than he did; more horsemen than he did; but that shouldn't cause too much of a problem. Maximus had his artillery with him today and although it was more useful against strongholds and army camps, the wild asses could kick a few holes in field formations too.

The rain had plastered Maximus' hair to his forehead and his scarlet cloak was saturated, clinging heavily to his shoulders and dangling down below his boot-tops. The grey shifted under him as he changed position, tossing her head and flicking her tail. Some of the Picti breaking into a jog at the head of their army had seen him now. A man with a red cloak under a silver eagle and riding a white horse. Was this man asking to die, or what?

'In your own time, Valerius,' the Caesar called and waited while the two onagers were winched into position. His hand came down, just in case Valerius had missed the point and the asses bucked, hurling their stone balls high into the air. One hit the ground in front of the Picti running line, then bounced up, still deadly in its ricochet and ploughed into them. Men were flung in all directions, stumbling over each other in their attempt to get out of the way of the stone's momentum. The second landed seconds later, driving straight through the front line and ploughing into the mass of moving soldiery behind.

The attack had slowed and men running at full speed were reduced to a jog again, all shape and cohesion gone. Again Maximus' arm rose and fell and this time the archers of the II opened up, their shafts flying like hail into the enemy.

'Shields!' a centurion yelled. The Picti slingers were whirling their leather slings around their heads as they ran, the murderous stones shattering and bouncing on the oval shields and driving some men to their knees under the impact.

'The Heruli will advance,' Maximus yelled to the horsemen on his left. 'Shake hands with those bastards on foot.'

Heels rammed against horses' flanks and the half Ala rode out, bits jingling and tails flying. They were moving at a walk, riding knee to ham because Maximus had no intention of exhausting his horses in the face of enemy cavalry. The men on the far left flank rode diagonally across the Roman front and those on the right held their reins tight, letting the line form up again. Now the horsemen rolled up the floundering infantry, hooves smashing down as the Painted Ones went down before them.

As he could have predicted, Maximus saw the Painted cavalry break forward. There was no cohesion in their line, no solidity, just individual heroes galloping hell for leather to relieve their comrades in the centre. He pointed to his left and his archers wheeled out of formation and took post behind the battling Heruli, hacking down anything in front of them. As one, they loosened their shafts high into the air. They sailed over the fight in the centre to pepper the Picti cavalry coming forward. Horses went down with screams of agony, some riddled with arrows, their legs kicking uselessly in their death throes. Their riders, those who had not been hit, were flung under the hooves of the men riding alongside them. Bones broke, skulls shattered and the cavalry of the Picti right wing had ceased to exist.

Wounded men were at the mercy of the Heruli now. Obeying the blast of the Caesar's cornicines, they pulled away from the struggling mass of infantry and rode right through what was left of their opponents. Riderless horses panicked, breaking in confusion and lasing out with their hind hooves, trying to kick the empty saddles off their backs. There was a kind of poetry in it and Maximus watched grimly as the Heruli went through their routines like dancers, leaning out of their saddles and hacking with their long-bladed spathas to slice through flesh and bone.

The Caesar wheeled his grey in the tight space in which he found himself and pulled back with his staff to higher ground. It was time for the main bout of the day and he wasn't going to miss this for the world. The Painted cavalry dithered on their left. They had seen what had happened to their comrades on the other side of the field and their bowels had run to water. They had had a moment and it was a brief one, when their attack might have checked the Caesar's tactics, but that moment was gone; that door had closed and Maximus knew it.

The Painted infantry were running again, but their lines were ragged and some were already staggering with the pain in their lungs, the ache in their legs.

'Now, II Augusta!' Maximus bellowed, bringing his hand down. 'Now's your time!'

The barritus rose like thunder from the infantry and the lines moved forward as one, the calcei thudding on three hundred feet and the spears coming to the level. The first Pict to hit the Roman line took a spear point in his throat and he was lifted off the ground, writhing like a hooked fish until he disappeared under the sheer weight of numbers. A second fared better, ducking under the spearheads and slashing at the shields. He was trampled underfoot and skewered where he lay. By the time the numbers had reached the Roman lines, the shock rang through the valley, men grunting and cursing as the shields locked and iron rang on iron, as though in some mad blacksmith's forge. And the killing had only just begun.

'He's started without us.' Andragathius reined in his black and took in the field ahead. Several hundred horsemen milled on the gentle slope ahead of him while the infantry were locked together in the centre. There were no showers of arrows now, for fear of hitting their own side. Now it was all about sheer guts and stamina.

He half-turned to Justinus. 'Looks like the Caesar's enjoying himself,' he grinned. They saw the silver eagle standing erect and already triumphant in the centre. If that standard had been wobbling, worse still, falling back, both men would have galloped like madmen to the rescue. But this was an action involving the Caesar and there was no cause for alarm.

Justinus looked at the German. 'Which of us, I wonder, holds precedence here?'

Andragathius threw back his head and roared with laughter. 'You Walhaz,' he said, 'always sticklers for protocol.'

'Walhaz?' Justinus had never heard that term before.

'Britons,' Andragathius explained. 'Specifically those well and truly shat on by the Romans. It used to mean any foreigner, but that applies to you all, doesn't it?'

Judging by the thickness of the German's accent, that wasn't even worth a reply. 'You haven't answered my question,' he said.

Andragathius sighed and folded his arms. 'Your territory, Wall commander,' he said. 'You take precedence. Or could we do it turn and turn about; one day on, one day off perhaps? No?'

Justinus ignored him. 'All right,' he said. 'Put the XX through their paces. Wipe out those Painted bastards pretending to be cavalry.'

'I shall be delighted, Commander,' Andragathius bowed. He clapped his spangelhelm over the long hair and wheeled his horse back to the column. Taran and Edirne sat their horses alongside Justinus. They heard the German's barked orders, saw the dragon standard come up and the column form into three lines ready for the attack. 'Watch and learn,' he murmured to Brenna's boys. 'Learn what made Rome great.'

'The XX Valeria Victrix will advance, cornicen. Walk. March.' And Andragathius led his men to glory.

The rain came on again as night fell. Victory had gone to the Caesar but he was taking no chances. His rearguard, who had seen no action today, built the camp, shovels slicing into the wet earth and throwing up the ramparts. The wooden palisades, solid trunks carried on the pack animals, were hammered into place and lashed together as the heavens opened.

Deceangli women had appeared from nowhere, clutching their wet rags around them and prowling like wolves over the fallen, slitting throats and helping themselves to trinkets, clothes, armour, *anything* that might have value or purpose in the days and weeks ahead.

'Sorry we're late, dears!' Andragathius had been scanning the cavalry lines of the XX Valeria Victrix and only now, with the flames licking the night air, did he haul up the flap of the Caesar's tent. Maximus sat there, surrounded by his officers and those of the XX. He smiled.

'So good of you to call,' the Caesar said. He clicked his fingers and a soldier-servant poured a cup of wine for the Master of Horse. Maximus was on his feet. 'The position as I see it, gentlemen,' he said and spread vellum out on the table in the centre of the tent. 'Here's the coast. Ships destroyed here. Villages taken here … here … and here.' His fingers danced over the calf-skin with its lines and circles. 'We're here. We know the Deceangli have held the Scotti … here. And we stopped the Painted Ones today. Which leaves …?'

Justinus raised his hand. 'The Hibernii,' he said, solemnly.

'Do you know these people, Justinus?' Maximus asked.

'I know *of* them, Caesar,' the Wall commander said, 'but I've never faced them.'

'Better ask the Deceangli girl,' Andragathius suggested.

Maximus rounded on him. 'If you mean the princess Elen of the Armies, then say so!' he snapped.

The German stopped in mid-swig of his wine. 'Yes, of course,' he said. 'Forgive me, Caesar.'

'I know the Attacotti,' Justinus went on, 'who ride with them. They're cannibals.'

The officers of the II Augusta and the XX Valeria Victrix had heard of those men too, men who loved the taste of human blood on their tongues and swallowed men's eyes on the battlefield. Maximus smiled grimly. 'Well,' he said. 'Perhaps we need to give them a lesson in cooking.'

There were embarrassed chuckles around the makeshift principia.

'And then, of course,' the Caesar smiled, stabbing the vellum with his finger, 'there's Segontium.'

CHAPTER TWENTY-TWO

Segontium

For the past two days, Colla Mor's Hibernii had been pulling back their tight circle around Clodius Vettens' lonely outpost. This morning there was no sign of anybody, just piles of rubbish and horse-shit to remind the beleaguered Romans that there had once been an army threatening them from every side.

It had been weeks and Vitalis' supplies were running low. All the meat had gone but the tribune was loath to order the slaughter of any horses; he would need them for attack or retreat. Men had prayed to whichever god was listening, lying flat on their faces before the Christian altar, kneeling before the great bull of Mithras, gazing at the broad golden disk that was Sol Invictus, the unconquered sun. And the sun was shining today, gilding the ramparts of the fort and the rotting corpses of the Hibernii that still lay untended and unburied, strewn over the vallum.

Clodius Vettens clattered up a ladder to the wall walk. Vitalis had released him from house arrest on condition that he did not try to reclaim his command; on condition that he kept his mouth shut. He looked older than his years in the glow of the morning and he nodded to the tribune who had taken away his purpose in life. He saw the ground stretching away to the forest. He turned, to the east, the west, the south. Nothing. There wasn't an enemy in sight.

'Have they gone?' he asked, incredulously.

'They outnumber us twenty to one, commander,' the tribune still accorded the old man his status. 'Would you leave? In this situation?'

But Vitalis never got his answer because there was a noise coming from the east. His sharp ears heard it first and he raised a hand for quiet. He dashed past Vettens and ran along the parapet. A guard there clicked to attention.

'What do you see?' Vitalis asked him.

'Nothing,' the man said. 'But I hear it.'

'What do you hear?' The tribune could do with a second pair of ears this morning.

'Sounds like …' the colour was draining from the sentry's face. 'Sounds like the legions of Hell.'

Standing next to another Christian this morning was perhaps not the greatest comfort that Vitalis could have hoped for. But the man was right. A rolling thunder was rising in the east, beyond the darkness of the pines that fringed the vallum.

'Cornicen!' Vitalis yelled to the trumpeter. 'Sound to quarters.'

The horn brayed in the morning and the fort's command came alive. Men tumbled out of their contuberniae, hauling on mail tunics, buckling on weapons, clapping on helmets.

'East wall!' the tribune shouted and the cry was taken up by circitors and semisallises all across the parade ground. Within minutes, the ramparts that faced the mountains were bristling with men, spears aloft, waiting for orders. For weeks now, the tribune had been doing this, crying wolf, turfing the men out day and night with alarms real and imagined. They all cursed him every time, as soldiers will always curse their officers until the dice have fallen, until the enemy is at the gate. Now, it was different and men squinting into the distance tried to calm themselves.

The sun was glinting on spearheads as an army came on through the trees, flashes now and then as leaves rustled and bracken crunched. Vitalis slapped the rough wood of the palisade posts in front of him. This was the camp's weakest side, with the forest closest to the building and little room for manoeuvre. It would take a running infantryman less than two minutes to cross the vallum, one struggling with a ladder perhaps twice that. Vitalis didn't have enough ballistae to man every wall, but he had placed two here, just in case.

'Artillery, arm,' he shouted, his voice steady. He looked along the line. He had come to know these men tolerably well over the past weeks. Claudius had a wife and three kids back at Isca; Lobelius was so lucky at Hand nobody would play with him; Titus was a practical joker whose pranks were legend. Before all Hell had broken loose on this frontier, every month, regular as the mountain rain, a lovely girl had arrived at the fort, a present from a 'well-wisher'. And, as regular as rain, Clodius Vettens had turned her down in a kind, fatherly sort of way. The well-wisher? That would be semisallis Titus, of the II Augusta. They all had names, friends, families, Vitalis knew. And had he now condemned them all to death?

'They're back, all right,' somebody said.

'No, they're not Hibernii.'

'Scotti. Got to be,' somebody else volunteered.

'Don't you know the Painted Ones when you hear them?'

'No, by God!' Clodius Vettens was pounding the palisade. 'They're Deceangli! They're ours!'

'Even better,' Vitalis said, pointing to where a silver eagle was emerging from the depths of green darkness. 'They really *are* ours!'

Cheers broke out along the ramparts. Spears were rammed butt down on the wall-walk and the helmets were unbuckled and thrown in the air. Vitalis turned to Vettens. He unclipped his sword and handed it hilt first to the old man. 'Your command, sir,' he said.

'Oh, no you don't!' Vettens laughed. 'If that's the Caesar out there, I think you've got some explaining to do, don't you?'

'So,' Magnus Maximus sat in Vettens' principia later that day. 'Let me see if I've got this right. You, commander,' and he turned to the old man who stood in full armour before him, to attention, with his helmet in the crook of his arm, 'defied my express orders and refused to surrender Segontium.'

'Yes, Caesar.' Vettens was staring into the middle distance and into his future. He was of the old school and knew that disgraced officers were expected to fall on their swords.

Vitalis was poised to interrupt when Maximus cut him short. 'And you, tribune, took away the commander's command, knowing full well what my orders were. In all my years in the army, I've never known such insubordination.'

'Caesar, I ...'

'Shut up!' Maximus stood up, sharply. He spun to the old man. 'Commander,' he said softly. 'I am arranging your escort to Isca. There you will be stripped of your rank and you will leave the army. You will have a pension of sorts – enough for you to crawl into any bottle you please. Alternatively,' Vettens clicked to attention, 'you can do what's fine, what's Roman.' He glanced down to the man's sword, the one he had not drawn against the Hibernii. 'I leave it to your conscience. Now, get out.'

Clodius Vettens saluted. He nodded at Vitalis and left. Neither man saw him again.

Magnus Maximus circled the tribune, looking him up and down, shaking his head. 'When I saw you last,' he said, sitting down again, 'you were a basket-maker.'

'And you were the Caesar,' Vitalis countered.

Maximus laughed. 'Well, that's me for you. Last of the great constants in this fluid life of ours. I sent you to find Theodosius.'

'I didn't get there.'

Maximus poured himself some wine but he offered none to the tribune. 'That's twice you've disappointed me in the last few minutes, Vitalis Celatius. A lesser man than me might start to see a certain pattern here.' He paused. Vitalis hadn't moved. He too wore full armour and stared into the middle distance, as Vettens had. 'At ease, man,' the Caesar said. Now he *did* pour wine for Vitalis and passed it to him. 'What the Hell are you doing here?' he asked.

'Looking for you, Caesar,' Vitalis said. 'I've come from Gratian.' He was careful not to use the word 'Emperor' in this man's presence.

'So I see,' Maximus nodded to the uniform that Vitalis was wearing. 'The Schola Palatina. Very prestigious. Got your knees under Gratian's table, did you?'

'He sends you a message, Caesar,' Vitalis said. He had taken the cup but had not yet drunk the wine.

'Really?'

'He says you can have Britannia.'

'Does he now?' Maximus laughed. 'That's good of him, but I've got that already. What else does he say?'

'That if you march on Augusta Treverorum, it will be to your grave.'

The laugh had turned to a grim smile. 'Yes, that sounds like Gratian. Snot-nosed kid.'

Vitalis looked at the man. 'I don't need to tell you how dangerous he is, Caesar,' he said, 'or how powerful.'

'No,' Maximus sipped his wine. 'No, you don't. Well,' he leaned back in Vettens' chair, 'you've caused me considerable inconvenience, tribune of the Schola Palatina. My intention was to let those barbarians come south, help themselves to this dung-heap and ride into a trap carefully set by me. You come along, all squeaky clean and proceed to bugger everything up. Now, we've had to do it the hard way and it's not over yet. My immediate dilemma is what the Hell I'm going to do with you.'

The Hibernii banners rattled in the wind that moaned through the mountains. The men of the snow were there, the men of the green swords, the men of the lion. They stood in their long lines, the harsh light of Novembris flashing on their mail and their spears, the cruel iron blades with the hooks designed to drag a rider down from his horse and rip a man's intestines. The Painted Ones were with them and the Scotti and the Attacotti, remnants of the armies that Maximus and Elen had put to the sword. Colla Mor, their king, sat his horse in the centre, his stolen banner of the red hand flapping above his bare head.

Across the broad valley from them, the II Augusta and the XX Valeria Victrix had fanned out into battle formation, the Alae on the wings and the artillery behind the infantry. Under the silver eagle in their centre, the Caesar sat his grey. Alongside him sat Justinus Coelius, commander of the Wall and to his left, Elen of the armies. Maximus turned to her. 'You know this man?' he asked, pointing to Colla Mor across the field.

'I know him,' she nodded. 'He was raiding Eudaf's land when I was still suckling at my mother's breast.'

'Do you speak his language?'

'Some,' she said, frowning. 'But I thought …' She looked around her. Every man she and Maximus had was standing on that field. Surely, the time for talking had passed.

'Justinus,' he turned to the man on his right, 'if the princess and I don't come back in the next few minutes, you have command of the army. And you know what to do.'

Justinus nodded and saluted the man, thumping his chest and holding his arm out straight. He watched as the two of them walked their horses out from their lines. The bewildered soldiers of the XX and the II Augusta looked at each other. Had the Caesar lost his mind?

Justinus watched the enemy. They looked as confused as his own men. Battle-hardened warriors turned to each other, gripping spear shafts and shields. Colla Mor's own bodyguard, the fianna, stiffened. What kind of ruse was this? The Romans, they'd heard, came on in silence, at a walking pace. But all they were offering today was one man and a girl. Is this how it was? Did Roman generals bring their whores to battle?'

Colla Mor knew better. The name of Magnus Maximus had gone before him. He ate babies for breakfast and sparks flew out of his arsehole. The girl he knew all too well. Elen of the armies, old Eudaf in long skirts. The Deceangli had run before his Eriu weeks earlier, but now he knew why. It was all part of a plan, playing for time until Maximus arrived with his legions. Colla Mor was outnumbered and he knew it. His allies, the blue-painted bastards to his left, had let him down.

The riders halted and swung out of their saddles. They let their horses wander, the grey and the roan, munching the grass, oblivious to what was happening. Maximus drew his sword and threw it tip first into the ground. Elen did the same. Her heart was pounding. She was walking, unarmed, towards the monsters that had haunted her dreams since she was a girl. And the man beside her, the man who filled her dreams now, the man who had lain with her and fought with her, what was he up to? She had no idea.

To the horror of the fianna and those of his army who were near enough to see, Colla Mor dismounted too and strode out across the short grass, his long cloak trailing the ground and the sheep shit. He drew his ornate sword and held it high. He kept it there

399

and stood still until the dark mutterings of his own men stopped. Then he drove the blade tip into the ground and was as defenceless as Maximus and Elen.

'All hail, Colla Mor,' the Caesar greeted him in Latin. 'I am Magnus Maximus.'

The king looked at Elen for a translation and she obliged, looking him squarely in the face.

'I know who you are,' Colla Mor said. 'And I know the pretty one, too.' He grinned his gap-toothed grin at Elen. 'What do you want?'

'I want to offer you a job,' Maximus said.

For a moment, Elen stood there with her mouth open. When she had translated, so did Colla Mor. Then he pulled himself together.

'What nonsense is this?' he asked.

'No nonsense,' Maximus said. 'You have … what … two thousand fighting men. I have three thousand. Oh, we could fight. I would win. You would lose. You'd probably die.'

'I'd be proud to,' the king said, defiant as always.

'Yes, yes,' Maximus said, 'very Hibernii. But this is the real world. And it doesn't have to be this way.'

'What do you mean?' Colla Mor's eyes narrowed. A man who ate babies wasn't likely to be straight with him.

'I mean, Colla Mor, king of Laigan …'

'… and Ulaid,' the king interrupted as fast as he could once he'd heard Elen's rapid translation.

'And Ulaid,' Maximus conceded. 'What do you hope to gain here? A few villages? Some sheep? That's small change, isn't it, in the scheme of things – oh, begging your pardon, Elen Llwydogg.' He winked at her and she shot him a glance that would have withered anyone but a Caesar. 'And to get that, you've got to beat us and take Caer Llyn. All rather … uphill, wouldn't you say?'

Colla Mor would. But he had his pride. 'My men and I,' he said, 'have sharpened our swords on the Pillar of Combat. I cannot go home empty-handed.'

'Nor will you,' Maximus assured him. 'Put your two thousand alongside my three thousand and we have an army to be reckoned with, Colla Mor. An army that can win itself more land, more silver, more gold than any of them have ever dreamed of.'

Colla Mor let Elen's words sink in. He blinked. He licked his lips. Then he beckoned with his left arm and sat down, cross-legged on the ground. Maximus did too with Elen beside him. Three of the fianna walked out from their line, dropping their swords as they came and sat around their king, cross-legged like him.

'Tell me more,' the king said.

'Well,' Maximus leaned forward, smiling like a conspirator. 'Tell me, have you heard of Flavius Gratianus Augustus, Gratian, for short?'

Colla Mor shook his head.

'No,' Maximus smiled. 'I didn't think you would have.'

Caer Llyn

It was not perhaps the easiest of truces that bound the Romans, the Deceangli and the Hibernii together, but the promise of the riches of Gratian's empire shone like gold in the eyes of Colla Mor. And among his people, the word of Colla Mor was law. He had thrown in his lot with the Caesar and now he must stand the hazard of the dice.

The year turned. The dead were buried and peace came to Britannia Prima. Old Eudaf, king of the Deceangli, did not live to see the spring, with its ripening shoots and its snowdrops carpeting the woods beneath the trees. As the heather began to show its colour from the dead fronds of the last year, so they buried him, as his people had buried their kings for centuries, wrapping the old man's frail body in his finest clothes, with a torque around his neck and a crown on his head. They clasped his hands around the hilt of his sword and laid him on a bronze bed where carved eagles soared and salmon leapt. For three days, they kept watch on his body in its mound, guarded by ancient stones carved with symbols most men had forgotten. The II Augusta and the XX Valeria Victrix mounted guard too, the standards of the legions standing alongside those of the Deceangli and the red hand of Colla Mor. Flames guttered on it all as the priests sang and whirled, their drums rattling through the long, still-dark nights.

They waited until a decent interval had passed and then Magnus Maximus took Elen Llwydogg for his wife. She already knew she was expecting his child; the soldier in her had hated the idea, the woman was happier than she had ever been in her life. She would tell Macsen Wledig soon – but not too soon. It would seem a lifetime to wait and things moved fast in the world of the Caesar; she didn't want him making any decisions based on a forthcoming child who might not even live to see a first spring; she had seen that happen only too often and hugged her knowledge to her, until the time was right.

The sun warmed the earth and the dancers flew, flutes and pipes playing the loving couple to their bedchamber in the royal palace. Among the honour guard that lined the route, a tall German spat copiously after the pair had passed.

'Don't you care for Elen of the armies, Andragathius?' Justinus smiled. He had got the measure of this man after months in his company.

Andragathius spat again. Then he broke formation and strode off in search of ale. Justinus laughed and went with him. 'They can stay there all night if they want to,' he jerked his head back to the guard, 'listening to their lord and master grunting and making his woman squeal. Me? I've got some serious drinking to do.'

'I'm no politician,' Justinus said, taking the cup the German offered him, 'but I understand what this is all about. He can buy Colla Mor with Gratian's gold, but Elen is different. He needs a force here in

Britannia, to hold the line for him. And anyway,' he sipped his ale, 'have you ever considered he might actually love her?'

Andragathius grunted. Then he became serious and leaned towards Justinus. 'It's a weakness, Wall commander,' he said, 'and it may be a fatal one. Consider this. He consults weird books that don't make sense. He consorts with a sorceress from the East who whispers rubbish in his ear. Now this Deceangli slut's got him tied to her by her apron strings. It's not healthy, Justinus; trust me.'

'But you'll go with him, nevertheless,' the commander of the Wall said.

Andragathius sighed. 'Either that,' he said, 'or it's back to counting sheep pens for the vicarius. You?'

Justinus shrugged. 'If he asks me,' he said. 'It's funny. For all the fighting I've seen, I've never once left Britannia. Abroad, they tell me, is a bloody place.'

'Oh, it is,' Andragathius assured him. 'Except Germania, of course. That's paradise.'

Both men laughed and Justinus finished his ale, slapping the man on the shoulder and wandering off into the night. There was still laughter and music among the huts of Caer Llyn and the torches burned bright. The commander of the Wall walked the ramparts that faced the north, to Britannia Secunda, which had been his home for more years than he cared to remember.

A twig snapped behind him and he turned, hand on his sword hilt. 'Vit,' he smiled, relaxing. 'You're dressed for the road.'

He was. The tribune had his field cloak over his mail and a haversack slung over his shoulder. 'I remember,' he said, 'hunting the deer with you far out there in Valentia, that day when Hell broke out.'

'The outpost at Banna,' Justinus nodded, 'the Valentinus rebellion.' He looked more closely at his old comrade. 'You, you bastard, haven't changed at all in that time. What's it been? Fourteen years?'

'Fifteen,' Vitalis said. 'And, yes, I have. Oh, not here, maybe,' and he gestured towards his face, 'but in here.' He tapped his chest. 'In here it's different.'

'Yes,' Justinus sighed. 'It always is. The Caesar has let you go?'

Vitalis chuckled. 'With my head and both bollocks, yes. It's a miracle.'

'You Christians!' Justinus laughed. 'So, what are your plans? Are you still in this man's army?'

Vitalis shrugged. 'Technically, I'm still on Gratian's staff with the Schola Palatina.'

'You're going back?' Justinus wasn't laughing now. 'Vit, that will put you right in Maximus' path. You know he's going to kill Gratian, don't you, just before he pinches his throne?'

Vitalis nodded. 'And I've got to get there quickly,' he said, shouldering his kitbag. 'Conchessa's still there, as far as I know, looking for her husband.'

'So, this time it *is* goodbye?' Justinus asked.

Vitalis smiled. 'We've said goodbye before,' he said. 'We didn't mean it then. We don't mean it now.' He held up his left fist where the Wall ring shone. Justinus raised his too. 'Here's to the Heroes of the Wall,' he said.

'The Heroes of the Wall,' Justinus echoed. They hugged each other and broke away. 'How will you go?' the Wall commander asked. 'Via Londinium?'

'Probably.'

'Do something for me, will you, when you get there?'

'Name it.'

'Pay my respects at the tomb of Leocadius Honorius; you know, for old time's sake.'

'I know,' Vitalis nodded. 'And I will.'

Londinium

The lights of the city winked in the chill of the spring evening. The bells of Bishop Severianus' church tolled for the faithful and another kind of faithful rolled among the tabernae, looking for an hour or two's escape from their cares.

In the house of Calpurnius Succatus, it was different. In the little room at the head of the stairs, with dark cloths hung over the windows to keep out the noise and the chill, Adelina approached her mistress with a cooling cloth and was immediately batted away.

'Adelina!' Conchessa said, through gritted teeth, 'if you come at me with that cloth again, as God is my witness …'

Palms up, the slave woman stepped back, to be immediately replaced by the midwife. 'How is our little mother?' To Conchessa, the woman's smile was verging on the imbecilic.

'*Not* a mother, yet,' she said, her smile acid. 'Which, I fancy, is most of the problem.' She broke off with a howl. 'Holy Mother of God!' The pain ripped through her and her abdomen tensed. She drew up her heels and arched her back.

'Bring more herbs,' the midwife snapped to Adelina. 'And goose fat.' Turning to Conchessa, she smiled again, her false, encouraging smile. She rarely lost more than one child in five in an average week, and as for mothers – sometimes she could go a month without a single death. But this one ... she pasted her smile on more firmly ... she was tense, the child was breech, it wasn't going well. The physician was on his way, but in her opinion he had just minutes to arrive or it would all be up with the baby; more than ten minutes and there would be a new widower to comfort.

The women set to with a will, Adelina's face set in grief already. She had seen her own mother die, giving birth to her tenth child, and knew the signs. Conchessa, it was true, was not exhausted as Adelina's mother had been, and the science of child birthing had moved on, with more herbs to comfort and soothe, to open up the way for the child. But still ... but still ... Adelina dashed away a tear and massaged her mistress' belly for all she was worth.

After the stabbing pain and the contraction that gripped her body in a red-hot vice, Conchessa flopped back, too tired to speak. Wordlessly, the midwife gestured to Adelina and between them, they hauled the frightened woman off the hard bed and onto the birthing stool.

'Adelina.' The midwife was now all efficiency. She wouldn't get paid if at least one of her patients didn't manage to get to the end of this. 'Kneel behind your mistress now and take the strain. Madam,' she tapped Conchessa lightly on the cheeks to get her attention, 'Madam, do exactly as I tell you, no more, no less.' None of the little mother business now – no need to tempt fate. The midwife gave up a prayer to Artemis, goddess of her craft, and put her hands lightly on Conchessa's belly, just above the parts she had always tried to keep private except for her husband and, just the once, Pontus. Although she was faint with pain and fear, she tried to move away. She had had enough of women's hands all over her for the last ten hours and more and she wanted it to stop.

The midwife put her hands more firmly. 'Stop that, Madam,' she said, sharply. 'You must do as I say or your baby will die.'

The room, which had been filled with Conchessa's panting, went silent. The midwife was not to know, but if Conchessa lost this, the only thing of Pontus she had left in this lonely, sterile life she was living with Calpurnius, she would die herself, and would be pleased to do it. She leaned back, presenting herself to the midwife, head turned to one side, her tears soaking Adelina's gown.

'That's better.' The midwife felt the tell-tale flutter of a contraction beginning and braced her knees against Conchessa's planted feet and screamed, 'Push! Push for all you're worth.'

Conchessa threw her head back, screaming and her baby flew into the midwife's linen wrapped hands. There was silence. A heartbeat. Two. Then, the best sound in the world filled the room. The lungs of Conchessa's son had filled with air and now he was expelling it, with all the noise he could. The midwife dropped back onto her heels, cradling the little one to her breast, rocking him to silence. Adelina knelt behind her mistress, taking her weight. She knew there was more to come before she could get back on the bed, more ministrations, more pain, even. But for now, Conchessa lay back, crying silently.

She held her arms out to the midwife. 'Give him to me,' she said, softly. 'Give Patricius to me.'

'You have chosen a name,' the midwife said with a smile. 'And a good name it is, too.' She looked down into the baby's face, screwed up and howling. 'Noble.' She held him out to Conchessa, who took him and cradled him in her arms.

'Noble, yes,' she murmured. Adelina looked over her mistress' shoulder as the baby boy suddenly stopped howling and opened his eyes. She had looked into those eyes before and gasped. 'Yes,

Adelina,' Conchessa went on, 'he does have a look of his father already, don't you think? Around the eyes.'

'Yes, mistress,' Adelina agreed, adding, silently and to herself, please God and all the gods that Calpurnius never notices that.

The midwife called for more water, towels, clean gowns and soon the mother and child were tucked up in bed, neat and trim as any pair could be who had not looked death in the face half an hour before. The midwife took Adelina to one side as she left to go to her next birthing, which, she prayed to Artemis or whoever might be listening, would be easier than this.

'Tell the father that I won't charge the extra,' she said, despite the fact that the labour had been as long as three or four normal ones. 'This is too near a miracle for me to tempt fate. Long life and health to the little mother and her child.' She looked over Adelina's broad shoulder to where Conchessa lay back, suckling her son at her breast. 'Take care of them.' And she clattered down the stairs, leaving Conchessa with her child and her dreams.

CHAPTER TWENTY-THREE

Llyn Tegid

The lake at Llyn Tegid lay silver and silent under the moon. The Egyptian stood before the fire that roared and crackled into the night. The logs split and spat, the tongues of flame running out along the branches and twigs that Justinus had cut and gathered and placed there. She was naked under her fur cloak because her ceremonies demanded it and, cold as it was at that hour, she let the fur fall and stood under the moon. Her skin prickled with cold but she did not shiver and she shook her sistrum rattle, murmuring in her alien tongue as she did so. Her feet slid sideways and she swayed, eyes closed, head thrown back like a wolf baying the moon.

Magnus Maximus let his cloak fall too, but he was dressed in the full uniform of an Emperor, one he had had made in Londinium and had not worn until now. His hair had been combed forward and cut, in the style of all Caesars since the deified Julius, he who was bald; he who was vain. Elen of the armies unclipped the gold brooch at her shoulder and stood in her regalia of queen of the Deceangli, gold torques at her throat and wrists, silver discs dangling from her ears and dancing on her fingers. Justinus Coelius, commander of the Wall, had brought no finery with him. He wore the uniform he wore day in, day out, defending the edge of the world, his grimy mail-coat and worn leather. The spangelhelm was still tied to his saddle with the animals tethered to the gorse nearby.

This was the sacred pool of the Deceangli, home of the water goddess. She lived in the depths and to look on her was death. But she gave life and good fortune to those she loved. And everyone knew she loved Elen Llwydogg – had it not been proved it a hundred times by coming home from all her battles? She knew her, the water goddess and she trusted her. She smiled on the queen and the queen smiled on Macsen Wledig. All would be well.

Maximus drew his sword with a flourish. This weapon had been at his side or in his hand for more than twenty years. It had brought his enemies low and had kept him alive. But now it was to serve another purpose. He reversed it in his hand and held it out to Elen who laid her hand on the brass hilt. Justinus did the same, with his hand over hers. And finally, the Egyptian laid both her hands on theirs. Maximus drew the blade back slowly out of their grasp. Then he thrust the weapon into the flames.

'Iron to the fire,' he and Elen chanted together, in her tongue of the mountains. He pulled the blade back. 'Iron to the water,' they said as one. Then he drew his arm back and tossed the sword high into the air. It spun in the firelight, flashing silver under the moon and splashed into the blackness of the pool. Bubbles frothed briefly and it was gone.

'She has it,' Elen murmured, 'the lady of the lake. And she has your heart, Macsen Wledig.' Her eyes were bright with tears. That was one of the many things he loved about her – a warrior who cries.

'Mark where it landed, Justinus,' Maximus said. 'When I come back, I want you to get it for me.'

'Me, Caesar? Won't I be with you?'

Maximus shook his head. 'No,' he said. 'I need you here. You are my watchman, Justinus; you always have been.' The commander of the Wall's face had not changed. He remained as stoic and dependable as ever. 'Well, cheer up,' Maximus laughed. 'It's not every day I appoint a new Dux Britannorum.'

Now, Justinus *did* react. His mouth fell open but no sound came out. Maximus was still chuckling. 'Let me spell it out, Justinus,' he said. 'You are military commander of Britannia. All of it. You'll have to work with the vicarius, of course, but there's a fly in any ointment. When we've said our goodbyes here, will you come with me to Londinium? I'm sailing from the Saxon shore just as soon as I can get the provisions I need.'

'No, Caesar,' Justinus said. 'I've some unfinished business in the north.'

Maximus shrugged. 'Suit yourself,' he said. 'It's your command now. But,' he closed to his man, 'you won't do anything rash, will you? Nothing hot-headed?' And this from a man who was going off to overthrow an Empire.

'No, Caesar,' the Dux Britannorum said. 'I wouldn't dream of it.'

Britannia Secunda, Aprilis

The high clouds left their shadows on the hills that lay south of the Wall. The new born lambs frisked and gambolled in the short grass, never straying too far from their mothers. The three horsemen plodded north, shields slung over their backs, a day's rations dangling from their saddle bows. From the saddle of the red-haired rider, a wolf's head hung, its skin dark brown, its fur matted with what had once been red, free-flowing blood.

It was Justinus who saw them first and he called Edirne to his side. It wouldn't do to let the lambs wander too far away. This may be Magnus Maximus' Britannia now, but it was still a dangerous place. It had not rained for days after that long, wet winter and a dust cloud spread across the valley that shel-tered between the hills.

'Taran,' the Dux Britannorum said, 'your eyes are younger than mine. What do you see?'

The prince of the Votadini squinted into the light. 'Warriors,' he said. 'Maybe fifty horses.'

Justinus nodded. That was what he saw too.

'Who are they, Justinus?' Edirne asked. He had felt safe at Eboracum, in old Flavius' house, loved by the old man and his slave. He had felt safe in the marching column with Justinus and his Wall soldiers. He had felt safe when he watched Andragathius' cavalry wipe out the Scotti. But now there were just the three of them and the Caesar had taken his best men far to the south. This was the territory of the Brigantes, always a difficult tribe. But there'd been no trouble with the Brigantes for years. Even their pony-queen, Cartimandua, had thrown in her lot with Rome against the terrible Boudicca. On the other hand, Justinus knew better than the boys with him that outlaw bands were everywhere. It would not be too long before the rumour spread that the Caesar had gone and he had taken the best part of the army of Britannia with him.

Justinus reined in his horse, keeping the animal's head up, ready to ram his heels home and ride like Hell. This time, it was Edirne who shouted, 'That's the Shining One.' He slapped his saddle-bow and looked at his big brother and at the soldier he would follow to the ends of the earth. 'That's Belatucadros.'

It was. Above the leading horsemen, fanning out as the valley broadened, the horned sun god flashed in the spring light.

'They're our people, Taran. They're Gododdin!'

He was already urging his horse forward, shouting in his breaking voice, using the native tongue he hadn't spoken out loud for so long. Taran galloped with him, racing his brother and laughing, lashing his bay with his reins, the cloaks flying out behind them both.

'Jupiter highest and best!' Justinus muttered. Had old Flavius taught these two nothing? He had no choice but to race after them. In his hurtling vision, as the ground angled right and left in his gallop, he saw the leading horseman dismount. The boys nearly rode right into the mass of cavalry, but hauled rein just in time and leapt from their saddles. Was Justinus seeing things? He thought he saw Elen of the armies at their head, her tawny hair streaming in the wind. Then he saw the hair was dark, a lustrous brown and he felt the sting of tears in his eyes.

He hauled back in the saddle and swung to the ground. Three people were kneeling in front of him, the princes of the Votadini and the woman they were hugging. All three of them were crying and laughing at the same time, much to the amusement of the horsemen looking on.

'My boys!' the woman said, over and over again.

'Brenna?' Justinus *still* didn't believe his eyes.

He dropped to his knees too, staring into her face and he felt the tears fall.

'My boys,' she murmured softly, kissing them through her tears. '*All* my boys.'

Londinium

The basilica was humming that morning, with petitioners coming and going. The vicarius was up to his neck in river drainage disputes and of course *something* had to be done about the stench from the cemetery before it became unbearable all over again once the summer heat arrived. It would be the birthday of the Eternal City in three days' time and the Mithraians were insisting on the traditional cow sacrifice. Bishop Severianus was bending the vicarius' ear of course, in the opposite direction. All in all, Chrysanthos didn't really have time for a tribune of the Schola Palatina who was just passing through on his way east.

'Can I help?' a decurion with narrow-set eyes came out of nowhere.

'Perhaps,' Vitalis said.

'You're from the Schola Palatina,' the decurion said, looking him up and down. 'The Emperor's bodyguard.'

'I am,' he said. 'And you?'

'Sorry,' the man extended a hand. 'Calpurnius Succatus.'

Vitalis' hand had not touched the decurion's yet and he stood there, open-mouthed.

'Is there a problem?' Calpurnius asked.

'That depends,' Vitalis smiled, 'on whether or not you are my brother-in-law.'

There was laughter that night in the decurion's house along the Via Orientalis. Stories old and new came from them all, even Adelina, who shrieked louder than anybody else. There were tears, too, at the memory of loss and separation. Yet even now, when all was right with the world and Calpurnius had been accepted into Chrysanthos' fold and there was a beautiful baby boy to fill their moments, even now …

The lamps burned low, the gentle breeze wafting the curtain over the crib.

'He's very like you,' Vitalis said, smiling as he stroked the sleeping child's cheek. Little Patricius stirred, feeling for his lips with his starfish fingers in the half light. He sucked on them sleepily, dreaming who knew what.

'He's more like Pontus,' Conchessa said. She wasn't smiling. She was looking at her big brother, waiting for his explosion of fury. It didn't come. 'You've only really seen him half asleep. But the eyes … and when he grins; oh, I know it's only wind, but the mouth, that little lop-sided twist …'

'You love Pontus, don't you?' Vitalis asked.

Conchessa pulled herself up to her full height. 'I am the decurion's wife,' she said.

'And you must be above suspicion,' he nodded. 'Yes, I know.'

'Now that you've found us,' she said, 'will you still go to find Theodosius?'

'I gave Maximus my word,' Vitalis said. She took his hand and sat him down in the atrium. The moon shone here, silvering the tables and the chi-rho high on the wall.

'Before we left Augusta,' she said, 'In fact, just as we were passing through the gate, we saw Theodosius.'

'You did?' Vitalis frowned.

'He was riding openly under the Porta Nigra, as though he'd been sent for.'

'By the Emperor?'

'Who else?' she shrugged. 'So, you see, there's no point to it now, Vit. *Somehow* Gratian has bought the younger Theodosius. He's not likely to throw in his hand with Maximus now.'

There was a long silence. She looked at his face, the brother she loved. Uncle Vitalis. The new status made her smile.

'So,' she patted his hand. 'What will you do? I'm sure Calpurnius can find you a post in the basilica, on Chrysanthos' staff. The Londinium garrison, perhaps. He'd welcome you as commander.'

'Did I ever tell you,' he asked her, 'about my friend Pelagius?'

'The missionary? Yes, you did.'

'He went north, to spread God's word. Somebody told me he'd crossed the German Sea, gone to Gaul.'

She nodded, remembering. 'They could do with God's word in Gaul,' she said.

'I might follow him. I promised I would years ago but somehow it never happened.' He reached out and stroked her cheek. 'Be happy, decurion's wife,'

419

he said, 'if not for Calpurnius' sake, then for little Patricius.'

She nodded. There was an iron lump in her throat because she knew she would never see her big brother again. He stood up quickly. 'Now,' he said, 'I made Maximus another promise. I promised I'd pay my respects at Leo's tomb.'

'Ah.' Her face darkened.

'Ah?' He raised an eyebrow and lifted her chin. 'Something else you haven't told me?' he asked.

'Leo isn't in his tomb, Vit,' she said, although she had no reason to feel guilty about that. 'It's a long story, but he found me at Augusta. In fact, he saved my life.'

'Augusta? Is he there still?'

'No. We don't know where he is. He came back with us, here, to Londinium. We haven't seen him for weeks. He'll have gone back to his usual haunts; you know Leo.'

'Yes,' Vitalis nodded. 'Yes, I do. But there's some-one who knows him better.'

'There's a tribune at the gate, my lady,' the slave said. 'From Augusta Treverorum.'

'A tribune?' Honoria looked up from her embroi-dery. 'To see me?'

'To see you, Honoria,' came the voice from the doorway.

She leapt to her feet. Honoria was always ready to play hostess to tribunes, especially handsome ones.

But not this one. This one brought a ghost with him. 'Vitalis.' She tried to smile. 'It's been a while.'

'It has.' He waited until she had sent the slave away.

'If it's the vicarius you're looking for …' she said, hopefully.

'No,' he said, looking at her with his level gaze. 'No, you're the only one who knows what happened to Leo.'

'Oh, of course.' The consummate liar was prepared to brazen it out even now. 'You'd left Londinium before … He drowned, Vitalis. A fisherman found his body. He's buried …'

'No, he isn't, Honoria,' the tribune said. He had never really known this woman, but he knew where she came from and how she had got where she was today. It was knowledge he would very much rather not have. 'I don't know who's lying in that tomb, but it's not Leocadius Honorius, the man we both loved once.'

'I don't understand, Vitalis,' she said.

He reached out suddenly, like a snake and caught her hand. He bent her wrist round painfully and looked at her fingers. 'Pretty jewellery,' he said. 'I see the vicarius is very generous to you.'

'Yes,' she winced. 'Yes, he is.'

'I particularly like this one,' and he pointed to one of the rings. 'I have one just like it.' He placed his Wall ring of the four helmets alongside hers.

'It's Leo's,' she said, trying not to cry out with the pain. 'I thought he'd want me to have it.'

'When, Honoria?' he asked, bending her over still further. 'When did you think that?'

'When they found his body, in the river.'

'Ah, but that's not quite true, is it, Honoria? You see, I happen to know that Leo wore this ring in Augusta Treverorum. That was *after* his body was found in the Thamesis. Odd, that, don't you think?'

'Stop it!' she screamed at him. 'You're hurting me.'

'Why don't you reach for your knife, Honoria?' he asked her, 'or offer me a cup of poison, perhaps. That's your style, isn't it? You killed Leo with one or the other of those.'

'No, I didn't!' she shrieked and pulled herself free of him.

Her slaves had come running, cudgels in their hands. Vitalis whirled to face them, his sword in his hand. 'I haven't killed a man in fifteen years,' he said. 'Don't make me start again now.'

'It's all right,' Honoria sobbed, holding her wrist, purpling into a nasty bruise. 'Let him go.'

Vitalis turned to her. 'I'm leaving Londinium,' he said. 'As for whether your secret is safe with me, only time will tell, won't it? But, just in case,' he shot a glance at the slaves, 'they find me floating in the river one of these nights, I shall be leaving a little letter with Bishop Severianus; you know, the one who talks to God.'

Britannia Secunda

That evening Brenna and Justinus, now they were alone, felt suddenly, stupidly shy. They sat opposite each other across the fire and looked anywhere but at each other. They both had much unsaid, but a man sat between them, smoky and insubstantial, but no more loved and important to them for that. Eventually, Brenna raised her head.

'You looked for me,' she said, quietly.

'You know that I did,' Justinus said. 'And if you hadn't ridden out today, to me and your boys, I would be looking still.'

'I saw your messengers, once. They came to Selgovae territory when I was there.'

Justinus half rose. 'Why ...?'

She held up her hand. 'Please, Justinus. I wanted to, I wanted you and my boys to know I was safe, but I have been ill since I lost Din Paladyr. I wandered in a dark, dark place, peopled with who knows what demons. I blamed myself. I thought that Taran and Eddi were dead, dead because of me and my ambitions. They told me they were dead. They ...' She hung her head, then, swiping furiously at the tears with the back of her hand, she carried on, 'they showed me a body. It had no head, no hands. No anything to make it a man. They said it was you, but I knew better.'

'How did you know?'

'The wounds were on the back. I knew you would never die like that.' Her eyes were glittering in the firelight and they still were dark at the corners, her skin was not as bright and fresh as he had remembered it in his dreams. Her hair, just at the temples, was showing the silver among the russet brown that told of hard times.

He patted the skins on which he sat, but she shook her head. 'Come, Brenna. Come and sit with me. I will wonder if you are truly real if I can't touch you now and then as we speak.'

Slowly, like iron to a lodestone, she moved around the fire. The ghostly soldier watched her go, a smile on his face. She sat beside Justinus and slowly, their fingers entwined.

'A long time has passed, Justinus,' she said quietly. 'Bad things have happened to me.' She felt his hand clench hard on hers. 'Not as bad as you might think,' she said, 'but bad enough. I have just moved through each day as best I can, one step at a time. Sometimes, not even a step. I was fed. I was clothed, but I was like a ghost. Someone to avoid, as though I carried the mark of the plague on my forehead. It wasn't living. It was existing. A voice in my head just kept repeating the boys' names, over and over. It echoed through my waking, it stopped me from sleeping.' Again, she raised her hand to dash away the tears. 'Even with them sleeping in the next tent, I hear it. I can't believe I have them back again.' She looked up at him. 'That I have *you* back again.'

In the circle of firelight, the ghostly soldier stiffened. This must surely be the moment, the moment he could stop worrying about this woman who he came to love so much, the moment he could join his

Flavia and Quin, his first family who had waited for him so long.

'I've got something for you,' he said. He held it out in the firelight and watched her eyes light up.

'Pat's ring,' she said.

He nodded and looked down at her tear stained face and he smiled. When her smile began to grow, he bent to meet it, covering it with his own.

A gentle sigh filled the tent and Paternus was finally gone.

Valentia

The Dux Britannorum had stripped his Wall command again, but this time it was his idea and there was a purpose to it. Five days march to the north lay Din Paladyr, ruled by the usurper Malwyn, his left hand man Aelfrith and the renegade Fablyr. Half a legion was marching over the rough turf that day as the month turned, a vexillum of the VI Victrix fluttering at its head. Justinus had few cavalry, but his infantry and artillery were heavy and well-armed. He was preparing for a siege.

Brenna led one wing, marching in a wide arc to the west. Edirne rode with her, delighted to have his mother back and proud now to be the man at her side. The boy's thirteenth summer had just passed and he was wiry and strong for his age. He was too young to remember Brenna before the coup that had toppled her in anything but the sketchiest of detail.

He remembered her soft, strong arms around him when the fever burned. He remembered her soothing the ointment onto his skin when he fell. But the general walking her chestnut over the heather now; he had no memory of that. But here she was, clear-eyed and determined. And he loved her all the more for it.

Somebody else who loved her, although it almost hurt him to admit it, was leading the right wing, heading east towards the grey, rolling sea of the estuary. Justinus Coelius had Taran with him, the grim-faced heir to Valentia, prince of the Gododdin, Lord of the Votadini. The vexillum of the VI fluttered over their heads as the horns of Belatucadros floated over Brenna. Vengeance was coming to Din Paladyr and the sleeping people there turned in their darkness, muttering.

There were no Saxon ships along the estuary, no fleet to bring reinforcements or carry out an escape. So far, so good. Justinus sent a galloper on a fast horse along the estuary to tell Brenna. The only aid to the besieged would come from the west, from Fablyr's Din Eidyn and she must be watchful. He had argued long and hard with her that *he* should lead the left flank, but she had shaken her head. 'My kingdom, Justinus,' she had said softly and he couldn't argue with that.

In the morning, Din Paladyr lay like a turtle on the landscape, its curved dome of grey rock dotted with huts, great and small and its walls a double thickness of northern pine palisades and ditches. It was here that Edirne had first met Justinus all those years ago, when the Roman had shown him how to beat his big brother with a wooden sword. The weapon at the boy's hip now was iron and old Flavius, Justinus' father, had taught him how to use it. For half a day, the Dux Britannorum's little army manoeuvred itself into position, forming a ring of iron around the fortress of the Gododdin. Justinus had no forests to hide in, nowhere to conceal the fact that he was woefully short of troops. But he had no intention of taking the place in a direct assault; that was a command too far. He had promised the boys; he had promised himself and now he had promised Brenna that Din Paladyr should fall and that Malwyn the malcontent should fall with it.

He had the perimeter camp dug fast, with trenches and palisades going up under the shovels and axes of his engineers. The men watching from Din Paladyr couldn't tell how flimsy they were; they were not to know that a strong gust of wind would blow them down. The cornicines blasted every hour and men ran pointlessly backwards and forwards. Brenna's cavalry wheeled and counter-wheeled, raising dust clouds on the far horizon. Just how many men did those bastards have?

'Rider,' the sentry called to Malwyn on the lower ramparts. 'Flag of truce.' The man who called himself king of the Gododdin dashed up the steps and watched the solitary horseman canter out across the turf. He leapt the stream and followed the old, dry watercourse to a position below Malwyn.

'Do you know me, Malwyn?' he shouted. 'I am Justinus Coelius, Dux Britannorum.'

'Dux Britannorum?' Malwyn chuckled. 'Well, well; promotion, eh? We are honoured. The Romans' biggest shit riding all this way to see us. Won't you come in?'

'Not yet,' Justinus smiled, easing himself in the saddle. 'Not until we're all here.'

'All?' Malwyn sneered. He wasn't about to fall for the oldest trick in the book. 'Going to get old Ammianus out of bed in Eboracum, are you? What's that? A thousand men? Look at me,' he held out his right arm, 'I'm quaking.'

'No, I won't bother Ammianus,' Justinus said. 'You're right. The Praeses is a little long in the tooth for active service these days. No, I'll let the VI stay where they are. What's a thousand men when I've got … well, let's not get into a numbers dispute, eh?'

'He's bluffing,' Fablyr had heard the commotion on the ramparts and had joined his lord. 'Look. He's got nothing.'

Justinus couldn't hear the muttered conversation, but it was obvious from Fablyr's pointing what the topic was. 'Don't worry,' he called. 'It won't be a long siege. The Caesar will be here in … I estimate two days.'

'The Caesar!' Malwyn spat. 'Yes, we've heard of him.'

'Yes, he's got the II Augusta from Isca, the XX Valeria Victrix from Deva. Then there's his Heruli cavalry, of course. Oh, and I nearly forgot.' He put two fingers in his mouth and whistled loudly. Three horsemen cantered out from the Roman lines, wild men in plaid and with braided hair. One of them had blue dragons coiling over his chest and neck. Another had three human heads bouncing on the chest-strap of his horse. As they reined in alongside Justinus he introduced them. 'My very good friends the Hibernii,' the flame-haired man bowed in the saddle; 'the Picti,' the tattooed warrior bowed 'the Attacotti.' The cannibal licked his lips ostentatiously and roared with laughter.

Malwyn and Fablyr looked at each other. They turned to hear a whoop to Justinus' right and a knot of horsemen cantered across the field. 'Where are your manners, Dux Britannorum?' Brenna shouted, iron on her head and iron in her heart. 'You forget the Deceangli.' A couple of her riders waved, their horses pawing the ground, read for battle. 'And of course,' she stared at Malwyn long and hard, 'my loyal Gododdin.' They all roared now, every soldier in Justinus' command, whatever their tribe.

'You told me that bitch was dead,' Fablyr hissed to Malwyn.

'I thought she was,' the man scowled. And the only sound that the king of the Gododdin could hear now was the thudding of his own heart.

'Do you have terms?' Fablyr bellowed, in that his lord and master appeared to have lost his voice.

'No,' Justinus said, smiling. 'I just thought I'd say "Hello",' and they wheeled their horses away.

Chapter Twenty-Four

Lugdunum, Gallia Lugdunensis

A battle lost. An empire in ruins. Andragathius walked his blood-flecked horse over the corpses of Gratian's legions. A rider had reached him from Maximus an hour ago. All was secure and the Caesar had entered the town unopposed. They had stood in the huge amphitheatre and roared their approval. Those were the men who had cheered Marcus Aurelius and Caracalla; the townspeople of Lugdunum were used to backing Emperors. And now there was a new one. Magnus Maximus Augustus had ridden his grey horse through the forum and accepted the homage of southern Gaul. Gratian? Never heard of him. And the stonemasons were smashing his statues already.

The Caesar now Emperor had fought his rival to a standstill. He had driven him out of Augusta Treverorum, beat him back at Paris on the Sequana and now, here where the olives blossomed under a cloudless blue and the birds sang no matter who wore the laurels, Gratian had to face his maker.

The man had lost weight in the past weeks. Twice – or was it three times – he had lost. He had held his own at Vesontio against the upstart's Gallic allies. He had given Maximus' rag bag of painted barbarians a bloody nose along the Rhodanus. But he had not stopped the onslaught and now it was too late.

For days Gratian had kept on the run, dodging and hiding with his cavalry and his staff. He'd lost count of the gallopers he had sent to Theodosius somewhere in the east. He needed him now. He needed his legions. The devil was at his gate. Whole units had deserted. Men who fought for pay could fight for anybody and Maximus could afford to pay more as Gratian's treasury dwindled. Some flocked to Maximus' standard. Others just went home. There was no cause to die for here; hadn't everybody always said it? Gratian was mad as a snake.

'It's over, Sire.' Septimus Pontus was exhausted. He had stayed with Gratian through thick and thin, although for the life of him, he couldn't explain why. Gratian valued loyalty, that was true, but looking at the man now, his armour ripped and dirty, his face grimed with the sweat of fear, what price that? The man had the look of death on him.

Gratian looked down from his gentle hill. The clouds of night were gathering in the east and he had nowhere else to run. He watched the big German trotting forward, his cavalry at his back. He saw him pause to lift a vexillum from the ground, the flag of the Schola Palatina. Gratian couldn't remember when its commander, Alfridus who loved boys, had gone down fighting. Pontus couldn't remember when he'd last seen his crony Milo Belarius, but wherever it was, the man had been wandering naked on a battlefield, singing softly to himself, his mind gone.

The Emperor who was no longer an Emperor hauled himself upright. 'It isn't over,' he snarled at Pontus, 'until I say it is.' He broke out of the tight circle of what was left of the Schola Palatina and walked down the hill, his boots sending up puffs of dust as his heels slipped on the shale. His guard shifted to follow him. What was the Emperor doing?

'Stand fast,' Pontus snapped at them. He had never held a commission in this regiment, but the men of the Schola had lost so many officers, they responded, in their exhausted state, to any barked command.

Andragathius reined in and sat in the saddle, his arms folded, watching Gratian. 'Have you come to surrender, Flavius Gratian?' he asked. There was no 'Augustus' added to the name now.

'You tell me.' Gratian stood still, his arms by his side, his sword at his hip.

'You have a choice as I see it,' the Master of the Horse said. 'You can hand me your sword and I will take you back to Rome in a cage where the mob can spit at you and tear you apart.' He smiled, half bowing in the saddle. 'Or you can take your chances with me.'

There was silence, apart from the snort and whinny of the horses ringing the field. Then Gratian laughed. It was a chilling sound that Pontus had heard before. He had heard it when his Emperor had leapt into the arena at Augusta that day he faced the leopard. He had heard it when he sent the Schola Palatina into the tunnels to burn out the Jews.

'So be it,' Gratian called and drew his sword.

Andragathius swung out of the saddle, bringing his right leg over the horse's neck. The long heavy spatha gleamed in his fist. 'You might want to make your peace with your God, Christian,' the German said.

'No need for that,' Gratian grated. 'I won't be seeing Him any time soon.

They circled each other on the slope of the hill, beyond the outer line of the newly dead. Pontus and the Schola Palatina stood on tiptoe to get a clear view and Andragathius' horsemen fanned out into a semi-circle. Gratian lunged first and his blade scraped on the German's. Andragathius had the height and the strength, but he was older than Gratian and no one could predict how it would go. Iron rang again, a spark flashing in the sunset. Gratian parried and jerked sideways, his blade licking under Andragathius' guard and grazing his thigh. The German hissed an oath and stumbled backwards. This man was good. He blocked the next attack but Gratian's eyes were blazing now and the man fought like the demons of the Hell in which he believed. Steadily, slowly, he was driving Andragathius back towards his own lines. The German's lungs were bursting and his legs felt like lead as he parried hit after hit. Then Gratian lunged, putting all he had left into the move, going straight for the bigger man's chest. Andragathius had never moved so fast in his life. He dodged aside and brought his sword in a backhand sweep that took off the top of Gratian's head. A flitch of bloody hair and skull bounced to the ground and the Emperor who was no longer an Emperor went down. Once, twice, he twitched, his face contorting and his blood trickling dark over the ground he had failed to defend.

Andragathius knelt and hauled him over, but Gratian was gone, his teeth gritted, his eyes staring sightlessly at the sky. The German rested on his sword hilt until he could breathe again. Then he fumbled inside his tunic and pulled out a coin, one of the new ones that Maximus had had struck at Augusta. He grabbed Gratian's jaw and forced his mouth open, placing the silver on his tongue.

'Just in case you're wrong about your God, Christian,' he wheezed, 'you might want to take this, to pay the ferryman.'

High on the hill, Septimus Pontus gave his last command as chief decurion on Gratian's staff and the battered Schola Palatina hit the road for the long retreat to nowhere. He watched as the German's cavalry rode their horses forward, trampling the body of the living god into the dust of Lugdunum. Forty thousand men could not defeat

Septimus Pontus – everybody knew that. Neither could Andragathius. He smiled his lop-sided grin and vanished into the coming night.

Din Paladyr

'They've gone.' Fablyr hurtled into Malwyn's hall as the cocks were still crowing and the sun was crawling over the fortress of the Gododdin.

'Gone?' Malwyn threw the girl off his lap and put the ale down. They both ignored her outraged squeal and made for the ramparts. Malwyn's men stood guard here, looking intently to the east.

'See?' Fablyr pointed, wanting a second opinion on whether or not his eyes were playing tricks on him. 'Nothing. The ramparts are empty.'

They were. Justinus' Romans had dismantled the palisades in the night, wrapped up their leather tents and had gone. To the west, the Deceangli and Brenna's Gododdin had upped their stakes too, leaving no sign that they had ever been there.

'It's a trick,' Malwyn muttered. 'And they expect us to fall for it.'

'No,' Fablyr argued, 'what they expected us to fall for was that the Caesar is on his way with his legions. That was bollocks and the Dux Britannorum knows it. He can't take this place with his pathetic little command and he's had to give up. I'll prove it to you.'

The Lord of Din Eidyn dashed down to his stables and led his horsemen out of the gates of

Din Paladyr, trotting in formation down the slope that led to the vallum that Justinus' men had created. Malwyn watched with trepidation, ordering his archers to be ready to give covering fire. Fablyr reached the first ditch, his sword drawn, his helmet on his head. Here were the post holes, black and empty. There were ashes here and there – the cooking fires of the VI Victrix, a little brushwood, a broken pot.

Fablyr rode round the camp, his men with him, prodding soil heaps and corners with their spears. Malwyn saw him wave and ride north and he crossed to those ramparts as the horsemen swept across the headland with the estuary churning grey and silent far beyond them. There were no fortifications here, just horse shit dotted along the ridge where the Deceangli had camped for the last two days. They were not there now.

Fablyr rode on, sweeping at a canter around the perimeters of Din Paladyr. Here, in the west, Brenna's camp had stood, its tents folded now and gone. And so to the south, where Valentia stretched wide and silent to the Wall. He wheeled his horse to face Malwyn's gate. 'You see,' he said, laughing and pounding his saddle. 'The cowardly bastards have run.'

There was a hiss and a whine and the air was alive with fire, flaming balls hurtling out of the sky to crash into the fortress' palisades and explode among the horsemen dithering before the gate.

'Belatucadros!' Malwyn hissed. He hadn't seen – none of them had – Justinus' ballistae roll out of the low woods to the east. All the watchers on Din Paladyr's walls had been so intent on following Fablyr's progress they had not looked behind them. The gate of the fortress roared into flame, the fire-tongues licking up the bone-dry timbers and hurtling across the lintel. 'Put that out!' Malwyn roared and chaos came to Din Paladyr. Men, women, even children, dashed to put the fire out, falling over each other in panic. This place had been sacked before and the older ones remembered it. Malwyn had brought this on them. The streets were choked with people, unhappy, terrified, mutinous.

This was exactly what Brenna had been counting on. Most of her people had deserted her before and had gone over to the usurper. Malwyn had executed the loyal members of her council. He had ordered their heads cut off in front of her and Fablyr's riders had hacked down any opposition. Anyone who had spoken of the queen in those dark days was held a traitor.

But all that was then, another time. And this was now; the VI Victrix were rolling forward, creeping like ants over the ditches and ramparts they had so recently deserted and they stood, presenting a shield wall to the east. Brenna and her people, with the Deceangli alongside her, drew up their shields to the west.

Fablyr wheeled his horse round and drove his heels home, galloping up the slope and forcing the terrified animal to leap through the flame and smoke. Some of his men followed him, others hung back, to die under the hissing, biting arrows of the VI Victrix. Inside the gate, Fablyr bellowed to anybody within earshot, 'Din Eidyn,' he yelled. 'Mount up. We're going home.'

Malwyn was on the steps, running down to him. 'Stop!' he shouted. 'Are you mad? You wouldn't get thirty paces.'

'Fool!' Fablyr snapped, taking his shield from a lackey. 'I was right all along. Justinus hasn't got Caesar with him. He's got a woman and two boys. If I move now, I can cut my way through. You stay here and starve if you want to.'

'Fablyr!' Malwyn yelled. 'I am your king. You will obey me!'

Fablyr threw back his head and laughed. 'You're no more my king than you were Aelfrith's,' he said. 'He buggered off, didn't he, with a lap full of silver. Well, think yourself lucky this time. You can keep the silver. If I'm going to die, I'll do it on my own ground, not yours.'

He wheeled his horse for the gate, but it was the last thing he did. Those watching saw him suddenly straighten in the saddle and blood spurt from his nose and mouth. His eyes widened in shock and disbelief. Then he toppled forward, over his horse's neck and lay twitching on the ground, Malwyn's knife in his back.

'Anybody else want to ride out?' Malwyn shouted.

Nobody moved. Nobody spoke.

'Put that bloody fire out!'

The camp fires twinkled in the short summer night. Justinus Coelius, Dux Britannorum, sat with one leg hooked up on the table, looking at the maps the VI Victrix had brought with them. He knew that Din Paladyr had been taken before, that the ditches and palisades presented nothing like the obstacle of a Roman fort. In the nearly three years that had passed, Malwyn had grown careless, sloppy, even. There was no sign of his Saxon allies now, of the cold, greedy bastard called Aelfrith. But Justinus was short of men. His Deceangli would want to go home for the harvest soon. Battles and bravado didn't feed empty bellies and these men had children of their own. As for the Hibernii, the Picti and the Attacotti, those three men didn't make very much difference to a fighting force in the scheme of things.

'Is this going to work?' Taran looked up from sharpening his knife blade, his eyes glinting as cold as the iron in the firelight.

Justinus looked at him. If truth were told, he didn't really like this boy. Little Eddi was Pat through and through, honest and friendly and good. But Taran was another man's son and twice in his short life, he had been forced to run south through the smoke and tears of a world turned upside down.

'Have faith, boy,' the Dux Britannorum said. 'Rome, they say, was not built in a day.'

'No,' Taran said, looking hard into his face. 'But will it fall in one?'

Justinus had no answer. Taran got up and sheathed the knife. 'I remember,' he said, 'when you took us to Eboracum, when we left this place.'

Justinus nodded. He remembered too. It all seemed a long time ago.

'Old Lug, the priest,' Taran went on. 'Remember what he said? "To the fortress of fate," he said. "May it keep you safe." Has it, Justinus? Out there,' he pointed to Din Paladyr, black against the night's purple, beyond the flaps of the tent, '*there* is the fortress of fate. And it may kill us all yet.'

'It may,' Justinus nodded.

'Lug also said "To the great mother. May her love hold you." Well, my mother is back now, but where was she, Justinus? When Eddi and I needed her, where was she?'

'Lost,' Justinus said. 'More lost than you've ever been. Be glad you've found her again.'

'"To the deep things," Lug said. "May you find them in wisdom."'

'And you haven't,' Justinus looked up at the boy. 'You haven't learned yet that this world of ours doesn't shine out of *your* arse, Taran. We'll take Din Paladyr. And you'll be lord of it one day, king of the Gododdin.' He stood up, nose to nose with the lad. 'And you're not ready. I wonder if you'll ever be ready.'

The boy's right hand snaked out, but Justinus was faster. He too had been taught by old Flavius and he had learned better. He caught the boy's fist and slapped him around the head. 'Your mother may have to listen to your sob stories, boy, but I don't. Now, get out of my sight.'

Lugdunum

The Egyptian writhed on the floor of the Emperor's palace, the cold of the mosaic chilling her skin. Through her diaphanous robes she felt the little tile fragments prickle and she felt the incense burn her nostrils and her lips as she stared into the flame. She was on her knees now, bowing low before Osiris, his green, sightless eyes unreadable in the half light. The slave behind her rattled the sistrum and brought the whip down hard across her back. She hissed as the leather cut her flesh and blood spattered over the saffron robes. A second stroke and she arched her back. The thong had landed in exactly the same place and tears filled her eyes. One last lash and they fell, dashing her olive cheeks and trickling into her mouth. The slave bowed and left and a gentler hand helped her upright.

'Sire,' she bowed.

Maximus slipped the bloodied robe off his priestess' shoulders and scooped up the soft, cooling ointment. She lay face down on the couch and he knelt beside her, like a nurse, like a lover, dabbing the running cuts across her back. She winced but said nothing. 'Well?' he asked her, leaning down to smooth her braided hair and kiss her ear. 'What does your god say?'

She lifted up her face and he kissed her, full and hard on the lips. She smiled. 'It will be well, Sire,' she said. 'You will meet Theodosius in the field. Where the sea rolls inland. You will triumph. And he will die.'

Maximus chuckled. And his chuckle turned to a laugh. He poured wine for them both and threw himself back on the couch beside her. He didn't see the look on her face. He didn't read the pain there. And it was not the pain of the whip.

Din Paladyr

Another night. But this one was wild, with one of those freak storms that sweep in from the German Sea sending the rain battering the shutters of Din Paladyr and fighting with the flames of the torches that the guards carried. They crept close to the wall, their armour wrapped in dark cloaks; Brenna, the queen; Taran, her eldest son; and Justinus Coelius, Dux Britannorum.

It was, like much else in life, a risk. Perhaps the biggest any of them had taken. Certainly, if they had mistimed it, the end would come quickly and their heads would join those of Brenna's council that had once stood on the slope beyond the fortress's main gate. Last night might have been too soon; Malwyn's people still ruled Din Paladyr and they were on their guard. Tomorrow night might be too late – Malwyn would know for certain that there were no reinforcements coming and he would have the numbers to take the fight to Justinus. Now was the moment. And for every step of the way, as their feet slipped in the mud below the ramparts, Justinus heard Taran's voice whispering in his ear. 'Is this going to work?'

Brenna and her son had been born in this fortress. They knew its every inch and that knowledge would be vital now. They pressed themselves into the north wall where the wind from the estuary cut like a knife. Justinus slipped off his cloak. He didn't need that tangling his legs in the next few minutes. He watched for Brenna's signal and she watched the parapet, Taran another pair of eyes to make doubly sure. The men patrolling the palisades worked to a routine. They plodded the wall-walk at a steady pace, their torches guttering in their hands, their spears wearing a groove in their shoulders.

Brenna's hand came down and Justinus climbed. He felt the jutting timbers wet, cold and slippery under his fingers and he felt his boots slide. Brenna's hand again and he flattened himself against the timber uprights. A guard had doubled back. Had he seen anything? Heard anything? The man stopped, looking out across the open ground to the Roman camp to the south east, mere pinpricks of firelight in the driving rain. Then he walked on and Brenna signalled again.

When he inched his head over the parapet, Justinus knew he had seconds to move. If he stayed there, clinging on until the guards made their turn, they'd see him and it would all be over. It was now or never. He hauled himself over the sharpened stakes and landed on the wall walk. The noise made both men turn. Justinus sent a dart hissing out from his belt into the throat of the man to his left. Then another into the chest of the man to his right. They both buckled at the knees, moaning and collapsed opposite each other. Justinus checked them both, then leaned over the parapet and helped Brenna climb up. Taran was last and now all of them were on the wall. Across the fort, the other guards patrolled unaware of this deadly breach of their security. They muttered to each other and whistled to while away the boredom of a wet night.

Now Brenna took the lead. She padded down the steps into the almost total darkness below the wall and the others followed, Justinus and Taran carefully and quietly rolling the guards' bodies onto the dungheap below. They would be missed and probably soon, so speed was vital. She hurried across the open ground and up between the smoky thatched huts towards the great hall that stood at the top of the hill. She kept her cloak drawn around her and her hood over her head. Nobody would know Justinus Coelius here and in the darkness he could pass for any other soldier. Taran had not been here for three years and few would recognize him either. It was the queen who had to keep to the blackest shadows.

There were guards at the hall's entrance where the torches guttered. The three crossed the open ground, hearts thudding. It was now or never.

'Who goes?' the sentry challenged, his spear prodding the darkness.

'Brenna, your queen,' she called loudly, sliding her hood back to show her face, the golden torque and the crown she had smuggled out when she had fled this place for her life. Justinus had a dart in his hand, ready to bring the man down. For what seemed eternity, the guard stood there, staring open-mouthed into her face. Then, he fell to his knee and his comrade did too.

'Lady,' they chorused.

Her heart leapt. She laid gentle hands on their shoulders. 'Come on,' she said. 'You're with us.'

They gathered up the hall flap for her and she swept in. In the centre, a fire crackled and roared against the wildness of the night. Beyond it, at a long oak table, heavy with the remains of a meal, Malwyn sat with his council. The talking stopped, as if someone had closed a door. As if someone had taken their last breath. No one moved, except Malwyn. He slowly rose to his feet and stood there, a cup of ale half-forgotten in his hand.

'Who is this stranger?' he asked, his face a mask of fury.

'I am Brenna, your queen,' she answered him, her head held high, her voice strong. She lashed the council with her glance. 'The queen of all of you,' she said.

No one in the chamber was a Christian. No one there believed in miracles carried out in the name of the Lord. But that night, Brenna of the Gododdin performed a miracle herself. One by one and without a word, the members of the council, some of whom she had appointed herself, all of whom had rebelled against her, dropped to their knees. 'Lady,' they said in an embarrassed and ragged chorus.

Malwyn slammed down his goblet, looking at the cowards all kneeling there. 'Are you sheep?' he screamed. 'She's a woman. The Gododdin don't take orders from a woman. You take your orders from me.' He drew his sword and raised it, kicking a stool aside and making for Brenna. Justinus' blade was in his hand in a second, but there was no need for that. A knife flashed across the hall and bit deep into Malwyn's chest. Blood sprayed from his nostrils, spotting his beard and he tried to steady himself. He was frowning at the dagger hilt jutting from his tunic, not understanding why he couldn't breathe, why he was already drowning in his own blood. Then he sank to his knees, his eyes crossed and he pitched forward.

Taran crossed the hall in a couple of strides, turned the body over and wrenched out his knife. He held it upright, glistening with Malwyn's blood in the firelight.

'Well, Justinus,' he said in a voice his mother barely recognized. 'Do you still say I'm not ready?'

Aquiliea

The sea rolled inland as it had for centuries, rippling up the sand dunes and drowning again the villages that had once stood there. The sun burned like a demon that day and the ravens were already wheeling over the wreck of the Emperor's army that lay below them.

Magnus Maximus Augustus was bleeding heavily, his arm ripped from wrist to shoulder and he was trembling with shock and exhaustion. It had been days since he had heard from Andragathius and that didn't bode well. The man had taken half the army to outflank Theodosius, but he hadn't done it. If he had, why was Theodosius here, with his back to the land, outnumbering Maximus three to one? He would have done so many things differently if he could have his time over again. He had destroyed Gratian and taken his throne, just as he said he would, just as the Egyptian had prophesied. And the Egyptian was never wrong, was she? Osiris; Jupiter highest and best; Mithras, god of the morning; the Galilean carpenter, all of them had heaped their blessings on the head of Magnus Maximus Augustus, the Emperor.

'Remind him,' one of Theodosius' letters had said over the last few months, 'that he is Emperor in the West by force of arms. I am Emperor in the East by divine intervention. He would do well to stand aside.'

Maximus struggled to his feet. His battered army could take no more; he knew that. The II Augusta who had marched with Vespasian, the XX Valeria Victrix who had destroyed Boudicca the flame-haired, lay broken. His faithful cavalry of the Heruli had dismounted, they had hung their saddles and bridles in the trees of an olive grove and they had slapped their horses' rumps for one last time, watching the animals trot away into legend. Colla Mor, who had sharpened his sword on the Pillar of Combat, would never see his Winter Lands again; neither would most of his followers. Nor would the Painted Ones, with their wild, lime-washed hair and their blue demons. And as for Elen's Deceangli, their bodies lay in rough-dug pits from here to Lugdunum, under a different sky.

Elen. He saw her smiling in the haze out to sea where the bodies of his men were washed by the tide. He heard her laugh above the sound of the soughing wind, he saw her as she slapped her saddle and threw back her head. Elen Llwydogg. Elen of the armies. He shook the image from his mind and strode for his horse, the grey that had carried him faithfully and well now for five long years. He caught the reins and hauled himself into the saddle. He took the sword a soldier handed him and saw the man had tears in his eyes.

'Now,' he murmured, 'none of that. You'll need your vision clear, pedes. You're going to see how an Emperor dies. How Magnus Maximus dies. How Macsen Wledig ...' He shouted and rammed home his heels. Theodosius' men stood to their arms across the body-strewn field. He was riding straight at them, one man, with just a sword. He wore no helmet and he was wounded. Was he mad?

Theodosius sat his horse under the purple flag of an Emperor. He unbuckled his helmet and watched the lone horseman galloping over the open ground. 'Archers!' He raised his hand.

The hand came down and a hundred arrows hissed into the blue.

And the dream of Macsen Wledig ended that day.

Llyn Tegid

She watched her dabbling her little starfish fingers in the dark water. Elen of the armies would always be a general, but now she was a mother too and the little girl with the dark eyes and black hair of her father took up most of her time.

'Mama,' the little girl said, looking at her own reflection in the water.

'Yes, little one?' Elen leaned back on the warm grass of summer.

'Is it true that a goddess lives here?'

'Oh, yes,' her mother said, smiling at her. 'She's looking after the sword of your papa for him.'

Sevira had never seen her papa, but she had heard stories about him. He was a hundred feet tall and men trembled at his name, but he was also soft and gentle and he loved both his girls more than life itself.

'Is he coming back for his sword, mama, one day?'

'Yes,' Elen said, smiling at her little daughter. 'One day.'

Glossary

Ala: Cavalry regiment

Alemanni: Germanic tribe

Attacotti: Celtic tribe

Ballista: Roman siege weapon, similar to a giant crossbow

Belatucadros: Celtic god of war

Cena: Mid-afternoon/evening meal

Chi-Rho: Christian symbol and monogram

Circitor: Rank above semisallis in Roman army

Contubernia: Army barracks

Cornu/cornua: Roman trumpet

Deceangli: Celtic tribe of North Wales

Decurion: Member of the aristocracy

Dux Britannorum: Military officer commanding Britain

Eriu: Irish tribes' name for themselves

Gododdin: Celtic tribe north of Hadrian's Wall

Goidel: Celtic term for the Irish

Gustatio: First course in a meal

Heruli: Germanic people serving in the Roman army

Hiberni: Roman term for the Irish

Libra/Librae: A Roman unit of weight (340 gm)
Lorica: A term used to describe Roman armour
Onager: 'Wild Ass' - A type of catapult
Ordo: Council/ local government
Pallium: Clothing typically worn by members of the nobility and the clergy
Pedes/Pedites: Foot soldier(s)
Picti: Celtic tribes north of Hadrian's Wall
Praeses: Governor of part of a province
Primus Pilus: 'First Spear', senior centurion of a legion
Rivros: Feb-March in Celtic calendar
Saex: A curved blade from which the Saxons take their name
Schola Palatina: Elite Imperial Cavalry Guard

Scotti: Roman term for the inhabitants of Ireland
Semisallis: Rank above Pedes
Signifer: Roman military standard bearer
Spangenhelm: Helmet worn by Roman soldiers
Spatha: Sword carried by Roman army
Ulaid: Irish-Celtic tribe of northern Ireland
Vallum: Defensive earthworks
Vexillation: Detachment of soldiers
Vexillum: A military standard
Vicarius: The governor of a province
Vicus/Vici: Neighbourhood(s)
Votadini: The Roman name for Gododdin
Walh/Walhaz: A Germanic word for Romanized Celts.

DATES & TIMES

Dies Lunae: Monday
Dies Martis: Tuesday
Dies Mercurii: Wednesday
Dies Jovis: Thursday
Dies Veneris: Friday
Dies Saturni: Saturday
Dies Solis: Sunday

Januarius: January
Februarius: February
Martius: March
Aprilis: April
Maius: May
Junius: June
Julius: July
Augustus: August
Septembris: September
Octobris: October
Novembris: November
Decembris: December

PLACE NAMES AND MODERN EQUIVALENTS

Aesica: Greatchester, Northumberland
Aquileia: Italian city near Venice
Augusta Treverorum: Trier, Germany.
Belgica: Tribal region that roughly covers modern Belgium
Bremenium: Rochester (Northumberland)
Britannia Prima: One of five provinces of Britain, covering Wales and south-west England
Britannia Secunda: One of five provinces of Britain, covering north England
Calleva Atrebatum: Silchester
Carthago: Carthage, Tunisia
Cilurnum: Walwick Chesters, (Northumberland)
Constantinople: Istanbul
Deva: Chester
Din Eidyn: Edinburgh
Din Paladyr: Traprain Law, Scotland
Eboracum: York
Flavia Caesariensis: One of five provinces of Britain, covering central England
Fletus: River Fleet
Gallia Lugdunensis: Part of France
German Sea: North Sea
Hibernia: Ireland
Hispania: Spain

Horrea Classis: Carpow Fort, Scotland
Isca Dumnoniorum: Exeter
Isca Augusta: Caerleon, Wales
Laigan: Region of Ireland (today's Leinster)
Lugdunum: Lyon, France
Luguvallum: Carlisle
Maia: Bowness-on-Solway
Maxima Caeseriensis: One of five provinces of Britain, covering south-east England
Mona: Anglesey, Wales
Mosa: River Meuse
Mosella: River Moselle
Onnum: Halton Chesters, Northumberland
Pontes: Staines
Rhenus: River Rhine
Saxon Shore: Coastal defences from Norfolk to Hampshire
Segedunum: Wallsend, (Tyne and Wear)
Segontium: Caernarfon, Wales
Tarraconensis: Catalonia
Valentia: One of the five provinces of Britain, perhaps north of Hadrian's Wall
Vindovala: Rudchester, (Northumberland)

BRITANNIA: Late 4th Century

THE
GERMAN
SEA

Din
Eidyn

Din
Peladyr

VALENTIA

The Wall

BRITANNIA
SECUNDA

Eboracum

FLAVIA
CAESARIENSIS

Segontium

Deva

Caer
Llyn

BRITANNIA PRIMA

MAXIMA
CAESARIENSIS

Londinium

THE SAXON SHORE